A Kiss for Big Bill

Brian Howard

For Dan, Thanks for the support Jees Ducky

In the annals of the Western Novel, many is the work that chronicles the hero, the principal actor, the mover and shaker. The man who "makes history." But for every real Hero in the popular literature, there were dozens of men, and women, who stood on the same stage as the Hero, and whose blood and sweat and emotion made up the real story, the steed of truth upon which another rode to glory. This is the tale of several such men.

Acknowledgements

Without the following folk, this book would never have come to be. I wish to gratefully mention and thank those whose moral and technical support made it not only possible, but a joy to do:

Lee Johnston for his editorial expertise and keen insight.

Alexis Cruikshank for her artistic genius and excellent technical skills.

And the RUCAS posse for their unstinting support and encouragement—
Mike "Latigo" Lenci
Derek "Cedar County" Mirkle
Kathleen "May B. Shecann" Loucks
Grant "Riverwalker" Tanye
Dave "Bonesteel Badger" Breed
Ron "Portagee John Phillips" Periera

And most of all, Diane, for providing the "Boot".

Chapter 1

He first spotted them silhouetted atop a low rise to the west, just the heads showing like a row of dark pumpkins along a fence rail, and at first he couldn't make out what they were. He reined in his big roan horse, the animal hauled down from an easy lope across the prairie, and studied the shapes off to his left, maybe half a mile away, he judged.

The horse stamped and snorted, impatient to be moving toward the water he smelled on the west wind, and the man patted his great neck absently, watching the dark shapes. He could see tiny bits of white on what he now was certain were heads, and as they slowly rose up in the heat shimmer of the late autumn plains they became heads on torsos, then the horses they rode began to come into view, and in a moment they finally halted atop the distant rise.

He counted seven, eight of them, all in a row, and two, maybe three led horses, some of the mounts painted and streaked in reds, whites, one with a blue streak. Indians. They started down the slope, coming at him in a line abreast.

The man scanned the horizon to the north and east. Hills rose in the northwest, and beyond in the distance mountains stood purple in the afternoon sunlight. He had been headed for those hills, six or seven miles out. Nothing between where he sat and those hills but gently rolling grassland, brown in the slanting light. To the north a smoke cloud hung low on the prairie, blowing in out of the west, and he guessed it might be a prairie fire, but he could not see any flames.

Custer had got himself butchered the year before, and now it seemed that every bunch of painted dog soldiers on the plains thought they owned the world. The man shook his head and sighed. They might own this one, for sure, unless the big roan stallion between his legs could out pace them. He could let them come up and see what it was they were about. Or he could run. If he waited, and he was wrong, he was a dead man. If he ran, he at least had a chance.

"Hey Bill!" the man said, patting the horse's neck once more, "Let's show 'em what you got!" He gave the horse a little spur and the animal started off with a lunge, heading into the northwest toward the smoke and the hills beyond. The stallion settled into an easy lope, and the rider looked over at the distant Indians.

They changed course on the long easy slope they were descending and began to parallel his path. He swore softly, and gave the horse another jab with his spurs. Bill kicked it up a notch, and began to run, easily, his long body rippling along to the rhythm of his pounding hooves. The Indians matched his pace, their ponies angling in slightly to close the distance between their column and the white man. The rider leaned over the neck of the horse, poised just off the seat of the saddle, letting the horse work beneath him, glancing again and again at the Indian line closing on his left.

The man used his spurs again, and the horse picked up the pace once more to a full gallop. The Indians stayed with him, gradually easing their course out to the east to cut him off. The man knew it was just a matter of timing, now, and he slapped the reins on Bill's shoulders, growling out, "Come on you big bastard, don't let me down!"

The warriors were strung out in a line abreast of him, now only a quarter of a mile away, and several of their fastest riders were a little ahead and angling in to cut him off.

He heard a war whoop or two as they gradually closed the distance. Then it seemed that they had all they could do to keep abreast of the big roan and his rider, and all along their line came the whooping of their exaltation. The man knew he'd beaten them to the cut off, and now it was a matter of stamina. They could not close with him without losing ground and going behind, and the fact gave the man hope.

He could see that most of the Indians carried rifles, and at his next glance he saw the lead rider briefly shrouded in a white puff of smoke. He heard the whine of the bullet and the distant pop of the rifle at the same time.

He instinctively hunched his shoulders as if ducking, and immediately felt foolish for it. No place to hide on the back of a horse. He spurred Bill again, slapped the reins across his heaving shoulders, but he knew the stallion was going just about all out. Bill surprised him and surged ahead, blasting across the dry prairie grass at a dead run.

His rider felt the rhythm of the horse even out and steady. He reached down behind the cantle and yanked a brand new '76 Winchester out of its scabbard. The long rifle was heavy in his hands as he swung it up across his chest. Two more Indians fired, the bullets singing by the front of the horse to skim the prairie and kick up dust twenty yards to the right.

The lead Indian ponies once again edged to the east, trying to close the gap. The man knew that if they got close enough, even by dropping back some, they would shoot him out of the saddle out of pure luck if nothing else.

He hooked the reins over the pommel, and, using his knees to absorb the pulsing gait of the pounding horse, levered a .45-75 cartridge into the rifle chamber. He leveled the gun and lined up the sights on the lead rider, letting the rifle float in his hands, watching the brass bead of the front sight gyrate past his target with the jolting of Bill's hooves. He swung half a horse right and an Indian head high, timing the rise and fall of the sight as he squeezed the trigger. The big gun boomed and smacked his shoulder. White smoke bellowed, then was instantly whipped away by the wind of their passing, and he watched the lead pony fold like a house of cards, its rider skittering across the prairie grass end over end.

The man racked the action of the rifle to chamber another round, steadied himself a moment with a hand on the pommel, then leveled the gun and fired again, this time at the new leader. He saw the rider slump suddenly, but not fall. Abruptly the whole column of Indians came to a bunched halt and veered off toward his back trail.

He clung to the saddle with his knees, took up the reins again with his free hand, and Bill just kept on bounding over the plains. Two miles later, after Bill had slowed and was working pretty hard with what he had left, the rider looked over his shoulder. No Indians. He slowly reined in the big horse and stopped on a mild knoll, wheeled about to face his back trail. While the horse blew, the man rested with the rifle across the saddle. He finally spotted them in the distance, still bunched.

"We sure as hell got lucky on that one, Bill old man!" he said, patting the horse's neck. He levered open the rifle carefully, removed the extracted cartridge casing from the action and put it in his pocket. As the next round came up on the carrier, he removed that, too, and then closed the action on an empty chamber. He pushed the live round back into the gun's magazine through the loading gate, then two more from his belt. He lowered the hammer, and slipped the rifle back into its rear-facing scabbard.

He looked again at the Indians, and could see that they were either going away or coming at him. After a moment he could see they were coming, not going.

"Damn!" he muttered. So they weren't about to go away after all. He wheeled the horse about toward the hills. He knew he would have to get to some place he could put his back to something solid, or they'd have him eventually.

Years before he had scouted this country, and knew pretty much what lay ahead. There was water from several springs in the hills, but the two he knew of lay to the southwest. In the north and west the land broke up into gullies and washes as it rose to a low ridge, then descended into the Cinch River breaks. If he could make that broken country, he would have a chance to lose them, or ambush them. The question was, could he make the two or three miles to the hills, then the few miles more to the head of the breaks. Not much choice. He turned Bill into the north again and urged him into an easy canter.

He mentally counted up the cartridges he had on hand, how many rounds for the army Colt on his belt, how many for the big Winchester. He knew he would have to pick his fight; if they ran him to ground they had the numbers to be at him all day and all night, and he would be a dead man in two days. He went over the hills ahead in his mind, knowing he would have to get through quickly, that he must not be headed, where he could hole up if they cornered him. Every few minutes he looked back at the dog soldiers in the distance. Coming.

The afternoon wore away, and the stench of the fire on the wind thickened. The grey brown haze stretched out along the land, obscuring the round knobs of the hills ahead. The man still could not see the fire to the west, just the streaming smoke. If the fire cut him off, he would have to run to the east, or straight back into the redskins. Either way, he was cooked.

8

The smoke thickened and he rode in a world of yellowed white, seeing only a few yards in any direction. He kept a sharp eye on the ground ahead, looking for any obstacles that might trouble Bill. The smoke stung his eyes, burned his throat. Surely it wasn't doing Bill any good. Then they cleared it, like a veil being lifted, and the hills loomed a mile away. In the west the sun was nearing the range of jagged peaks. As horse and rider came up on the low, brown mounds of the hills, he reined in Bill again, to give him a chance to clear the smoke from his lungs and blow.

He looked back for the braves, but the smoke lay like a fat snake over the prairie, obscuring everything to the south. He had an urge to take the rifle and get down, wait for them to clear the smoke and pick off as many as he could. They would break out of the smoke suddenly, eyes smarting, and he was sure he could get two, maybe three before they knew what hit them. But he had no idea of exactly where they would break out into the open, and if they were a few hundred yards off of where he hoped they would be, they'd be around him in an instant and that would be that. Custer made that mistake, he would not.

He spurred Bill toward an opening in the hills. If he could get out of sight among the knobs, he might be able to circle around and set up an ambush from a point he could easily abandon and slip away after doing them some damage.

Bill was tiring as they entered a shallow draw. They pounded up the sandy wash as the man's last glance at the plain told him it was empty of all but the billowing smoke. Then they were in the hills and hidden from view.

The ground began to break up a little, with low scrub brush clumped on the hillsides. The rider stayed in the bottom of the wash as it wound deeper into the hills. The lowering sun cast shadows in the bottom of the draw. Soon they were moving in the shade completely as the surrounding hills blocked out the sun.

The man finally stopped, then turned Bill straight up a long, brushy slope. He knew that over the crest of that long mound was a downhill run through the Cinch River breaks. Once up there he would have a fine view of his back trail.

The horse slipped and scrabbled its way out of the bottom wash and onto the slope, and worked hard up the slope in great bounding leaps. As they climbed the rider could feel the energy go out of his mount as each bound grew a little shorter, took a little longer. Bill was about played out.

As they neared the crest, a war whoop sounded behind them. The man knew he had been spotted, and swore. Just over the crest, he reined in the hard blowing horse, jumped down, went around to the rifle scabbard and dragged the big Winchester out. Bill stood trembling, blowing hard, and the man knew that without rest they would never make it to the river, even downhill all the way. He had to buy them some time.

He crouched beside a sage brush clump on the ridgetop. He could see them coming down the far slope. They had come directly cross country while he had stayed in the meandering wash bottom. They had worked much harder up and down the hills but had shortened the distance and now they had their quarry in sight. They came sweeping down the opposite bank, maybe 300 yards out. He counted six, seven, eight. All that lucky shooting hadn't accounted for much after all.

He checked the rifle sights, set the rear sight elevation for 150 yards. It would be a downhill shot, and he knew the rifle would throw a little high because of that. He judged the bottom of the gully at about 200, maybe 250 yards out. Sun at his back, but they would be in shade down there, so he had no advantage.

He crouched, then lined up the long, heavy barrel where he figured the lead rider would hit bottom. The wind was coming in over his right shoulder and flowing down to his left. That would be where the smoke would trail away. He could try for the left most of the lead riders, then swing quickly to the next one right without being hindered by the smoke from his shot. Everything depended on his being able to do as much damage as possible as quickly as possible.

He bore down on the sights, front bead in the rear notch, left hand holding the fore end with its elbow braced on a knee, watching the lead horse and rider drop down in front of the gun, then they were in the bottom of the wash. He made an effort to focus on the front sight as the warrior crossed the draw, his finger gently tightening on the trigger. Boom! The buck of the gun slapped his shoulder, and he worked the lever smoothly as the barrel settled back in, this time to the right slightly, the sights sliding together and centering the second warrior, who had already crossed the draw and had his pony struggling up out of the wash onto the near slope. The rifle boomed again and all the world went white with smoke. The man levered in another round as the smoke wafted off to his left. He caught sight of the rest of the Indians in a bunch rounding the curve of the wash to his left, disappearing at the run. He threw the rifle up, but no chance for a shot. Then they were gone around the slope of the hill.

Below him, a downed horse lay in the bottom of the wash on the right. On the left, a standing pony, and one dead warrior at its feet. As he watched, an Indian suddenly emerged from below the rim of the wash and leaped onto the standing pony, and, gripping the horse on the off side with his heel and a fistful of mane, got the pony going down the wash after his brothers. The man threw the rifle to his shoulder once more, but did not fire. Then the warrior rounded the bend in the wash and was gone.

The man quickly gathered up the empty cartridge casings and pocketed them. He racked open the action of the rifle, lifted out the live round, closed the action, lowered the hammer on the empty chamber, then stuffed the magazine full of cartridges again. He slipped the Winchester back into its scabbard. He swung up on Bill, patted his neck, and gently spurred the horse westward down the slope of the hill to start a descent into the Cinch River breaks. The last of the sun blinked away over the purple mountains in the distance.

Chapter 2

Darkness had come and a rich, full moon had risen by the time a slow moving Bill and his rider reached the Cinch River. The man urged Bill into the shallows, let him drink. He looked up and down the dark, moon sparkled river. The trees and brush along each bank were black in the shadows of the moon.

He got Bill's head up and turned the tired beast upriver, walking him in the shallows. They moved along for half an hour in the rippled water, the man careful to keep to the shallows, until they reached a clump of willows on the western bank. He could see the sparkle of water trickling over rocks in the moonlight as a side stream emptied into the Cinch. The rider turned Bill in among the trees, where they clattered up a rocky stream bed, then into a little canyon. They followed the stream up the canyon for another ten minutes, and finally stopped at a small widening of the canyon walls with a pool of quiet water.

The moon was well up and peeking over the rim of the gulch as the man stepped down and began to unload the horse. The base of one bank of the little canyon was shadowed from the moon by an overhang of rock, and he stashed the gear in the shadows. He used his rope to set Bill out on a long lead, and tied the other end to his saddle set against the darkened bank.

"No grass tonight, Bill," he said softly to the horse as he patted his neck, "If we've thrown 'em off, we'll take the time tomorrow to find you the best there is. Sorry about that." The horse snorted and stepped to the pool and began sucking up water noisily.

The man went to his gear and arranged the saddle against the gully bank, pulled his rifle out of its scabbard, and sat back against the saddle with the Winchester across his lap. He knew they could not track Bill in the dark, through the water, but he had not lived the last dozen years in Indian country by taking anything for granted. He would have no fire this night, for though they could not see the flames down in this little hole in the canyon, they might smell the smoke on the wind that drifted easily down from the heights to the west.

The clear air had turned cold, and the man got up to spread the wet saddle blanket over a rock to dry. He fetched a rolled-up coat from his gear bag, shook it out and put it on. He got his sleeping blanket, some jerky from the bag, and a tin cup. Bill was done drinking as the man went to the pool and filled the cup, drank it down, filled it again, and returned to the saddle. He settled in, chewing the jerky and washing it down with water.

He dozed through the night with the Winchester at hand, waking often in the stillness. The only sound was the gurgle of the little stream as it emptied into the pool. Bill was asleep in the moonlight, standing next to the pool. The moon climbed along the southern rim of the gully and then was gone over the peaks in the west. The man slept better in the starlight, and jolted awake once to a distant chorus of coyotes laughing at the stars. Then, with a faint hint of dawn blushing the eastern horizon, he came fully awake. Time to go.

Chapter 3

The first day out of the cold camp the man eased Bill along at his own pace, and though the horse was tired, he kept at it. They stopped at every opportunity for water, grass, whatever browse the man could find on the mountain slopes. As the man let the horse graze from time to time, he kept his eyes sweeping every ridge, skyline, and canyon mouth in sight. The occasional deer or buffalo or elk that came into view got his immediate attention, and he felt the urge to grab for the rifle in its scabbard under his leg. But these figures he ignored once he had identified them as animals. It was human forms he looked for, warriors on horseback.

By the morning of the second day, Bill was stronger and seemed eager to pick up the pace. They traveled briskly throughout that day, and during the night the camp was inundated by a rainstorm. Packing his gear in the morning, the man had to drain and twist water out of everything, and when he got up in the saddle, the warm autumn wind was already drying his rig.

By mid day the man was guiding Bill down the muddy main street of Quandry, Wyoming. The horse's hooves made sucking plops in the goo as he plodded along. The man had mostly dried out, but the wind had died, and scattered clouds rolled apart to reveal a new blue of crisp autumn sky.

Quandry was not a large town, but did boast a hotel, a bank, two saloons, a livery, a dozen small houses, and a general store. And, at the west end of the main street, a brand new railroad station. The rider took in the sights as he moved up the street toward the station, and noted that the street seemed sort of quiet for mid-day. As he passed the hotel nearest the station, loud voices caught his attention.

Three men were arguing with a fourth man, and a fifth man was looking down over the rail of the second floor veranda at them. As the rider passed, the three had just yanked a shotgun out of the hands

13

of the fourth man, and shoved him off of the porch. He kept his footing, but shook his fist at them as he turned and walked up the street. The expression on his face was one of ruddy rage. The rider could just catch a glimpse of a badge on his vest as his brown coat swung open. The shortest of the men on the porch stepped into the street and tossed the shotgun up to the man on the veranda. That man grabbed the gun and sat back in one of two chairs there, balancing the gun across his lap. He put his feet up on the other chair, looking for all the world like a napping rattlesnake draped on the rocks.

The four men all eyed the rider as he passed. Bill plodded on to the rail station, and the man got down and tied up the big roan to the hitching rail. He stepped up on the station platform, and then went inside the small office, which bore a sign stating "Tickets, Freight, Telegraph" over the door. Inside, he found a clerk hunched over the telegraph gear, writing quickly as the tap-tap-tapping of the key dictated. The newcomer found a blank telegraph pad on the counter, and a stubby pencil. The pencil had a newly whittled, sharp point. The man put the point to the paper to begin a message, and it snapped off at the wood. He pulled a well-worn Sheffield bowie from the scabbard on his back belt, and began to whittle a shorter, stouter point.

The tapping stopped, and the clerk acknowledged with three quick taps of his own. He laid down his pencil.

"Hello," he said brusquely, "what can I do for ya?" He stood to the counter.

"Like to send a telegram up to Missoula."

"Sure. Go ahead and write it out."

The man finished with the point, sheathed the knife, and began writing.

"Looks like the station here is new. Been here long?" the man said as he wrote.

"One month. I was the senior assistant at the Cheyenne office, then they sent me here to break in a new man. Track goes on to Journeyville, stops there."

"Where's the new man?"

"Ain't you heard? Most of the town is out at the cemetery layin' under the Stoeger family. Kilt by Injuns just four miles from here! Tragic thing, all those kids. Hell, we ain't had no Injun trouble in years, it's this war goin' on up north that's got every redskin all het up!"

"Well, I surely do know that. Had to shoot my way through just getting here." He put down the pencil and shoved the pad to the clerk.

The clerk read it off. "To: General O.O. Howard, Missoula, Montana Territory.

"Have reached Quandry, WT. Stop. Last message stated Nez Perce headed Yellowstone. Stop. Awaiting contact with Fifth Cavalry. Stop.
Signed: Jon Beck"

"Yep. That'll pretty much do it," Beck said.

The clerk totaled up the cost per word, worked out the sum on the back of the paper, and Jon Beck paid the bill.

"Recommend a good hotel?" he said.

"Ransom House, just up past the livery, other side of the street, probably your best bet. We've two boardin' houses in town, but the Ransom House has the better food. That's where I eat, anyway."

"All right. I'll be up there if a reply to that comes through."

"Might take a day or two. No direct line up to Montana, got to send it back down through Cheyenne, around the horn, so to speak."

"Do what you can."

"Sure enough. Say, you an Indian fighter or some such?"

"Something like that."

"We could use a little help in that regard around here, you know. Sheriff and his posse are out after the redskin scum that did for the Stoegers, but they ain't Injun fighters. They might be able to use some help."

"I'll see what I can do. Mean time, you get a reply to that, I need it pronto."

"Sure enough, Mr.—" and the clerk glanced at the message, "—ah, Beck."

Jon Beck left the office, untied Bill and walked him up to the livery on the right side of the street. He led Bill in through the big open doors. A man was in the loft forking down hay into the mangers of two stalls, where horses chewed amidst the food shower.

"Got room for one more?" Beck called up to the man. The hayman stopped work, leaned on his pitchfork, and peered down at Beck. He wore three weeks of beard, a dirty tweed vest over a once

15

white shirt, and a crumpled stovepipe hat. Hard to tell he wasn't in the hat when it got crumpled.

"Yeah, I got room. Just put him in number three, there, next to the bay." The man went back to pitching hay, this time dropping some into the manger in stall three.

Beck began unloading his gear, stacking it next to the main doorway. "Got any oats?" he called up to the stableman.

"Yeah, I got oats. Cost ya, though."

"This big feller saved my life a few days back. I figure I can pay for oats." The saddle came off, and Jon heaved it easily over a saddle rail with several others along the wall. He led Bill into the stall, took the bridle off of him, patted his neck, and closed the stall gate.

"Any chance you could curry him good this afternoon?" he asked. The stableman was climbing down the wooden ladder built up one wall. He hit the ground and walked over, rubbing his hands.

"Yeah, cost ya, though."

"All right."

"You staying in town long?"

"Two, maybe three days, I guess."

"Couple of bucks in advance wouldn't hurt nothin," the stableman said.

Jon Beck fished a small gold coin out of his pocket and handed it over. "There's five, on account. You take good care of that horse, or I'll be looking for change."

"Yes sir! That horse'll think he's died and gone to critter heaven!"

Beck went to his gear, took up the rifle scabbard and tied the ends of its tethering straps together. He slung the scabbard over his left shoulder, then pulled his long bowie knife from its scabbard behind his right hip and slipped the blade, handle first, up his right sleeve. The tip rested in the palm of his hand. He gathered up the saddle bags which he slung over his left forearm, and his gear bag, clutched in his left hand.

The stableman had been watching this, and as Jon prepared to step out the door, he glanced back at the horse, and saw the stableman looking at him.

"Expecting trouble?" the top-hatted man asked.

"You never know," Beck said, "And he needs that curry today, all right?"

"Yeah, I can do that."

Beck passed out of the livery and angled across the street for the Ransom House Hotel. The three men still occupied its porch, and the fourth still sat on the balcony with the twin-barrel gun across his lap. Beck's boots squished in the deep mud of the street, and he could feel the mud sucking at each sole, trying to pull the boot from his foot.

Jon could feel the eyes of the four on him as he came up to the steps, then climbed them. Two of them were leaning on the porch rail, the short one was standing near the door. The two leaners were off to the left. As he topped the steps he heard a small noise from above, and figured the veranda cowboy had shifted position and was trying to watch what went on below. As Jon crossed the porch, the short man stepped over to block his way. The smell of whisky permeated the air.

"Well hold on there pardner, you look like you come a long way! You're almost home, 'z only a few more yards to a hot bath and a clean bed. Least as clean as ol' Miz Ranson can get it," the short man grinned. "And it's only a few yards to her, too!" the kid leered. The other two laughed, one poked the other.

"'Cept ya gotta pay the road toll, yes sir, it's a dollar a head to get in!" the kid continued.

"Oh?" said Jon Beck softly, "And why would I want to pay this "toll" of yours?"

"Why, a dollar'ld do it! Injuns about, bad hombres and mean men, but we here cowboys'll make sure nobody's gonna get in yer way!" The young man giggled. His face was flushed, his eyelids drooped. He swayed a bit on his feet.

"Well, pardner, it looks to me like you're in my way," Beck said as he stepped very close to the kid, winking at him as he did so, "I figure you boys have had enough fun for the morning, and it's time to go sleep it off. Wouldn't you agree?"

"Hell no! Maybe you didn't hear—", the drunken cowboy began quickly, then froze. He glanced down at what was tickling his belly. His eyes widened. Beck's Sheffield bowie was just about nibbling its way through his shirt. The other two toughs could not see it, their view blocked by all the gear Beck had draped over his left arm.

17

"Tell your pards to step off the porch to the south side there," Beck said very quietly, staring straight into the now alarmed eyes of the younger man. The kid licked his lips, glanced down again, and said, "Boys, this here hombre has a point, a very good point." He looked again into Beck's face and tried to smile

The other two looked at each other, and one of them stepped toward Beck.

"Now Henry, I ain't joshin' here!" the young man blurted out. "Let's us go get a sasparilla over to the saloon."

"Sasparilla...?!" one of them cried, "What the hell—"

"Just shut up and get movin!" the redhead said loudly, smiling all the more brightly into Beck's face.

The two leaners looked at each other again and moved past Beck down the steps and into the street.

"Meant no harm, stranger, just funnin' with ya, no offense!" the small man said, and edged around Beck to join his friends in the street.

"No offense taken," Beck said, and slipped the knife into his belt. He stepped to the hotel doors and was quickly through and inside, shutting the door carefully behind him.

Once in the small lobby, Beck dumped his gear in the corner next to a stuffed chair. He slipped the Bowie back into its scabbard, then drew his army Colt and stepped to the window. Very carefully he peered out the space between curtain and post, and saw the three men standing in the street. They were all looking up at the second floor veranda. Beck stepped across the room to the hallway that led into the interior of the building. He quickly went down the hall to the first door, opened it, looked in. The room contained a bed, a wash stand, hooks on the walls for clothes. No personal possessions were in it. Beck stepped in, closed the door until a tiny crack remained between door and jamb. He waited.

After a few moments, he heard the floorboards of the hallway creaking, and then a shape passed by the crack. He could see the back of the man from the balcony moving down the hallway past the door. He quickly opened the door and stepped into the hallway two paces behind the cowboy, who was nearly to the lobby and had the shotgun at the ready. The man stiffened at the sound of the door and the noise of Jon's boots on the wood. The loudest sound of all was the four little clicks of the Colt revolver coming to full cock.

18

"Well, hey, I was just—"

"Shut up! Lay that scattergun on the floor very carefully. If you so much as twitch, you're dead meat." Beck took a pace closer to the man.

"Why....why sure, pard, I—"

"Now!" Beck said low and hard, the barrel of the Colt touching the back of the man's head. The man took a sudden, deep breath, paused, and Beck could see him swallow. He gradually bent over and laid the gun on the floor.

"Now walk straight out of here, and don't look back. You look back even once, and I start shooting. Understand?"

"Yeah. I understand." The man moved slowly, stiffly toward the door, then was at it, then had it open, stepped through, and closed it behind him. Beck could smell the odor of the whisky in the hallway, and smell of sweat, and a deep, acrid stench. Fear.

Chapter 4

Jon Beck sat in the overstuffed lobby chair, which he had placed in the corner on the front wall so that it was behind the front door as it opened into the room. He examined the scattergun that lay across his lap, noting the "W. W. Greener" etched in script along the top rib between the barrels. He worked the lever and opened the breech, where two 10 gauge shells raised their brass heads. When he heard a noise on the porch outside, he snapped the action closed and checked the hammers—both at full cock.

The doorknob turned, the door creaked open slowly. A head protruded into the room, wearing a Derby hat. Beck recognized the ruddily complected profile of the lawman he had seen lose the shotgun earlier.

"Come on in, marshal," Beck said. The man started, looked around, caught sight of Beck in the chair. Then he noted the shotgun. His eyes lingered on it for a moment.

"It's all right, marshal, I'm just holding it for you," Beck said, rising and letting the hammers down one by one. The man stepped into the room as Beck let the shotgun slide down to rest its butt on the floor.

"Well, thank you, stranger, I'll just take it, then," he man said, stepping toward Beck and reaching for the gun. Beck made no move to hand it over, and the man hesitated, paused, then looked Beck in the face.

"Those four boys friends of yours?" Beck said as he hefted up the gun and handed it over.

"Hell no, them bastards is just hands out at the T Bar W. They's drunk as polecats…you see which way they went?"

"Nope. I'm Jon Beck, just got to town." Beck held out his hand.

"Oh. I'm Nate Chalkin, deputy marshal around here," the lawman said, and shook the proffered hand. He winced a little.

"Deputy, hunh? Where's your boss?" Beck said.

"Who?"

"The marshal."

"Oh, well, he's out tracking them Injuns what done for the Stoegers. Left me in charge. Those T Bar boys about the only folks left in town, what with the funeral and all."

"Those cowboys always drink like that?"

"Naw, they ain't really bad sorts, just get to be real little pricks when they drink too much. But I suppose they earned it, this time. They's the ones found the Stoegers."

"They seemed to be having a little too much fun for men that needed to be drunk."

"Well, maybe so, they did run off two drummers that tried the hotel afore you did. They ran out of cash over to the saloon and were looking for a liquor stake. Roustin' folks was their way of getting it, I suppose. That's why I came over here to break it up, them drummers come a-runnin' all het up."

"And what were you going to do with the shotgun?"

"Well, it was for just in case."

"You normally the deputy around here?"

"No, I'm normally Mr. Connolly's teller, over to the bank."

"Well Nate, just a word of advice. If you're going to pack iron, you'd best be prepared to use it. Otherwise it will just get you killed."

"Oh I don't think them boys was in a killing mood. I figured I'd just roust 'em a little."

20

"Then why'd you take the shotgun?"

"Well, there's four of them...."

"Why'd you take the gun?"

Chalkin stared at Beck for a moment.

"They wouldn't listen to me if'n I had no gun. I'm just a bank clerk, fer God's sake, they weren't about to do what I said lest I had a gun."

"Did they do what you said?"

"No."

"No. They took your gun. If you rely on a gun for authority, you have no authority."

"But I'm just a bank clerk. They know that."

"Yep. I guess they do."

"Well how'd you get rid of 'em, then?"

"I just asked politely. They recognized the error of their ways and went away."

Chalkin looked Beck up and down. He saw a man of average height, stockily built, with a strong featured face and grey, steady eyes. His lean chin and jaw bore the stubble of several days on the trail, and his mustache was brown and bushed out his upper lip. It was the eyes, Chalkin finally decided, that gave him the uneasy feeling he had in his gut from the moment he first saw the man. It was a feeling that something was about to happen, an edgy, unbalanced feeling, as if he was in the presence of some great beast about to go for his throat. He blinked. No, this Jon Beck was just a man, just a man. But still....

"You some kind of lawman?" he finally asked Beck.

"No. On my way north to see about some Indians. Work for the Fifth Cavalry at the moment."

"Injun fighter? Hell, we sure could use you around here, never seen anything like it, everything peaceful as a pasture, then all of a sudden we got blood all over the place!"

"So I hear. When did all this happen?"

"T Bar boys came tearin' into town three days ago, found the Stoeger place all burned out, family dead. We went out with wagons and brought 'em in, then the marshal got up a posse and they lit out the next morning. This morning the whole town went out to the cemetery to lay 'em under. Should be back any time now, so....in fact, I think I hear 'em now."

Beck had already stepped to the window, and parted the curtain to peer into the street. There he could see three wagons, a buggy, and a dozen horsemen, as well a several dozen people on foot, strung out as they came up the street. Most were dressed in black. The buggy stopped before the hotel, and a lady wearing black and a veil stepped down onto the porch steps. Deputy Chalkin opened the door wider.

"Howdy Mrs. Ransom," he said, stepping out of the doorway, as the lady entered the room, "are the Stoegers now resting in piece?"

"Yes, Mr. Chalkin, they are, may God rest their souls" said the woman, lifting her veil. She glanced over at Beck.

"That there's Mr. Beck," said Chalkin, "going to be a guest of yours I guess."

"Pleasure, Ma'am," said Beck, removing his hat with a nod.

"My apologies for not being here to greet you, sir," said the woman, "but if you will just come this way, I will get you the best room in the house." She bustled over to the other side of the room and went behind the little counter, reached beneath it, and placed a large book on the wood. Behind her were a sideboard and a tall open-faced cabinet with mail cubbies across its front. She fetched up a small inkwell and pen as Beck stepped up, and set them on the counter.

"Well, I've got me two more for you Mrs. Ransom, I'll just go and fetch 'em over," said Chalkin, and stepped out the door, closing it behind him.

Beck picked up the pen, dipped it, began writing his name where Mrs. Ransom pointed.

"Will you be in town long Mr., ah, Beck, is it?" she asked, peering at his signature.

"Few days at most. On my way north, scouting for the army. I was instructed to wire General Howard's command from Quandry for further instruction. 'Spect he's most likely caught and whipped those Nez Perces by now, though."

"Perhaps not! You have no doubt heard the tragic news of the Stoegers? Some think the murdering savages who killed those poor people were with those northern renegades.

"Begging your pardon, Mrs. Ransom, but I don't think they could have traveled this far south so fast. Last I heard they were still just east of the Bitterroots, maybe headed for the Yellowstone. Even if they've still managed to elude General Howard, they could not have come this far south in so short a time. No, if it's Indians that killed your Stoeger family, they are most likely a local band, or passing through. Have they done any other damage around here?"

"I certainly hope you are correct, sir, and the evil savages who have done this shameful deed are few in number and long gone from the country! And no, we have had no reports of any further killings or burnings in the three days that have passed since the horror became known to us."

"That's good. Hope it stays that way."

"And I, sir, pray hourly that it is so. Please come this way, I will show you to your room."

Beck collected his gear from the corner and followed Mrs. Ransom down the hall, where she let him into the last room on the left. She placed the key on the wash stand as he set his belongings beside the bed. He asked for a basin of hot water, which was promised him as soon as his hostess could get up the fire in the kitchen and heat the water. Mrs. Ransom went out, and Beck could hear the voices of others coming into the lobby, along with the whiney tones of Deputy Chalkin.

He found the pitcher on the wash stand was full of water, so he poured some into the basin and, taking a neckerchief from his pack, proceeded to wash his face and neck. This done, he hung the rag on a bedpost, and removed his rifle from its scabbard. He opened the butt trap and took out a cleaning rod that was in three pieces and wrapped in soft deerskin. He screwed the three pieces together end to end to make one long rod, then threaded a slotted tip to one end. He took a little wad of bunting from his kit, and attached a piece of it through the slot. He opened the rifle's action, racking the rounds out on the bed one by one. When the rifle was empty, he left the action open, and, dipping the bunting in the water basin, ran the wad down the bore from the muzzle, and pulled it out again. The wad came out black with fouling. He plucked it from the slot, rinsed it in the basin, put it back on the slot, and repeated the process, scrubbing the bore of the rifle and then running a dry cloth patch through it until he could place his thumbnail behind the chamber and look down the bore at the reflected light gleaming off of shiny steel rifling. He then attached a piece of oiled deerskin to the slotted tip, and ran that through the bore several times. He inspected the action, and using the tip of this Sheffield with a bit of the cloth, cleaned up the last of the fouling he could see in the moving parts. He inspected the gun in detail, looking it over for rust, dirt, fouling, and wear. He saw that several weeks in the saddle scabbard had already started to scuff the bluing off of the sides of the barrel at the muzzle, and at the stock boss near the wrist.

"They don't stay new for very long," he muttered as he picked up the rounds from the bed, looked them over, and slid them back into the rifle's magazine.

Mrs. Ransom tapped on the door half an hour later, and handed him the basin of hot water when he opened it. She smiled as he thanked her, and let him know supper would be served in the cook shed out back at about six o'clock.

He used the hot water to shave and clean himself more thoroughly.

An hour later he found Mrs. Ransom at the front desk, handed over his key, made arrangements to have his laundry done, learned that the menu for supper included crabapple pie, and remarked on Mrs. Ransom's good spirits.

"I hesitate to say it, Mr. Beck, but Indian trouble always seems to guarantee a full house! Drummers hate to travel at such times, and local families come to town for safety. And we've several railroad men from up the line who tell me Journeyville's hotels are all full for the same reasons! I only pray that you are right in your opinions and whatever vicious beasts that did this thing are running for their lives at this very moment."

"Could be, Mrs. Ransom, could be. I'll be back for dinner, you have convinced me with that promise of apple pie!" He tipped his hat and went through the door.

Chapter 5

Jon Beck stepped out onto the hotel porch. His grey eyes quickly took in the details of the town, the pock-marked mud of the street rapidly hardening in the mid afternoon sun, two men loading a wagon at the mercantile, a lone rider walking his horse out of a side street, the open doors of the livery down across the way near the train station, the railroad depot itself at the end of the street, the several men talking on the depot porch.

He stepped down and walked toward the side street, and at its intersect noted the saloon on one side of it, and the several small shops opposite. One of those was a harness shop or saddlery. Beck walked to the front of the saddlery as a wagon came up the street, loaded with several women and a bunch of kids, two men on the driving seat and two more on horses coming along behind.

Beck stepped past a couple of saddles on stands outside the shop and into the darker interior. One wall was hung with new bridles, another with cartridge belts, holsters, whips, coiled riatas, and quirts. Shelving on another wall held pairs of boots. As Beck looked over the merchandise, a squat man stepped out of a back room into the shop.

"Welcome, senor, have you come for a new saddle today?" the stubby man said with a small smile. His skin was dark, and his face clearly showed Indian blood. His thick arms hung out a little from his sides, as if he were in a perpetual shrug.

"Good day, senor," Beck said, "No, not a saddle. Can you make me a pair of moccasins?"

"Of course, senor! I make the finest moccasins in all of Wyoming Territory!" His smile broadened. "And most of Colorado as well!" he said, sweeping his arm toward one wall where hung several pairs of boots and moccasins.

Beck smiled in his turn. "Excellent!"

"Please sit down and remove your boots," said the half breed. "I will take your measure." He swung a low stool out from a corner, and Beck sat. As he pulled off his boots, the 'breed ducked into the back room and returned a second later with a wooden shingle and a knife.

He knelt before Beck and placed the piece of shingle flat on the beaten earth floor, and guided Beck's foot onto the wood. He marked the length of the foot with a nick of the knife on the wood, then did the same for the width. He quickly placed the other foot on the wood, confirmed that both feet were about the same.

Sitting back on his haunches, he said, "Would you care for the hide of the cow, the horse, the deer, the elk, the buffalo?"

"Whatever will last," Beck said, pulling on his boots. "They must tread quietly on the rocks, not stiffen after wading rivers, carry me a thousand miles after stray horses...and let me run very fast when I see an Indian."

The half breed laughed, a low guttural cough.

"Senor, you do not seem the kind of man who runs from anything," he said, almost in a sneering tone.

"I did not say I would run from an Indian, senor," Beck said with a smile, "Sometimes they are hard to catch."

The half-breed laughed even harder.

"Then come to my bench, catcher of Indians, I will let you pick out the best of my skins. I would suggest a young elk for the ankle, and an old elk for the sole. The one will bend with every step, while the other will give less easily but will last like iron."

They went into the smaller room at the back of the shop, which had a workbench along one wall beneath a small window. Stacks of hides filled a corner, shelves were piled with scraps of leather, shoe lasts, patterns, boxes and jars. Tools were arranged on the bench. The half-breed told Jon Beck that his name was Samuel Gland as he showed some of the hides to his customer. Beck chose the materials and Samuel went to work. He pulled down a last from the shelf, determined it was the correct size by holding the stick up to it, and fitted it to a rack on the bench. He went to work on the moccasins as Beck seated himself on one of the piles of hides. The shop reeked of the stench of tanned leather.

"What brings you to our little town?" said Gland.

"Indians."

"Surely you do not come here to hide as all the others do."

"No. I will be leaving soon, when the cavalry arrives. I will lead them to the north, where we will talk to the Crow. I hear that the Crow are friends of the Nez Perces."

"Ah, I hear this too."

"Do you have friends among the Crow?"

"The Crow work their own skins."

"I mean as an Indian."

"I am a poor Spanish worker of leather, that is all."

"Gland is not a Spanish name. So your mother was an Indian. Of which tribe?"

Samuel looked over his shoulder at Jon Beck, his black eyes flat. Then he went back to the task at hand.

"When there is talk of Indians on the warpath," he said, "my business is poor. Men would have me mend their harness when they know my cousins will not kill them for it as they ride home. But let the first farmer come running to town with cries of Indians, Indians, and I am at once friend to every skulking red bastard on the northern plains!" He spat in the dirt to the far side of where Beck sat.

"What brought you here from Arizona?" Beck said.

Gland looked at him again quickly.

"Are you not Apache?" Beck went on.

"Si, I am of Apache blood, but how...?"

"Your own moccasins, Apache. A man who can make any moccasin he wishes would only wear what he knows best."

Gland went back to work chuckling. "You are right, senor, I am a simple worker of leather. In the Chiricahua Mountains, no white man would buy from me. And the Apaches just steal what they want. I left that land to find a place where a man can work and feed his family and not have to beg or kill to make a living."

"When these farmers you spoke of come crying of Indians, who are they crying about? Surely the Nez Perce cannot have come this far south. Is it the Crow, are they now rising up against the white man?"

"No no, senor, nothing at all like that," Gland said, shaking his head over his work. "The iron road has brought the singing wire, and the news of the Nez Perce comes to us by the day. They approach, it is said, but they are still far away. And the Crow, they squat over their cooking pots eating the white man's beef, they chase nobody. I know of one Arapaho camp not far from here, a day's ride, but it is not they who make the farmers cry out."

"Who, then?"

"That, senor, is a mystery to me."

"I saw the burial party return, I heard from the people that a family was butchered, not far from the town. Burned out, they say, a family with children. Who would do such a thing if not Indians? If these farmers come to town crying Indians, Indians, it would seem that a poor worker of leather as an Indian would want to know the truth of it. For the sake of his business, if not his hair."

Gland worked on without a word for a few moments. Then he said, "That is true."

"And what did you find out?"

"I only know that Indians did not do this thing, senor."

"Is that all you know?"

"It is enough. But it is still bad for my business, anyway. The crying farmers believe what they will. No one listens to a half breed Spanish who is only protecting his cousins."

Within an hour the shoemaker had finished his work. Beck tried on the new moccasins, declared them an excellent fit although stiff. They discussed curing the leather and the final set it would take with use, which hot fat to apply for waterproofing. The price was negotiated, and Beck paid in coin.

"Thank you, Samuel, these will do fine."

"To help you catch your Indians," Gland said, offering his hand, "but you must be careful what you chase, sometimes the catching is only the beginning."

Beck chuckled. "Very true," he said, and took the offered hand in his own. Their grips tightened. The man who filled his days bending tough hides to his will, tugging stiff sinews through tight holes punched in the leather, kneading stubborn skins into pliant submission, used the crushing force of his grip to impress a memory into the flesh of the grey-eyed stranger's hand. But as his fingers clenched in practiced force, he found his palm gripped in fingers of steel, solid, unyielding, matching his strength with a surge of greater power, tighter, harder, like the unfeeling jaws of a vise.

Their eyes met, did not blink, as their hands pressed home the inexorable contest of sheer power and crushing force. Finally, the half breed dropped his gaze and backed off his grip. Beck released him instantly.

"Thank you for the moccasins," Beck said, and with a slight smile stepped through the shop and out into the street..

Samuel Gland shook his right hand as if he had just pulled it from the fire.

Chapter 6

The sun hung low over the buildings along the west side of the street, and the shadows were half way up Beck's middle as he turned and strode back towards his hotel, boots in hand. A shriek sounded from the saloon across the street, and as he glanced in that direction, three cowboys burst through the doorway, stumbled across the plank porch and tumbled into the street. Two of them went down hard in the dirt, one of those skidding on his face, and the third caught a roof support post and swung around it neatly, staying upright. The cowboy who had skidded the furthest sat up and shrieked again, a cross between a rebel yell and a Comanche war whoop. The one face down in the dirt rolled over and laughed.

A very large man in a white apron appeared at the door. The cowboy wrapped around the roof post gave a half-hearted yelp, and, seeing the bartender take a step toward him, unhitched himself from the post and leapt into the street, where he caught a spur and stumbled, fell, laughed.

"You boys go sleep it off!" the bartender said from the edge of the porch. "When I tell you no credit I mean that, so don't come back less'n you got something to spend!" He turned and went back into the bar, and a fourth cowboy came out, looking over his shoulder at the passing barkeep. The fourth cowpoke was moving slowly, chewing on a toothpick. Beck remembered him with a shotgun in his hands. The cowboy grinned at the three in the street and leaned against the roof post, shaking his head. His eyes lifted and he saw Beck.

"Well lookee there, Simon," said the cowboy sitting in the street, "There's that sneaky bastard got the drop on you in the hotel!" He, too, had found Beck with bleary, bloodshot eyes, and grinned as he spoke. Beck kept moving, crossing the street on a diagonal that placed him in the shadow of the lowering sun on the west side of the street. He watched the cowboy on the porch, and shifted his boots into his left hand.

The man sitting in the street was the short, red headed tough who had felt the tickle of Beck's bowie knife on the hotel stoop. His smile faded as he got to his feet, swaying a bit, and the other downed men got up too. "Boys," the redhead said, "I think we need to collect that dollar right here and now!" The three in the street began to close on Beck, while the man on the porch just leaned on the post and watched.

"Hey, Simon!" the leader said over his shoulder, "You want to plug him when we're done with him?"

The three were grinning as they came within arms length of Beck. The man to the left never saw the fist that released the boots and slammed into his nose with startling quickness. The blow stunned him, stopped him, buckled his knees. Before either of the other two could react, Beck's right plowed into the redhead's solar plexus, doubling him over with a grunt. Beck shifted his weight to the right as his left swung across the back of the doubled man and connected with the jaw of the third man, who only had a chance to begin raising his hands to protect himself. The blow twisted his head and he seemed to pause like a hovering bird, then went down like felled timber, out cold. The redhead was on one knee, where he groaned and then threw up in the dirt of the street.

The first man hit was sitting in the dust, holding his face, blood oozing from his nose, cursing. Beck had his eyes on Simon on the porch. At the edge of his vision he saw the bloody nosed man try to tug his revolver out of its holster, but the hammer was tangled in his vest and watch chain. Beck crouched before him, looked him in the eye, shook his head slowly back and forth and said, "No." The bloodied man, cursing with pain, slowly focused on Beck's face. He stopped mumbling as he gradually began to comprehend. He turned loose of the gun.

Beck picked up his boots and stood. He stepped around the three casualties and approached the man on the porch.

"So, you must be Simon?" Beck said.

"Maybe."

"Seems like I just keep bumpin' into you boys all over town. I don't want any trouble, never gone looking for it. You fellows keep pushin', somebody's gonna get hurt. Bad."

"Looks like you already started down that road."

"They're all drunker'n a whisky barrel rat, they most likely won't even remember this when they sober up, 'cept for the bruises."

"They won't always be drunk."

"Well the sooner they sober up, the better I'll like it."

"Maybe you won't."

Beck eyed the tall young man leaning against the post. There was no smile in his eyes, but he wasn't sober, either. Beck decided to let the implied threat go by.

"I'm willing to find out," Back said.

The cowboy named Simon heaved himself off the post, turned, and went back into the saloon.

Chapter 7

Jon Beck had just deposited his boots in his room when he heard the distant hoot of a train whistle. In the lobby he found Mrs. Ransom pulling on her coat.

"Supper will be delayed to seven o'clock, Mr. Beck," she smiled, "Mr. Ransom had better be on that train, and with him my new stove!"

"Let me walk you down, Mrs. Ransom," Beck said, opening the door for her.

"You are a gentleman, sir!" she said, going out.

They reached the station in time to watch the small locomotive come chuffing across the river flats and steam up to a stop just past the new station platform. Beck stepped away from Mrs. Ransom and went to the telegraph office window. He asked the telegrapher if any messages had come for him, but none had.

Behind the locomotive and its tender were passenger cars, then freight cars and a caboose. Mrs. Ransom had met with one of several men getting down off of the first passenger car. They hugged and off they went down the platform to see about their freight. Beck could see the faces of soldiers peering from the windows of the second passenger car.

Several more persons stepped down from the first car, among them a young lady in a grey satin traveling dress with a feathered hat set at a rakish angle. The soldiers soon had her squarely bracketed with their glances, some grinning. Two portly gentlemen greeted the woman, who was taller than both, and who smiled and shook their hands. Her chestnut hair, pinned up under the hat in a tight bun, gleamed in the late afternoon sun slanting in under the station landing roof.

"A purty gal always did get you to lookin', Jon," came an amused voice from behind him. Beck turned, and grinned. "Hardy, damn your eyes, you still sneakin' up on a man just like always!" Beck said, sticking out his hand to the shorter, grizzled man before him.

Hardy was about a foot shorter, bearded, buckskin clad, brown eyed, broad in the chest and bandoleered with twin cartridge belts. He took Beck's hand with a smirk.

"Easy! Easy! Dammit all to hell, easy on that paw!" cried Hardy, and Beck gently shook the hand offered him. Hardy wore two pistols on his belt, and a large bowie knife in a beaded scabbard. His beard was grizzled brown with tobacco stains at the corners of his mouth. His eyes, squinting in the afternoon light, wrinkled at the corners in the pleasure of meeting an old friend. Hardy jerked his hand out of Beck's grasp and shook it as if to cool it off.

"Now Lige, you know I wouldn't ever go and hurt you none," cooed Beck.

"My bleedin' Aunt Tilly you wouldn't!" said Elijah Hardy. "What's the latest on them redskins? Howard caught 'em yet?"

"Not so's you'd know it. Last I heard they were bearing down on the Yellowstone, we figure they're heading for the Crow country. They're old friends of the Crow, relatives and all that, hunt buffalo with them every year. That's why they sent for you, I'm guessing, you bein' brother to the Crow and all. How's the misses, by the way? She obviously left your hair alone up to now," Beck said, reaching out to lift the battered old hat up off Hardy's head and looking critically at his pate.

"She's doin' just fine, thankee," Hardy snapped, and grabbed the hat and shoved it back down over his thinning locks.

"Looks like she'd have to hunt around a bit for enough fur to make a scalp lock, there, old pard," Beck grinned.

"Well just you never mind about my hair, Jon Beck! Fightin' Injuns is a sight easier when you ain't got something they want. They'll plug you first off, rather'n me, just to get at them curly locks of yourn!"

"Maybe so, maybe so. Where is your lovely bride, by the way?"

"She's already up at the Crow camps, visiting relatives. Been up there about a month. The boys are both at the agency school. I been off in St. Louis taking care of a little business."

"Well, I've been back east, too, Chicago. Amazing how it's grown, ain't it."

"That's certain." Both men turned to look at the commotion of the soldiers getting off the train. They carried bedrolls and rifles, the short cavalry carbines. A sergeant was loudly getting them shaped into a squad, rank and file.

"That our detachment?" Beck said, nodding at them.

"Yep. Fifth Cavalry, two companies. Horses in the box cars."

"Who's in command?"

"I am!" came a voice from the right. Beck turned to find a captain of cavalry approaching from the telegraph office. "Captain Frederick Peachbow, at your service." He had pulled a gauntleted glove from one hand and extended the hand to Beck. Jon took it, firmly shook it. "I am assuming you gentlemen are my scouts…?"

"This here's Jon Beck," said Hardy, "an old friend of Gen'l Howard and a right fine scout! Almost as good as me! I'm Elijah Hardy"

"A pleasure, sir!' said the captain, shaking Hardy's hand. "My orders did indeed name the two of you. As soon as I get the men bivouacked and settled in, I would request your company at a meeting. We will discuss our strategy, and my orders so far as they go."

"At your convenience, captain," Beck said with a nod. The officer turned and headed for his now lined up and waiting men.

"Any other scouts hired for this little excursion?" Beck asked.

"From what I gather, it's you and me and whoever we can round up. We'll need at least two other white men, one each on the pack mules, somebody to cook, and maybe two more for runners. I figure the Crow will be happy to send along a few braves once we get up that far," Hardy said.

"The Crow? What if they decide to side the Nez Perce? Wouldn't we be bedding down with rattlers while we're huntin' rattlers?"

"Naw, no such thing. I know the Crow, they've always been a savvy folk, they've known for many years that the white man is too strong to fight. Hell, they tried to warn Custer after the Rosebud, before the Little Big Horn, but the damned fool wouldn't listen to his own scouts. And besides, my wife would tell me if her folks were fixin' to take my hair."

"What little there is of it."

"Oh you jest keep on a sniggering about it, your day will come!"

"I hear Fischer is with Howard. He the boss this trip?"

"Yeah, some such. Paisley and Forman were with Gibbon, and Tom Gordon's already up on the upper Missouri having a look around. They say Miles has the Seventh east of Miles City thinking the Sioux might come south out of Canada to get in on the fun. I think he's just prayin' they'd do it, too. He'd just love to get his teeth into Sittin' Bull for sure! Personally, I don't think Sittin' Bull's that stupid."

"Well, Howard's pushing from the west, Miles is sitting on the north, and here we are getting ready to go at 'em from the south. With two companies, no less. Sort of makes you wish Oliver would hurry it up some."

"Hell, if he catches 'em he'll most likely have to baptize the lot of 'em affore he sends 'em off to Jesus! He may be a fine, upright Union man, but he can't run worth a lick!"

"He might surprise you, Lige. Once he sets his teeth into something, he don't turn loose."

"Well, I jest wish he's chew a little quicker. Two companies and a half dozen scouts ain't a lot of capitol when yer playing table stakes fer keeps."

"Last word I got was from up around Missoula. The Nez Perce broke out of the Bitterroots and overran a local garrison they had forted up there. Or so they say."

"Any kilt?"

"Didn't say."

"Howard's men?"

"No, bunch of raw recruits from the new post at Missoula. Was a bunch of civilians with 'em, I heard, and they took off like rabbits."

"Figures."

"Why don't you gather up your gear, let's go down to the boarding house where I'm staying, get you some quarters. Maybe we can go hunt up a whisky before supper, eh?"

"I do like the way you think, Jon Beck!" said Elijah Hardy.

The soldiers were unloading their horses, mules and tack from the boxcars, and Hardy went to claim his own mount and gear. Beck helped him by carrying his saddle and scabbarded rifle over to the livery stable. The soldiers herded their mounts to an open area behind the livery corral, and began to lay out several tents for erection.

Elijah led his horse into the stable, and found an empty stall. Three other mounts nickered and stamped as they passed. Beck hung the saddle on a wall peg next to several others and his own, and handed the rifle to Hardy.

The stable was quiet except for the horses. Beck noticed that the water buckets in each stall were empty. He gathered them up and went to fill them at the big tank just outside the large double doors leading into the corral. He placed a bucket in each stall that contained an animal. The last one went into Bill's stall. The manger was empty. Bill nickered and tossed his head. Beck looked around the building, but did not see a sign of the stablemaster. He went to a board-rung ladder fixed to the timbers next to the corral door, and climbed into the loft. He found the loft mounded with hay, and a pitchfork leaning against the wall. He pitched hay over the edge of the loft, made a pile of it on the livery floor, tossed down the fork, and climbed down to it. He then pitched the hay into the various mangers for the hungry animals. The sound of chomping horse jaws filled the stable.

"See ya still got the big one," said Hardy, the rifle butt on his instep and his forearms crossed over the cased muzzle.

"That I do. He saved my hide just getting to this mudhole of a town, outran a passel of redskins down near the Cinch River. Nothing like him for flat out speed, that's a fact."

"Injuns down there on the warpath too?"

"You know how it is. One man alone can't ever take the chance they'll be friendly, be they red or white. Just as soon have my back to something solid whenever I say hello."

"So it is. Do any shootin'?"

"Indeed I did, and that reminds me. Got me a new Winchester, a .45-75. Newest thing, picked it up in Chicago. Throws a nice heavy slug, takes a horse down better'n a Government round."

"You don't say!"

"I do say. Only problem is finding the cartridges to feed the beast. Have to keep a close eye on the brass and reload 'em when I can. But she's a long range piece and hits hard, and that makes up for a lot. Come on over to the hotel, and I'll introduce you!"

Chapter 8

Beck and Hardy walked on down to the Ransom House, and found no one at the desk in the lobby. Two drummers stood on the porch smoking cigars in the blue evening light. In Beck's room Jon got out the Winchester, and Elijah's eyes lit up at the sight of it.

"Phillip's Hardware in Chicago had this one," Beck said, "They call it a Centennial Rifle. Some sort of big do at the Philadelphia Exposition when they introduced it last year, so Winchester called it that. Sort of a grain fed '73."

Hardy chuckled, hefting the rifle and looking it over end to end. "Got a bit of meat to her, that's for sure," he said, throwing the rifle to his shoulder and sighting along the barrel. "but sweet, very sweet." He lowered the rifle and thumbed in the loading gate to reveal the gleam of the brass cartridge head in the action. "Loaded, I see."

"Yep," said Beck and fetched a cartridge from the belt hanging over the bedpost. "And this is what it likes to eat." He held the cartridge out to Hardy. Elijah handed over the rifle and took the cartridge, examining it closely.

"Well ain't that odd," the shorter man said, "Looks like the .44, but all growed up!"

"Called a .45-75. New thing with the rifle. Throws a 350 grain pill, pretty much flat out to two hundred yards."

"That would do it!" said Hardy, handing back the cartridge. "Tried it on critters?"

"Puts most anything on four legs down in a heartbeat. And, it has a most satisfying effect on Injuns."

"Bet it does," chuckled Hardy.

"I'm still working out the hold on it, though. So far, I've killed about as many horses as riders. Just haven't had enough time to get the long range drop worked out."

The clanging of a bell sounded dimly.

"That must be the supper bell," said Beck, slipping the cartridge back into its belt with the others. "Come on out back, they've got a cook tent set up, we'll have some grub and see about a room for you. And maybe a bath?" He wrinkled his nose.

"Now why on earth would you say something like that to me?" said Hardy quizzically, "I already had a bath this month, and that's a fact!"

Beck slid the rifle back into its scabbard, and leaned it in the corner. They stepped out of the room, and Beck used an iron key to lock the door. They went down the hall and out the back door, stepping down from a small stoop into a courtyard. Three smaller buildings ranged on the right, and a large tent open on the near side faced them across the dirt space. On the left another tent with two smokestacks protruding from its top, both billowing smoke into the still evening air. Mrs. Ransom was lighting a lantern at the entrance to the open tent. Two long tables were inside it, rowed with chairs, boxes, small barrels, even a mason's wheelbarrow, places for the patrons to sit. Half a dozen people already had found places at the tables, and several more came out of the hotel as Beck and Hardy headed for the tent. The drummers came around the building, a family of seven came from around the cook tent, roomers came down the staircase at the back of the hotel building, all converging on the supper tent as ducks to a pond.

The two scouts found perches along the outside of one of the tables, the drummers on the same side, the children of the large family found themselves across the table from the men. More people kept materializing from the hotel, and coming in around the buildings. Soon the mother of the family shooed the kids to the wall so adults could occupy the seats at the table proper. The kids were soon joined by children of another family, and as Mrs. Ransom and a young female assistant brought in the first platters of food, the tent was fairly bursting with diners. Mrs. Ransom glanced about the crowd and her eyes widened slightly. She took a deep breath.

"Ladies and gentlemen, I was not expecting such a crowd!" she began, speaking loudly over the murmur of the diner's voices. "But not to worry, I will make sure all of you are fed. In the mean time I ask your patience, and I must set forth the rules of the house! There will be no foul language at table, gentlemen, and I ask that you mind your elbows and your reaching! If you must smoke, you shall not do so at table! Please use the courtyard for your cigars. Mr. Ransom will have spirits available after supper for those of you so inclined."

The speech was greeted with a general grunt, and a dozen hands shot out for the platters in unison. Mrs. Ransom and her helper were kept hopping, bringing in the bread and the steaks and the steaming potatoes, the jugs and the mugs and the milk for the children, the beans and the biscuits and the gravy, and as each platter or plate was laid down it was quickly grabbed, its contents assaulted, and passed round the table like a well-cooked tornado. For the first ten minutes her efforts were like tossing stones into a well, everything she brought disappeared nearly instantly. The only sound was the munching of jaws and the grunting of eager feeders.

Soon every plate was full and the men were sawing away at the beef with every manner of cutting instrument from Hardy's massive bowie knife to a drummer's dainty pocket pen knife. Beck listened to the smacking and tinking of hardware on the tin plates and thought of the tired company of soldiers he had tramped into The Wilderness with during the war, the slogging of their shoes in the thick undergrowth and the tinkling of their gear, the boots snapping and slapping the foliage underfoot, no one saying a word in anticipation of an enemy just ahead, or maybe not, the tangled forest too dense to see beyond a yard or two. Intent men, instantly waiting for death, to give it or receive it. He came back to the present from his reverie as Hardy spoke.

"Where'd all you folks come from?" he said to a plainly dressed man across the table.

"We have a place just north of here. With them redskins on the prod, we thought it best to come in for a spell."

Several others around the room grunted at that with full mouths. Mrs. Ransom busied herself with the children along the tent wall, making sure they each had a plate and enough to eat. Two of the family women helped her.

Gradually the desperate tempo of ingestion lessened, and one by one the cleaned plates were shoved back. The chewing became reflective.   The serving girl brought in pies, and soon new enthusiasm was applied to them.

"My but it has been a cool autumn," said a woman at the table, daubing at her lips with a napkin. Four men in working clothes rose from the table, dropped coins onto the plain cloth tabletop, and left the tent.

"Track layers," said a man in an apron who had appeared at the opening near the kitchen, looking after the departing diners. "Can't wait to get over to the saloon." He began to clear away the empty platters and plates.

One of the drummers pulled a cigar from the inside pocket of his coat. He bit off the end, then glanced over at Mrs. Ransom who had paused in gathering empty plates from the table to glare at him. He glanced at the cigar, smiled, and put it back into his pocket.

"Would you be Mr. Ransom?" he asked the aproned man.

"I am, sir," Mr. Ransom said, his arms laden with dishes.

"I believe refreshment was mentioned earlier?" said the drummer.

"This way, sir, please," Ransom said and turned and left the tent. The two drummers also rose and went out.

In ones and twos the other diners finished up and rose to leave. Beck and Hardy sat back and worked easily at a piece of apple pie each. Two little girls were brought over and seated on the bench across the table from them, next to the man who had the place to the north. They were dished up pie and each tore into it like ravenous badgers.

"Seems a waste of good pie, letting a kid have it like that," said Hardy.

"Indeed," remarked Beck, "I think it would be better given to a raccoon."

The two children stared at Back and Hardy with large, unblinking eyes, shoveling in the pie without pause.

"In fact," said Hardy, "I think there's a raccoon come sniffing around for some of that pie right now!"

The little girl nearest Hardy shrieked and dropped her fork, and jumped backward over the bench. She looked under the table like a miner looking at a squib dynamite fuse, then fury filled her face. She jumped back onto the bench and went to work on the pie, glaring at Hardy.

"Must have been my imagination," smirked Hardy, "nothin' under there but feet."

The pie done, Beck and Hardy left the tent. In the courtyard they found that Ransom had set up a makeshift bar on a plank set over two barrels. Several bottles were set out, and a few glasses. The drummers were each holding a glass, cigars lit, laughing at something Ransom had said. A jar with cigars also graced the bar, and as Beck came up he reached one out and one of the drummers offered up a match.

"Mrs. Ransom get her new stove?" Beck said as he bit the end off the cigar and took the offered match. He struck it on the wood bar, and lit the cigar.

"Why, yes, indeed she did, brought it up on the work train with the troopers. But how…?"

"Oh she has talked of nothing else for days and days!" Beck lied. "However, judging by the quality of tonight's repast, I would venture to say that she has already achieved perfection with the stove she has now."

Ransom smiled and chuckled a bit. "Kind of you to say, sir. But the "perfection" you so kindly note is due to a husband who does most of the cooking over a wire grill and dutch oven, I am proud to say! But once the stove is brought up from the depot, we will begin to build a proper kitchen around it, with our new dining room! We intend to expand, sir, and build a first class hotel right here where you stand!"

"Well, you have a grand start, sir!" offered one of the drummers, as two more of the diners joined them at the makeshift bar. Ransom set out glasses and poured drinks. "No brandy, I am afraid, gentlemen, but some of the finest corn whiskey ever made in these parts!" he said with a small smile. "What brings your gentlemen to our fair little town?"

The two newest drinkers snorted a bit. "Why hell, Fred, you know us!" one of them said, "And I'll have one o' them fine see-gars," and he reached one out of the jar.

"Well I wasn't meanin' you railroad boys," said Ransom, "how 'bout you other gents?"

"I'm Henry Stone, late of New York, New Orleans, New Bedford and new to Quandry, Wyoming Territory!" smirked one of the drummers. A few small laughs resulted. "I am here in passing to

Miles City, as a dealer in fine linens, calicos, general millenary and dry goods. My card, sir!" and he drew a small white card from a vest pocket and handed it over to Mr. Ransom.

"Bill Bailey, brandy, wine and fine liquors!" said the second drummer, also producing a card. "Perhaps your lack of good brandy can be remedied forthwith, sir, and at very attractive prices!"

Ransom smiled and said, "Thank you gentlemen, and these railroad men are Jason Pearly, chief construction engineer, and Bradley Downs, his section boss," nodding to the pair of railroad men. "And you gentlemen?" Ransom said to Hardy.

"Oh we're just here to see about a few redskins," said Hardy, "what with Gen'l Howard taking his sweet time on the Clearwater, somebody has to tell the army what to do. That would be us."

"Are you with that troop of soldiers that arrived today?"

"We will be soon enough. Scoutin' for 'em."

"What can that little troop of soldiers do against a whole nation of Indians?" said Bailey, "Custer had hundreds of men, and look what happened to him!"

"It ain't how many you got," said Hardy, "it's how you use 'em."

"With the whole northern plains rising up to the warpath, forty or fifty troopers won't account for much, no matter how well used," scoffed Stone.

"Well I don't rightly think the whole northern plains is a'boil with Injuns," Hardy said, "they's a bunch of 'em know their place and are stayin' peaceful. We only know that some of the Nez Perce are runnin' mad, no others."

"But everyone knows they are going to join the Crows," said Downs, "and what about the Sioux just north of the border? If they come back to get in on it, there'll be no stopping them!"

"The army should just field the men to wipe them all out. And that includes a raid into Canada, I say!" said Bailey.

"Indeed," Downs said, "wipe them off the face of the earth! We've suffered enough of this constant rising and massacring and back stabbing from this rabble, best we hunt them all down and get it over with!"

"I'll drink to that!" said Stone, raising his glass. It was clinked by his fellow salesman and the two railroad men.

"Women and kids too?" said Hardy.

"Of course!" said Downs, "Why leave lice to breed more lice? They are only animals anyway."

"I'll drink to—"began Stone, his glass rising. Beck's hand reached out to his forearm, gripped it.

"I propose another toast," he said, looking into Stone's face, which had suddenly taken on a look of concern as Beck gripped him. "Here's to sensible men acting like good Christian gentlemen, and may God guide the hand that holds the reins."

A pause calmed the night as they thought about it for a few seconds. Hardy raised his glass, Beck also, and the others slowly followed, clinking them all together. The man called Pearly made no move to join in.

Beck took his hand from Stone's arm. Cigars were puffed, whiskey sipped, the cooling night air enjoyed. No one spoke for several minutes. Stone rubbed his forearm a bit, absently.

Ransom cleared his throat. "Where are the Nez Perce now, Mr. Beck? We have only heard that they are headed south, and some say they are in the Yellowstone country even now."

"That's what we are here to find out, Mr. Ransom," Beck said, "We and the United States Fifth Calvary."

"And what of the Stoeger family," Ransom went on, "you did hear of that, did you not? If the Nez Perce are somewhere to the north, what Indians did that awful deed?"

"Was it Indians? For sure?"

"The cabin was burned. Arrows were found. The stock run off, who else could it have been?"

"Perhaps you are right, Mr. Ransom," Beck said. "I only suggest that the Nez Perce are too far away to have had anything to do with it."

"But not the Crow!" burst out Downs. "If they are fixing to join the Nez Perce, this is just the kind of thing they would do!"

"Now how the hell·do you know what they would do?" said Hardy.

"It's the thieving, killing, sneaking thing all Indians do!" shot back Downs. "I've been laying track on these plains for ten years now, and I've never seen a single Indian any man could trust not to stab him in the back the moment opportunity presented itself!"

The whiskey was beginning to loosen the tongues of the little gathering.

"And I still say they should be shot down to a man, woman, and child!" said Bailey, glaring at Beck as if to dare him to disagree.

"They were here first," said Hardy.

"Well, we're here now!" Downs declared, "They just ride through a country once a year, don't stay, don't raise a thing, don't build a thing, and somehow come to the conclusion that they own it all and at the same time don't have any particular use for it either! They get all riled when someone comes along who can make something of the land, build on it, improve it, make it what it is supposed to be!"

"And what is it supposed to be, Mr. Downs?" Beck said.

"Part of the country! Part of the United States of America! A country founded by white men for white men, and peopled by white men able to take it and make it something! Something great!"

Four of the men cried "Here! Here!" and clinked glasses. Ransom reluctantly added his clink. Beck and Hardy looked at each other.

"So, is there no place in your great land for the people who lived in it first?" said Beck.

"Not if they're murdering savages who will not change their ways!" Downs said, very satisfied with his speech and its response. "Besides, they do not even claim to own the land. They say no one owns it. Why then should not the government take upon itself the guardianship of the land, to apportion it among the uses it is best suited for? All benefit from that, don't you think?"

"Except the original owner," Beck said. "Of course, he does not think of himself as the owner, but in the context of his life and his religion, he is part of the land upon which he lives. We would call it ownership, he would call it a part of his being. His soul. The land is his mother, from which all things come to him. Would you take money for your mother?"

"That's absurd!" said Bailey, "The government has purchased the Indian lands fair and square, and paid good money, too! Why, I read in the papers just last week in Denver that this Nez Perce squabble is just an argument over the price of the land! This is a hell of a way to transact business, I can assure you of that!"

"Business, is it? Let me ask you a question, Mr. Bailey," said Beck. "Let us say that you own a house, a big one with twenty rooms. One day, a stranger comes and moves into one of the rooms. You say to him, why are you in my house? Get out! But he says to

43

you, you are not using this room, you haven't even visited this room for a year. I will make good use of it, I plan to turn it into a bordello. You have nineteen rooms left, you do not need this one. Here's one hundred dollars for the room.

"But you, as owner of the house, do not want to sell the one room. So the stranger goes to your neighbor, who agrees to sell the room for one hundred dollars. The stranger comes back and sets up his bordello. He shows you a bill of sale from the neighbor. You say to him, he is just a neighbor, he does not own this house. But the stranger has paid his money to someone, and so he has the papers that make him feel like the owner of the room. You protest. You threaten him. He calls his friend the army colonel, who comes with his troops and occupies seven other rooms, to protect his friend who has become the owner of one room. So, Mr. Bailey, what do you do now?"

"Preposterous!" muttered Bailey, looking off into the night away from Beck.

"Balderdash!" said Downs. "Where Indian lands have been purchased, a good price has been negotiated in good faith, and paid in full! Our Government would not intentionally cheat the red man, it is certainly the other way around! No sooner have we paid for these lands than we have to fight to take possession!"

"Because it's the neighbor doing all the selling," said Beck.

"You, sir," spoke Mr. Pearly for the first time, speaking to Beck, "seem inordinately fond of the red man's point of view, for an employee of the U.S. Army. Does the captain in charge of our local contingent know of your sentiments?"

"Oh, I expect not," Beck said. "I haven't found an army feller yet that was looking to see both sides of the issue. Sort of like you railroad people, you only know one thing, and that's building track. Who you lay it atop of is of no concern to you, is it?"

"You mean where we lay it, don't you?" Pearly said evenly.

"No, I mean who," Beck said. "When it comes to Indian lands, you're shoving these people around like they don't even exist. Then you wonder why they take a shot at you from time to time."

"Maybe someone should take a pot shot at you, Mr. Beck," Pearly said, gesturing at Beck's face with his whisky glass, "Or at least let the army know they've hired an admirer of the Noble Savage to go scouting for them. Makes one wonder what you'll find out there on your scout, Mr. Beck, and whether you will in fact report what you see." He stood up from leaning on the bar and placed his glass on the wood, glaring at Jon Beck as he did so.

"Now Mr. Pearly, sir," said Hardy, quickly, "you folks have been right quick to speak up against the Injuns, and this being a free country, you've all of a right to do that. But if you are comin' around to figure on buttin' heads of a personal nature, I'd best warn you, our Mr. Beck here has a mighty hard head."

"Well now, 'Lige, you may be right about the head," said Beck, blowing out a long plume of cigar smoke into the night air, "but Mr. Pearly is only concerned that the U.S. Army is not impeded in its duty to protect him and his construction crew. Am I right, Mr. Pearly?"

Pearly stared at Beck for a moment.

"I do have a railroad to build, sir. And it does concern me when those forces with which I find myself allied appear to be more sympathetic to the common enemy than to our own cause. I merely asked if your superiors were aware that you love redskins more than white men."

"Oh well, since you put it that way," Hardy said, and stepped away from the bar. "I tried," he muttered, shaking his head.

Beck looked at Pearly, whose eyes were nearly hidden in the shadow of the brim of his Derby hat. Pearly was half a head taller, but slimmer through the middle and broad in the shoulders. He wore his hair close cropped, his nose was broad and straight, and his jaw prominent and square. A small mustache flowed across his upper lip. His head was silhouetted by the lantern on the cook tent pole at his back. His neck was as broad as his head. Jon Beck looked him over, and then Pearly leaned on the bar with one elbow. Beck realized that he himself was in the full glare of the lantern, and any move he made would be instantly apparent to Pearly.

He reached out and doused his cigar butt in Pearly's drink.

"Guess it's time we Injun lovers turned in for the night, 'Lige," he said. He did not move, but watched Pearly's face and waited.

Chapter 9

A yellow flash like lightning and a smashing clap of thunder startled the men at the bar, as the lantern on the post behind Mr. Ransom exploded. Beck dove for the ground and turned to look from whence the shot had come, for he knew instantly it had been a gunshot that exploded upon the night. As he looked across the courtyard, another fireball flashed from between two of the little buildings, its thunderous concussion coming at the same instant. He caught a glimpse of a face behind the flash, beneath a low hat, then darkness.

He realized then that someone had been shouting, and it was one of the railroad men. He rolled off to his right, and rose to one knee while drawing his big army Colt from its holster under his coat. Ransom was shouting, too, and he .glanced at them to see that the kerosene from the smashed lantern was on fire and the flames were licking at the wall of the cook tent. Ransom began beating at the flames, and others joined him.

Beck rose and moved across the courtyard toward the point of the firing. He held his revolver in front of him, thumb on the hammer, ready in an instant to return fire, expecting at each second to see the splash of light and the boom of a shot coming at him. He reached the mouth of the little alley. Darkness filled it, then a lighter area beyond, a wood yard for the hotel.

A light came up behind him, then Hardy stood at his side holding a lantern in one hand, one of his revolvers in the other.

"See anything?" he said. The alley was empty save for a pair of crates against one of the walls.

"Naw, whoever it was is long gone by now."

"What you figure that was all about?"

"Don't know," said Beck, holstering his six-shooter, "maybe just some drunk havin' his fun."

"Well aren't you going after them?" said Downs, coming up to join them at the alley.

"Why? If he, or they, wanted to stick around and shoot it out, we'd all be full of holes by now. Naw, they're gone. Or, he's gone. Got a look at one man in the muzzle flash."

"Who was it?" Downs demanded.

"Don't know."

"Well who would do such a thing?" Downs said as they started back toward the bar. The flames in the tent had been smothered, and smoke still rose in the light of two more lanterns brought near to survey the damage.

"You got any enemies might want to get some lead into you?" Hardy asked Downs.

"Of course not!"

"Fire anybody off of your rail crew recently?" said Beck

They reached the bar. Ransom was wiping his hands on a towel. The two drummers had disappeared. Pearly leaned on the bar again, the glass with the cigar in it at his elbow.

"We hire and fire all the time!" Downs said, "Men don't go to shooting over it!"

"Perhaps it was one of those dirty little savages you speak so highly of," Pearly said evenly, looking at Beck. Jon stepped up before Pearly, face to face.

"Pretty sure it was a white man," Beck said, "looked an awful lot like a railroad feller."

"And what does a "railroad feller" look like?" sneered Pearly.

"Oh, you can always tell 'em in a crowd," Beck said, "all puffed up and proud as roosters, full of self importance and perfect opinions of themselves. You see, they only know one thing, which is track. You get 'em off the rails, and they're lost little sheep, bleatin' for their mommas."

Beck, on the balls of his feet, knew that Pearly would have to shift his weight off of the bar to organize his first swing. He did, and Jon flashed a left into his nose in the same instant. The blow staggered Pearly, but he came back with a quick roundhouse right, which Beck dodged. Beck got in a hard right to Pearly's midsection, then a left cross to his jaw as the big railroad engineer stumbled past him with the momentum of his punch.

The left to the jaw had stopped Pearly, who straightened up and shook his head, his fists held at belly level. Beck did not follow up, but waited, letting Pearly make the next move.

"And that will be enough of that!" said a big man, coming across the courtyard from the hotel back door. He wore a dark suit, a black hat, and a large silver star on one lapel.

"Was it you two doing all the shooting a moment ago?" he demanded.

"Why hell no, marshal!" said Pearly, dropping his hands, "Somebody was taking pot shots at us from the alley over there. Ran off I guess." He rubbed his jaw absently.

"So you two are just slugging it out to pass the time?" the sheriff said. "I warned you about this, Pearly. Ain't gonna have you tearin' up my town no more!"

"Seems we disagree on a few points of common interest," Beck said, "no harm done."

"And who might you be?" said the lawman.

"Jon Beck. Scouting for the Fifth Cavalry. And this here's Elijah Hardy, also scouting." Hardy nodded to the marshal.

"Well, pleasure to make your acquaintance, gentlemen," said the sheriff, "But no more fighting, you hear? You hear that, Pearly?"

"Mr. Beck and I will have a chance to carry on this conversation later, I am sure," said Pearly. "But for the mean time, Will, there will be peace."

The sheriff turned to Beck. "Come see me in the morning at first light, Beck, you too, Hardy. I need a couple of scouts to help me on this Stoeger killing."

"Be happy to, marshal, anything we can do," said Beck.

"Good. Now I figure it's time you all turned in. Enough shootin' and fightin' fer one night. Ransom, shut this bar down. The saloon down the street is open if you want to whoop it up some, and the bartender there knows how to keep the peace." He turned and headed back toward the hotel.

"Come on, Lige, lets go see about your room," Beck said, turning to follow.

"Just remember what I said," Pearly growled. "You and me ain't finished yet."

"Suits me," Beck said, smiling at Pearly.

Beck and Hardy went into the hotel, where it was discovered that all the rooms were full, several people had bedded down in the lobby, and several more on the porch. Hardy ended up in Beck's room, where they were to share the bed. Later, as the candle was dowsed and they settled into the dark, Hardy said, "That was a good 'un, that part about the Christian gentlemen and reins of god and all."

"Oh, you figure?"

"I ain't never heard you mention God in all the years I've sided with you, pard. You taken up prayin' and such?"

"Not lately. Last time I hollered at my maker was at The Wilderness. I was tootin' the boys forward, captain leadin' us, when we located the Rebs in the fog and the brambles. They couldn't of been mor'n thirty feet away, when the whole world blew up in fire and thunder. Sort of like tonight, only magnified by five hundred muskets. Dozens of men all around me fell, our captain went down, I got three holes in my uniform but not a bullet touched me. I tried to blow the charge, but I couldn't get up enough spit. I prayed to God, then, prayed that I could do my duty, toot that horn and get the regiment moving forward. I could hear the clink and clatter of five hundred ramrods shovin' home five hundred bullets just a few feet away in the mist and smoke. I could hear the screams and groans of the dozens of wounded around me. The rest of the men were coming up an then they began to fire in return, around me, over me, under me, the flash and the fire in the mist and smoke, and then the Rebs began to reply, and I went to earth like a bayed badger, flattened out behind any lump of cover I could find. The leaves were dripping from the mist, and I wetted my lips from the leaves and blew the rally for all I was worth, and the boys came 'round, and they kept up the firing, and so did the Rebs, 'til night came and the dark. And all the while men were screaming for their God, both Rebel and Union, and all the while I was blowing them forward so's they could kill and die. All of them with the name of God on their lips.

"We never saw a one of those Rebs, and they, I believe, never saw a one of us. We had six hundred men in the regiment on the morning of that day. By the morning of the next, barely two hundred answered the muster."

Hardy lay silent in the dark for a time, then said, "The Lord must have liked yer music, Jon, He spared you for it."

"Maybe. Ain't had much truck with Him since."

Chapter 10

Beck and Hardy rose before dawn and found the cook tent already half full of patrons shoveling down flapjacks, bacon, fried potatoes, biscuits and gravy. They joined in the jostling and clattering of cups and plates and fed like hungry wolves. Leaving coins on the table, they rose and left as others came on to jamb the tent.

As the grey blue of the dawn light filled the street they walked across to the marshal's office, and met the constable coming down the boardwalk.

"Come in, gents," the lawman said, "thanks for coming over." He unlocked the door and pushed it open for them. He followed them in, took off his coat and hung it on a wall peg, and went to the stove. He opened the stove door and began stirring around in the ashes with a piece of kindling.

"I'm Will Gerline, the town marshal," he began, speaking over his shoulder as he tried to get a fire going. "Few days ago we had a farmer and his family killed, 'bout four miles up the valley. Burned the cabin with the family in it, whoever done it. Looks like Indians, since there were arrows found, and the stock stolen. Trouble is," he said, tossing several pieces of wood onto a new flame, and shutting the door, "we poked around out there when we went out to investigate and fetch the bodies back to town, and we couldn't find any sign. I mean, the kind of sign you would expect if it was a war party. We found plenty of tracks from the boys who found 'em, but not much else. It was four hands from a ranch further out, coming in to get supplies, they saw the smoke and went in for a look-see. But no Indian sign to speak of."

"You figure it was Indians, even with no sign?" Hardy said.

"Right now I don't figure nothin'. That's why I wanted to see you fellows. Could you come out to the place with me, have a look around? I know you got the army to attend to, but it ain't far, and it wouldn't take but an hour or two."

"We'll go see the captain, find out what the plan is for the detachment. If he says we have the time, we'll be glad to go out there for a look see. But with the recent rain storm, and all the folks trampling over the area, might be a waste of time."

"I know that. And I appreciate your help, all the same. Our posse spent the better part of two days trying to come up with something, and we got nothing. Right now I just don't know which way to jump."

"All right. We'll check with the army and let you know."

"Good enough."

Beck and Hardy left the office and walked down to the train station. Several wagons in the street had folks in and around them, some rising from sleeping in the wagons or under them. From the railroad platform they could see the dozen tents of the army's encampment. Smoke from the cook fires curled up in the morning air. The first rays of the morning sun streaked in from the east. The men at the cook fires made frosty clouds of breath that silvered in the sunlight.

They went to the camp, found the captain, learned that the command was awaiting the next train for the last of their supplies and horses. The equipment had to be brought up on the work train for the narrow gauge line, which used a light duty engine and was not a main line hauler. There were not enough cattle cars for all the horses, so the second trip was necessary. They agreed to meet with the captain to go over the orders and the maps at noon.

They went back to the marshal's office, but he was not there.

"Lige, you wait here for the marshal, and I'll go down to the stable and saddle up the horses," Beck said.

"Sounds good to me, pard!" Hardy grinned, pulling a chair up to the stove. "That little sorrel of mine is due for a good run."

Beck left the office and walked down to the stable. The big street doors were closed, but he found he could ease one of them back and slip through the opening into the stable. Inside he found the horses nickering in the stalls, the doors to the corral out back open, and the water tank just outside the doors full. He went to Bill's stall. The oat bin was empty, the hay was gone, the water bucket empty. He could hear the thump and rustle of the other horses in their stalls. He opened Bill's stall, and the horse backed out into the stable, then went immediately to the water tank and began to slurp up the water. Beck shook his head, his teeth clenched, as he went to each of the other stalls and turned out the horses. All of them plodded directly to the water tank. As they drank their fill, they wandered on out into the corral. The stalls had obviously not been cleaned in days, and the odor of manure was strong in the stable.

Beck went to the wall ladder and climbed into the loft. He found the pitchfork where he had left it the previous evening, and began to pitch hay from the heaped stacks in the loft out the open loft doors. The hay fell into a mound near the tank below, and the horses immediately came to it and began feeding.

He had a good pile over the side when he heard what sounded like the snorting of a pig. He paused, and moved around the mounded hay in the direction of the sound. There, on the side of the mound, lay the stable man, on his back, seemingly asleep. At his side lay a nearly empty whisky bottle. His crumpled tophat lay in the hay just above his head. As Beck watched, the sleeping drunk let out another snort.

"Mr. Pickworth! Mr. Pickworth, are you up there?" came a screechy call from outside the stable. Beck moved back around the hay mound and peered over the edge of the loft door into the corral. A small woman in calico stood just outside the ring of feeding horsed, peering up at the loft door.

"Sir!" she hollered in desperate tone, "Have you seen my Mr. Pickworth? Is he about the premises at all?"

"Would that be the stable man?" Beck said, leaning on the fork handle.

"Yes, sir, my Mr. Pickworth owns this enterprise, that he does! He did not come home last night at all, and with all the folks crowding into town because of the Indians, I must assume he has been working the night through. I have brought him his breakfast," she said, holding up a covered pail to demonstrate, "and now, sir, can you call him up for me?"

"I'll go you one better," Beck said with a grin, "I shall deliver him to you."

He dropped the pitchfork, strode back around the hay pile to the prostrate stable master, and, taking the bottle up in one hand, with the other grabbed the stable man's coat front and hauled him up. Pickworth was a slight man, and Beck had him up on his feet as he just began to wake, then toppled him over a shoulder. Jon gathered up the hat with the bottle, and strode back around the hay to the loft door. Without hesitation, he pitched Pickworth out into space, and tossed the bottle and hat after him.

The splash of Pickworth's arrival in the water tank spooked the horses from the hay momentarily, but they were hungry enough from their neglect that they returned to it immediately. Mrs. Pickworth eyed the sputtering livery man, the bottle floating beside him, and the breakfast pail. As she helped her husband crawl out of the tank, she lit into him with a broadside of prickly invective, dropping the breakfast pail in the process. When she had tugged his soaking carcass over the edge of the tank, she grabbed him by one ear and marched him off across the corral like a miscreant schoolboy, he all the while protesting weakly, she all the while gaining volume and rancor like a skyrocket on the way to the big boom.

Beck chuckled, picked up the pitchfork, and went back to forking hay over the side to the horses chomping away below. He worked around to the other side of the hay mound from where he had discovered the passed out Pickworth, and as he jabbed in the fork for a new load, he heard behind him the unmistakable four clicks of a Colt's revolver being cocked.

He paused, gripping the haft of the fork, considering the revolver in its holster under his coat, and deciding on a quick turn and jab with the fork. But how far away was the shooter who, he was certain, pointed a pistol at his back? Would he be able to reach him with a jabbed pitchfork? Would a quick run and jump out the hay door be a better ploy? As these thoughts raced through his mind, a gentle snore also reached his ears.

"He sound's right contented, don't he?" came a voice that Beck remembered but could not place. He turned slowly, fork held lightly in his hands.

Sitting in the hay in the light of a side window was the young cowboy called Simon. In one hand he held the frame of a Colt's revolver, working at it with a rag in the other hand. The barrel assembly lay on a small cloth in his lap. He dipped water out of a tin can before him in the hay, working at cleaning the gun. He grinned at Beck.

Behind him a soft snore emitted again from the sleeping form of the short, red headed cowboy, out for the count in the hay. Beyond him, Beck could see the legs of the third cowpoke, and he surmised it would be the one with the wrecked nose.

"Don't go down well, havin' somebody cock a gun at your back, now do it?" grinned Simon.

Beck looked at him for a long moment, then tined the fork into the hay at his feet. He leaned on the handle, casual like.

"I just keep runnin' into you boys like a farmer swattin' at a plague of locusts," Beck said, letting his eyes roam around the loft, looking for any more surprises. He sighed. "All right, we done traded drops, now what?"

"Ain't no "what" to it," Simon said, "we're done. Finished. Zach there," Simon said, jerking his head over his shoulder to indicate the red head, "finally finished all the rotgut he could pay for, borrow, and steal. Jim back there, hell, he's just along for whatever Zachary's into. We never meant you no harm, it just worked out that way. I 'spect we'll be headin' back out to the ranch sometime today, if'n them two gets it slept off."

"What's the celebration been about? You four..." and Beck looked about again for the fourth man, "You four been riding high and handsome for a time, at least every time I seen ya."

"No celebration, no sir, nothing like that. We were on the way in from the ranch, saw the smoke at the Stoeger's place. Zach there, he was sweet on the Stoeger girl, Anna was her name. Just seventeen, we was at her birthday party couple of weeks ago. She and Zach, well, they was fixin' to get hitched, and her folks were for it, sort of. Zachary was saving his money fer to get a little spread of his own, some of us was gonna pitch in and help him, then work for him to get it goin'.

"Well, when we seen that smoke, Zach took off like a scalded cat, got there first, the cabin all burnt out, fire still going. We caught up with him just in time to keep him out of the ashes and what was still burning, he was going to go in there after his gal. But you could see it wasn't any good, and right then we didn't know if anyone was in there anyway. We got the well bucket going and managed to get most of the last of the flames out, and we found 'em in there, all four of 'em...."

"Marshal said it was Indians. That what you figure?"

"Musta been. Arrow stuck in the wall near the front winder, another on the ground around the side of the cabin."

"Family have much stock?"

"Pair of plow mules and a milk cow. Chickens. But all them was gone, musta been taken by the Injuns what did it."

"See any sign?"

"Didn't take the time to look for none. Hightailed into town to get the marshal," Simon said, concentrating on wiping the last of the fouling out of the revolver frame.

"So you fellows just decided to let the posse see to it? Didn't feel like going out after the ones that did it?"

"You gotta understand," Simon said, pausing in his cleaning to look up at Beck, "Zachary, there, was mighty sweet on Anna. When we made certain she was in the cabin with the rest of 'em, he just went cold. Like you snuff out a candle, just like that. We came on into town, and I went over to the marshal's office and told him about it, and Zachary stayed out at the place to keep watch. He was like stone, sittin' there against the well house, just about dead sittin' up. He was mighty sweet on that gal."

"He come out of it by the time you got back?"

"Well, there's the funny thing, he wasn't at the farm when we got there. Took the marshal a bit to get together a posse and get 'em all saddled up and out there, had to get a wagon along too. Zack was gone when we showed up. Everything else was just like we left it, cabin even still smokin' some. We got the bodies into the wagon, and me'n the boys rode with them back to town. Posse went out looking for sign. We unloaded the Stoeger family over to the railroad sheds, and then we come over to the marshal's office to wait, heck, I figured the posse to come back any time.

"Well, Zach rode in about sundown, but no posse. Said he was out lookin' for the bunch that did it, but no luck. First thing he heads for the saloon, we all mosey along with him, and he dove straight inter a bottle of rotgut and never popped out again for four days. He was awful sweet on that Stoeger gal."

"And the rest of you? All of you splashin' about in that bottle to keep him company?"

"You might say that," Simon said, smiling a little, "He's our pard, for all that."

"I noticed you bein' the one that kept an eye out on the rest."

"Somebody has to nurse them kids, time to time." Simon picked up the barrel of the gun and looked through the bore against the light of the little window.

"So that little meeting at the hotel, you boys just cadgin' up a little drinking money, is that it?"

"Sort of."

"And later, at the saloon, more of the same?"

"Well by then Zachary didn't like you much any more," chuckled Simon as he fitted the barrel assembly back on the pistol frame and fingered in the retaining wedge. He pulled out his belt knife to tighten the retaining screw.

"How about last night? That you, out behind the Ransom House tryin' out that there open top pistol?"

"Me? Ransom House? Why, whatever do you mean?" Simon grinned, and he began thumbing cartridges into the revolver. He loaded five, indexed the cylinder, and lowered the hammer on the sixth, empty chamber. The pistol rested in his hands in his lap.

Once again Beck began to consider his options, thinking of using the pitchfork on the seated cowboy if the gun barrel came up in his direction. But something in the smiling face of the young man seemed benign, like a well fed cat ignoring the fat mouse running by his feet. But cats will pounce for the pure joy of killing. Would Simon?

"Oh, THIS gun?" Simon said, as if discovering the pistol in his hands for the first time. He twisted around and slipped the gun into the holster on the belt of the sleeping red head.

"Just cleaning it for a feller. Can't abide a dirty firearm, just like our daddy always taught us."

"Who was it got it dirty, him or you?"

"That I don't recollect," Simon said, laying back on the hay, his elbow on the mound and his palm supporting his head. He snatched up a strand of hay and stuck it between his teeth, and smiled again at Beck.

"You boys going to pop back into that bottle when he sobers up?" Beck said.

"Don't think so. We has about worn out our welcome around here, time we moved on. Zach's used up all his money, and mine, and just about everybody else's he could lay a paw to. No, I may have to persuade him some, but I figure it's time we got out of town."

"Back to the ranch?"

"Maybe. If they'll have us. Don't think he wants to stay around this country, now, what with his feelin's fer that gal and all. Can't say's I blame him. How about you? I heard you was a scout for that cavalry troop that just pulled in. Goin' after them renegades?"

"That's the plan." Beck studied the supine cowpoke for a long moment. "You looking for a job of work to do?"

"Might be. What'cha getting' at?"

"I need two or three good runners, men that can ride long and hard. Army will provide men from their end, but I need some on mine. Interested?"

"Might be. How long's the trip, and what's the pay?"

"For as long as it takes to get those Nez Perces rounded up. And the pay is forty dollars a month."

"After all the trouble I been to you, why you asking me to hire on?"

"That's a damned good question…Simon, is it? Don't know if I have an answer as yet."

"Yep, it's Simon, Simon Pocket. And I don't have one, either."

"One what?"

"Answer. But I will let you know soon's I do." He grinned around the hay twig jutting out through his teeth.

Chapter 11

Beck climbed down out of the loft and went to the oats bin in one corner of the stable. He found a bucket and ladle, and filled a bucket with oats. He went into Bill's stall and dumped half the bucket into the feeding trough. He stepped out of the stall and whistled for the big horse, whose head came up from the hay at the sound. Another whistle and Bill came across the stable to the stall. Beck took hold of his ear and gently steered him into the stall, slapped his rump as it went past. But Bill had sniffed out the oats and needed no encouragement to go to the trough. Beck closed the stall gate.

He quickly dumped the rest of the oats in his bucket in the next stall, and went back to the bin for more. Soon he had most of the stall troughs supplied with oats. As he worked, the horses began to notice what he was doing, and since most of them knew the sound of the oats sliding out of the bucket into the troughs, they needed no encouragement to start for their stalls, too. As each one went in,

Beck closed the gate on the horse. He was nearly done when Hardy and Marshal Gerline squeezed through the street doors.

"Well now Jon, I figured you to have them horses all saddled up and ready to go by now," Hardy said, looking around the stable. "You too busy kissin' that big roan of yours to do anything useful?"

"Well he do smooch right nicely, 'Lige, and that's a fact. But no, I've been catching up on a little of the stable man's work here, seems the stock has been somewhat neglected."

"Where's Pickworth?" said Gerline, "Didn't see him around last night when I stabled my horse."

"Oh, I found him this morning, all right," Beck said, "But it seems he had caught a bit of chill from the damp, and went home so's his wife could tend to him."

"Wife?" Gerline said, "How'd you know he had a wife?"

"She come by with his breakfast."

The marshal was looking out into the corral when he said, "Would that be it, out there next to the water tank?" Beck and Hardy turned and saw the overturned breakfast pail, food strewn out from it, and nearby the whiskey bottle.

"That would be it," Beck said.

"She don't take to his drinkin' too well," Gerline said, "I 'spect he's gonna be tied up for a spell. Let's get them horses saddled up and get out to the Stoeger place."

Hardy's mare was still out in the corral, so he went off to fetch her. Beck and Gerline saddled up their horses, and, mounting up, walked them out through the corral and its outer gate and down to the army camp. Hardy caught up with them there, and the Marshall led them out past the railroad station, across the tracks, and onto a rough wagon road heading to the northwest between low-lying hills. The new sun was on their backs and shoulders, and quickly warmed them from the chill of the morning.

"You been marshalling out here long?" Beck said as they rode along.

""Bout a year, now." Gerline said. "Did some prospecting up in the Tetons, then over in the Black Hills. Didn't cotton much to all that diggin', too much like real work."

"Didn't strike it rich, then?"

"Nope. I was always one of them fellers who staked out ground right next to the mother lode. Close enough to smell it, but not taste it. Come up here with the new rail line, worked for Downs and Pearly for a spell, but that was too much like work, too. When the camp was established where Quandry is now, it was a pretty rough place. Before they could make up their minds as to which route to take north, settlers was coming up the line, and a couple of ranches got going, and affor you know it, they actually had a town. Been building on the frantic for over a year now. At any rate, we had some trouble with the railroad people and the new settlers not getting along, and I didn't particularly care for the way Pearly handled it. Figured the regular folk needed a little help and all, and when they decided to hire some law, I up and volunteered. We got those railroaders tamped down some, but as you boys found out last night, Pearly don't hesitate to mix it up. What was you two fightin' about, anyway?"

"Our Jon, here, is a stanch advocate of the Indigenous Tribesman of the Plains!" spouted Hardy, "He'll stand for the redman through any storm of abuse or rancor, through the worst of any prejudice or bigotry, he'll champion the Nobel Savage to the bitter end of—"

"Hardy, shut your trap!" Beck growled.

"What he did, that Pearly feller," Hardy grinned, "was call Jon an Indian lover."

"I was merely explaining to the learned gentleman how the Indians might feel about what has happened to them, and to their land."

"And he called him an Indian lover!" Hardy repeated.

"He was looking for a fight. I don't mind what he said, but he said it just to get a fight going. I've always been a right obliging feller in that regard."

"Well you being a scout and all," Gerline said, "seems sort of strange to be taking the Indian's side of it."

"Ain't taking their side of it," Beck said, "just explained what some of them have told me about it. The more I can learn, the better off I'm going to be scouting, and maybe fighting them. It pays to understand your enemy, as the scholar once said."

"Well, I suppose you're right about that," Gerline said. "And from what I could see, you have a powerful enemy in Pearly. He's the line engineer for the road, but he's more of a gang boss than Downs is, and that's a fact. He's got no hesitation to settle any matter that comes up with his fists, and from what I've seen of him, he's pretty good at it. I think he even fought professionally back east, maybe Boston, from what I heard, when he was schoolin' to be an engineer."

"He one of the reasons you quit the railroad?" Beck said.

"Matter of fact. And I didn't exactly quit, I was fired. By Pearly. Objected to him beating down a farmer who had just put a couple of his track layers on the floor. Farmer got cold cocked by Pearly from the side, staggered him. Pearly just worked him over, got him against the bar, kept at it almost methodical like, wouldn't let him fall. I finally had enough and grabbed Pearly, and he promptly knocked me down too. But the farmer hit the floor, and that was the end of it. Pearly was mad as hell at me, kicked me when I was getting up. Now, I'm not a small man, but that kick got me where it hurt, and before I could collect myself I was knocked down again. And kicked. And fired on the spot.

"Next day I went out to the rail head and found Pearly again. I wanted to take him on one to one, fair fight. He wasn't having any that time, and he had half a dozen layers behind him, so nothing happened. Shortly after, I got the marshal's job. Pearly and I have crossed trails several times, but he ain't game to go against me fair like. But I know him, and I figure he's just waitin' fer his chance, sometime when he's got an edge of some kind. He's like that, canny as an alley cat, knows when to fight and when not. And when he fights, he's pretty sure he can win."

"Well, we ain't got no call to butt heads with him again, I 'spect the army will be pullin' out tomorrow or the next day, and we'll most likely be pretty busy up north."

"Just watch out when he's around, I'm telling you. He's a mean one, when he's got the upper hand."

They covered the miles to the lane leading into the Stoeger place, as the wagon road narrowed to a broad horse trace, and then to a trail. They cut through low hills all brown with the fall grasses, and followed a small creek crowded with high brush and small trees as it wound its way up a grassy canyon. The creek bottom widened out then, and the farm lay in the hollow, tucked into the low hills.

The house was a part log, part rough frame structure, with a chimney of field stone that comprised most of what was left. The log walls still stood, leaning outward from the blackened rubble that had been the family's home. A small well house stood ten yards from the door. A lean-to barn crowned a corral across the farmyard. Two small shanties close by it could have been a chicken coop and hay shed. The three horsemen rode up to the ruins of the cabin and halted.

"'Lige, Marshal Gerline and me'll take a look around here, why'nt you look about for some sign."

"Sure 'nough" Hardy said, and turned his horse for the corral.

Beck leaned on his saddle horn, and said, "You folks came and got 'em out?"

"Yep. All four of them in the cabin. Pretty much all we did was get the bodies out of there and into the wagon. Didn't mess with much else."

"Well, lets have a look. Come on in and tell me where you found 'em," Beck said, swinging down off of Bill. He led the horse to the well house and tied the reins to a hitch rail the rancher had built over a small water trough. Bill nosed the water in the trough. Marshal Gerline tied up his mount, too, and the men went to the front wall of the cabin. Beck pointed to a solitary arrow sticking in the corner post farthest from the door.

"That your Indian sign?" he said.

"Well, yes."

Beck stepped to the arrow and yanked it out of the wood. He looked it over end to end.

"Another one on the ground round that side," Gerline said. Beck stepped around the cabin, along the wall, found a second arrow lying on the ground.

"This all of 'em?" he said.

"Yep."

"Well, these were mighty curious Indians," Beck said, handing an arrow to the marshal. "Notice the fine arrowhead made out of what appears to be a six-penny nail. And those are most likely chicken feathers at the tail, not your usual Indian make-up, at least not in my experience."

The marshall chuckled. "I'll be damned, I do believe you're right."

They went to the front door, where the doorframe was partly burned away and the remains of the wood-plank door hung askew by its lower leather hinge. Inside they moved into wreckage and ashes, the stench of the charcoaled cabin permeated with a rancid smell of cooked meat.

The cabin was a two room affair, with an additional lean-to built out of the right wall. The dividing wall between the two rooms was on the right, and was of wood framed with flat-cut poles. Most of that wall was burned away. Ahead against the back wall was the fire place and chimney. A Dutch oven sat on the raised hearthstone, and a kettle was suspended from an iron crane on the left side.

In the center of the room, some of the debris had been cleared away, and the round top of a rough table could be seen on the ash heaped floor, the stick remains of several chairs under and around it.

"We found Mr. Stoeger there at the table," Gerline said, "looked like he'd just been sitting there calm as you please when he died. Mrs. Stoeger was over there at that cupboard," he said, pointing to the burned out ruins of a cupboard cabinet to the left of the fireplace. The doors had been mostly burned away, and cups and plates showed their white china through the debris like the bones of a rotted beast.

"She look like she was putting up a fight?"

"Well, not really. Sort of slumped down there next to the cupboard."

"How about the kids?"

"Both of them was in the lean-to over there," Gerline said, kicking aside some of the burned boards and stepping to the right side of the cabin. The lean-to portion had been made of frame lumber and boards, and was nearly consumed down to stub walls. The remains of two beds could be made out, and one of them showed a long imprint in the rubble. "Stoeger girl was found in that bed," Gerline said, "and the boy was over there next to that chest along the wall."

"Either one look like they was puttin' up a fight?"

Gerline thought for a moment. "No, nobody in the whole family looked like they was doing anything special."

Beck kicked aside debris to get to the smaller of the two beds. He reached down and grasped a stick protruding from the rubble, and pulled it free. It was the nearly intact remains of a bow.

"I think I found the "tribe" who stuck that arrow in the house," Beck said. "Looks like the boy was doin' a little play actin'."

"Yep. That would explain the nail arrowheads."

Beck and Gerline kicked around through the rubble for a time, lifting debris here and there, searching into the bedroom things in the parent's sleeping room, where they found a purse with two gold coins in it, and a small revolver. They found a Winchester rifle standing in one corner of the main room. The kitchen cupboard sideboard had the ruins of some vegetables on it, a carving knife, and in the pot slung over the fireplace was the remains of a stew. The Dutch oven held the blackened remnants of the dinner biscuits.
Jon poked around in the fireplace with the carving knife.

"I'll be durned," he said, "looks like they were cooking with coal!" Marshal Gerline shuffled over to have a look. "Humm," he murmured, "it do indeed."

"You folks do that much around here?"

"Well, not in my experience," Gerline said, "use mostly wood. When the railroad come up, they had a depot here for coal and water, among the other building materials they was using for the construction."

"I grew up in Pennsylvania," Beck said, "father was a blacksmith, his before him. Used coal in the forges all the time, but not for cooking. Stink up a meal real bad, and if you burned it indoors, it would kill you, like as not. Unless you kept the windows open and the wind coming through. I wonder if they didn't fall victim to the vapors of it."

"But why the fire?"

"Not sure about that," Beck said. He went out of the cabin, followed by Gerline. They could see Hardy up on a nearby hill, crossing the grade, looking to cut sign. Beck walked around the cabin slowly, looking it all over.

"See that sack of coal next to the wood pile?" he said, pointing. Gerline looked.

"Yeah?"

"Mostly full. I figure they were trying it out, maybe first time. Looks like they bought a sack of coal in town, or borrowed one, either way." He eyed the blackened field stone of the chimney stack, and the half chord of firewood stacked next to one of the leaning, charred log walls. The fire had not eaten its way through the wall, and the stack of wood was still intact.

"When you got the bodies into town, did anyone do an autopsy?" Beck said.

"Autopsy?"

"Well, you know, check 'em over to try and figure out what killed 'em?"

"Oh, well, sure, Doc Bender had a look at 'em, but he's a horse doctor by trade, and I'm not so sure he knows what he's doing 'round a real person and all."

"Well, what did he say?"

"That's just it, he couldn't find any bullet wounds or arrow marks and such."

"Any of 'em scalped?"

"No. No, they wasn't scalped."

"Well, it's been my experience that if they had been killed by Indians, scalps would have been taken. It never ceases to amaze me that even "tame" Indians, the ones we think of as civilized, and can even speak white, they'll still take a scalp at the drop of a hat. So to speak."

"So what do you figure happened here?"

Beck thought about it for a time.

"Well, you notice that the fire seems to have taken the roof, and then commenced to burn down from there when the debris caved in. Everything covered with ashes and burned wood coming down from above. No sod roof on this house, I take it?"

"Nope. He done it all in wood. There's a little stand of lodge pole pine just up the valley there, and that's where all the wood came from."

"And the girl was found in bed. And the old man sitting at the table. Rifle in the corner. They were not in a fight, that's certain. I think they were all in for the night, and the misses was cooking supper, using coal for the first time. Now, I know that coal, if used in a closed up room, can be pretty dangerous. I think they were overcome by the fumes, and all of 'em were knocked out, just as if they'd been put to sleep."

"And the fire? How you figure that came about?"

"Well, there's a considerable pile of clinkers left in the fireplace. I figure Mrs. Stoeger wasn't familiar with using coal, and she got too much going. I noticed that pile of wood that remains outside looks pretty green. If they had been using green pine that hadn't had a chance to cure, the chimney was probably pretty badly tarred up. I've seen in happen more'n once, family burns green wood all summer, and since it's hot during that time they use a low fire, which means more smoke and more tar in the chimney, then in the fall they build a bigger fire for heat, and the flames get up in the chimney and touch off all that collected tar, and 'fore you know it, the chimney's belchin' flame like a roman candle. Now, coal cooks out a lot hotter'n wood, and if they had a good coal fire going when they passed out, and it got into the chimney, it's a sure bet it would have touched off anything burnable in that chimney."

"But the fire? That would have just shot up the chimney and out."

"That's the thing. A chimney stack fire like that is usually pretty spectacular, from what I've seen. Sparks and debris flying all over the place. My bet is, sparks ignited the roof, and the family being knocked out from the fumes, they didn't know it, and couldn't do anything about it. The whole thing burned down around their ears."

"Well I'll be damned," Gerline said, looking away across the hills. "And we spent nigh onto two days looking for the dirty redskins who did it."

"And twern't a single one in sight, nor a track to be found," said Hardy, walking his horse up to them in the yard. "No Injun's did this one, gentlemen, but we have a mystery on the card."

"And that would be?" Beck said.

"Stock gone, chickens gone, where'd it all go? I have a trail. Of sorts. If you will mount up, I'll give you a little tour."

They did, and followed Hardy into the corral. He led them to the side of the corral where a gate existed near the stream that bent near the farm structures on its way down the little valley flats. Hardy reached down, slipped the rawhide latch, and swung the gate open. They proceeded down to the water.

"Lots of tracks through here, stock led down to water time and again. But look over there on the upstream side, see how those tracks curve from the corral down to the water? They are all outbound, and you can see in the gravel and sand there by the stream, maybe three, four animals walked down and into the water and all headed up the stream."

"So they are," Beck said. "Your posse search up thataway much?"

"Some," Gerline said, "I mean, we followed the stream both up and down for a bit, but most of the time we were over in the hills looking for any tracks where they came in. We did find the cowboy's trail, the four that found 'em, but that was all."

"Could these tracks have been made by your posse?"

"I don't think so. We were split up, mostly, looking all over the place. These tracks sure do look like several horses moving out together."

"And I found a lot of your posse's sign, and the trail you found of the cowboys. I think we need to go upstream a bit and see where this leads," Hardy said.

They began to work their way up the creek, Beck on the left bank, Hardy on the right, and the marshal traveling in the water. They paused frequently at every place that looked disturbed for any reason, conferring over every scrape and dent in the soil. Finally, several miles from the cabin, at a spot where a small waterfall made an impassable barrier, they found sign.

"There she be, plain as day," said Hardy, halting his horse over the obvious marks of several animals climbing the creek bank onto the slope of the hill.

"Could it have been Indians after all?" said the marshal, "Maybe this is their get away track."

"Not unless one of them is riding a cow," said Hardy. "Looky here, see that set there in the soft ground? That's a durned cow print or my name ain't Elijah!"

They got down and stared at it for a few moments.

"So, they was making their getaway with the stolen cow!" said the marshal.

"Might have been," Beck said. "I still don't see foul play here. It looks like somebody is making off with the cow, all right, but I would be willing to bet a nickel to a double eagle these other tracks are from the mules this farmer had. And from the looks of it, one galoot is leading the whole pack."

"All right, all right," the marshal said in exasperation, chuckling a bit, "so we jumped to the conclusion it was Indians, and we was wrong. Let's get on down this trail and find out where the critters went."

"Good enough," Beck said. "We got about two hours left 'till noon, and then we need to be back to town to attend to the army. Whoever done this has two days head start at least. I don't figure we're going to get very far, but it's worth a shot."

Chapter 12

They spurred their horses up and over the shoulder of the long hill, spreading their positions out a little to blanket the area that the trail covered. It was not hard to follow, even after several days, as the dry, brown grasses had been combed evenly by the constant northwest wind, and the animals that had gone before had plowed and broken the grass carpet with a well defined furrow. Over the brow of the hill the trail led them down to the stream again, but did not enter it. After several miles the trail merged with another.

"I figure that's the four cowboys," said Gerline, "the spread they work for is off thataway." He pointed up the valley of the stream.

"Maybe one of 'em is taking the stock to the ranch?" said Hardy.

"Let's go see," Beck said.

Within another two miles, the trails diverged again, the incoming trail leading away from the creek and up toward a shallow divide, while the outgoing trail continued on up the valley. The three pursuers followed that.

The trail soon began to angle away from the creek, and then wound through a cleft in the hills to the east and down into another valley. There they could see another stream bed marked by trees and brush winding its way through the bottomland. Far down the valley was a swatch of green and brown foliage that indicated broader water. And trailing out from one edge of that swale was a low, windblown wisp of smoke. The trail seemed to be headed directly at the smoke.

The riders urged their mounts into a canter and rode over the rolling, brown hills down into the valley and finally to the stand of scrub oak and spike hickory that surrounded a small pond. As they came up, they could see two tepees in the trees, and horses tethered nearby. The smoke was coming from a low fire spread along a shallow pit, and over the pit was a rack made of laced hickory stems, holding many strips of drying meat. They halted their horses at the edge of the trees. Just then four Indians on paint ponies came out of the heavy brush to their left. Each of them carried a rifle.

Hardy held up a hand in the classic sign of greeting, and grunted several words. Gerline edged a hand off of his reins and rested it on his hip next to his pistol.

"Take it easy, marshal," Beck said easily, "if they was hostile we would never have seen the smoke, nor made it this far. Let Hardy palaver with 'em."

One of the braves answered, and Hardy laughed. He kept up a conversation, and then the braves turned toward the camp. Hardy started after them.

"They ain't Crow but they speak it," he said. "I think I found your cow."

They followed the braves into the trees and dismounted near one of the tepees, tied up the horses with the Indian's mounts. As they approached the tepee, an old man stepped out of it and raised his hand.

"Howdy!" he said, and smiled through crooked teeth. "You come for white man's buffalo."

Hardy looked at Beck and Gerline and grinned.

He spoke to the old man in a guttural tongue, as the four braves who had led them in came over and sat on logs nearby. The old man sat, and waved the white men to seats of their own. Hardy kept at it, and laughed several times more. Finally he turned to his two companions.

"That meat over the fire is the cow. What's left of it. This bunch are Arapahoe, on their way to trade with the Crow. The Crow have white man's goods, ammunition, blankets, knives. This bunch will trade 'em skins, buffalo robes, medicine feathers. They ran into those four cowboys four days ago about a day's ride back. Cowboys had nothing to trade, so nothing much came of it. Then two days ago one of them wranglers caught up with this bunch here. Leadin' two mules and the cow. Traded for hides, took off with a load on one of the mules. Other mule over there by the pond. Cow made a high feast for 'em last night, jerked the rest this morning. That chief, there," Hardy concluded, nodding at the old man, "he figured somebody would come 'round about the cow, that's why they ate it quick."

"Howdy!" said the chief, grinning through teeth that looked like a picket fence after a hurricane.

"Who was it told you about the wreck out at the Stoeger place?" Beck said to Gerline.

"One they call Simon, I believe."

"And the other three? When did you see them?"

"Never really did, actually. Deputy told me about the hotel, and your part in it. Said there were four of 'em. Bartender at the Downspout Saloon told me about them getting kicked out, and your part in that. I ain't actually seen all four of 'em together."

"Well, one of 'em was here, that we know. So that explains what happened to the stock. Except for the one mule."

"Say, I think I know what may have happened to that mule, too," said Gerline, reflectively. "Yesterday when the army hit town, first thing the Captain Peachbow did was ask around for mules. Said they needed more of 'em for supplying the company than they were able to bring. Wouldn't be surprised if that mule is now wearing an army brand."

"Speaking of which, let's go have a look at the mule these Injun's have," said Beck, rising. "Hardy, ask him if we can have a look see. Make it plain we are only looking, we don't want it back."

Hardy did so, and one of the braves led them through the trees to the pond. The mule was tethered there. It was a large mule, which eyed them calmly as they came up.

"Well looky there," said Beck, moving to the mule's shoulder, "U.S. Army surplus." On the mule's hide was a "US" brand with a branded diagonal through it.

"Probably a safe bet its partner had the same brand," Gerline said. "Maybe if we check with the army, we can find that animal and maybe find out who sold it to 'em."

"If that's where it ended up. Worth a try, anyway," Beck said. They moved through the brush back to the camp. Hardy had a few more words for the old chief, who grinned and bellowed "Howdy!" at them as they untied their horses and led them out onto the grasslands again.

"So far, it looks like one of them wranglers made off with the Stoeger's stock, bartered most of it here, maybe took the rest back to Quandry, or thereabouts," Beck said as they set off cross country for the town.

"With a load of hides, to boot!" said Hardy.

"Question is," put in Gerline, "were the Stoegers dead before or after he took the animals?"

"You figure there's really a question about that?" Beck said.

"I do. There was four of them cowboys. If they was known to the Stoegers, they could have got real close, all friendly like, and hit 'em with something, all sudden like. Then just set fire to the place to cover it up," Gerline said.

"Could be," Beck said. "But why? We found that bag of money you got in your saddlebag, and that little Colt pistol. And the rifle was still there. Why would those four have hurt anyone? And then come to town to tell you about it? Nothing from the house seems to have been taken, and the family didn't seem to be puttin' up a fight, or so you said. No, I think the story of one of those boys being sweet on the Stoeger girl was more like it. They were on their way into town, swung by the farm so's that boy could see his gal, and they found the place already burned. Some of them went on into town, and whoever stayed at the farm got to thinking. He probably recalled meeting those Arapahoe, who were on their way to do some trading. I figure he just tied all the animals nose to tail and trailed 'em out of there, and caught up with the trading party where we found 'em. They only told us about one cowboy, not three. That one, he probably figured that since nobody owned those animals any more, no one would care. He was looking to get him a stake for something, that's what I figure."

"You may be right," Gerline said. "But I want to talk to all four of 'em, see what kind of story we get. After all, the love angle may be true, but it may have been love gone bad, she may have turned him out for a better catch. Maybe it's revenge or some such."

"Could be. But I don't see three boys who ain't known as desperados turning on a farmer and his family just because a fourth one of 'em is love sick. That don't pan out."

"Jon, what do you know of love sick?" Hardy put it, "The only thing you ever loved is that durned horse of yours!"

"'Lige, sometime I will tell you a tale about love," pronounced Beck, "and it is sure to convince you that a good horse is sometimes worth its weight in pretty gals."

"He's a big horse. That would be a bunch of gals!" Hardy chuckled.

70

"And cheap at twice the price," Beck said, gently spurring the big roan into a canter.

Chapter 13

Hardy and Beck reached the stable in town just after noon. Inside, they found the stableman shoveling horse apples into a rank smelling wooden wheelbarrow. He watched them dismount, and came to a sort of attention as they approached him, shovel in one hand, other hand at his side, battered stovepipe hat at a precarious angle atop his disheveled hair. He was quaking slightly as Beck looked him over.

"Why Lige, I do believe Mr. Pickworth, here, has come to grief of some sort. Notice his ear, if you will. Looks like wolves have been a gnawin' on that side, there," said Beck, reaching out to indicate Pickworth's left ear. The stableman quickly raised his free hand to his ear and flinched back. The ear was red and swollen.

"Tween't no wolves and you know it right well!" he whimpered.

"More like a mountain cat, then? Female?"

"She can be a terror, I will say!" Pickworth blurted.

"She'll seem like a cuddly house tabby next to me if you fail me this time!" Beck growled, looming over the suddenly cringing hostler, "We'll be leaving the horses with you once again, and they will get only the best of care."

"Yes sir!" croaked Pickworth.

"And oats!"

"Yes sir!"

"You see to it! If these horses ain't treated like equine royalty, I will sail you out of that upper door like the buzzard you are, and this time there will be no water tank to break your fall!"

"Oh yes sir, Mr. Beck, I'll see to it, I will!" said the hostler, doffing his hat and nodding like a spasmodic mechanical toy.

Beck turned to leave, and Hardy, over his shoulder to the stableman, said, "Best you do like he says. You get him riled again, there will be blood!"

71

The stableman scurried after the two horses, moaning to himself.

The two scouts walked out to the army camp, and found the officers gathered at the captain's tent. Captain Peachbow was seated with one of his lieutenants, and another lieutenant bent over a chart table set up under the tent flap awning. As the men came up, the captain rose to introduce his two lieutenants, Morgan and Phelps, then stepped to the map table. He pointed to a spot on the chart.

"Here we are at present, gentlemen. Dispatches this morning place the Nez Perce band very near or possibly inside of Yellowstone Park, we think about here. To the northeast, about here, is the Crow agency, and this area, here, is known to have several Crow camps. So far as we know, the Crow have taken no warlike action. Sturgis with his Seventh Cavalry is in this area, here, and Colonel Miles with his command is to the north, in this area.

"Now, it is my understanding that General Howard has come to the verge of Yellowstone Park, that the renegade band is in fact somewhere in the Park ahead of him, but not yet among the Crow. Our mission is to locate the renegades, and prevent them from linking up with the Crow. We must find them, and stop them, and above all keep them from turning south."

"If you will excuse the observance, captain," said Hardy, "You've got about forty, fifty good men here, and the Nez Perce are said to number over a thousand. You really think we'll be stopping them? Or even slowing them down?"

"They have women and children with them, Mr. Hardy," replied Captain Peachbow, "I hardly think they will be in position to put up much of a fight."

"Oh, they'll fight," said Beck, "and no doubt of that."

"Mr. Beck, I understand you have a better than passing acquaintance with this tribe," the captain said. "What of them? We've fought the Sioux and the Cheyenne, and no better mounted warriors ever galloped over the plains. Are the Nez Perce the same?"

"No two tribes are the same, captain," said Beck. "When I walked among them, they were on our side, so to speak. They scouted for me, and the army, during the Yakima and Cayuse campaigns. Got to know a few of 'em right well.

"Now your average Nez Perce, he was born atop a horse, so to speak, and the women ride as well as the men. They love fine horses, and have been breeding them since the days of the Spanish. But they're not like the Sioux or the Crow for fighting, they can fight from the back of a horse, sure, but they'd just as soon lay for you in the rocks or woods. They're a mountain people more than a plains Indian, so to speak, and they're a pack of dead shots. They been shooting rifles since Lewis and Clark met 'em in '04, and they don't waste ammunition.

"My advice to you for fighting them would be to go to cover at first contact, no matter how far out there you figure they are. If you can see them, they've already been watching you for some time. And if you're within shooting distance of them, chances are they'll get lead into you 'for you get any into them."

"I'll take that into advisement, Mr. Beck," said Peachbow with a hint of a sneer in his tone, "You just get us in contact, and we'll take care of the rest. Our job is to find them first, and find out what the Crow intend to do. Ultimately, we must prevent them from coming south. With Miles in the north, and Sturgis in the east, Howard will flush them into our net, which we will all participate in closing. The biggest question, besides where they are and where they are going, is, what will the Crow do."

"I don't figure you'll have much to worry about from the Crow," Hardy said, "they've been pretty peaceable through all of this. They've known for many years that the white man is the future. They've already settled pretty peaceably up around the agency, and I just can't see 'em getting' too het up about their cousins' troubles."

"And have they been disarmed, Mr. Hardy?" said one of the lieutenants, Morgan.

"Hell no," said Hardy, "how would they hunt and eat without guns?"

"Then if they are armed, they are dangerous," Morgan blurted angrily, "and there is every possibility that they will join in the fight."

"Ridiculous!" Hardy snorted, "I know the Crow, and they won't get wound up in this mess."

"Oh?" Morgan sneered, "You know this because your squaw has promised you it is true?"

"Maybe," said Hardy evenly. "What my wife tells me is always true, for unlike the white man, she was never taught how to lie. But that ain't what tells me they'll stay peaceable in this, I been around the Crow for twenty odd years, I know how they think. Oh they'll talk it over, about joinin' in all right, and some of the young bucks may just go and do it. They love a good fight, no matter who it is they're fightin'. But in the end, they'll not go against the white man, they've signed the treaties and they'll keep their end of it. In fact, we'll probably get some of 'em to scout for us in this deal!"

"And you would trust them to assist us in hunting down their brethren?" Morgan said.

"I would," Hardy said, a little irritation showing in his tone. "The Crow have had to live twixt the Sioux and the Cheyenne, the Blackfoot and the Comanche all their lives. They know how to get along, and they know how to fight. They have negotiated with and fought with all of those tribes for their entire history, so scouting for us against them is just second nature."

"I believe it was Crow scouts with Custer on that fateful day a year ago," Morgan said, "didn't do him much good, did they."

"From what I heard tell, if Custer had listened to his scouts he'd be sportin' his hair today just like you and me. Only a fool ignores good advice."

"A fool, sir?" sputtered Morgan, "Why, damn you, sir! I'll not stand by and have you speak ill of one of the finest Indian fighters on the frontier!" He loosed the flap of his pistol holster and was dragging the gun out when Lieutenant Phelps grabbed his gun arm. Captain Peachbow grabbed his other.

"That will be enough, Morgan!" bellowed Peachbow, then to Hardy, "Sir, you will not speak so of the dead while you are a member of my command! Colonel Custer died in service to his country, and so deserves the honor due any fallen soldier. Do I make myself clear?"

"Yes, captain, that you do," Hardy said, "My apologies to the lieutenant, there, and to you. Almost seems like you was related to the good colonel, lieutenant. Didn't mean no disrespect toward your kin."

"We were not related, sir!" said Morgan stiffly, re-buttoning the holster flap. "We wear the same uniform, with pride, sir. He was good at killing Indians, an avocation to which I aspire in the keenest way!"

"Well, I suppose a young man fresh on the frontier might find it a grand adventure, killing Indians and all, but—" Hardy began.

"It has nothing to do with adventure, Mr. Hardy!" exclaimed Morgan, "It has everything to do with what is coming to them, what they justly deserve!"

"Which is?" posed Hardy.

"Extermination! To the last woman and child and camp dog! You see, Mr. Hardy," Morgan went on bitterly, "I lived in Minnesota as a boy, with my family. The rising of '62 brought the Sioux to our door with their knives and guns and hatchets in hand, and before we could even blink they were on us like a pack of wolves! My family was slaughtered before my eyes, and they left me for dead as well. God blessed me to survive, while hundreds of white men and women and children did not. Hundreds, sir, whose only crime was the farming of land that had been legally purchased from those same noble savages! I swore as a child that I would dedicate my life to justice. There is only one justice that I can possibly see, and that is wiping them out!"

Captain Peachbow stood close to Morgan and looked him in the face. "Simmer down, Morgan, you'll get your chance to fight Indians, God willing. In the mean time," he said, turning back to the table, "Mr. Hardy. I understand your wife is a Crow. Can she get us into the Crow camps without bloodshed?"

"As I said before, she tells me there ain't going to be any trouble. But, getting you military boys into the Crow camps may be impossible. At least without trouble. With blood running high all around, " and he eyed Morgan in saying it, "some young buck just might take a pot shot at a uniform, any uniform, just to show his medicine. I would suggest you let me palaver with the Crow. We'll most likely be able to spy out the lay of the land and get some real idea of which way the Crow will jump. Although I'm still saying, they are not going to get into a fight with the army."

"And if you discover otherwise," blurted out Morgan, "would you admit to us that you have been wrong? Or rather, that your squaw has been wrong?"

"Why would I not?" Hardy said. Beck, standing just behind him, could see a slight tension gather in Hardy's shoulders.

"Because so far we have heard that your Indians are such paragons of virtue, all peace and light, and never lie. I should think it would be difficult for you to relate the truth, should it turn out otherwise than what you have stated," said Morgan with a sneer.

"Well don't that beat all!" Hardy said. "I do believe this pup is calling me a liar," he spoke over his shoulder to Beck.

"You have given us nothing but your opinion so far," went on Morgan, "I believe the army is paying you for what you see, not what you think. Perhaps you will see the truth if you can get by the blanket your squaw has draped over your eyes!"

"Well right now I see a wet behind the ears popinjay lieutenant who's gonna get a lesson in manners..." said Hardy, starting around the table for the young officer.

Beck grabbed Hardy from behind, wrapped him in his arms and lifted him off of the ground. The Captain stepped in front of the lieutenant and stayed him with a hand to his chest.

"Mr. Hardy! Lieutenant Morgan!" barked the captain, "That will be quite enough! If I hear one more word spoken by either of you, I will place you under arrest! Shut your mouth, lieutenant," said the captain to Morgan, who had begun to protest. "I mean it, one word. From either of you!"

Beck lowered Hardy to the earth again, and loosed him from his bear hug.

"Mr. Morgan," Peachbow said gravely, "I am aware of your history and your great loss in the uprising of 1862. But we are here to do a job of work, and it is our duty to see that job through. Whatever you think of Mr. Hardy or his wife is to be kept to yourself. I will not tolerate your jeopardizing our mission with your hostile feelings toward our scouts! Control yourself, sir, or I will relieve you and send you back to the fort, where you will find yourself on report and subject to disciplinary action! Do I make myself clear, sir?"

Morgan came to attention. "You do, sir!"

"And Mr. Hardy," Peachbow said, turning to the scouts, "as an employee of the US Army, I expect you to conduct yourself with the same self control as any of my officers. Do you understand me, sir?"

"Well captain," Hardy said, clearing his throat, "I'm generally a pretty easy going feller. But one thing should be made clear. No man calls me a liar and goes unmarked for it! I'll let it slide for the time being, but there will come a reckoning—"

"Mr. Hardy!" Captain Peachbow growled, "That's not good enough. If you cannot put this behind you, now, I shall release you

76

from your contract this very moment! I will not have quarrelling men in this command who might be at each others throats when I need them most! Mr. Morgan, apologize to Mr. Hardy."

"What? But captain, I—"

"Just do it, lieutenant. That is an order!"

Morgan glared at Peachbow, then at Hardy. He then fell to attention again, looking straight ahead into space. "Mr. Hardy," he said firmly, "please accept my apology for intimating that you might be less than truthful in any aspect of your communication with us."

"Well now, sonny—" Hardy started, when Beck elbowed him in the ribs. He grunted, eyed Beck out of the corner of his eye, and went on. "All right, all right, apology accepted. No hard feelings."

There was a moment of silence as each of them cooled out and glanced at the others in the group. Then the captain said, "Now then. Let's get into the logistics. Lieutenant Phelps, what of the mule supply?"

Phelps stepped up to the table.

"Yes sir. With the dozen we brought with us and the six more we procured last night, that gives us a total of eighteen. Now, of those, three, maybe four of them may not be fit for packing, as they seem to be plow mules. One of those had an old army brand on him, though, so that one may do. Only way to tell is to load them up and see what happens."

"Where'd you find that old army mule?" Beck said.

"Sergeant said they were in a corral over to the south side of town, little barn over there where folks coming into town can leave their animals. Seven mules there, of which we bought five. That one was among them."

"They of interest to you, Beck?" said Peachbow.

"Might be. Family on a small farm northwest of here was killed a few days ago. They had two plow mules, which were missing when the family, or what was left of them, was discovered. We tracked those mules to a local Indian camp, but the Indians were not involved in the death of the family as near as we can tell. And, they told us it was a white man who trailed the two mules and a cow to their camp. The Indians had the one mule, and what was left of the cow, and said the man bringing the mules left with one of them, headed in the general direction of Quandry. Lieutenant Phelps, any of the other mules you looked at have old army brands?"

"No, just the one."

"Even money says that's our missing mule. Who did you buy him from?"

"That I don't know. I will have to ask the sergeant."

"I'll have the sergeant brought up for you, Mr. Beck. In the mean time, we pack the outfit and move out as soon as possible after daylight in the morning. Mr. Phelps, please fetch the sergeant for Mr. Beck. Mr. Morgan, come with me," said Peachbow, gesturing toward his tent.

Morgan glared at Hardy, then turned and followed his captain through the tent flaps. Beck and Hardy waited at the map table, idly looking over the layout of the country bisected by longitudinal and latitudinal lines on the heavy vellum. The sound of a heated discussion, in low but urgent tones, rumbled out of the captain's tent.

"You know, Lige," Beck said casually, bending close to observe the course of a river line on the map, "I heard tell that Custer wasn't scalped at all at the Little Big Horn. Had his hair cut so short there was nothing fit to take. So I hear."

"True. But that popinjay jackass lieutenant didn't know that, and I sure got him hummin' with that remark, don't you figure?"

"Maybe not the wisest course of action, my friend."

"Maybe not. But these holier-than-thou Injun killers give me a butt pain," Hardy said in soft tones, bending to examine a river line of his own on that side of the map. "He may have a good reason to hate Injuns, I'll allow, but not all Injuns in the same."

"You mean your wife ain't just waitin' for a chance to lift your hair while you sleep?"

"Well, maybe she is at that. She is my wife, after all."

Chapter 14

The sergeant had little to say about the procurement of the mule, in that he had arranged the sale of all the animals through a man living on the premises of the little barn, but the sergeant did not

78

know his name. He did say that the man needed a day to clear the sales with several owners.

Beck went off to find the mule salesman, and Hardy went to supervise the cutting out of the mules they would be using, and see about packing and crew.

Beck found the small corral and its little barn on the south end of town. The corral contained a dozen horses, and another five mules. Two boys were forking hay from a wagon into a manger on one end of the corral. Beck approached them.

"You boys know where I can find the owner of this corral?" he asked them.

"That would be me," said a man emerging from the barn. He was wiping his hands on a rag, and was smiling broadly. He extended a hand. "Jules Finnigan's the name, what can I do fer ya?"

Beck took the hand, shook it. "Beck's the name. I'm looking for the owner of a mule you sold to the army yesterday. Had an army surplus brand on it."

"Sure, that was one of 'em. Belonged to that half breed, that saddle maker feller."

"Was it here long?"

"Nope. Came in the day before, out yesterday. Folks been coming into town from all around the country, skeered of them Injuns coming down from the park. Most just board their stock here, or at the stable up yonder. Army come around looking fer mules, found a few folks was willing to sell."

"That half breed feller say where he got that mule?"

"Why, no...and I didn't ask. Was it stole?"

"Don't know, yet. May have been."

"Well I didn't know that, all I done was arrange the sale—"

"I'm not looking for somebody to hang. Just yet. Thanks for the information."

Beck left the corral and walked up to the saddle shop where he had purchased his moccasins. He entered the shop, and found no one in the front room. He heard a pounding from the workshop, and pushed aside the buckskin curtain that formed the partition between the two rooms. He found Samuel Gland, mallet in hand, imprinting a piece of leather. Gland looked up from his work as Beck entered.

"Ah, senor...Beck, isn't it? Good to see you again. What may I do for you today, senor?"

"I understand you recently sold a mule."

"The hide was unsuitable for boots."

"A live mule. With a surplus army brand."

"I buy, I sell, I do what I can to make my living here."

"If you want to keep on making a living here, I need a straight answer. Who sold you that mule?"

Gland looked at Beck for a long moment with his flat black eyes. Finally he laid the mallet and the leather punch on his workbench.

"I do not wish to get anyone in trouble, senor," he said, "I am a peaceful man, and as you say, I do want to continue making my living here. If I bring trouble down on anyone who lives here with me, I bring it down upon myself."

"It is not trouble I will bring to you over this mule," Beck said. "I simply want to know who brought it to you. I know where it came from, and you do, too. I think I know who brought the mule to town. I have met him twice already. Each time he has thought to do me harm, but each time he has been unlucky. If I describe him for you, will you at least tell me if I am right?"

"I will."

"Short, about your height. Red hair. Wears a blue shirt, a very nicely made deerskin vest, and—"

"Some of my best work!"

"I thought as much. Thank you for your help. I will never tell anyone that you remember your best work."

"I am grateful, senor."

"And if I might ask, what was the price you paid for the mule?"

"He had skins also, elk, deer, one buffalo. I gave him ten dollars, senor, for the lot."

"Not much for a mule."

"He did not want to pay to feed it, senor."

"Thank you, Mr. Gland."

"De nada."

Beck returned to the stable to check on his horse. He found Pickworth busily currying the animal, and oats in the stall feed trough, upon which Bill was lazily munching. His big brown eyes were half closed, and he indeed appeared to be in the critter heaven he had been promised. Beck smiled slightly. He looked at Pickworth with a frown.

"We'll be along before dawn to pick up the horses. Make sure they're ready," he growled.

"Oh yes sir, yes sir!" Pickworth blurted and curried all the harder.

Beck found Hardy in the corral behind the stable with two mules and three army privates. One of the privates had packing experience, and Hardy was going over what they would requisition from the army stores. The other two privates would be the runners, needed for constant communication with the main army column. After Hardy got them squared away, he and Beck turned their attention to the mules. One of them was the army surplus animal he had been inquiring about.

"Think that old veteran remembers how to carry a load?" Beck said.

"We'll soon see," said Hardy. The army packer came back with a pair of pack saddles and rope, and then all of them went to the commissary for the supplies. They carried hardtack, bacon, ammunition, one small tent, and sacks of necessaries back to the corral. The afternoon was spent pack saddling the mules and loading them with the gear. The surplus animal took to the saddle and its load with calm indifference, while its partner made a bucking circuit of the corral before settling down to acceptance of the saddle. Hardy and the army packer worked out the packing arrangement, then all of the material was unloaded and stowed just inside the barn door. Hardy instructed the privates to be at the corral by four the next morning, with their horses and gear. He and Beck went to the army camp and found Captain Peachbow.

"Come in, gentlemen," he said at the tent door, as two sergeants and Lieutenant Phelps eased past them to exit the tent. The captain seated them in camp chairs, went to a side chest, and poured out three cups of whiskey, handing a cup to each of his scouts as he sat down.

"Gentlemen, here's to a speedy conclusion of this affair, and to your health!" said Peachbow, raising his cup. The scouts saluted with theirs, and all drank of the whiskey.

"I will furnish you with copies of our central operational map, and we can coordinate the search via the runners as we go. First in importance is a visit to the Crow camps, and as you so bluntly noted, I do not think it wise for uniforms to be seen there at this point. If we go in force, the Crow will most likely construe that as a hostile gesture. We don't want them thinking that. So, I will leave it to you gentlemen to visit the camps and find out what the Crow intend."

"Gambling with our hair, are you, captain?" Beck smiled.

"Not at all, Mr. Beck. Mr. Hardy is certain you will be safe—"

"And we will be!" grumped Hardy.

"—so I see no reason for worry over this. If we run into the Nez Perce before we get to the Crow villages, then we will simply do what we can to fight them and contain them. But we must know where they are, and what they intend."

"Still planning on moving out in the morning?"

"Yes indeed! Your detachment will precede us with a direct approach of the Crow camps. The main column will head for the Yellowstone, and we will coordinate movements once you have determined the Crow intention. We will have four wagons in the supply train to follow us up, and I will establish a base of operations on the Yellowstone, or beyond, as the situation warrants. I am informed that another two companies of the Fifth Cavalry will be coming up in two days time to support us. We may be in a position to make a good fight after all."

"May be?" said Beck. "What were you planning to do if no support were available?"

"Our job, Mr. Beck. We are soldiers. We do what we are told, and we do our best."

"Well, here's to your best, then," Beck said, raising his cup, "let us hope it is good enough." They all drank to that.

Chapter 15

Beck and Hardy found that two other men had been assigned to their room when they went back to the hotel to turn in that night, both of them railroad workers. The hotel was packed with refugees of the Indian panic, with the lobby housing half a dozen men and their gear, the hallways strewn with a dozen more, and the sheds out back filled by several farm and ranch families. The scouts worked around the railroad men as they checked, cleaned and packed their gear. Hardy had a good time impressing the spike drivers with his prowess as an Indian scout and Hero of the Plains. Beck had a hard time keeping his mouth shut when the stories began to border on the ridiculous. The scouts made arrangements with the hotel keeper for an early breakfast, and turned in. The snoring throughout the hotel reminded Beck of the first time he had witnessed a buffalo run, with the thundering of the hooves shaking the ground like an earthquake.

He did not sleep soundly or long, and shortly after midnight rose, dressed, strapped on his revolver, and, managing to step on the men asleep on the floor only a few times, and those lightly, made his way out the back door to the cook shed. The hotel owner was already there building up the fire in the cook stove. Seven people were asleep on the floorboards of the cook tent.

"You feedin' all these?" Beck said softly to Mr. Ransom.

"Anybody that comes, we'll feed 'em. Until the grub runs out."

"Seen anything like this before? Everybody coming in like this, I mean."

"No. We had a busy time of it when the railroad had their camp here, hundreds of men all around. But they've been twenty miles up the line for months now, working on the McGinty Grade and some pretty tall bridges. Naw, this is the first real Indian scare we've had in years. Hard to believe there's so many folks in the neighborhood, until they all come callin'".

"Ain't that the truth. How soon can we get some grub?"

"Give me half an hour, you'll be first in line."

By the time Ransom had the stove top hissing and popping with bacon and potatoes frying in the pans, and biscuits coming out of the oven, his wife had joined him. Together they worked frantically to get the food on the tables. Beck was joined by Hardy, then others, and as they got the first plates heaped with food the line was already twenty people long. Five of the sleepers still snored on the cook tent floorboards, and everyone just stepped over them as need be. Beck and Hardy gulped their food, washed it down with hot coffee, and after gathering their gear from their room, headed for the stable.

The three army men were already at the corral, and they had one of the mules nearly packed as the scouts came up. By the time they had saddled the horses, packed the mules, and stowed all the gear, soft light was seeping up over the earth to the east. They mounted up and headed down the street. As they passed the marshal's office, Gerline came out on the boardwalk in the soft morning light.

"Headin' out, then, are ya?" he said.

Beck reined in Bill, and the little column paused.

"Yep, going to find us some redskins," Beck said. "We even have with us that mystery mule, the one taken from the Stoeger place. Have a pretty good idea of how it got to town."

"So do I," Gerline said. "Been doin' a little scouting around of my own. Pretty sure it was Zak Tibbits that brought it in. I recalled he wasn't with the cowpokes who come in with news of the Stoeger raid, but he had been out there at the place when they discovered it. I figure he saw a chance for a little profit, and he was the one what stole the stock."

"May have been. But you called it a raid."

"I still ain't so sure that bunch of redskins we tracked didn't have anything to do with it. I need to talk to Tibbits and his bunch to make sure. In fact, I need to bring 'em in for questioning on the theft of that stock. And funny thing is, I been lookin' for 'em most of the night, and they seem to have disappeared."

"Probably headed back to their ranch, after all."

"Maybe so. At any rate, you have good luck out there, and take a scalp for me, will you?"

Beck looked over at Hardy, who looked away with a disgusted expression and a shake of his head.

"Never took a scalp in my life, marshal," Beck said. "'Fraid you'll have to collect your own."

The column started again, and the light in the east grew steadily as they passed out of town a few miles and turned north. Hardy led the way, climbing up the valley of Station Creek to the northeast, following a game trail as the light came up. Less than a mile from the east road they stopped when two horses moved out onto the trail in front of them from behind a thicket of witch hazel. On the first horse sat Simon Pocket. He was leading the second horse, which appeared to be draped with his supplies.

"Howdy Mr. Beck!" said Pocket, "I have decided to take you up on that job offer. If you'll still have us, that is."

"Us?" Beck said.

"Sure, me and Zak. He ain't feeling none too prime at the moment, but he'll come around, I'll see to that. And he'll do his job, I promise you!"

Beck took another look at the led horse. It wasn't gear piled atop it, after all. It was Zak Tibbits, the red headed trouble maker, lying along the horse's neck, and draped with rolled slickers fore and aft, a sack of necessaries next to his shoulder, a rifle scabbard partly shielding his face. He looked to be dead.

Beck sighed and shook his head.

"Don't know about this, Simon," he said. "This ain't no picnic we're goin' to, I need men who can get it done. Is he even alive?"

"Sure 'nough, and he'll be right as rain come sundown! You have my word on it, I'll get him squared away right enough, just give us a throw at it! You can dock his pay for a day or two, and if he don't come to shine, you can dock mine too!" Simon had a pleading look to his eyes. "I need to get him out of that town, don't you see? He's pissed off too many folks, and there's a few come lookin' for him. If I don't get him out of there, he's gonna get hisself shot, and that's a fact."

Beck sighed again.

"You're a fool if you do this," Hardy muttered at his side.

Beck looked at Hardy, then at Pocket.

"Tell you what, Simon," Beck said, gritting his teeth and looking at the trail for a moment, "Here's the deal. You tag along with us, but you ain't hired until he's able to do a day's work. And the first time he mangles the job, you're both gone. Clear?"

"You're a generous man, Mr. Beck," Pocket said with a grin, "You won't regret it, that I promise you!"

"All right then," Beck said, "Let's get on with it."

Pocket eased the horses to the side of the trail, and the party moved through. Simon wheeled his mount to bring up the rear after the last pack mule, and as the led horse swung around to follow its tether, the human form lashed to its back let out a low groan.

As the light came up, the pace did too.

They climbed into the headwaters of Station Creek, then over a low ridge into the valley of the North Fork of the Stinking Water. The country was broken by the many streams and washes feeding the Fork, and the scouts stayed high on the ridges seeking faster travel over the rolling grassland. The end of the first day found them descending a long slope into the small valley of a creek. They made camp on a flat near the gurgling water, amid a grove of lodgepole pine.

In the last light of the day, Beck sent the three army privates off toward three different high points within sight, with instructions to await the dusk and report back any sighting of lights. He and Hardy unpacked the mules, watered and staked out the stock on good grass, and set about working up a meal. Simon and Zak Tibbits, who was sitting upright in his saddle for most of the last part of the day, came riding slowly up to the camp then. They had been lagging just within sight, about a mile back.

"Well, ya lived through that, now dincha!" Pocket said, swinging down tiredly.

"You go to hell," muttered Tibbits, sliding out of the saddle like a sack of dead cats. He sank to the ground, then rose unsteadily and made his way to a fallen tree a dozen yards from the fire that Hardy was building. There he sank once more against the log.

Pocket unpacked their gear, unsaddled the horses, watered them, staked them out, and reported back to the camp. Beck sent him out for firewood as the last of the sunlight left the near peaks and the shadows began to deepen. Soon Hardy had the pans out and biscuits cooking, along with bacon and beans. They would save the hard tack and jerky for more hurried times.

The riders came in one at a time, and by an hour after dark all had reported. The one private sent to the northeast reported several fires in the distance further in that direction.

"Most likely a Crow camp," Hardy said over his tin plate of food, "Maggie said they'd be somewhere along the Stinking Water until first frost."

"Who's Maggie?" said the trooper named Fitzsimmons. He was a slim, black haired kid, barely old enough to shave. His fellow soldiers were about the same age, a blond boy with blue eyes named Gloy, and a smaller, darker fellow named Benson. All three were packing in the chow like it was their last meal on earth.

"Magpie Woman," Hardy said around a mouthful of beans, "my wife. Actually they call her Bird with the Big Voice, so to speak. She figures Magpie Woman is close enough."

"Have you been married to her long, Mr. Hardy?" said Fitzsimmons.

""Bout twenty years, lad, and it ain't like we was married, proper like," Hardy said.

"Not married at all," Beck said, "more like you and me owning a horse, Fitz."

"You bought her?" said Fitz.

"T'other way around," Beck said, "she owns his sorry hide, pelt, claws and tail complete!"

"Well, she do have a way about her, sorta gets your attention," Hardy said with a smile.

"Yep, usually with a big stick, and when he ain't lookin'! Pow, right up side the head!" Beck said, grinning.

"Aw, she ain't that bad!" Hardy said, stabbing the last bit of bacon on his plate with his knife.

"How'd you meet her, Mr. Hardy?" said Benson.

"I was out on the Bozeman Trail, private in the army just about your age," Hardy said. He ate the bacon and chewed reflectively.

"We was going round and round with Red Cloud and his people in those days, they was mighty het up about all the settlers traipsin' through their parlor, so to speak. After I got that situation all worked out, my enlistment was up. Liked the country, so stayed on to do a little prospectin', worked for the army hauling freight, cuttin' wood and the like. Got to know the country right well, and so just before the war I was up in the Bighorns, pannin' a little color, digging around for a strike, when a passel of Cheyenne took a hankerin' for my scalp. By that time, the Bozeman had been closed off, so any white man in the country was considered fair game. They jumped me just about sundown, dozen or so of 'em, came a screaming down on me like a flock of crazy turkey buzzards, figured they had me cold. And they did. Kilt my horse right off, winged me in the arm and the leg, I got one shot off before they were on me, wrassled three of 'em at once knife to knife, and as luck would have it took two of 'em over a cliff with me into the Tongue River. One of those never came up, but the other one was like a she-cat with younguns ta feed, fought me tooth and nail as we washed down the river. His pals ran along the bank as best they could, but the current was swift right there and we lost them ones on the shore.

"But not each other. We was each holding the other's knife hand. Kickin', bitin', twistin' like two snakes in a death dance, all the

87

while rolling in the current against rocks, logs, sucked into whirlpools, smashed against boulders—"

"Hardy—" grumbled Beck.

"I'm getting' to 'er, Jon, these boys needs to know how it was! Now, all this time I know'd I was goin' down hill, so to speak, my left arm was going numb from a bullet in it, my leg was hurtin' somethin' fierce with a bullet in it, and that young Cheyenne dog soldier just had no quit in him! But fate, well, she's a fickle ol' bitch, and on that day she had me in mind! We swept round a bend right into a snag what had fell in the water, right about the time that Injun got me under and was keepin' me there! Now, that snag was all broken branches and sharp stakes, and when we slammed into 'er the Injun was caught up in the branches and I was swept through a gap underneath, like. Of a sudden I was free of 'em, and off down the river I went, just about played out fer keeps. Took me a mile or two ta find a place I could fetch up on the rocks, and the last thing I recalled was feeling the blackness come over me and looking up to see an Injun looking down at me! My last thought in this world was, dammit, I couldn't outrun 'em after all!

"Well, that Injun looking down at me was Magpie Woman. To this day, I always recall that my first look at her was upside down. She thinks it's good medicine, when I call her my upside down woman. She took it as a good sign that she had found a husband washed up on the rocks like a belly-up fish, and she and her friends got me to her camp, which is where I come 'round. She dug out them bullets, bound up the holes, fed me and wiped me and kept the flies off for a week till I opened my eyes. Let me tell you, upside down or right side up, the sight of an Indian right then was none too cheery fer this old codge, I can tell you! I was so sore I couldn't move, I was runnin' a fever, I knew right off they was just keepin' me fed up and breathin' so's they could cook me and eat me first chance they got! So when the darkness came again I thought my last thought, which was damn, I'm a gonner...but that squaw is kinda purty. Just a dyin' reminiscence, you understand.

"Well, couple of days later, I woke up again, and there she was again. This time the fever had broke, and I was hungry as a bear. She fed me and we spoke to each other, I knew a few words of Injun at the time, but it soon was plain as day she was working to save my sorry hide. Never did know why. Got well, came and went and came again, and married her. Injun weddin'. It was the soup, I reckon. Never had better before, nor since."

"You boys take that as a lesson," put in Beck, "When it's your turn to cook, don't do too good a job of it, lessin you get Hardy, here, fastened on you like a tick on a hound!"

Simon Pocket had joined the group during Hardy's tale, and squatted at the fire while one of the troopers poured coffee into his offered cup from the pot at the edge of the coals.

Tibbits remained at the log, just at the fringe of the furthest fire light.

"So what's the plan for tomorrow, Mr. Beck," said Pocket, tasting the coffee.

Beck stepped to their gear and retrieved a long cylinder made of leather. He extracted a roll of maps, and, sorting through them by looking at the corners, found one he wanted, pulled it out and unrolled it. The hands all bent in to look in the light of the fire.

"First thing, we're going into the Crow camps tomorrow, maybe the day after. Hardy, here, is going to seek out his lovely bride, who will help us get to whoever knows what we need to know. If the Nez Perce have not come into the country yet, we'll then head north and northwest and look for 'em. If they have, they may have already met with the Crow. The question is, if they have talked to the Crow, and if the Crow are meanin' to help them, will we come out of there with our hair."

"You mean we're going into the midst of the Crow Nation without even knowing if they are friends or enemies?" said Fitz.

"Some of us, yes," Beck said, "Just me and Hardy. We don't want you boys showing your uniforms just yet, if they've decided to go to war, you'd be the first to die. On the other hand, Hardy is part of the family. Many of them know him. A lot more of them know Maggie. We have a better than even chance of coming away with our hair if we go in there alone, just the two of us. We've got to find out which way the wind blows, and get a message back to Peachbow whichever way it is. So here's how we'll do 'er, come sunup...."

Chapter 16

Beck went over the map with his crew, gave them a good impression of where they were, where they were going, where the next spot for rendezvous might be if they became separated. They discussed what the soldiers were to do if Beck and Hardy did not return from the Crow camps. It was known that Colonel Sturgis and elements of the Seventh Cavalry were operating to the north and east, and contact with those units was discussed. The maps were put away, and as the last of the coffee was shared out among those around the fire, Simon took a cup out into the darkness to Tibbits. Tibbits had not come in for food.

Hardy got the three troopers talking about themselves, where they haled from, why they had found a home in the army. Fitzsimmons joined to escape the squalor of a Boston slum. Benson was a Maryland farm boy who didn't like farming. Gloy mentioned New Orleans and a girl, and a bit of trouble he couldn't go back to. He spoke of it lightly, and shrugged. "Seems she had a beau she never told me about, until it was too late," he added. "Them southrons is a might quick on the trigger, sometimes."

"Sometimes?" said Beck.

"This feller was one of the slower ones, I guess."

The bedrolls were fetched, and the crew turned in. Beck took first watch, and moved off into the trees within sight of camp. He found a spot where he was hidden in the shadow of a clump of bushes, and settled in to keep watch. The horses snorted a bit in the nearby grassy swale. It was a clear night, and cold. The stars in their billions cast a silvery wash over the landscape. Beck could hear at least one of the men snoring.

When the stars had wheeled half the night away, Beck moved to Hardy's bedroll and touched the sleeping man's foot. Nothing moved, but a moment later, Hardy rolled out and put on his boots. He took up his coat and rifle, and moved off toward the trees without a word. Beck went to his bedroll and turned in.

Dawn had still not splashed its golden light on the nearest peaks when the camp woke and rose and Beck rustled up a breakfast of biscuits and coffee. They packed the mules and loaded up their gear, saddled the horses and were moving off when the sun first touched the mountain tops.

They moved north down the valley of the Stinking Water, keeping to the high ground and out of the many small canyons and washes that fed the main river. In the early afternoon they trailed down to the river and forded at a wide, gravelly shoal, then up the north canyon ramparts to the northeast. They had sighted the confluence of the north and south forks from the heights, when Hardy spotted two riders on a neighboring ridge. They were Indians.

"Crow?" said Beck, following his gaze.

"Can't tell from here. Let's go find out."

Beck gave instructions for the four riders, not including Tibbits, one to go to each of four high places he pointed out, while he and Hardy made the trek into the valley toward the two Indians. Tibbits was to proceed with the two mules to a high point further along the river. If the two Indians were hostile, they might have friends hiding nearby, and perhaps the scouts would spot them. If they were friendly, they might come into the valley between the two ridges for a palaver. The group split up, and Beck and Hardy rode down the slope into the valley.

The two far horsemen watched them come, then started into the valley themselves. A short time later they all met in a small meadow between the ramparts.

Hardy spoke to them in a guttural tone, using hand gestures from time to time. They spoke in turn, and Hardy translated for Beck as they did.

"Crow of the River Clan. Magpie Woman is known to them. Yes, I am Magpie Man. Yes, this is the Red Bear. Magpie Woman is in the camp of Many Wolves, another day's ride. Nez Perce? Some Nez Perce. Soldiers? Away east, several...days. Come to camp of Many Wolves, Magpie Woman knows."

The two Crow warriors promptly wheeled their horses and took off at a gallop back up the slant of the valley slope.

"They say my wife is happily terrorizing the family, and awaits the arrival of her noble husband. Or something like that. They say they have seen a few Nez Perces, but they only come for a visit. When I asked if they intend to help their cousins against the white man, they did not say. But, they said to come on in to the camp of Many Wolves."

"Well, the Nez Perce are here," Beck said "And it isn't just a little social call, not this time of year." He sat for a moment and surveyed the surrounding heights. "What do you think, Lige? They laying a trap for us after all?"

"I don't figure it that way. If they was fixin' to do us harm, they'd be out here hunting scalps. We'd be prime meat by now, that's fer certain. No, I figure whatever them Perces is talking about, it's still up for grabs. Maybe we can have a say in it, after all." Beck and Hardy rode up a slope toward a nearby promontory, where it had been agreed the scouting party would all meet again and travel on.

The dispersed scouts came in, and they awaited Tibbits who was coming along the ridge with the mules. When all had gathered, they moved off again, keeping the river in sight. It was late in the afternoon when they had passed the confluence of the forks and reached the main river about a mile below it. They found a camping place set back in a little gorge to the northwest of the running water, with good grass and a small stream running through it. As before, they unloaded the mules, watered and picketed the stock, and Hardy set about cooking the evening meal. Fitzsimmons pitched in to help, asking questions about the simple process of cooking as they went along. And once again, Tibbits and Pocket set up a neighboring camp a short distance away from the cook fire.

Beck approached them in the waning light of the early evening.

"Simon, would you come with me for a bit?" Beck said. Tibbits sat on a rock, his head in his hands, staring at the ground. Pocket got up and came with Beck as they left the camp and walked the short distance out of the side canyon to the river.

"Tonight or tomorrow," Beck said, "Hardy and me'll be going into the Crow camp. We figure it will be all right, what with his woman there, all in the family as he likes to put it. But you never know. So, what I need from you is, if we run into trouble, take over the command and get word back to Captain Peachbow. Send one runner to do that. Then take the men north and northwest, heading for Heart Mountain. Like we talked about before, if the Nez Perce don't hook up with the Crow, they'll most likely head north, maybe try to link up with Sitting Bull in Canada. Or, they may head south, or even toward the Black Hills. They're out of their home lands now, and there's no telling which way they'll dodge. I'm betting on Canada."

"All right, Mr. Beck, if'n you and Hardy get scalped, I'll get word to the captain. If they let us alone long enough, that is."

"There is that. If they do us harm, they won't be far behind coming for you, too. So you're going to need to be ready. I figure we'll go into the Crow camp tonight, test the waters. They won't be able to see where you go, in the dark, so after we leave, break camp and go to another place you and I will work out. No fire, and leave a fire burning at the old camp. That way, if you hear gunfire, or we just don't come back, they'll have to find you first to finish the job. That'll give you a running start, at least."

"Good thinking, Mr. Beck. Always like to hear a plan that considers keepin' my hair in place."

"And when you leave a decoy fire behind, make sure it'll die of its own accord and not set the whole country on fire."

"Sure thing."

"All right, then. Let's go have a look at the maps, and get a rendezvous worked out. By the way, how's Tibbits coming? He gonna make it?"

"Well, he ain't too pert, but he's game. He hates me right powerful fer draggin' him out here, but he ain't quit yet. I told him I'd knock him off his horse if he tried, and he could walk back. He ain't got over the drunk well enough yet to stand up to me, but I figure that will come."

"Can we count on him?"

Pocket looked out over the river, watching the purple gloaming of the evening deepen.

"Mr. Beck, like I told you before, he just can't seem to shake that gal's dyin'. Most of us have lost someone at one time or another, God knows, but this one has got him by the tail and it's twistin' him somethin' fierce! He just needs some time, I figure, and a job of good hard work to do."

"Well, I don't have the time, but I have the work. Keep him on those mules, and use the soldiers as your runners. Once you head to the north, keep at least two men on the ridges at all times, and find out what's in every valley. If you sight any redskins, watch out! If they see you, they'll most like come sniffin' round to get a shot at

93

you so you can't report. If you confirm they are Nez Perce, send a runner, and then stick to 'em like pitch on a porcupine's ass!"

"That's if'n you don't come back."

"It is. I need a man to take command, and you're it!"

"I'll do my best, Mr. Beck," Simon said, "I shorly will!"

They returned to the camp and got out the maps, studying their position by firelight, and worked out a new meeting place. Hardy had the grub ready, and this time Tibbits came into the firelight and joined them. He ate a plate of beans and biscuits like it was his momma's cooking, and washed it down with hot coffee. But within minutes he grimace and grabbed his gut and stumbled out into the night. Pocket rose to follow.

"Let him alone," Beck said, "three days of whiskey takes a little getting used to."

"More like five days," Simon said, sitting again. He looked out into the night after Tibbits.

"Why, I recall once in Nawlins," Gloy began, smiling after swallowing his last bite, "had a feller I knowd come up with a new barrel of Kayntuck bourbon, fresh off a flatboat from the river. He bet me and a pal o' mine that he could...."

Beck left the fire and the story telling, and went to the horses picketed in the grass. He found Bill there, munching on grass through his halter. He patted the big horse and rubbed his shoulder, and the horse raised his head and snorted. Beck rubbed his nose.

"Feel like a little more work tonight, old boy?" he said. The horse snorted again, and his ears perked up and began scanning the night. Beck eased his coat back and felt for the handle of his army Colt, scanning the night in the direction the horse was looking, down past the fire toward the mouth of the gulch they were camped in. He saw movement against the sheen of the river water.

A voice called out, words that Back could not hear clearly. Hardy, rifle in hand, stepped out of the firelight toward the river. Beck left the meadow, skirted the fire, moving through the thicket of willows to one side of the canyon. He came up on Hardy talking Indian to two mounted braves.

"Come on over, Jon," Hardy said. Beck joined him.

"They bring word from my wife, we need to come in tonight. She says the Nez Perce are already there, and they have indeed come to talk war."

94

"Let's go, then," Beck said, turning for the camp.

He went to his saddle, hoisted it onto his shoulder, picked up the saddle blanket and bags, and, over his shoulder said to Simon as he left the firelight, "You're in charge. We're going in now."

He and Hardy saddled up and left the camp with the two Crow braves.

They traveled slowly in the night, out along the river to the north, moving on the sandy bars and beaches of the low running stream After an hour of the two Crow leading them silently on, they rounded a bend in the river and saw the light of campfires ahead on the south bank. The braves led them across a shallow ford to that side of the river, and as they came up on the camp the two Indians turned off into the night with a word to Hardy. He and Beck paused in the darkness outside the camp.

"We're to wait here for a bit," Hardy said, leaning on his saddle pommel, "Seems to be a situation developing."

"Situation?"

"That's all they said. Little strange, though. They know me, I'm family after all."

"So you keep telling' me."

"And usually I just ride right in, they don't take no fright in it atall."

"So what you figure's goin' on?"

"I think the Nez Perce is still in the camp, that's what I think."

They sat their horses for a time, then they could see a figure silhouetted against the light illuminating one of the tepees leave the camp and come in their direction. The scouts slid down off of their horses as the figure negotiated the hundred yards to them.

"What carrion eaters lurk here in the dark, afraid of the camp of mighty Crows?' came a soft but high pitched voice of the approaching figure.

"Just a pair of rangy coyotes, lookin' fer easy pickins'!" Hardy said. In the starlight Beck could see the figure then as a woman, and Hardy wrapped her up in a big hug, gladly returned by Magpie Woman.

"How you been, Maggie?" Hardy said, "My blankets have been mighty cold of late."

"They better be!" Maggie said, "I catch you with some Arapahoe trash woman I cut off your flag pole!"

95

"You always was a gentle soul" chuckled Hardy, and kissed her forehead. "What's with the meetin' out here in the dark? Am I not family any more?"

"Sure you family anymore!" Maggie said, and turned to Jon Beck. "I see the Red Bear is here too, and him family anymore too!" She stepped to Beck and gave him a big hug.

"Maggie, my blankets are cold, too," Beck said, holding his arms around her, "What you gonna do about that?"

"Your flagpole I just bend a little!" she said, kneeing him lightly between the legs. He grunted and let her go. "And what do you do with the beautiful maidens I send to you, anyway?" she scolded, "Little Otter was ready to go away with you, all you had to do was give horses to Many Wolves!"

"He wanted too many horses. I couldn't pay," Beck said protested.

"I heard he only wanted five horses," Maggie scolded, "What is five horses to a man like you?"

"He wanted Bill."

"What, you married to that damn horse?" she cried, "Little Otter go steal you ten more just like him, all by herself! Nobody goin' to guard a horse that ugly! Even she could steal you ten ugly horses, maybe twenty!"

"Well, I'm back. Maybe Many Wolves will bargain for something I can pay."

"Pffst!" spat Maggie, "Too late. Little Otter soon be gone, many warriors come to woo her. And they all have pretty horses, many pretty horses."

"Guess I'm just out of luck," Beck grinned.

"Guess you just too blind to see," Maggie said. "But now you must go ahead of us into the camp. See that tepee there with the Great Sun on the side? Go to that tepee, go in. Wait for me."

"You coming along?" Beck said.

"Me and flagpole here stay behind for a little," she said, stepping close to Hardy. "You never mind, we be along by and by."

"Don't hurt him none," Beck said, tying Bill's reins to a bush. He retrieved a small bundle from his saddlebag, and headed for the Crow camp in the dark. He heard a giggle behind him.

Beck moved slowly in the dark, carefully placing his feet so as not to make noise. As he came up on one of the tepees, dogs began

96

to bark. He skirted the encampment, staying in the dark outside, moving toward the tepee with the Great Sun symbol painted on it. He could see cooking fires before some of the skin huts, women tending them, pots sending up curls of steam, braves squatting at the fires, several children running about, and the dogs, barking, barking. The Indians in the camp paid no attention to the dogs.

He reached the Great Sun tent, entered the light of the several fires as he moved toward its entry flap. Half a dozen big dogs converged on him, several of them growling, but they sniffed him quickly and soon found other things to do. The general barking died down. The Indians in the camp paid him no heed.

He ducked into the tepee, let his eyes sweep the dimly lit circle. A small fire burned in its center, skins and bundles ringed the space against the tepee walls. Three Indians, all men, sat at the fire.

"He who comes is Red Bear," said one of the men, looking up at Beck. All three wore buckskin shirts and leggings, and the buckskin was decorated in fine bead work. The man who spoke was older, with a wrinkled face. His hair was braided, one to each side, and his braids showed the grizzled white of age. His dark eyes gleamed in the firelight, and his mouth frowned.

Beck said, "Standing Tall, it has been many moons since we rode together."

"Yes, Red Bear. Sit."

Beck lowered himself to a seat by the fire. The old man studied the flames.

"Magpie Woman has told us of your coming," he said. "It is good to see you again. When we rode against Red Cloud and his warriors, the buffalo were as the grass, everywhere many and strong. Now we must travel many days to find them. We find less and less buffalo, more and more white men. It is a bad time. The young men cry out for war, yet they do not know who to fight. The young men cry out for they are angry, but they do not know what they are angry about. They are afraid, but they do not know why.

"When the Son of the Morning Star was killed, some of them rejoiced. Others did not. Those who had been with the long knives came back to tell of it. There was much talking in the camps of the Crow, but no one made war.

"Now our cousins from the Snake come to us—"

"Are they here?" Beck interrupted.

97

"Maybe. Wait a bit. They come to ask us to join them. Fight the white man. Hunt buffalo with them. But they have no place to go once the buffalo are killed. Some of our young men want to go with them, and fight. This is a bad time. If they go, they can only die. There are too many white men. This I have seen, this is what I know. I have said this to my Nez Perce cousins. They tell me they have beaten the white man in battle many times. They have no fear of the white man. I say to them why are you running from them if you have no fear? They answer they have come to hunt buffalo, as they have always done. They tell our young men they can come hunt buffalo, and everything will be as it was. The young men are not fools. They know that the soldiers cannot be far away. Now you come. You are of the soldiers. This is a bad time, and you must help us. You must tell the young men the truth. They must not go and die."

"So," Beck said, "They are here."

"Will you help us, Red Bear?" Standing Tall said. "I have seen many winters. I have scouted with you against Red Cloud, and again when we rode against the Cheyenne. I have seen many winters and I have seen many white men. It is not good. The young men do not listen to me. They are angry and they want to fight. You must tell them the truth. They must not ride off to die with the Nez Perce."

"Can you take me to them?" Beck said.

"Yes. But first I must go and prepare the way. You are expected. Many Wolves speaks to them even now in the council. I will go, and when I come again, we will go there together."

"Agreed," said Beck, rising as the three men did so. "And Standing Tall, I will do what I can. I do not want my Crow brothers to die with the Nez Perce. I want my Crow brothers to help me scout against the Nez Perce, not to kill. This whole thing can end in peace if they will help."

"We will see," Standing Tall said. The three warriors left the tepee.

Beck seated himself at the fire once more, with his face to the tepee entrance.

As he gazed into the embers of the fire, he heard a rustle at the entrance flap. He let his gaze slowly rise to that spot, and saw half of a small face peek in through the flap slit. A second small face slowly appeared below that, then a third lower down.

98

"Raccoons infest this lodge, and foxes! Pretty soon the skunks will come and make their home, too!" he growled.

The three faces disappeared and giggling sprinkled the air at the tepee entrance.

"Come, enter the lodge, little people. Come in, come in!" Beck said in a growl, taking the bundle he had removed from his saddle bag out of his coat.

Slowly, three Indian children came in through the flap and stood shyly before him. Two of them were girls, one boy.

"Me Red Bear, eater of children. What are you?" Beck said.

They spoke not a word, but looked at him with big black eyes. He recognized the largest child, a girl named Shining Water. He said her name in Crow, and she grinned from ear to ear.

"Here, take some of the honey rocks, give them to your friends," he said, and took a handful of rock candy from the pouch and held it out. The three approached him carefully, stretched out their hands as if reaching in to pet a rabid coyote. They took a fistful of candy each, and Beck let out a fierce growl. They jumped, and scurried from the tent, laughing. Beck chuckled as he put away the candy pouch.

Hardy ducked into the tepee and came to sit at the fire. He sighed.

"They here?" he asked.

"Yep. Standing Tall said they are at the council. He's gone to get the ambush ready for us."

"What?!" Hardy cried, jerking his head up to look at Beck.

"Just jerkin' yer lead, ol' pal!" said Beck with a laugh. "You and Maggie get those blankets warmed up a bit?"

Hardy glanced to one side in exasperation. A bit of color came to his cheeks.

"Ain't no puttin' her off, that's fer sure. So what's the skinny on the council, we goin' over there or not?"

"Just as soon's Standing Tall comes for us. What's Maggie say about the general feeling around the camp? Standing Tall says they're arguing it both ways, the young bucks want to fight, the old hands say no. Sort of like it always is, eh?"

"Maggie tells the same tale. Only, I get the feeling a lot of the young bucks would rather chase after their cousins and steal a few horses first, no matter what they do. I figure it this way. If the Nez

Perce get close enough to the border, or beyond it, Sitting Bull may come down and pitch in. If that happens, it will be all out war until one side or the other is wiped out. I figure if Sitting Bull comes south, the Seventh Cavalry will not stop even at the border to go after 'im. They've got a score to settle, and Miles and Sturgis are the pile drivers to pound 'em firmly in the mud. If the Crow see it going the Indian's way, they may join in after all. I'd hate to see that, I don't want to see any of the family kilt, you know how it is. But the young bucks, they're all het up, they're looking to get in on the fracus, one way or t'other."

"I don't think Howard would let Sturgis and Miles go completely crazy if it came to that. I think he would respect the border, if they get that far. And if Sitting Bull doesn't do something stupid like come south."

"But Howard is at least two days back, so they say. Maybe more. If'n the Nez Perce can talk the Crow into helping them, they might have enough guns to make a real fight of it. And it might all be over before he can come up."

"Well," Beck said, "We got to do our damnedest to make sure the Crow don't get in the middle of it. What we'll do is—"

Standing Tall ducked through the tepee flap and stood up.

"Come. The council will hear you," he said.

Hardy spoke to him in Crow, was answered, spoke again. Finally the Indian said, "Yes. Come." He ducked back out of the tepee.

"What'd you say to him?" Beck asked.

"Just asking if our deaths would be quick and clean," Hardy said, straight faced.

"And?"

"You heard him."

Chapter 17

They followed Standing Tall out of the tepee, and as they crossed the camp the dogs commenced to bark and spin and make short charges. The hue and cry of the children went up at the appearance

100

of Jon Beck, and he had to wade through a passel of them as they neared the council lodge. Hardy spoke gruffly to them in Crow, and they stood aside, all eyes on the two white men. Several women and a dozen braves stood about the entrance to the council lodge, and Standing Tall ducked inside. Hardy glanced at Beck, and in he went. Jon Beck followed him in last.

The large tepee was packed with Indians, a dozen of them seated cross-legged around the central fire, another dozen standing or sitting at their backs. A space was made for the two scouts at the fire. As Beck stepped up to be seated, his eyes fell on the face of a grinning Indian seated across the fire pit. He paused.

"I see my brother Two Shirts has come to sit at the council of his cousins," Beck said as he lowered himself into place beside Hardy. Hardy translated into Crow this statement.

"Red Bear is my brother," said the grinning Indian to all of the council, showing his smiling face around to all of them, nodding. "I know this Red Bear well! We have taken scalps together, we have stolen ponies together, we have made the maidens smile at us as brothers!" Grunts and a laugh or two greeted this as Hardy sent it over.

"Two Shirts knows that he speaks too well of Red Bear," Beck said. "Two Shirts has taken all of the scalps, Two Shirts has stolen all of the horses. And Two Shirts has also stolen all of the maidens, for they would not have the Red One who is white."

More laughter as this was said again.

"Many Wolves," Beck said, looking at the warrior beside Two Shirts, "You know the man of Magpie Woman, you know his heart. He comes to you in peace, as do I. We know of the Nez Perce and why they are here. We are not at war with you, we do not want to be at war with you. We come to smoke the pipe of peace." Hardy made it plain in Crow.

"Hungh!" grunted Many Wolves, "We smoke!"

The pipe was produced, tamped full of the sacred tobacco, and lighted by Many Wolves with a flaming twig taken from the fire. The pipe passed around the circle, first to the left of Many Wolves, and ending with Two Shirts. As it came to each warrior, he would gesture with the pipe to the four winds, then take a puff, and pass it to his left. When all had partaken, Many Wolves spoke. Hardy translated the words.

"Many Wolves says the Crow have heard the words of their cousins, who war with the Bostons. They have traveled three moons, and have battled the whites three times. Each time the whites have been defeated. One Arm comes behind, with many Bostons. The white man makes war on the women and children as well as the warriors. The white man speaks the rifle, and only knows the rifle. Our cousins have come to ask us to hunt buffalo with them, and to bring our guns to the fight. If we do this, the white man can be defeated and we can live in peace. So say our cousins."

A murmur arose from the Indians in the lodge. Two Shirts was not smiling, but was staring at Beck.

"Two Shirts has fought at my side, a true warrior, a man of honor," Beck said slowly. Hardy followed along in Crow. "He comes to you from a proud nation, men of great courage, men who speak from the heart. His heart is true, his talk is straight. I cannot tell you what he says in not true." He paused, Hardy caught up, the Indians murmured among themselves.

"But what I can tell you is this," Beck went on, "The Great Father in Washington is not pleased with what the Nez Perce have done. The soldiers are sent from all sides, and they come by the thousands. They come like the flocks of ducks in the time of first snows, that gather by the countless numbers and swoop down to darken the surface of the lakes and ponds. This is how they come, to gather all around the Nez Perce and stop them. The soldiers will come until the Nez Perce can go no further, until the Nez Perce cannot see anything but a wall of blue coats, all around them."

"And then these Bostons will wipe out the last of the People!" cried out Two Shirts. "They kill our women and our children and they kill our old people! They kill our horses and they kill our dogs! What are we to do but kill them in return? We will not stand there and die like our dogs! We will go to the Grandmother's country to the north, and we will join with Sitting Bull to fight the white man! If you will not join with us to fight the white man, perhaps Sitting Bull will do so!"

Beck looked at Hardy, pursing his lips. His eyes fell back to the fire. It seemed that some decision had already been made, as if the Crow had already refused the Nez Perce their aid. Beck spoke again.

"Two Shirts is a brave warrior," Beck said, looking at the Indian who had just spoken. Two Shirt's mouth was grim, his eyes glittered with passion. "I am proud to call him my brother. I respect his bravery and his willingness to fight. I, too, would fight, if my family and my clan and all that I knew were under attack. Every man at this council would do the same. There is no shame in dying a warrior's death.

"But the women and children should not have to die. If the Nez Perce stop now, General Howard will stop the killing by the whites. He has promised to do this."

"So you say!" spat Two Shirts loudly, "But it was he who spoke the gun from the beginning. It was he who brought the Bostons to our camps in the beginning. It was he who would do nothing about the whites who killed our young men for no reason, until there was nothing left for us but to fight back! Why should we trust him now? Why should any of you trust the whites?" the warrior shouted, looking around at the seated braves.

"Two Shirts, you have called yourself my brother," Beck said, "And I have said to you I am your brother. Have you ever known me to speak with a double tongue?"

Two Shirts glared at Beck across the fire, the light of the flames glinting from his black eyes.

"I do not say to these braves that what you have in your heart is not true," Beck went on. "I was not there with you when this war began. I do not know what happened. From what you speak, you were wronged. So be it. General Howard can bring justice to your people in the end. The whites have killed Nez Perce. Nez Perce have killed whites. You say you have beaten the soldiers in battle three times. Surely you have killed enough whites to even the score."

"We have killed many whites. We have seen the Bostons run."

"Then let it stop here. Go to your chiefs and tell them..." and Beck paused, calculating carefully what he would say next, "tell them that General Howard wishes an end to the fighting, and will stop all the killing by the white soldiers. Tell them that the Crow are a peaceful people, and will not go to war to help the Nez Perce."

As Hardy finished the translation, the council fell completely silent. Beck held his breath, knowing he had gambled with that last statement, hoping that Two Shirts already knew it to be true, as he did not. Hardy looked at him and raised his eyebrows.

"Two Shirts," Beck said quietly across the fire, "I know that you went to the mission school at Lapwai, that they taught you the white man's tongue and the white man's god. Did you not find the whites there to have good hearts?"

"They are not the whites who killed us."

"No. I am sure they were not. But as you know from this, all white men are not the same. We do not all speak with the same heart. General Howard has been plain to you. If he must use force to make the will of the Great Father in Washington known to you, then he will do so. He will not trick you or speak to you with a double tongue. If he spoke the rifle, he had no choice. He does the will of the Great Father. He has no choice. But he has always spoken to you with a straight tongue, has he not?"

"What do you know of him? How do you know of this?"

"I have served with him for fifteen years. I have never known him to lie. When you and I scouted for him against the Yakima and the Cayuse, did he not always act as a brave should? Was he not always a warrior of honor?"

Two Shirts made no comment to this.

"I tell you again. Go to your chiefs, tell them that General Howard will stop the killing at once. All you have to do is trust him and stop running. Your women, your children, your old people will be spared. Your warriors will be spared. You can all go home again, and live in peace. You have been killed, you have killed in return. Let it end now."

Two Shirts looked at the faces of the council around him. The Crow warriors and elders about the fire would not meet his gaze. He snorted, and rose to his feet.

"The Crow are a nation of women!" he sneered, and shoved his way through the murmuring warriors to the flap, ducked through it and was gone.

Beck scrambled to his feet.

"Talk with Many Wolves," he said to Hardy, "Find out what they really will do." He went to the entrance and ducked through it, emerging into the fire-lit darkness of the camp.

"Two Shirts!" he called after the back of the Nez Perce just disappearing into the darkness on the other side of the clearing.

Before he could take a step, a brown wave of small bodies descended on him like a gaggle of giggling geese, dozens of children flinging themselves on his legs like warm leeches, jumping up and grabbing his arms, heaping on, a mass of dark faces in the semi-darkness of the camp, each face slashed with a white grin of their teeth as they laughed and squirmed and swarmed to conquer the Red Bear and the wonderful packet he carried beneath his coat. He finally tried to fling them from his arms, paw them from his back, but he dared not hurt them, could not dislodge them without harm. The weight of the mass of squirming children finally howled him over, and they rode him down like triumphant wolves on the carcass of a buffalo.

The original three children had quickly conspired to conquer the Great Red Bear even as they left the tent originally with their candy. He had given it out before, he had growled before, and they had come back with reinforcements before, and the battle always went against the Bear. So they had scattered through the camp and gathered all of the children young and old, and were nearly ready when he had come to the council tent. But the man of Magpie Woman had warned them, not now! They did not fear the man of Magpie Woman, for he, also, had brought them sweet things in the past. But they did fear Magpie Woman, for she could be cunning in her revenge. So they waited.

Now the pile of squirming bodies had their quarry at their mercy, and a dozen little hands snaked into his clothing to find the precious bag and its sweet nuggets. But the Red Bear, who by now was flushed with the tussle of the ton of children clinging to him like a score of determined raccoons, rose to his hands and knees, then to his knees, then lurched to his feet and shook, and screeching children shed him like the droplets of water from a shaking dog. And in this deluge of flying bodies was one small girl who had managed to clutch the sacred bag just at the moment of her ejection into the night! She landed on a heap of kids, laughing, and screamed to one and all that she had the goods! The others immediately left Beck and made for her.

Beck took one glance after the now disappeared Nez Perce, then at the children who were converging on the girl.

"No!" he roared, wading again into the mass and snatching up the child just as the rest of the children crested against him again like a wave of human surf. The children paused slightly, awed by the roar of the Great Red Bear. In the firelight, Beck's face was indeed flushed red, and fierce.

He snatched the bag from the clutches of the little girl.

"First, the biggest piece of all to the brave woman who captured it!" he said, reaching into the bag for a piece of candy. Behind him, Hardy repeated this in Crow. The children all fell silent, and Beck handed out the largest piece of candy to the girl folded in his arm. Twenty hands immediately reached out to him, and he filled them as fast as he could from the bag. Soon all the hands were filled, and the children scampered off by ones and twos, giggling. Beck set the tiny candy thief on the ground. She flashed him a smile and disappeared like a streak of brown shadow. The bag was empty, save for one piece. Beck stuffed the bag back in his coat.

"Well, he got clean away. Was hoping to hold him back some, maybe get him to give us a clue to the main body of 'em," Beck said.

"Good thing you snatched that little one," Hardy said, "She was gonna get trampled for sure."

"Yeah, got a little out of hand there," Beck said. "What of Many Wolves? They with us, or agin?"

"With us. They'll scout for us, if we let 'em have any horses they can steal. They'll have a party waiting at first light, north of the river. Right now we need to go see my wife. She has news."

"May as well, no tracking Two Shirts in the dark."

They crossed the camp again, then walked out on a path beside the river, silver in the moonlight. Within a few yards another camp opened out, a dozen tepees, cook fires, women tending them, old men squatting at the heat. The dogs yelped and barked and growled, marking their passage to one of the lodges. They ducked inside.

Magpie Woman was dishing food from a pot over the central fire into a gourd bowl. She handed this to Hardy, who sat at the fire. Beck sat beside him as she dished up a portion for him. She sat next to Hardy as she handed the bowl to Beck.

She began to chatter in the guttural language of the Crow. Hardy followed along in English.

"Two Shirts has been here two days. Others of his band have been in the camps along the river. Some even have gone to the camps in the valley. Everywhere it has been the same. Some of the young men want to fight. But even they do not see a happy end to the war. They only want to steal some horses, get rich, buy wives. Can you blame them?"

She grinned at Beck, then said in English, "With enough horses a man can get a wife. If he is no warrior, the bride price is too steep for him."

"You tell her a warrior must first want a wife," Beck snarled, rolling his eyes upward.

"I think she can hear that for hers—" started Hardy, and Maggie cut in again.

"Sometimes the bear must think of his winters. When he has too many winters to chase the buffalo or the deer, when he cannot dig for grubs, when the berries are too far up the mountainside for him to eat," she went on, "he will need a woman to bring him his supper. The bear must think of his children, he must not wait for a woman too long, or he will not be able to train his cubs as he should. Cubs need the strong hand of the bear to show them what a bear should be like. An old bear with no teeth can only sit in the lodge and tell stories, not show the cubs what a bear should be like."

"I have plenty of teeth, woman, make no mistake about that," Beck growled. "Now enough of this about wives, what of the Nez Perce? Do you know where they camp?"

Magpie Woman answered in Crow. Hardy gabbed along.

"Two Shirts did not say. He and a dozen of his clan came ahead, scouting into our lands to find out what we would do. We were glad to see him, and sad to see him. We know of the trouble, the word of this is among all the people. So we had already talked about it. We did not turn him away, his is our cousin. Many of his people are our cousins. We could not turn him away. We let him speak of war, and many of the young men spoke of fighting at the side of our cousins. But the young men know that this is not a good fight. There is no blood on our land, so we do not choose to spill any. In the end it is as you saw, we will not go with them to fight."

"But you will go with us to scout?" Beck said, eating stew with his gourd spoon.

"That is a different thing. The young men see a chance to steal some horses. The Nez Perce are rich in horses. It they lose a few, it will not matter to them. The young men want to grow rich and pay the bride price. They have not had a chance to go raiding for many

107

moons, and winter comes. It is a good time to find the warmth of a new wife."

"So you say!" Beck nodded, "Will the young men steal the horses of the soldiers as well?"

"A horse is a horse. If the rider does not need it any longer, then a young man may make use of it."

"Just so we understand the matter," Beck said. "I must speak with Many Wolves tonight. If your young men come to scout for us, I see no reason why they may not take what horses they can find. But they may not steal army horses."

"Many Wolves will understand, and he will tell the young men. The Crow have been friends to the soldiers for many winters. They will not fight the soldiers now. Many Wolves will tell you this, as well as I."

"Well let's go talk to him. I want to be sure," Beck said, putting down his empty bowl and rising.

"Now that the council is past," Maggie said, rising also, "the daughter of Many Wolves will be at his fire as well. Perhaps she knows where you can find some more ugly horses, after all."

Beck sighed and shook his head. "As long as Bill ain't part of the deal," he muttered.

Magpie Woman followed he and Hardy out of the tepee, trying to suppress her glee.

Chapter 18

The dove grey light of early dawn brightened the swath of sky to be seen between the mountaintops as Beck and Hardy waded their mounts across the river. The peaks were dark, the valleys veiled in the vestiges of the fast fading night, but on the far shore a mottle of muted color marked the waiting mass of Crow scouts. Pinto ponies were much in evidence, browns and grays and whites also, the warriors atop them a polychrome of buckskin brown, reds and yellows and blues streaked in with bleached bone white of dyed porcupine quill and beadwork breastplates, adorned skin vests, buckskin leggings. And feathers, some in full head dresses, most in ones and twos and threes, at all angles, adorned the heads of the fighting men of the Crow. The two army scouts drew up on the river bank before the assembled braves.

"Ain't they purdy!" Hardy grinned, folding his arms across his saddle pommel and turning his head to grin at Jon Beck.

"Who among you leads?" Beck said loudly to the Indians. Hardy translated. Two warriors walked their horses to the scouts. They spoke to Hardy.

"This here's Man-On-High-Place and Jumping Fox," Hardy said, indicating the Crow warriors left and right. "They will...translate for the others, pass along our orders."

"Isn't that what you do?" Beck said to Hardy.

"Actually," said High Place with a smile, "Mr. Hardy's Crow leaves a little bit to be desired."

Beck stared at the warrior before him.

"Yes, it speaks!" High Place said, still grinning. "We have a very good agency school. I was one of the first pupils. I also work for the agent, Mr. Allen. He has been very good about teaching me your tongue."

"Well don't that beat all!" Hardy muttered. "This mean I can go home now?"

Beck laughed.

"Man On High Place, I am Jon Beck. You know Mr. Hardy."

"And I know of you, Red Bear. I was not at the council fire this last night, but I know. My daughter came to me with a nugget of the candy taken from you. She will make it last for many days. Sometimes we get candy at the agency, but it is rare. Even the beef is rare. The flour has worms. The barreled pork is sometimes rotten. It is my job to explain all of this to the people when they come for their allotment. And to convince them that tomorrow it will be better."

"And has it ever gotten better?" Beck asked.

"Sometimes. Sometimes not. But the people have hope."

"And you will help us against the Nez Perce?"

"That is why we are here."

"Then here is what we will do...."

Beck gave instructions to the braves with both Hardy and High Place translating. The Indians were to search out the trail of Two

Shirts and his band, and also scout up the valleys of Syash, Snow and Alder Creeks, all of which fed the immediate valley of the Stinking Water. They would meet the following day at a point north of Heart Mountain. High Place and Jumping Fox turned their ponies into the warrior party and began instructing them of the scout's wishes.

"We better high tail it to the rendezvous point, find out if anything came up last night," Beck said to Hardy. The Crow began galloping off in small parties, whooping and screeching a few parting war cries to the remainder. As they dispersed, Beck and Hardy started their mounts back toward their low camp of the day before.

As they came up on the camp, they found the trail of about a dozen horses converging there also, then moving off up the valley into the higher country to the north. They also found the trail of their own men's shod horses and pack mules, these moving up slope on a divergent course.

"Looks like the camp had visitors last night," Hardy said. "Our men must have moved out ahead of 'em, though."

"My money says it was Two Shirts and his cousins, come to make sure they wasn't followed. I figured on something like that, and our boys had the good luck to get moving before Two Shirts came looking for 'em. Couldn't track 'em in the dark, so they had to high tail it. And now we got a trail to follow," Beck said, starting Bill along the route of the larger party.

"Well hold on there, pard," Hardy said. "If you go to tracking the Nez Perce, how you gonna get word to Peachbow about what happened here?"

"That's where you come in, Lige," Beck said, holding up Bill.

"No, now wait just a minute, I came along on this little soiree to track Nez Perce, and to interpret Crow for ye! You is supposed to be the big chief, the man making all the command decisions. You can't do that runnin' down Two Shirts and his cousins. 'At's what you got me for, and them soldier boys, and all them Crow braves up yonder!"

"Two shirts and me got a little something to settle," Beck said. "I do aim to find him, and I do aim to get it finished, twixt him and me."

110

"That may be," Hardy growled, "but that still don't ignore the fact that you is in charge of this outfit. If you try real hard, I's right sure you can manage to get yer head shot off in due course, but right now, you need to get to the rendezvous point and get one o' them soldier boys trottin' along back to Peachbow with the news. Now, you know it and I know it, so you take that trail there to our people, and I'll take this here Nez Perce pike right on up the hill after 'em."

Beck looked at Hardy with an expression of sheer disgust. He cursed under his breath.

"Just keep in mind they don't want to leave no witnesses," Beck said, turning Bill along the trail of the shod ponies and mules. "If you run across them Crow scouts out in the hills, get them to ride ahead of you, they can track better and faster. And they can take the first bullets for you, too."

"Always a cheery soul, ain't cha," Hardy chuckled, starting his horse along the Nez Perce track.

"Just do it," Beck called, moving away up the hillside.

He followed the tracks that rose along the valley and up the valley wall at the same time. After several miles the trail crossed the crest of the ridge, then paralleled that crest for several more miles. The trail led him down off of the shoulder of the hill into a broad valley, with tall grass and a stream winding through its belly. Wooded slopes ramped up on either side. The stream entered the valley through a steep walled canyon, and the trail left the valley some distance from this canyon, winding up again into the heights. Then he crossed another ridge and down into yet another broad, shallow valley. There were fewer trees on the heights, and the grass was lower, beat down in clumps. He could see the mark of buffalo all about, but none fresh.

On the gradually rising ground to the north he moved Bill in among the trees again. The sun was low in the west, and then behind the mountains. Long shadows gave way to deepening gloom in the valleys, while the clear blue sky directly overhead shown brightly.

Bill snorted and stopped, his ears scanning the thin forest ahead. The trail led up the easy slope winding through the trees. Beck sat for a time, listening in the silence of the late afternoon. Finally he reached down and slid the big Winchester out of its saddle scabbard. He steered Bill to one side of the trail, cutting up the hill at an angle away from it. The big horse moved easily on the slope, his long

111

body bunching and stretching as he moved with the uneven ground. Beck took him slowly into heavier cover, then turned to follow the general direction the trail had been going. Half a mile along he gently stopped the horse within a stand of mountain sorrel.

Down the slope, he could see a blue-clad figure sitting against a tree. He had a rifle across his lap, his hat tilted down over his eyes, his legs stretched out before him. He did not move, and Beck could not see his face. Jon turned the horse and eased him down the slope toward the figure. He glanced all about him as he moved, stopping Bill frequently, choosing easy walking for the animal so that very little sound was made. He brought his horse to a stop ten yards from the blue coated figure. Beck looked carefully all around.

"What'cha figure, Bill, he be dead or he be sleepin'?" Beck said.

The soldier jerked awake, tossing his head up so that his hat hit the tree he was leaning against and toppled into his lap. Eyes wide, mouth agape, his focus finally took in the horseman looming over him.

"Got a keen eye on your back trail, Private Gloy?" Beck asked casually.

"Well suh," Gloy said, heaving himself up and fetching his hat, "I was keepin' an eye out for ya'll, that's certain." He slapped the hat on his leg, causing Bill to toss his head, and put it on.

"Well you sure enough found me," said Beck dryly. "Where's the camp?"

"Just over the hill a bit," Gloy said. He started walking in the direction he had pointed.

"We was up all night getting' up here," Gloy said. "Sort of tuckers a feller out, that kind o' thing."

"Son, this here is Injun country," Beck said, "you ain't got time to be tuckered, not if'n you be partial to keeping yer hair."

They moved across the slope and down another into a vale with grass and a trickle of water burbling along through it. The other two soldiers were there, and had a fire going with very dry wood, so that almost no smoke rose to be lost in the trees. Simon came in from the little meadow carrying a collapsible canvas bucket full of water. Beck swung down and began to unload Bill.

"Any trouble getting up here?" Beck asked Simon.

"Nope. Took most of the night, then again some this morning. I figure this was about what you had in mind. How about you? The Crow left you your hair, must have turned out all right."

"It did! There's about fifty Crow scouts out in these hills right now, looking for the Nez Perce. They're on our side in this one. The Nez Perce were in the Crow camps when we got there, but they couldn't persuade 'em to fight."

"No belly for it, eh?" Simon said.

"Not so much that, as they just ain't that stupid. As the man said, nobody's been killing Crow, so the Crow ain't gonna go killing no white man. They'd rather make war on their own cousins, steal all the horses they can. Simply matter of economics. And love."

"Love?"

"Horses to a Crow is money. Money is dowry. Dowry is some fair Indian maiden's hand in marriage. So, in all likelihood, the Crow are going to war for love."

Simon just shook his head.

"And speaking of love," Beck went on, "where's Tibbits?"

"On the hill, up above the meadow. Keepin' an eye on the stock."

"Good move."

Beck took Bill into the little meadow and picketed the horse in the grass with the other animals. He plucked fistfuls of rough, brown grass and rubbed the horse down with it. Bill munched away at the roughage in the deepening twilight as Beck returned to the fire.

He took a small notebook from his saddlebag, along with a pencil. He opened the leather cover of the book, and seated on a thick branch by the fire, wrote out a note concerning the Crow, the scouts, position, results. He tore the note from the book and folded it.

"Fitzsimmons," he said.

"Sir?"

"Think you can find your way back the way you come, then along the Stinking Water to Captain Peachbow?"

"Of course, sir!"

"In the dark?"

"Well, I have been known to do a little late work, sir," smiled Fitzsimmons, "Many's the chicken coop that—"

"Well can you or can't you find your way to the river in the dark?"

"Yes sir! Of a certainty, sir!"

"Go saddle your horse, then. Benson, a little supper soon?"

"Nearly ready, Mr. Beck," Benson said at the fire.

"All right then. Get that horse saddled, get some food in you, and off you go."

The beans and bacon and coffee came up within ten minutes as the last of the light left the glimmering sky overhead. The temperature dropped rapidly, and by the time all had eaten and Fitzsimmons had taken the message and left the camp, those left behind gathered closer to the fire. Beck sent Simon out to relieve Tibbits, who came and sat at the fire and ate the plate of food offered him. He said no word.

Beck got out the rolled military maps and went over them by the firelight. As he was rolling up the parchment and slipping it back in its leather canister, Gloy said, "Riders coming in."

Beck took up his rifle and moved away from the fire into the shadow. The two soldiers did likewise. Tibbits stood by the fire.

Soon Beck could hear the footfalls of horses coming across the slope from the west. In a moment a voice called out from the dark of the woods.

"Hallo the camp! Comin' in, Jon."

"Come ahead," Beck hollered back.

Hardy rode up to the firelight, and with him two Crow braves. Hardy dismounted, and stripped his horse of its gear, but the Crow did not. The two braves said a few words to Hardy, and rode out of the firelight to the east.

"Where's yer horses?" Hardy said.

"Just up in the meadow there," Beck said, nodding his head toward the little grass meadow up slope. "Mr. Tibbits, would you be so kind as to take Mr. Hardy's horse out and picket him with the others?"

"Sure thing," the cowboy said, and took the horse away. Beck dished up food for Hardy, and a cup of coffee.

"Lost the trail about five or six miles from here," Hardy said as he ate. "Them two Crow coming down the valley the other way, no sign of 'em there either. I figure they took care about their trail about time they went into camp for the night."

"Headed mostly north, though?" Beck said.

"Yep."

"So where'd those two Crow braves go?"

"Gonna make a camp of their own. White man's fire too big, easy to find, easy to attack."

Hardy finished up his chow, and Tibbits came back to the fire.

"Mr. Tibbits, would you please gather up the plates and wash 'em in the creek. Mr. Benson, thank you for a fine supper. Mr. Gloy, would you please gather in some more firewood. Gonna be a cold 'un tonight."

The chores got done, the camp settled in, the men in their bedrolls around the fire. At midnight Hardy went out to relieve Simon, who came in and went immediately into his bedroll. The fire was stoked up at the time, and as the morning hours wore away the dark, the flames died to embers. Frost formed on the grass and thickets out beyond the reach of the fire's warmth.

Beck woke in the small hours, his head on his saddle, thinking. He could see the stars in a crystal sky through the trees overhead. The glow of the fire was low, and soft snoring came from one of the other bedrolls.

Where had they gone? Why not keep heading directly back to the main body? If they had passed through their lower camp, they knew it was there, they knew they would be followed. They would have been able to see enough of the trail left by the soldiers and mules to get a feeling of where that group was headed. Why not follow that trail, even in the dark, if they feared the scouts? Leave no witnesses. Beck was sure they meant to do that. Yet here they were, the country crawling with Crow, but no sign of the Nez Perce who dared not lead them back to the family. Where were they now?

He rolled out of his blankets, rolled the blankets into a bundle, took his cup to the stream and dipped out a filling of icy water. This he downed slowly, listening to the night, the occasional pop of a coal in the fire, the sigh of a first morning breeze high in the trees, the hoot of an owl far off along the slope. He could see his breath in the starlight, like a cloud of steam chuffed from the little six-wheeler that had sat puffing by the station when the soldiers had come up to Quandry. He thought over the army maps, the valleys, the peaks, the trails. Where would he go if the Crow were denied to him? What would he do?

Two Shirts was one of the happier Indians he had known. When Beck had been chief of scouts for Howard during the Cayuse fracas, Two Shirts had been his best man. Two Shirts had a wife, three children, two small girls and a son about to become a warrior. Beck thought of the little family traveling with the main body of the Nez Perce, what it must be like living on the run like that, never knowing from which direction the next attack would come. He had been in the tepee of Two Shirts many times. He had held two of those children in his lap. The woman of Two Shirts had smiled at him, as a mother smiles. She had given him this name, Red Bear, for his great round shape and ruddy complexion when he played with the children and got his blood up from running around with them. The name seemed to precede him where ever he went to an Indian camp. But it was not because he became red when he growled and ran after the children.

And then he knew. He had been with Two Shirts when he had played a joke on another band of scouts, stolen their horses at dawn, then taunted them for being lax in their watchfulness. Anything for a good joke.

Beck strode back to the fire, dropped his cup, grabbed his rifle. He kicked the feet of one of the sleepers. Tibbits rolled out and got up.

"Get your rifle, let's go!" he said in low tones.

"What—"

"Hush. Get the rifle. Come with me!" Beck commanded. Tibbets quickly slipped into his boots, put on his coat, grabbed his Winchester and gun belt and followed Beck as he moved briskly toward the horse meadow.

They moved up the slope through the trees, the silver starlight fleshing out into a pale hint of an early dawn they could not see. They reached the meadow, and out in the mist the horses grazed peacefully. Except Bill. Beck could see the long-bodied stallion to the right of the mules, belly deep in mist, looking about, ears working the landscape. He would start to lower his head for a mouthful of grass, then come to alert again, searching for a hint of danger with those ears, then go back to the grass, but not getting there before coming back up on alert again.

The two men crouched at the edge of the meadow.

"They're here," Beck said softly, nodding at the horse. Tibbits remained silent, his eyes darting from animal to animal around the meadow.

"They're gonna try to run the horses off," Beck whispered. "I'm going out among them, see if I can't get my hands on as many leads as I can before they jump. I think Hardy's up there on the right somewhere. You get back to the camp, get the men up and armed, but do it quietly. Get 'em back up here as quick as you can, we just might beat 'em to the punch."

"What about Hardy?" whispered Tibbits, "Shouldn't we warn him?"

"Lige can take care of himself. I want them to come, but when we're ready for 'em. If we warn him we'll never see a whisker of 'em. Now go!"

Beck, crouching low, moved out into the mist toward the horses. The dawn was gaining clarity, and Bill started slightly and turned to look at him when he came up. The big horse knew him instantly and nickered. This brought the heads of several of the animals in the little meadow up to look, and as Beck rose to look up the meadow over the back of Bill, half a dozen mounted men materialized out of the greater dark of the woods at the meadow's edge.

A long flash of rifle fire erupted off to the right, and with this clap of thunder the six Indians, as they quickly proved to be, charged down on the herd. Beck grabbed the lead of one of the mules grazing near Bill, and Bill's lead, and hung on to the two animals as his rifle slipped out from under his arm into the grass at his feet. The Indians came on whooping and screeching, trying to stampede the stock. The rifle spoke again on the right, and then another flame leaped out from Beck's left, answered by firing from the braves on horseback, the long flashes like straight lightning bolts in the soft light of dawn.

Beck folded both lead ropes into one hand, and drawing his big army Colt, fired off a shot at the center of the Indian line as it reached the middle of the meadow. He fired again and again, and the flash of the muzzle blast and the cloud of white smoke blinded him to his enemies. The horse and mule were nervous but not panicky, and his grip held the ropes firmly. The Indians charged by on either side, and several shots were fired in his direction. He answered with two more pistol shots. The rifles spoke again from

117

the edges of the meadow, and then the Nez Perce were gone into the trees down the slope.

Beck holstered his revolver and got both hands on the ropes, thankful that the animals were veterans and used to some sort of gunfire. He looked around the meadow, and saw that most of the animals were still there, dancing nervously around their tethering pins. A figure came running across the meadow from up the hill. As it neared, Beck could see that it was Hardy.

Just as Hardy came puffing to a halt before Beck, firing could be heard from the camp, half a dozen shots, then silence.

"Goddammittohell!" Hardy spat out, "Those bastards almost snuck right on by me!"

"Well, you rushed 'em along some," Beck said, "they didn't have time to pull the picket pins, so I think we saved most of the stock. See any of 'em go down?"

"Naw, still too dark. Couldn't see my sights in this light, it was all just luck shootin'!"

"Let's gather up the horses and get down to the camp. Looks like we're gonna have a fresh trail to follow after all!" Beck said, picking up his rifle.

"Who was that firin' over on the other side?" said Hardy, going after the nearest horse.

"Not sure. Might have been Tibbits. He'd come up with me, and I told him to go back and alert the camp. Guess he didn't do it."

They unpicketed the horses and led them down into the trees, and left them to water near the camp. They approached the fire, where three men were standing in the light of the freshly fed flames. A fourth was lying at their feet.

"Who?" said Beck, stepping up to the light.

"Gloy," said Benson, "Never even got out of his blankets. We got one of them, though!"

"What? Where?"

"Right over there," Benson pointed. Beck went over to a buckskin clad figure lying a few yards from the fire. He knelt to the body, and rolled it over onto its back. It was a Nez Perce face he did not know. Beck rose and went back to the fire.

"They came down right through the camp!" Benson said.

"Lucky fer us you dusted 'em up some 'fore they got here," Simon said. "Just had time to roll out and grab our guns. Poor ol' Gloy, though, I don't think he even woke up."

"Just bad luck," said Tibbits.

Beck looked at Tibbits for a long moment. "Yeah, bad luck," he said levelly. Tibbits let his gaze drop to the fire.

"All right," Beck said, "Benson, figure you can rustle up a breakfast?"

"Sure 'nough."

"Let's get to it, then. We've got a grave to dig, and then we're after 'em."

Chapter 19

One man on the shovel kept the grave growing as the rest packed the mules and horses and prepared to move out. The two Crow came back, and shared words with Hardy, as Beck took his turn in the grave pit with the camp shovel.

"They heard the firing, all right," Hardy said to Beck, "And now they are congratulating themselves for not camping with us."

"Wonderful," Beck said, graunching the shovel blade into the rocky soil. "Tell them to find the trail, report back to us."

One of the Crow dropped from his pony and took out his knife as he strode to the Nez Perce warrior stretched out at the edge of the trees.

"No!" Beck said loudly. The Crow brave paused, and said something to Hardy in Crow.

"He says why let it go to waste," Hardy translated, "Some woman will smile on him if he takes it back."

"He did not earn it," Beck said.

"Don't think he cares about that," Hardy grinned, "A scalp is a scalp"

"Tell him to go find Two Shirts and his band and take all the scalps he is man enough to carry," Beck said, glaring at the Crow standing over the body.

119

Hardy did so, and the Crow warrior muttered something and sheathed his knife. The two braves quickly left the camp, scouting the trail of the Nez Perce as they did. They were soon lost to sight among the trees.

They eased Trooper Gloy into the grave, covered his face with his coat tail, and covered him up. They did not bury the Nez Perce, but left him laying as before as they mounted up and started in the direction the Crow scouts had taken. Beck put Tibbits on the mules, and sent Simon and Benson out as flankers, with instructions to work the ridgelines and investigate every valley within sight. Hardy went ahead with Beck to follow the Crow trail and sweep wide on either side of it as they moved to the north through the broken country.

At mid morning they came to a winding creek valley, the water flowing to the northwest. Beck called a halt, and they rested the horses as Tibbits came up with the mules. Soon Pocket came in with nothing to report. They rested a half mile from the water, and Beck suggested they go down and water the horses. They had only moved a short distance when a party of Indians entered the valley, coming from the north around a shoulder in the valley wall.

"Hold up!" Beck said quickly, holding up his hand. "We got company."

They sat and watched the Indians, counting eight in all, move along the stream. They were spread out and scanning the ground, obviously searching for sign. They moved across the valley half a mile away, oblivious to Beck and his party. As they passed out of the valley at the far end, another body of horsemen came into view around the shoulder of the valley wall, this time instantly recognizable as cavalry. As they trotted in column up the valley along the course of the stream, Beck gave a holler and waved his hat. They did not see him.

"Simon, go down there and introduce us, will you?" Beck said.

Pocket set spurs to his horse, which took off in a spurt but quickly settled into a cantering lope. The mount was tired. Soon they could see him angle up and make contact with a standard bearer halfway down the long column, then run his pony along the cantering troopers to its head. Shortly the whole command ground to a halt, and Pocket waved his hat in Beck's direction. The scouts headed down toward the army column, and as they did so, the troopers dismounted and led their horses over to the stream to drink.

Beck led his men to the head of the cavalry column, where he found several officers studying two maps on the grass while soldiers watered their horses. The colonel rose from the parchment as Beck swung down off of Bill.

"Jon Beck, colonel," Beck said, shaking hands with the colonel. "We're scouting with Captain Peachbow's unit, Fifth Calvary, out of Quandry, Wyoming Territory."

"I'm Sturgis, Seventh Cavalry," said the colonel, "Have you come from south of here?"

"Indeed we have, colonel," said Beck, "We've spent the last few days in the Crow Nation, and in fact chased a small party of Nez Perce out of there yesterday. We have about fifty Crow scouts out in these hills now, and expect to rendezvous with them north of Heart Mountain later today."

"We've just come from there. We have good information that the main body of the Nez Perce are to the south."

"Not south of here, colonel. We've just come through that country. Nothing there but us and our Crow scouts. Captain Peachbow is on the Stinking Water further west, with two companies. And I am told Howard is at out east of Yellowstone Park by now."

"Damn and damn again!" swore Sturgis, "Our scouts had definite news of the Nez Perce on the Stinking Water!"

"They may have exaggerated a bit."

"What do you mean?"

"Well, there were Nez Perce on the Stinking Water, all right, maybe a half dozen of them. They were in the Crow camps trying to drum up a little support for their war. Crow wasn't having any of it, though. What exactly did your scouts tell you?"

Sturgis looked out at the surrounding hills, thoughtfully.

"Only that the Nez Perce has reached the Stinking Water. This news reached us yesterday, and we have been moving south to cut them off."

"Yesterday? Seems a mite slow, to me. The Nez Perce have been in the Crow camps for several days. Who brought the word?"

"Crow scouts, some Arapahoe. Same bunch that are working up the valley ahead of us."

"Colonel, I don't mean to tell you your business, but it looks to me like your scouts was intending you to be elsewhere when the Nez Perce come along."

"So it would seem." Sturgis thought for a moment, then said, "Do you have any clear understanding of General Howard's position?"

"Only that he was several days back of the Nez Perce main body, and that they were in Yellowstone Park, both Indians and soldiers, as of a week ago. My guess is Howard is most likely on the Clearwater or the Yellowstone right now, or they're making for Clarke's Fork to head north. With Peachbow in the south, and you on the east, Howard'll crowd 'em the only way they have left, which is north. And Clarke's Fork is the way."

"Come on over here to the maps," Sturgis said, indicating his officer's cadre standing over the maps in the grass, "Let's get some idea of where we are, where you have been, where we must now go." .

As they went over the maps, Benson came in from the hills, nothing to report. Hardy got the horses to water, then let the animals graze. Sturgis and his officers laid out the route of their march, and all could see that the feint they had been responding to had left a huge gap in the circle of soldiers on the north.

"Nothing for it now but to join Howard and form a new plan. Who knows, maybe he has caught the red devils by now and is giving them a good licking!" said the colonel, rising from the maps.

"Well, if you don't mind it, colonel, I intend to continue to the rendezvous with my scouts. I will assume your journey will take you north, eventually, and I'll send my riders accordingly. Is there any of your outfit to the east of us?"

"I am told several companies of infantry have moved into the eastern reaches of the Crow reservation, possibly to the agency by now. And, a troop of cavalry is acting as their support. But as you know, infantry, God bless 'em, are slow. So, my concern is for that country to the northeast. At the moment, we have nothing there to cut them off."

"Mostly badlands out that way, colonel," said Hardy, "I don't figure they'll try that way. Nez Perce need grass and water for their ponies, they've got to go where they can get it."

122

"Yes. Well. Gentlemen, thank you for the excellent information, as distressing as it has turned out to be. By all means continue in your quest to the north and east, and I will give your compliments to General Howard," Sturgis said, pulling on his gauntlets.

The officers and men of the cavalry column mounted up, formed up, and moved on up the valley. Beck watched them go, the long column of horse soldiers cantering past him as he thought, scanning the surrounding, wooded hills.

"You figure them Crows drew him south on purpose? Get him out of the way?" Hardy said.

"Well, either that or something got missed in the translation. Wouldn't put it past some of your people to give their cousins a little help, even if they won't join 'em in war."

"My people? Since when are they my people?"

"Since you married into the family. Come on, we've got a rendezvous to keep. Benson," said Beck, as he swung a leg over Bill, "You take the mules for a spell. Simon, you get out on our left flank, Tibbits, take the right. Get up on every ridge you can, get a look-see into every valley beyond. If the Crow did lure Sturgis south to clear the way for the Nez Perce, chances are they aren't far away. Keep an eye peeled, Two Shirts and his braves are most likely close by, too. Let's go."

The scouts moved out, heading along the trail left by the cavalry.

The country became steeper as they moved to the north and east, ridge after ridge looming before them. The horses labored up the sharp slopes, blowing on the crests as the riders scanned the valleys below. By mid afternoon they had toiled up one long and gravelly slope to find, at the top, a rolling country ahead, and black in the northeast the blocky outline of Heart Mountain. At the base of the long slope, two riders were coming toward them, and out of a gulley to the east three more appeared, also coming up the long grade.

"Looks like our Crow comin' in," said Hardy, squinting at the approaching riders.

The sound of a rifle shot echoed out of the canyon to their rear. Then three more shots in quick succession.

"The damned mules" Beck said, wheeling Bill back the way they had come. "Gather them braves and come on as soon as you can!" He spurred Bill down the long slope toward the sound of the firing, which seemed to be sporadic but continuous.

Bill's long body stretched and bunched and stretched again as he pounded down the long slope, winding among the spaced out pines, then they were in the canyon bottom and among the brush and scrub of the flood plain. The horse worked the open spaces heavily, running but as if held back by some unseen harness, his great sides heaving with every bound. Beck took him across the bottomland, then as they began to work into another canyon, the sound of the guns stronger now, he guided the big horse up the left hand slope at an angle, looking to get to high ground over whatever battle was going on. Bill slowed gradually as they climbed, and by the time he reached the ridge line, he was nearly walking and blowing heavily.

In the little vale down below, white clouds of gun smoke clung in the still air over a pocket of thick brush and boulders, and more gun smoke along the ridgeline to Beck's front and left. He slid the big Winchester out of its scabbard and swung down off of the still moving Bill, running to a pair of crossed logs just ahead. He could see animals in the boulders down below, and guessed that would be his mules and Benson's horse. On the ridge, as he watched, he made out the forms of at least three Indians, firing down at the mules.

The nearest one was about sixty yards out. He levered a round into the chamber of the rifle and steadied it across the topmost log. The fine front bead settled into its rear sight notch and the distant form of the nearest Indian rose up to fire over the boulder he was hiding behind. Beck touched off the round, and the rifle bucked against his shoulder, white smoke billowing out to hide all before him. He racked in another round, waited a second or two for the smoke to clear, sighted on the same spot. No human form could be seen. As he shifted his gaze toward the other areas of smoke along the ridge top, a white puff burst out and a bullet smashed the log just to his right, gouging the top and sending splinters into his face. He cursed and ducked behind the logs.

He blinked, testing to see if anything had hit his eyes, and rubbed his smarting cheek. His fingers found a small sliver of wood in the flesh, and he pulled it out. No other damage seemed to have been done. He readied himself, rifle before his chest, then rose and fired with a hasty sight picture, ducked again. As he went down he glimpsed another white puff from the same position, and yet another to the right of it and further along the ridge line. Two bullets sang over the top log. They had him figured.

Down in the vale, rifle shots were popping off with regularity. Beck looked around at Bill, suddenly worried that the big horse was in the line of fire. But the animal had moved off down the slope a little, and was standing looking at him behind a mound of earth. Luck had placed him in a sheltered spot.

Beck peeked around the log to his right. Three shots answered his glance, two of them shattering wood from the logs. He rolled along the rocky soil to his left, keeping below the piled logs, and, levering in a fresh cartridge, popped up, sighted quickly, fired the round, and dropped. Two more shots answered, the bullets thunking in the dead wood.

He heard the sound of horses and looked back at Bill. Hardy and five Crow were coming up the slope behind the big horse. They dismounted, and the Indians spread out to find firing points. Hardy slid his rifle out of its scabbard, ducked, and crawled up to Beck.

"What you make of it?" he said.

"They got Benson pinned down in the valley. They're most likely after the mules, trying to slow us down or drive us out. Maybe four or five of 'em on the ridge line."

The Crow began to fire from places to the right and left. Answering fire came from the ridge, this time five or six rifles responding. A lively give and take of rifle reports filled the valley with echoes.

"You figure it's Two Shirts?" Hardy said, peeking through a chink in the piled logs.

"Most likely. They're real set on keeping us from heading north. The main body has got to be close, otherwise they wouldn't risk an open fight."

Hardy and Beck found places in the log pile to peek through, and managed to located the Nez Perce warriors by watching for the smoke of their firing and then for movement. They popped up and fired and ducked, adding their guns to the melee. The white puffs of gun smoke drifted gradually out along the ridge to the east. Bullets whined over head, or thunked into the wood of the covering logs. Benson, down in the little valley with the mules, had stopped firing. Then, on the slope behind him to the west, another rifle opened up. At first, Beck thought it was another Nez Perce and sighted on the smoke with his own rifle. But he could see the direction of the smoke and flame, and the rifleman was shooting at the Nez Perce. He smiled.

"What say you and me take a little trip?" he said to Hardy. "If we drop over the ridge to the east, we can get around behind 'em, maybe get to their horses."

"Risky business, the way them boys shoot."

"Well, that may be so, but we got to get Benson out of there. No telling how much damage they done him already."

Hardy shook his head, said, "All right, let's do it!"

"Now remember," said Beck as they crawled back to lower ground, and began to move crouched below the ridgeline to the east, "if they fire on us, one will lay down a covering fire, the other will move up. Once that man is in position, he lays down the cover, the other moves."

"We'll flank 'em, over run 'em, take 'em by overwhelming assault!" Hardy said wryly. "How many you say there was?"

"I don't know, maybe five or six."

"And how many are we? Oh let's see, I count about...two?"

"Oh shut up," Beck said, moving nearer the top of the ridge, using the trees and rocks as cover. Hardy moved off to his left, further down the slope. They had covered about a hundred yards, when a fresh volley of firing broke out ahead of them. The cracking of rifles came by the dozen, and no bullets whizzed through the air around them. Beck took off at a dead run up the slope and crested the ridge. The area where the Nez Perce had been firing from was shrouded in gun smoke, but the firing was now coming from further back in the trees. As he watched, two blue coated soldiers moved out of the trees on the run, took up firing positions on the ridge top, and shot down the ridge slope behind the little valley.

Hardy puffed up to where Beck was standing, took in the scene.

"See?" Beck said, "A good attack does it every time."

"Who the hell is that?" Hardy said.

"Beats me," Beck said. "Let's get down there and see about Benson."

They back-tracked along the ridge to the horses. The Crow had gathered, and, Beck and Hardy leading the way, they all mounted and crossed the ridge and moved down into the valley. As they rode up to the jumble of brush and boulders, Benson, carrying his rifle, came out to meet them. He stumbled a little as he moved.

"Ain't you boys a pretty sight!" he said, grinning. Blood was seeping down from under his hat, reddening the side of his face. "They had me cold, 'till you showed up. Just luck I was moving right by these rocks when they jumped me, got the mules in there and me too, otherwise I was a gonner."

"Looks like you been scratched a mite," Hardy said. "They hit the mules?"

"Don't know, been kinda busy," Benson said. He sat down heavily on a rock, took off his hat, began touching his head. Beck dismounted and went to see about his wound. Hardy moved into the boulders and led the mules out. The Crow, with a word to Hardy, moved back up the ridgeline the way they had come.

The mules were up and walking, and seemed unhurt. Hardy was unpacking them to check them over when Pocket came down the western slope.

"Get any of 'em?" he asked, swinging down off his horse.

"Them or us?" Beck said.

"Either," Simon said.

"Think we might have got one or two of them. Benson here tried to deflect a bullet that was aimed for one of them mules. A good use of his bean, it would seem," Beck said, taking down his canteen from Bill and wetting a kerchief with water. He began to clean the wound on Benson's head.

Simon helped unpack the mules. One of them had three bullet wounds, all of them just nicks. The other mule was untouched. The gear had taken the brunt of the damage, with bullet holes in the packing canvas, the bean sack holed, the bacon shot through, the coffee pot dented by a deflected shot. As they sorted the gear, riders appeared at the crest of the eastern ridge. As Beck paused in sewing together Benson's scalp to watch them, a column of soldiers materialized and wound down the slope. Beck counted nine troopers, and one additional rider. They hit the vale floor and moved up to the scouts as Beck tied off the suture.

"Well I'll be, if it ain't Lieutenant Morgan!" Hardy said, grinning. "I do declare, lieutenant, you come along just at the right time!"

"I am delighted to oblige you, sir!" he said, dismounting. "What's the damage here?"

Beck described the wounds, the holed goods, the Crow scouts.

"And don't go shootin' at 'em, if you please, they work for me and they'd take it right personal if you was to kill a few of 'em."

"Mr. Beck...and Mr. Hardy. I know we have had our disagreements in the past. I would like to say to you once again, I do apologize for my previous remarks. I realize full well that we have friends among the tribes, and I am not out here to paint the country red with Indian blood."

"Just joshing with you little, lieutenant," Beck said. "And if I might ask, what brought you to our neck of the woods?"

"Fitzsimmons came in with your note and his report. Captain Peachbow decided to send you reinforcements. Here I am. And at a fortuitous moment, I might add."

"That's for sure," Beck said, "Your boys kill any of 'em?"

"We may have wounded one or two. Your scouts were up there scalping the man one of you killed before we could get into position to attack. Filthy custom, that. I would suppose it was they who scalped the warrior back at your camp."

"You were through our camp?"

"Yes, about mid day. Ran into your man a few miles further on. He helped us to find you, at least until we heard the firing."

"Who--?" Beck began.

"Oh, that'd be me!" Tibbits said, moving his horse out from behind the body of troopers. He grinned down at Beck.

"What were doing back in that country?" Beck said, "You were to scout the country out to the east on our flank."

"Jest followin' the sign," Tibbits said, "thought I had a line on 'em, then these here soldier boys showed up."

Beck eyed Tibbits for several moments without speaking.

"This bunch of Nez Perce that jumped Benson, looks like they came in from the east," Beck said slowly.

"What're you trying to say, Mr. Beck?" Tibbits said, still smiling a little.

"Nothing much. Just that if I send a man out to scout the flank, I expect him to be where I send him. Or thereabouts. Not ten miles in the rear doin' God knows what."

"That's where the sign led me!" Tibbits said loudly. "You want me to scout, well, that's what I was doing!"

128

"If you found clear sign, clear enough to take you back the way we come for ten miles, why didn't you report in, so we all could have followed it?"

"I wasn't sure it was them Nez Perce. Wanted to be sure afore I come told you."

"And you met up with these cavalrymen near our last camp?"

"Yep. So what?"

"And the good lieutenant here tells me that Nez Perce we left in that camp lost his hair after all," Beck said.

"Probably one o' them Crow doubled back for it, they's mighty partial to scalps," Tibbits said lightly.

"Maybe. Mind if I take a look in your saddle bags?" Beck said evenly.

Tibbits face went sour, and reddened. Not a word was spoken in the bunch, and all eyes rested on him.

"Ain't nobody touching my saddlebags," Tibbits said, low and mean.

"And why is that?" Beck said, taking a step away from Benson's side, then a step toward Tibbits' horse.

"'Cause they're my saddlebags, and I don't like what you're getting' at."

"What I'm getting at," Beck said, taking another step, "is that I think you went back to that camp and took that scalp yourself. What I'm getting at, is that you disobeyed orders to do it, and because of you those Nez Perce nearly got Benson. What I'm getting at is when I told you in the meadow last night to wake the camp, you didn't do it, and they weren't ready when the raiders rode through, and as a result, Gloy is now dead!"

"Trooper Gloy?" Lieutenant Morgan put in, "Was that who was in that grave at the camp?"

"It most surely is," Beck said, without taking his eyes off of Tibbits. "Now Mr. Tibbits, I may be wrong about you, and I am willing to admit it if I am. All you have to do is let me have a look in those saddle bags..." and he took another step.

Tibbits drew his revolver and cocked it in one swift motion, the muzzle pointed squarely at Beck.

"You ain't lookin' at nothin' that belongs to me!" Tibbits snarled. Beck heard the racking of several rifle levers at his back. Tibbits eyes glanced briefly at the men behind Beck, then back at the big scout. "You got me all wrong, Mr. Beck! But you ain't gonna treat me like no wet behind the ears whelp, neither! You can all go to hell, and that's a fact!" With that he wheeled his horse and rode south along the valley, holstering his gun as he galloped out of sight.

Jon Beck watched him go, shaking his head with pursed lips.

"Well then!" said Lieutenant Morgan, "We've had an excellent day of shooting at Indians, and," he looked at the late afternoon sky, "I'd say only an hour or two of it left to enjoy! Where do you plan on making your camp tonight, Mr. Beck?"

Beck looked at the lieutenant as if seeing him for the first time.

"North of Heart Mountain, if the light holds," he said. They made preparations to move out.

Chapter 20

The Crow came off the ridge as the little column formed up. One of the braves wore a fresh scalp tucked through his belt. Beck, speaking through Hardy, sent the Indian scouts out in advance, and a couple of them off toward Heart Mountain to seek out the rendezvous point and report back. Lieutenant Morgan wrote out a dispatch and sent it back to his main command with one trooper. Benson had begun to stiffen up from his wound, and another trooper helped him mount. As Beck and Morgan led the column off to the north, Beck sent outriders to the flanks.

"So, did Peachbow run into anything?" Beck said.

"No. His scouts located Howard in the Park. We also ran into Sturgis' scouts on the way here. Say, there's nothing like shooting at them, is there?"

"What?"

"The Indians. Those murdering savages on the ridge. Nothing like driving them with good, solid marksmanship, making them run. Almost like shooting deer."

"'Ceptin' deer don't shoot back."

"Humph! I didn't see much cause for alarm there. We had them cold, drove them out, and I am sure we bloodied one or two. Ran like deer, too."

"Well, you caught 'em cold, that's for sure. And glad you done it. But don't go thinking it's always going to be that easy. Today was yours, tomorrow who knows."

"What of this rendezvous you have planned? Who are we meeting?"

"Crow scouts. Whole passel of them joined up back on the Stinking Water, they've been out in the country around Heart Mountain. Tonight we'll gather them in, find out what's what."

"And that man Tibbits? What was that about?"

"I figure you heard most of it. That feller has been off on a trail of his own ever since I met up with him. Not sure why I hired him on to this trip, most likely 'cause of his pard back there, Pocket. Now Pocket, I figure I can understand that feller. He's been riding with Tibbits for awhile, and when you get to sidin' a pard, well, you stick with him. Sort of wonderin' why Pocket is along with us now, allowin' as how he's been follerin' Tibbits' lead up to this point. Or maybe t'other way around. We may lose him yet. At any rate, we've got your men now, so things should improve some. The horses are nearly worn out, 'ceptin' for Bill, here," and Beck patted Bill's neck, "what with all this up and down the valley walls. But just over this ridge ahead, the country flattens out some around Heart Mountain, and we might have a better go of it."

But Bill, good reputation and all, labored up that same slope that they had climbed earlier in the day, and when they finally reached the top, his head hung just as low as the rest of the scouts' mounts. Once again Heart Mountain loomed square and black to the north in the fading light of the afternoon.

They rode down into the rolling country before the mountain, and guided by the Crow outriders crossed the sparse land and watched the last of the sun gild the mountaintop as the purple shadows grew around them. The pace slowed considerably as the darkness thickened, and the stars had come out sharply bright by the time the Crow led them into the camp of the Indians.

Lieutenant Morgan sat his horse for several long moments, looking at the dozen or so Crow scattered about the camp. Some watched him curiously. Three of them were butchering a freshly killed deer, and meat was set roasting on the fire. Finally, Morgan dismounted and set about the ordering of the soldier's camp. The horses were tended to, and two small tents set up. Hardy went to the Crow fires and talked with the braves as the soldiers prepared an evening meal. Benson was seated on a stone just within the firelight. Beck squatted at his side.

"How's that head?" Beck said.

"Feels like a buffalo stepped on it," Benson said. "My neck is so sore I can hardly move it."

"Well, just take it easy. Couple of days you'll be scratchin' and clawin' with the best of 'em! And by the way, good work with them mules. You saved our bacon."

Benson laughed, then grimaced. "Well, most of it, anyway," he said.

Hardy came to the camp with Man On A High Place. Beck rose to meet them, and they gathered up Lieutenant Morgan and stepped to a spot just outside the firelight. Simon Pocket joined them.

"We found Nez Perce," High Place said, "at least enough warriors to know main camp beyond little way."

"Get a fight goin'?" asked Beck.

"No. We saw them, they not see us."

"What exactly did you see?" said Morgan.

"Maybe thirty braves. They had wagon with them, much goods in it. Stole it, for sure. They come from east, go north. Maybe half a day from us. Some of my people watch them now."

"Did you see any soldiers?" Morgan said.

"No. Plenty soldier sign, much tracks. The Nez Perce go to buffalo country north of Yellowstone. Good grass there, water for horses. Meat. We find good herds today, much buffalo. Maybe Nez Perce take time to hunt, we catch."

"That would be the plan," Morgan said.

"Well, maybe not," Beck said. "At least not until we can get word to the main body of soldiers and they can come up. That would be the plan, wouldn't it, lieutenant?"

"If we can engage them, perhaps we can slow them down, give the army a chance to catch up," Morgan said eagerly.

"Or we could engage them, get wiped out, and furnish them with more guns and ammunition for their run to Canada," Hardy said.

"Mr. Hardy, I have no doubt you mean well, but our duty is to find and engage the enemy," Morgan huffed. "You saw how they ran today, all it takes is a good, swift attack and they'll melt before us like April snow on a warm spring day."

"You're right about one thing," Beck said, "Our job is to find them. Looks like we're getting close to that. Once we do, and we have sent dispatches back to the general, then we can figure out what to do at that point. But as I have said to you in the past, Lieutenant Morgan, do not underestimate the fighting ability, or marksmanship, of the Nez Perce. If you do, you will pay dearly for it."

"Humph" grumped Morgan, "We shall see."

High Place went back to the Indian fires, Hardy went to see about something to eat. Lieutenant Morgan set about organizing his men, posting a watch, detailing their relief.

"Well, Simon," Beck said, "What'll it be? You going to run out, too?"

"You got no call to say that, Mr. Beck," Simon said. "You know that I promised—"

"It's just a simple question, Simon, I just want to know what to expect."

"You can't go and blame him, not with what—"

"Simon, you heard me when I laid it out for him. You know what I think of him and what I think he did. I don't see how him agrievin' for that gal caused him to disobey an order that got Gloy killed, nor got Benson attacked, nor made him want to pick up a souvenir! I figure the little bastard has been playin' you all along, and you're swallerin' the bait."

Pocket looked off into the dark, his jaw working, thinking hard.

"And those mules from the Stoeger place."

"What of 'em?" Pocket said, looking again at Beck.

"Them and the milk cow was took from that place while you and the others was in town getting' the sheriff. It was Tibbits what took 'em, and—"

"Just how do you know that?"

"'Cause he sold one of 'em to the saddle maker, Gland! And the way I got it from Gland, I have no doubt it was Tibbits."

"Well even if it was Zak, I don't see—"

"What you don't see is Tibbits has been playing on your sympathy from the very first hour you boys found that burnt out cabin! He managed to conquer his so-called grief long enough to steal three head of stock, make a savvy trade with the Indians for one cow and one mule, and haul the hides he got for them into town on the other mule, where he sold the whole outfit to Gland. And you know damned well that's where he got the money to keep you boys drunk for a week! And just before the attack on our horses and camp, I told him to get back to the fire and roust you boys out, so's you'd be ready if Two Shirts and his bunch came down on ya. He ignored my order, stayed in the meadow with the horses, and took a few shots at the Nez Perce. I know that Gloy, or any of us for that matter, might have got killed in that raid, but if he'd got you all on your feet, at least you would have had a fighting chance.

"And that scalp! He knew them Crow coveted that hair, and I'm figuring he went back to get it to make a deal with 'em. Or to make him a big man at the next bar he manages to roost in. And because he wasn't out on the flank, the Nez Perce jumped Benson and nearly got the mules. Yeah, I know they might have got to him anyhow, but the whole point is, Tibbits is off on a trail of his own, and I can't afford to have a man like that eatin' my bacon and drinkin' my coffee when I can't count on him."

Pocket shook his head and said nothing, looking again into the dark.

"So my question is a simple one, Simon. You with us, or with him?" Beck said. He went on, speaking low and evenly. "We need you on this scout, me and Hardy. Oh I know, we got soldiers now to fetch and carry messages, but I need a man with your eyes and your guts. I figure tomorrow, maybe the next day, we're going to be up to our asses in Indians, and I need a man that will stick. Are you that man?"

"Mr. Beck," Pocket said slowly, "I hired on for the job. I thought Zak would come around. He and me got a few things to settle. But I hired on for the job. If you'll have me, I'll side you plumb into hell and back!"

"Good!" Beck said, sticking out his hand, which Simon took, "We may not be headin' fer hell, but I got a feeling the resemblance is gonna be mighty close."

.

Chapter 21

That night more Crow scouts came in. The sentries posted by Lieutenant Morgan were surprised again and again, as the Crow, seeing the camp fires from a distance, crept up on the camps and startled the sentries by appearing at very close range. Several times rifles were leveled, triggers pressed, and only a split second of indecision kept a friendly redskin out of the happy hunting grounds. The Crow of course thought it all great fun.

Near midnight the temperature had plunged to frost, and then the snow began. Beck and Hardy spent most of the evening with High Place and Morgan, listening to what each arriving scout had to say, and were still at it when the snow started. Within two hours the snow had changed to a cold rain. Even bundled in their heavy woolen greatcoats, the soldiers rose from their bedrolls and huddled at the fires for warmth. The wet soon got into everything, everyone.

An awning was rigged next to the soldier's fire, and Morgan got out and unrolled the army maps. He and Beck and Hardy went over the topographical sketches in detail. The Crow scouts had reported that several parties of Nez Perce had been sighted, and it was surmised that these were all foraging warriors. Most of their movement, once they had found food or loot, took them to the west and north. It was agreed that in the morning the scouts would head north for the Yellowstone, keeping their Crow scouts off to the west and traveling north. Several of the Crow braves were certain the main body of the Nez Perce were on Clarke's Fork and moving north as rapidly as possible. Several had seen some white scouts, but at a great distance, and to whom them belonged no one could say.

High Place went back to his people before dawn with the plans for the next day. Morgan rousted out what few of his men were sleeping, and the camp was struck in the cold drizzle of the dawn. The fires were smoldering, hissing coals by then, the rain having dampened them down to death, so that only hardtack and water were possible for breakfast. Beck went to saddle Bill, and rubbed the water off the great, broad back as best he could before seating the blanket and saddle on him. Bill had been eating the sparse, course mountain grass that he could get at, but it was not enough to fuel him

135

for long, Beck knew. He led the saddled horse to the mountain brook near the camp. The mules were packed, the light coming up.

Hardy came up beside him with his own mount as Bill drank from the stream.

"Sorta weather makes you want to burrow deep and not come out," he muttered.

"We've been lucky," Beck said, squinting at the lowering clouds.

By the time the little column of army and civilian scouts was formed up, the Crow had disappeared to the north and west. Troopers were sent out on the flanks, and the men spread out to cover as much ground as possible as the party started generally north and west. The horses plodded reluctantly into the wind and rain, a lowering grey sky offering no hint of sun or blue.

From the shoulder of Heart Mountain the land had looked rolling and easy. It was in fact crossed by innumerable gullies and water courses, most of them dry in mid September, so that the horses worked always on some up slope or down slope, through stands of scrub pine and tamarack, across rocky creek bottoms. The Crow came in during the day in ones and twos, spoke with Hardy and disappeared again. In the early afternoon the rain slackened to an intermittent, windblown drizzle. Beck and Morgan had just met on a ridge overlooking the Yellowstone breaks, when firing was heard in the distance to the west. A dozen shots, then silence.

"Well, whatever that was, someone got the best of it quickly," Morgan said.

"We'll be at the river by nightfall," Beck said. "Should be settlements there. Heard folks was coming into the lower Yellowstone valley this year."

"We shall be able to re-provision, and with luck, make contact with our main body, if they are indeed coming down Clarke's Fork."

They started their horses down a long slope among lodge pole pines.

"How long you been out here, lieutenant?" Beck asked.

"Two months. Our rescue of your party yesterday was my first action. The men performed quite admirably."

"Rescue?"

"Indeed! Without our flanking assault, you might have been badly mauled."

"Then I would guess I owe you my life," Beck said sardonically.

"Think nothing of it!" cried Morgan brightly, "Only too happy to be of service."

But the country was rough and the horses tired, and they had not reached the Yellowstone by nightfall. The rain had stopped as they chose a place to camp, near a small rivulet made to run by the recent rain. The mules came up, and Benson with them. He was doing all he could to stay in the saddle, helping to herd the mules along. The soldiers found some downed trees that remained dry on the underside, and the men stripped out this material to get a fire going. Soon all the soldiers were gathered at the blaze save two unlucky troopers positioned on nearby high points as sentries. Bacon and coffee were soon heating over a smaller cook fire near the main blaze. Steam rose from the coats and clothing of the men as they stood to the big blaze with lapels held wide, absorbing the heat like heavy vultures in the sun.

Crows found the camp, straggling in to report to High Place and Hardy. They had found tracks, trails, much sign, but nothing promising. Several of them reported a Nez Perce party, maybe six or eight warriors, traveling several miles ahead of the scouts. These warriors had been seen several times, but stayed out of range of the Crows, and the Crows were not eager to close within rifle shot of their adversaries. The firing heard earlier in the day turned out to have been just such an encounter, where three Crow scouts had been taken by surprise by another party of Nez Perce, number unknown, and had escaped with one of them slightly wounded.

The Crow did not camp near the soldiers, but instead made a camp further down in the valley, near a pond fed by the stream the soldiers drank from. Beck found a small meadow across the slope from the soldier's camp, and the animals were picketed there, with one of the sentries, now replaced with a fire-dried man, posted to watch them. Beck had stripped off Bill's saddle and blanket at the camp, and after picketing the big horse amid the brown, damp grass of the swale, rubbed him down with a spare shirt.

"Best I can do, big fellah," he said, scratching Bill's neck just back of his head. The horse lowered his head and nudged his face into Beck's chest as Beck took to scratching both sides with his fingers. "Yeah, ya like that, don'tcha?" he murmered.

The rain had stopped at nightfall, but the cold deepened. Soggy bedding kept most of the men either awake or fitfully sleeping, and some dried their blankets at the fire, then turned in for a few hours in warmed woolen comfort. Hardy and Beck went over the information the scouts had brought in. Lieutenant Morgan joined them, and they all supped coffee and talked.

"Main body of Injuns has got to be on the Fork," Hardy said, "Too many scouts out hereabouts for them not to be close. I'd come down Clark's Fork, it if was me with women and kids in tow."

"Looks like Canada for sure," Beck said.

"Our last courier this afternoon spoke of Sturgis on the Fork in hot pursuit," Morgan said. "We'll make the Yellowstone in the morning, and see if we can't join up with them. I do believe Captain Peachbow remains in the south, so I may be required to rejoin him."

"Well as it's going for now," Beck said, "we've pretty much certified they are not veering east. That party out in front of us has got to be Two Shirts and his bunch, and they're just lyin' around waiting for us to try and close up. And that I'd like to do. I figure we could make a solid two day push, maybe three, whatever the horses will stand, and try to get north and east of the main bunch. If we could get in close at that point, we might have something solid to tell Sturgis."

"And what if they dodge east below us when we're pushing hard to the north?" Hardy said.

"No, it's Canada for sure, I'd bet on it!" Beck said firmly. "If they get into that open country north of the Yellowstone, what with all those horses they're drivin', nobody will catch them then. They wear one out, just hop on a fresh one. We don't have that luxury."

"What we do have is orders," Morgan said. "We are to remain east of the fight, make sure that if they do come east, we will detect them and report. I don't mind catching them if possible, but I'd rather not get in their way."

Beck looked at the lieutenant for a moment.

"Well, now," he growled, "that's the first sensible thing I have heard you say this whole trip, lieutenant!"

"It only stands to reason," Morgan said, taking no offense. "The horses are getting played out, the men are tired, and if we succeeded in heading them, well, to what purpose? If they are going all the way to Canada, we can't do much to impede their progress. We will continue to shadow them on the east, as we have been."

"All right, then," Beck said. "Still like to close up with Two Shirts, though. We have a little unfinished business to take care of."

"Now Jon," Hardy said, "be patient. Who knows, Two Shirts might just come fer that powwow sooner'n you think."

Grub was cooked again before dawn. The last of the bacon was eaten, and only one tin of hard tack remained. It was a thin meal all around, and the men, who finally got a short rest in the small hours of the morning, were still exhausted and hungry as they packed and saddled up in the first grey light of morning. The cold had come down close to the earth, frost rimed the meadows, and the breath of men, mules and horses blew in clouds as the party prepared for the day's march.

The Crow scouts were gone into the hills by the time the army moved out, and they had been in the saddle for an hour before the sun finally peeked over the eastern table lands. Beck and Hardy rode point, with the soldiers on the flanks, and Lieutenant Morgan back with the mules and Benson, who rode silently, stiffly, his mouth open and eyes dull, staying with the mules and nothing more.

By early morning, the sun had turned the frosted grass wet with dew, and warmed the men on their right sides. They came down off a gentle ridge into the Yellowstone valley. Morgan came trotting up to Beck, who pulled in big Bill for a breather.

"Civilization at last!" Morgan said. "Look, over on the north bank, buildings there!" he said, pointing. He fetched a spyglass out of his saddle bag and snapped it open to peer at the distant structures. "Some kind of farm, looks like."

"Well, let's get down to the river, see about finding a ford," Beck said.

The reached the banks of the river at mid morning. As September lengthened, the Yellowstone had diminished somewhat, but still presented a deep, swift flowing obstacle. They decided to head downstream to the northeast to look for a ford. The mules came up and the flankers came in as they walked the horses along the river bank, and soon they found a place where the river broadened and shoaled over what looked like a rocky and graveled bottom. On the far side the cut bank rose five or six feet over the water level, and the flood plain stretched off a mile to the low bluffs of the plains.

"I'll give it a go here," Beck said, "If it's solid I'll give you a holler."

He turned Bill into the water and the horse waded out past his fetlocks, then his knees. The bottom was stony but firm. They came to the center channel where the water was much deeper but not swift. The horse went in up to his belly, then of a sudden he was swimming. Beck eased himself off of the saddle and floated beside the horse, hanging on to the saddle as Bill towed him along. The water was startlingly cold, and Beck caught his breath with the shock of it.

They floated down a bit with the current, and Beck could feel the powerful working of the big horse's body as Bill rhythmically churned away for the shallows. And then his hooves found purchase and he was lurching out of the water as Beck slipped back aboard the saddle and was hoisted free of the cold river. He turned Bill back up the river at a diagonal across the shallows, and soon was nearly to the far bank and almost even with the waiting men.

"Looks pretty good!" he hollered back at them. "Come on over."

Lieutenant Morgan ordered a soldier to lead each mule and another to ride along behind each one. Hardy and Pocket, along with the two remaining soldiers, were to stay with Benson, who was nearly comatose though upright in the saddle. The mules would go across first, one at a time, and then they would bring Benson over last.

While these arrangements were being made and the first mule started, Beck rode Bill to the north bank, and, finding a path up the bank through the silvered, worn driftwood trees and branches strewn everywhere, he steered the big horse up onto the flats above the river bed. He paused and leaned on his saddle pommel, looking back over his shoulder as the soldiers led the first mule out into the main channel.

Before him to the bluffs the flood plain of the Yellowstone was nearly flat, but furrowed where other channels had flowed and dried as the river level went down, the surface covered with scoured sand and sagebrush. More grass grew on it toward the edges where it met the low bluffs of the northern plains. Driftwood spotted the ground, great trees and logs, limbs and tangles, the wood scoured clean by the flooding waters of years past, bleached white like bones in the sun. Then Beck's eyes darted to the northwest, up the valley. In the distance, smoke. It began as a small, dirty black cloud, then streamed upward and whitened, quickly forming a column against the blue of the clear autumn sky.

He turned and looked again at the river. The soldiers had the first mule across the main channel, and Lieutenant Morgan was riding ahead of it through the shallows. He spurred his horse out of the water, across the flats of the river bed and up the bank to rein in beside Beck.

Before Beck could say a thing, Morgan's eye caught the smoke. The column was huge now, standing like a leaning pillar as the easy, ever present wind bore its top to the southeast.

"What the hell?" Morgan said.

"Looks like it's a couple of miles out," Beck said. "Haystack or barn or some such. Probably that farm you saw earlier."

As they looked, a second column of smoke began, this one slightly to the river side, closer.

"Indians?" Morgan said.

"I think we found our main body," Beck said. He looked back at the river, where the second mule was being led into the shallows on the far side, two hundred yards away. The near mule was coming across the shallows toward them.

"Not only that, Mr. Beck," Morgan said, smiling, "I think they have found us!"

Beck looked at Morgan, who had his spyglass out and was intently looking at the smoke. Or just below it. Then his own eyes detected color, moving, along the flat plain half a mile upriver. Horsemen. Quite a lot of horsemen. As he watched, they grew more distinct. Some moving along the bluffs, riding down river. Some nearer the water, riding down river. Some fanned out across the flood plane. Riding down river.

Beck wheeled Bill and started back for the head of the bank. "Indians!" he called out, "Get that mule over here now!"

"I'm going out to scout them a bit," Morgan said, starting his horse forward.

Beck wheeled Bill again to face Morgan's receding back. He could see the warriors beyond clearly now, and spurred Bill in pursuit of the lieutenant. Morgan was trotting forward, a grin on his face, as Beck charged past him, reined in Bill across Morgan's path. The lieutenant pulled up sharply, shying his horse from the collision.

141

"Damn you lieutenant!" Beck shouted, "There's a hundred warriors out there and they'll be on us in a second! If we're gonna live out the half hour, we need all the guns we have and we're gonna need to find a hole! For God's sake turn around!"

Mogan craned his neck, leaning out of the saddle a bit to try and peer around Beck. As he looked, the surly expression of irritation on face drained away, and his eyes widened. Beck looked behind him.

"All hell and damnation!" he growled and spurred Bill for the riverbank. "If you want to live you better come on!" he shouted to Morgan, who, with sudden alacrity, wheeled his horse and followed. The Nez Perce, who by now were closing fast, began to fire, and the distant pops of their rifles mingled with the whine of bullets flying by the ears of the two riders as they plunged over the bank and down onto the sandy riverbed. Beck yanked his Winchester from its scabbard and leapt off of Bill, legs churning sand as he ran up the low bank as Morgan passed him going down. At the top he found a drift log for cover, levered a round into the rifle's chamber and laid the gun across the log. There were too many targets and for a second he could not decide which of the thirty or forty Indians charging down in a line, now within a hundred yards of the bank, to aim at. He finally just gritted his teeth and lined up on the nearest brave and triggered the rifle. The gun bucked against his shoulder and the smoke cleared almost instantly on the wind as he levered in another round, aimed and fired, levered, fired, levered, fired, going for all he was worth as the line of braves swept nearer, nearer, the fear rising in his throat, his guts churning, making every shot count but knowing the gun was running out of cartridges. Warriors disappeared under his sights, horses went down, the center of the line thinned. He heard other shots being fired around him, his hat was jerked off, splinters showered his face, his ear suddenly burned, and the rifle was dry. He ducked behind the log, and began frantically stuffing cartridges from his belt into the loading gate of the rifle. He could see in his peripheral vision that Morgan was to one side of him, another soldier to his left, both firing rifles. Below the bank another soldier was coming from the mule, rifle in hand. Out in the river, he could see as he finished loading and glanced up, the second mule was in the main channel, two troopers with it, all swimming, sliding down with the current. Smoke trailed away from the men left on the far bank, as they added their firepower to the fray from long distance. Beck peeked over the log.

The Nez Perce had come within fifty yards of their position, then backed off. They had dismounted their horses, left them in a shallow depression in the flood plain, screened by a pile of driftwood. Now they fanned out across the ground, coming on in groups, some firing as the others ran forward. Half a dozen had clustered at the river bank a hundred yards upstream, and were firing at the men on the south bank. Beck searched briefly along the driftwood line and found another tree that offered better protection, got the big Winchester up on a new log with a second log protecting his left side, and went to work.

The fine sights on the big Winchester repeater allowed him to hold close and place his shots accurately. He waited for the braves to rise for their advance, ignoring the firing Indians, and got in two well place shots that he was certain has taken their toll. Then the firers found his position, and bullets whined close, some splattering splinters into this face. He kept is head down, and when the Nez Perce began to move, whipped the Winchester up and boomed out another shot here, another there, making each one count. He loaded as he went now, slipping new cartridges into the gun as he watched for his next target.

The third soldier was on the line now with the others, and their Springfield rifles spoke with authority. Beck glanced at the river, saw that the second mule was climbing out of the main channel, the men having a job to do getting the tired animal out of the deep water. As he watched, a sudden spout of smoke erupted from the brush line two hundred yards down river from his own men on the far side, and the mule went down. He heard a thunk and a cry of pain, and one of the soldiers at his side collapsed and rolled down the bank.

"They're behind us!" he yelled at Morgan and the other men, and scrambled for a large pile of driftwood above the waiting horses. There was a pool below it, a backwater left when the river retreated into its present flow, and Beck, leaving his rifle leaning against a log in the tangle, jumped down the bank and grabbed the reins of the horses and tugged them all into the pool, where they were screened from fire from across the river by driftwood heaped on the river bottom. He went for the mule, and bullets whipped geysers of sand into the air around him. The mule would not come willingly, and it

143

was all Beck could do to stand in the gunfire tugging at the animal's lead without flinching. Finally the mule walked after him into the pool, joining the tired, drooping horses.

The soldiers who had been with the mule in the river were sprinting over the riverbed now, leading their horses. The mule was still out there in the shallows, on its side, the rushing water not deep enough to move it. Morgan and the one remaining trooper from the bank dragged the wounded man to the edge of the pool. The two men from the river came in, adding their horses to the herd in the water. Beck could see that the part of his people across the river had burrowed into the driftwood piles on the south bank, and were exchanging fire with whoever was shooting from the brush downriver.

"We have to get back up there," Beck said, jerking his head at the top of the bank. "If they see we aren't firing, they'll rush us!"

Morgan thought for a moment.

"All right, here's what we'll do. Johnson, you stay here with Kilroy, see if you can't stop the bleeding. Keep your eyes on the other side of the river, if anyone comes from that direction let us know. The rest, spread out in the wood along the bank. Find a position that offers you some cover from the back, otherwise that bunch over there," and he nodded toward the south bank, "will pick you off even at this range. Pick your shots, make 'em count!"

Beck nodded, a smile on his face. "Good, let's get to it!" he said.

The men scattered along the bank, drawing new fire from the south side of the river, but at the range the shots were coming from, no damage was done immediately. Renewed fire came from the soldiers on the south bank, answering the bushwhackers directly. Beck scrambled up the bank, retrieved his rifle, found a concealed spot, and looked out at the flood plain. Half a dozen Nez Perce were up and running full tilt at his log pile, and as he threw up the rifle and fired, nearly all of the soldiers at his side fired too, and the volley cut down three of the Indians and sent the rest pelting back the way they had come. Beck sent two more rounds after them, and saw one of them flinch, go down, get up and scurry to cover.

The soldiers and Beck set about a careful aimed fire, picking their targets from cover, then getting the rifles up and firing quickly, then going to cover again. Someone was always watching, another always firing, and the Indians made no further move to close the distance. The group up the river to the northwest kept up a sporadic fire on the men at the south bank, but they were well hidden now, and the Indians were not achieving anything.

But the hidden foes in the brush down the river on the south bank were making closer shots, waiting for the smoke of Beck's men's firing to show where the soldiers were in the wood pile, then firing at the smoke. The soldiers did not have enough protection at their backs to risk staying up for more than a few seconds. The incoming bullets began to do damage, sending flying splinters about, nicking a man here and there.

Beck peered through the logs at the enemy's south bank position. It was all of three to four hundred yards away, too far to effectively return fire with any sort of predictable result. The solders on the south bank were about two hundred yards from the bushwhackers, but the angle was wrong, they could not get their shots low enough to get in among the brush where the attackers lay. Then, as Beck watched, someone mounted a horse and burst from the driftwood piles where the soldiers were holed up. He spurred his horse up the bank and disappeared over the rim into the rough sagebrush country beyond. Soon Beck heard firing from guns he could not see, and white smoke rose back in the brush. The bushwhackers had retreated back into the brush also, adding their own plume of smoke to mark their spot.

"Hardy you old fool!" Beck muttered, "Bless your heart, don't get yourself shot up! Maggie'd never forgive me."

Beck turned back to the fray before him. The firing had died, and he could see through chinks in the logs that the Nez Perce were pulling out. They were taking their wounded, gathering at the horses. The solders began to lay on the fire, their Springfield rifles barking loudly, and they hurried the Indians along even at the six hundred yards range they were attempting. Shortly the Indians were mounted and streaming for the foothills to the north, and as the soldiers watched, the dozens of braves curved around and headed down the river.

Beck turned back to the south bank. As he watched, half a dozen horsemen broke cover and charged down the bank a quarter of a mile down river, splashed into the water, swam the main channel and splashed out again. They charged up the bank from the riverbed and headed out across the flood plane after the receding warrior band.

145

"Whipped 'em again!" Morgan said, standing up and thunking the butt of his rifle into the gravel of the riverbank. "Good shooting, men!" he said, grinning.

Just then a bullet whined past his ear, as the report of a rifle came down the wind from the flood plain. Beck could see the plume of rifle smoke drift away from a pile of driftwood two hundred yards to the northwest. Morgan dropped behind the logs with a curse.

"Did those yahoos up on the north bank to the west of us go with the main band?" Beck asked one of the soldiers.

"Yeah, they pulled out," the man replied.

"So. Lieutenant Morgan," Beck said. "Obviously we have work yet to do. Chances are that one lone brave ain't so alone. They've probably left a few of their best shots to keep us pinned down while the rest go off and do more mischief. I say we bring over the other men, then see if we can't flush 'em out."

"Excellent idea, Mr. Beck. Can we signal them over?"

"Sure," Beck said. He stepped down the bank to the bottom, lifted his hat, waved it.

After a few moments the soldiers on the far back emerged from the driftwood tangles on their horses and made a dash for the river. They were keeping Benson in the saddle, and the horses hit and crossed the shallows at a weak gallop, then they were into the main channel, swimming for it. Someone was with Benson, keeping him in contact with his horse. They all reached the channel bank just above the dead mule, their horses lurching up into the shallower water, and Benson was slumped over the horse's neck. It was Pocket helping him, and they came across the shallows at a trot, Simon running his paint pony along side Benson's horse, which was being led by Hardy.

The soldiers on the north bank were waiting intently for the sniper out on the flats to take a shot at the coming troopers, but he did not expose himself. Then the coming party was under the cover of the bank, and Simon jumped down and eased the collapsed Benson down off his mount and laid him out in the sand next to the wounded Kilroy.

"That was some piece of work, Hardy," Beck said at Hardy swung down off of his horse. "You taking that bushwhackin' bunch off'n our backs saved our bacon, that's a certainty!"

"Twern't me," Hardy said. "Simon Pocket's yer man."

146

"Simon?" said Beck, his eyebrows rising.

"Went out after 'em all alone. I figured he was a gonner. Damned if he didn't come back like some lost puppy."

Beck turned to the still flushed and puffing Pocket.

"Well I'll tell you to yer face, that was the dumbest stunt I ever did see!" Beck said with a grin, "And thank God you were dumb enough to pull it off!"

"Jes trying to do my part," Pocket said, looking down.

"Part my ass!" Beck said, "That was the work of a dozen men! Or one crazy one! How many Indians were there?"

"Half dozen or so. I found me a perfect spot, boulder back there, old drift logs hung up on it. Perfect spot. Once I got 'em in my sights, why, nothing they could do but run. Perfect spot, that's all."

Beck stepped over and clapped Pocket on the back.

"Well, you had the poor judgment to try it, and the good judgment to make it work. Proud of you, Mr. Pocket. You've earned yer keep!" Simon's face began to flush again with embarrassment.

They set about tending to the wounded Kilroy. He had been hit in the back on the shoulder blade. The bullet had shattered the bone, but had not penetrated deep. Hardy, a good man with a knife, was elected to get the bullet out. Kilroy was awake, dazed, awaiting his fate quietly, dealing with the pain as best he could. They quickly got a fire going, and Hardy heated his knife.

Benson was lying on his back, and one of the soldiers rolled up his coat and eased it under his head. The bandage on this head was soaked through with blood, and from under it oozed a lighter, yellowish fluid. He stared at the sky, unblinking, mouth slack.

Two of the soldiers were in the driftwood logs atop the bank, scanning the flood plain for the remaining Nez Perce. The smoke columns in the northwest were three in number now, and to the south along the river another had appeared.

They rolled Kilroy onto his belly on a greatcoat, stripped off his shirt, bathed the wound, and Hardy took up the heated knife and went to work. Kilroy cried out once as Hardy felt with the point of the knife for the bullet, and luckily found it still embedded in the shattered bone. As he dug it out, Kilroy's body relaxed, for he had feinted. Hardy rinsed the flattened, distorted slug in the pool where the horses stood, tossed it to Lieutenant Morgan.

"Give him that as a memento, if he lives," Hardy said, rinsing his knife.

One of the soldiers fetched a needle and thread, and, after washing out the wound with canteen water, stitched up the flesh. They got his bloody shirt rinsed out, and another soldier produced a spare from his own kit, and they got Kilroy into it. The shirt was far too large for his bony frame but it would serve to keep him warmer until his own dried out. They pulled his unconscious body to a sitting position, and got his bloody uniform jacket back on him.

Hardy stepped in front of Beck, and looked over his face. "Hold still, Jon," he said, and with the tip of his knife and a fingernail, yanked several splinters out of Beck's face.

Several of the other troopers had minor wounds, splinters, gouges from near misses, and all were stripped, cleaned, sewed up, and dressed again. Beck found his hat out on the riverbed, a neat hole in the crown, plumb center, and a ragged hole in the back of the crown. He looked at it speculatively, and then felt along the top of his head with his free hand. He could feel a furrow in his hair, but it did not break the skin. He put on the hat, and bathed his ear with a wet handkerchief. The bullet wound there had merely taken the lobe off. It still bled, but not profusely. He had one of the men put a stitch or two in it for good measure.

Lieutenant Morgan climbed to the top of the bank, spoke with the two men watching there, came sliding back down the gravelly slope.

"No movement out there," he said. "I figure they'll lie in wait until we show ourselves. They've got us pinned down. We might be able to make a rush past them, or even overpower them. But, without knowing how many there are, or where they are, we're taking a risk. The big question is, where did the rest of them go."

"East along the river," said one of the soldiers.

"Yes, trooper   , east along the river," Morgan said, patiently, "But, are they going back to the main body, or are they going further afield looking for loot? Will we see them again, or are they gone for good? Is the main body up river, or down?"

"I think we might see them again," said Hardy. "They've left a few sharpshooters behind for a reason. It ain't just spite, they figure to keep us bottled up until them braves come back this way. I figure they'se got the main bunch hid up north and west, most likely beyond those fires we see up there. The braves we seen is out looking for food, horses and guns, whatever they can steal. After all, this group what run up agin' us was just fighters, no women or kids or lodge poles, so the families has got to be back up there, where they came from."

"All right then," Morgan said, "Let's suppose you're right. We can expect the warriors to come back this way sooner or later, collect the sharpshooters they left to watch us, and retreat to the northwest to the main force. That gives us several choices. We can stay and wait it out. We can break out of here and try to find a position from which we can stop...," and he paused as both Beck and Hardy began to shake their heads, mouths open to protest, "Or at least slow down the war party. Or, we can re-cross the river and head back upstream, where sooner or later we are going to make contact with whatever troops are in pursuit of the main body."

"Well lieutenant," Beck said, "keep in mind we have two wounded men to carry along. And, if we go charging out of here without knowing how many they have watching us, chances are a few more of us'll get winged. First thing should be, we need to find out who's out there, and where they are."

Morgan thought about this momentarily.

"And how do you propose we go about doing that, Mr. Beck?" he said at last.

"Why, me and Hardy are old Indian fighters, Lieutenant," Beck said with a small smile, "Scouts of the highest caliber. Him and me'll go find out for you."

"Do so!" said Morgan immediately. "But don't take long about it! I do not for a moment feel that the main party of warriors will be long in coming, if indeed they are just out on a foraging expedition. We are cut off here, and if they come at us in a determined fashion, or even re-cross the river and surround us, we will be badly cut up at least, if not cut down!"

"All right then!" said Beck with a nod, "Lige, let's go have a little chat with our friends the Nez Perce!"

The chat proved to be all one sided. When the two scouts attempted to move along the bank up the river, they left the protected area of the curved river bank and immediately came under fire from the position of the group that had engaged the south bank troops from the cover to the west. That sniper was well hidden in the driftwood tangles, and in order to drive him out, they would have to

149

cross a hundred yards of mostly open ground. Hot work for a squad of soldiers, but nearly impossible for two men.

They tried moving out east along the downstream reach of the river. There they got about a hundred yards before another sniper drove them back. As they were returning to the shelter of their outside curve of the river bend, one of the soldiers keeping watch stood slightly and turned to watch them, smirking. Two bullets clipped the wood log, one on either side of him, and he ducked quickly, smirking no longer.

"Well, they've got at least four of them out there," Hardy said, "And we know about where they are. Pretty good scoutin', wouldn't your say, lieutenant?"

"Mr. Hardy, you do not amuse me!" said Morgan.

"We can saddle up everything we got, make a charge at one of them, probably get 'im in the end. We know about where they are, but most likely they'll move about some. But then we'll have to come around and make a run at the next one, and the next," Beck said. "Each time we'll most likely get our man, but it'll cost us. We can't leave any of 'em alive as we move out, or that one'll draw blood for sure. We have to clear 'em out before we can move the wounded. So, in the end, we can take 'em one at a time, but I figure they'll get one or two of us in the bargain."

"The alternative," said Morgan, hands on his hips, looking out over the river, "Is to wait here like badgers in a hole."

"You ever gone after a badger in his hole?" Beck said.

"No. But I have seen it done, with a good dog," Morgan said.

"What happened to the dog?"

Morgan did not speak for several long moments.

"All right then," he finally said. "We need to fortify this position as best we can. We can shift some logs round, give some protection in case they cross the river and come at us from the south bank. Then we wait until dark, at which point we can attempt the river ourselves, if need be."

Beck looked at Hardy, who shrugged. They all got to work, with the sentries keeping watch. An axe was taken from the remaining mule's gear, and some of the driftwood was cut and wedged up into position. Several times shots came in from the sagebrush and driftwood tangles out on the flood plain, but no harm was done, and several good firing points were reinforced. They got a cook fire going and made coffee, and broke out the last tin of hard tack. The men who had been in the river dried their clothing in the new warmth. Morgan got the men who were off of the bank to cleaning their weapons, and the scouts did the same, taking turns so that all the rifles were not out of action at the same time.

By mid afternoon they had done what could be done, and waited on the gravelly bank under a sky gone gradually grey. No sun shown, but the weather had warmed somewhat, and they were not cold in their army greatcoats or buckskin jackets. Smoke columns bloomed in the east along the river, a grim testimony to the penetration of the warrior band. Those to the north and west and thinned and died as the day wore on.

Morgan had just taken a look at his watch and put it away in an inside pocket of his jacket when one of the men on the brow of the bank gave the alarm. They all scrambled up into the driftwood tangle and took up firing position. Out to the northeast they could see the movement of color against the brown of the autumn hills, and there the body of Nez Perce warriors flowed into view. They came up the valley hugging the bluffs, well out of rifle shot of the scouts. As the scouts watched, a handful of horsemen detached themselves from the warriors and came over the flood plane toward the river. They drew up a quarter of a mile away. One of them cantered forward toward the waiting fighters. He halted a hundred yards out, raised one hand, palm forward, and walked his horse toward the fortified brush pile. Fifty yards out he halted.

"Hey Jon Beck!" he shouted, hands on the reins as his horse skittered.

Beck looked at Morgan on one side, then over at Hardy on the other. He stood up from behind the wood pile.

"Man of the Nee-Me-Poo, will you come into our camp and share our fire?" Beck said loudly.

The warrior laughed. "You do not fool me, Jon Beck! But I come to give you good words."

"What would Two Shirts say to his old friend?"

"You are to live. We will not harm you. Go away from here and you will live."

"But we have business with your chiefs. We must go north so that we may speak with them."

"No! Do not come. You will live if you do not come!"

"We must come. You know that we must come."

"Then you will die. I say this, Two Shirts!"

"I know that you do not lie, Two Shirts. But we must come. You know that we must come."

"Waugh!" growled Two Shirts, and spat onto the ground. He shook his head, then shook his fist at the soldiers, at Jon Beck. "You are as the Two Days Behind! One Arm speaks the rifle, speaks death to all Nee-Me-Poo. You speak death as well. So be it! It shall be death!" He wheeled his horse and galloped easily away. As he passed across the flood plane, angling up river to pick up the handful of waiting horsemen and rejoin the last of the retreating war party, five mounted warriors materialized from five points on the broken ground, converging and forming up on the disappearing Two Shirts.

The other soldiers rose from their positions, letting rifles slide down to butt in the gravel.

"Looks like we can move out, lieutenant," Hardy said.

"Yes. So it appears. All right then, let's repack the mule. Anderson, take McDovy out in the river and salvage what you can from that downed mule."

The gear was brought in from the river, the remaining mule was repacked, the horses readied. They got the groggy Kilroy onto his horse, and went back for Benson. But Benson needed no help, now, for his stare was frozen and unseeing, his lifeless corpse beyond care.

Chapter 22

They heaved Benson across the saddle of his horse and tied him down, not wishing to bury him at the river where the next spring flood would wash out the corpse and carry him off to the mercy of scavengers. Beck scoured the brush piles for his spent cartridges in the mean time, rinsing them in the pool where the horses had stood, stowing them in a saddle bag. Lieutenant Morgan insisted on following after the departed Nez Perce, in the certainty that they would lead him to the main body of Indians, or his own soldiers in their pursuit, or some kind of action. Or all three.

As they left the river bank they passed by the three bodies of Nez Perce that had died charging the soldiers. Beck counted seven dead horses scattered about the area, which surprised him. He saw no other warrior bodies, which also surprised him.

"Thought we'd done more damage than this," he said to Hardy as they walked their tired mounts past the downed horses.

"Well, we got Trooper Benson in tow, don't we?" Hardy said. "They do the same for their folks."

By late afternoon they had reached the farmstead that Morgan had seen through his glass on first approaching the Yellowstone. The house was a smoking ruin, as was the barn, and a black circle on the earth nearby was all that remained of a grass hay stack. A dead cow lay in what was left of the corral attached to the barn. They paused before the house.

"Hey there!" came a hail from the brush on the bluffs. A man stood up from the sage, waved. He waded through the tangle of bushes and strode down into the farm yard. He carried a rifle, the butt of which he lowered into the dirt before the soldiers.

"Your place?" said Morgan.

"Yep. Was. Them thievin' bastards was on us pretty quick. I seen the smoke up the valley, figured they'd be comin', jes didn't figure on 'em getting' here so quick. Wife and kids up in the brush there," he said, nodding over his shoulder at the sage he had just come from.

"Anything at all left?" Morgan said.

"Yer lookin' at it."

"You might come with us, we're on our way to find the main army command chasing these red devils. You could state a claim against them, for your property."

"Ain't leavin' my place," the settler said. "It's my place."

"I'll pass along your location, what the situation is here," Morgan said. "What is your name?"

"Brockway's the name."

"You have anything to eat, Mr. Brockway?"

"Don't know. Have to look around, see what come through."

153

"Well, we have nothing to spare you, ran out of food this morning. I'll let the army command know you need help. I suspect this whole valley could use a hand about now."

"S'pect so," Brockway said, tiredly.

They began to move out, when the distant sound of gunfire came down on the wind from the west. Beck and Hardy looked at each other. The low, rumbling sound continued for a time as they rode. They tried to hurry the horses, but the animals would simply gallop a few steps, then go back to the slow, plodding walk of worn out animals.

The firing kept up for the better part of an hour, off and on again, coming in bursts. The valley of the Yellowstone widened out as they plodded west, and the flats were covered in grass, low trees, more sage brush. They came up on another smoking ruin, and as they approached several people emerged from the nearby sage flats. One of them was a woman, dressed in a close fitting grey tweed traveling habit. She carried a feathered hat, and smiled up at the soldiers, but only briefly. Two of the men carried rifles, another had two pistols stuck in his belt.

"Well it was the stage depot!" gruffly spat out the man with revolvers in his belt, "If'n that was what you was about to ask."

"Anyone injured?" Morgan said.

"Naw, they hit us right about the time the coach come in from Coulson. We high tailed it into the brush, they didn't come a'lookin' much, jes fired the place and ran off with the coach, stole the horses. I'm Ed Forrest, I run the place."

"We've been scouting their eastern flank all the way from the Crow agency," Morgan said. "Sounds like our boys finally caught 'em, up there a ways" and he nodded his head sideways further up the valley.

"Oh they been goin' at it heavy, that's certain," said one of the men with rifles, "And a good thing too, that bunch what hit us come back through moving fast, when they heard the shootin'. Probably kept 'em from comin' into the brush after us."

"Anything we can do for you now? We have no food," Morgan said.

The woman began to cry, and sat down hard on the ground where she stood. The men standing with her just looked at her. Morgan

154

scowled and swung down from his horse, took his canteen and went to her, squatting at her shoulder.

"Now ma'am, they're gone, you're safe now," he said quietly, patting her shoulder, "Here, have a little water." He unstopped the canteen and held it out to her.

"He killed Pookey!" she sobbed, "My little Pookey, never harmed a soul in the world!" She dabbed at her eyes with a handkerchief, her feathered bonnet in her lap.

Morgan looked up at the men, brow furrowed.

"Dog," said Forrest. "I had to do it, blamed thing was barkin' its head off, them Injuns was firing at the sound! Had to kill my own pup too, or tried to, he run off 'for I could finish him. He at least shut up after that."

"Her dog?" Morgan said, exasperated.

"I tell ya I had to do it! Twern't no pleasure, and it was jest a dog! If'n I hadn't done it we would ha been kilt fer sure!"

At the "jest a dog" portion of his protest, the woman broke anew into sobs.

"Come, come," Morgan said, taking the woman about the shoulders and helping her up, "Let's find some shade and get you some rest. Mr. Forrest, any hope of building a shelter of some kind?"

"May have some canvas left, we'll go see. Come on, Joe, let's have a look at the scrap pile, they may not have burned that." Forrest and one of the riflemen moved off toward the ruins of the barn and corral.

Morgan helped the woman into the shade of a small willow tree nearby the wrecked station house, and eased her down again. She took the proffered canteen and tilted it up.

They began to chat as she dried her eyes, the anguish still marring her well-painted beauty. Her tears had streaked her cheeks with the coloring about her eyes, mingled with the powder already there.

The rest of the scout party swung down. The station hands found a canvas piece, and several long poles and boards. They quickly fashioned a shelter using the willow tree to help support it, and framed in the now quiet woman as she sat. Morgan left the canteen and came over to the men.

"She's a vaudevillian, would you believe!" he said, "On her way to the mining camps to entertain."

"Hope that dog weren't part of her act," mentioned Hardy.

"Fanny Brice, her name is. A singer, and does comedy as well," Morgan went on.

"I hear them vaudeville women is whores," said one of the soldiers.

"Not at all!" Morgan protested. "I met several of them when on leave from the Point. Every one a delight, and not a single whore among them. Several quite prudish in their own way, as a matter of fact. One must keep the seeming from the fact of the person, as, after all, they are actors."

"Even the ones what lift their skirts and shake their butts at ya?" smirked another soldier.

"She isn't a chorus girl, she's a headliner. Or so she said."

"What's a headliner?" the first soldier asked.

"Why, that would be the actor at the head of the bill. The one advertised for all to come and see. The famous one." Morgan ran out of categories.

"Never heard of no Fanny Brice," muttered soldier number two.

"You've been in the west too long!" Morgan said. "Why, when I was last in Chicago—"

"Lieutenant I hate to bust up this fine tete-a-tete about that lovely Miss Brice over there, but I think we got company!" Beck said, looking up the valley over the back of Bill.

They all turned to look in the same direction, and there, coming across the flats half a mile away, were dozens of horses, and riders with them. The late afternoon sun was at their backs, and the soldiers could not determine who the riders might be.

"Quick!" shouted Morgan, mounting up with a leap onto his horse's back, "You people, back into the brush!" he shouted at the civilians. Miss Brice gave a shriek and jumped to her feet, and the three men helped her on either side as they scurried into the sage once more.

"Ain't no cover in a quarter mile, lieutenant!" Beck said. "I think we best join 'em, at least for now."

Morgan looked at the oncoming animals, then all around him. "Right!" he said, "Come on!" He spurred his mount, which responded sluggishly, to the edge of the nearby sage flats, dismounted, and the others tugged their tired horses and the mule along to join him. Two of the soldiers mounted up, and took the reins of the remaining horses and plunged deeper into the rolling brush land. Beck snatched his rifle from its scabbard as Bill was led off. The soldiers and scouts spread out into the brush and squatted down out of sight.

Beck could see through the few bushes to his front, and the herd of horses came into his view. Indian outriders moved the heard along with war whoops and prods from their rifle barrels into the flanks of the reluctant ponies. The riders did not seem to care that a group of potential enemies had just disappeared into cover as they approached.

"Well damme, they're Crows!" Hardy said, standing up. Two of the braves screeched at him in passing, and he hollered something in Crow at them. One of the last riders in the pack drew his pony aside and galloped up to stop in front of the scout party, all of whom had risen from the scrub.

"High Place!" bellowed Hardy, "What in tarnation you get yerself into now?"

"Hah, Man of Magpie Woman, we go to our lodges. The fight is finished!."

"Nee-Me-Poo finished?"

"Nee-Me-Poo run, go to Grandmother's Land. Leave these fine horses to Crow!"

"But what about scouting? You work for us now, you come scout with us now to the north!"

"No! Many fine horses, we take them to our lodges! Atsina, Stone People steal them if we do not take them to our lodges. The young men are rich with horses, they can marry now and be rich too."

"But you have a wife, High Place!" Hardy said, "You don't need more horses! Come with us, scout as you promised to do. Big medicine for him who comes to fight, much glory!"

"No! Cannot eat medicine, cannot ride glory. We take these horses to our lodges. Big medicine already rides with Man On A High Place!" he shouted, jerking two scalps from his belt and holding them high. With another shriek he heeled his pony into a gallop and headed down the valley after the receding herd.

Hardy shook his head, spat into the dust, mumbled curses. "Hell, I thought he was civilized. He's just as bad as the rest of 'em," he grumbled disgustedly.

"Well, Lige, you can hardly blame 'em. They came for horses, they got 'em, they went home. Besides, maybe he's wrong, maybe the army stopped 'em after all," Beck said.

Morgan hollered for the horses to come up, and they all mounted. He told the civilians now coming again from the sage that he would send an army detail back with food as soon as possible. The scouts started once again up the valley.

The broad flood plain of the Yellowstone broadened further still, and a flat valley flanked by high bluffs soon appeared in the northwest. They passed the remains of the stage coach half a mile from the station, on its side. Strewn about it was mail from several pouches, luggage smashed open, clothing in bedraggled heaps and ribbons on the sage brush. The horses were gone.

Another herd of horses was run past them down river by more Crow warriors. They paid no attention to the scouts, intent as they were in controlling their new found wealth. As the scouts came up to the mouth of the wide side valley, a party of troopers, in a column of fours, topped a low rise and cantered up to them.

The lieutenant in charge halted the column, and offered his hand to Lieutenant Morgan. Morgan took it.

"I'm Barrington. You the scouts on the east flank?" he said.

"Yes. Fifth Calvary, Captain Peachbow's command. I'm Morgan, this is Beck and Hardy, my chief scouts," he added, nodding over his shoulder at the two men. "What happened here?"

"Sturgis finally caught 'em!" said Barrington. "Or at least, we got close to 'em. Ran 'em up Canyon Creek, up there to the northwest. Crow scouts got to their herd, nipped off part of 'em, killed a few of the herders. We've gone into camp up near the mouth of the canyon, have a hospital set up. I believe the colonel will be waiting on Howard to come up, and for the supply train to get here. We're down on rations. My men and I are scouting the lower Yellowstone, make sure we are not surprised, see what the damage is. You come from that way?"

"We did. Had a little fight six or eight miles down the river. Maybe sixty, eighty braves ran us to ground, went on down the river, maybe ten, twelve miles all told, as we could see by the smoke of the fires they set. They came back the same way, bypassed us. We'd have been wiped out for sure if they'd set their minds to it. As you can see, they hit us hard enough," Morgan said, nodding to the wounded and dead men.

"What of the civilians down the river?"

"Everything we saw was burned out, but no casualties. One farm, a stage station. Coach taken and destroyed, all the horses run off. They tried to destroy the mails. Not sure about further down, we didn't go that way."

"We will. In the mean time, follow our trail back the way we came, when you hit Canyon Creek, bear to the north. You'll find Sturgis camped about four, five miles up, and the hospital for your wounded."

"Good luck, Barrington. We"ll see you up at the camp, I would guess," Morgan said.

The soldiers moved off down the valley, and the scouts in the opposite direction. They found the creek, running at just a trickle, and turned up its valley. The evening came as the grey light began to fail, and they finally found the army camp just as the last of the light disappeared from the land. A sentry hailed them, they identified themselves, and asked directions to the hospital. There they got the wounded man down and into the care of the surgeon, and unlashed the body of Benson and slid him off of his horse and into a row of covered bodies. The battle had been the last one for a dozen men. Their canvas covered forms were laid out like cartridges in a belt, uniform in the reflected light from the hospital staff's fire.

Morgan, Beck and Hardy led their horses to the colonel's tent, and tethered them with others along a picket line. They went in to meet with Sturgis.

Morgan braced, saluted, received the casual salute from Sturgis as he rose from peering at a map spread on his camp table, its upper corners held down by two lanterns. Two of his captains were with him, and a lieutenant.

Morgan made his report, detailing the scouting over the last several days, the crossing of the Yellowstone, the fight with the Nez Perce, and what he had seen coming up the valley after the fight. Sturgis, chewing tobacco as he listened, caused his officers to dance out of the way as he turned his head to spit tobacco juice, his attention on Morgan and his aim somewhat haphazard.

"And I should like to note, sir, that the actions of Mr. Pocket and Mr. Beck went above the call of duty and honor, sir, in the saving of my life personally, and in the saving of the detail as a whole," he finished up.

"How so, lieutenant?" Sturgis said, glancing at the men so named.

"Mr. Beck stopped me from riding into the face of an overwhelming hostile force, sir, turning me back in time to take up the defense of the command, and bring it to a successful ending. And Mr. Pocket, acting on his own initiative, single handedly attacked half a dozen Nez Perce warriors, diverting them from an attack on our flank which surely would have destroyed us but for his efforts."

"Well," said Sturgis, "Well, gentlemen, my congratulations on your excellent results. Lieutenant Morgan, your full written report will reflect upon the heroic actions of your scouts, I am sure. I am afraid I cannot release you to Peachbow just yet, and I request your further action on behalf of this command."

"Of course, sir!" Morgan said, still bracing.

"And stand at ease, lieutenant," Sturgis said.

"Of course, sir. Thank you, sir," Morgan said, relaxing slightly.

"Gentlemen, join us at the table, please. Or, perhaps I should ask, have you eaten?"

"No colonel, we ran out of food this morning," Morgan said.

"Henry," Sturgis said to his orderly, "Bring whatever we have left in the pot. Now gentlemen, here is the situation. We have chased the savages down Clarke's fork, through here," and he swept a finger along the crooked line of the river on the map, "and our scouts advised us earlier this afternoon of their presence a few miles up Canyon Creek. We have conducted operations against them most of the latter part of the day. Unfortunately our mounts were played out to the point of not being able to head them before they gained the canyon, and they have gone on ahead once again. Our rations are essentially gone, our horses are essentially worn out, the men are exhausted, and Howard, we are told, is only a day or so back. In light of all this, we have gone into camp as you see us, and will remain here for a day or so to re-victual the command and await General Howard. I have sent scouts out into the lower Yellowstone valley to see about forage for the horses. From what you tell me some grass in available in the field, but all cut hay has been destroyed by the Nez Perce."

"It would seem so, colonel," Morgan said.

"We have the scout Fisher with us, come ahead from Howard, and some of his people. I would like your force to join him and get on after the Nez Perce first thing. We must determine where they go, keep them under our eye at all times."

"Any fresh mounts to be had, colonel?" said Hardy.

"Only those captured from the Nez Perce. Fischer and his Crow scouts got into their herd during the battle, and I am told a sizeable number of animals have been cut out. We may have a source of mounts there, but hardly broken to our gear or way. I have a man out now assessing that situation. As for the army mounts, as I said, we are flat against it there. Can you leave at dawn, with Fisher's blessing, of course?"

"Colonel, our own horses are as your own," Beck said. "We'll do what we can, but it is nearly impossible to get more than a walk from the animals without resting them, and getting them some kind of feed."

"Well," Sturgis said, "Let's examine the situation and work out what needs to be done."

Food came in the form of hard tack and some beans. The latter was hot food, and the scouts dug in with gusto. More talk of the day's battles, both up river and down, and then the scouts left the tent for the bitter cold night air. Sturgis remained at the map talking with his officers. Beck, Pocket and Hardy unsaddled their mounts, and Beck rubbed Bill down with a tow sack one of the soldiers gave him. He led the big horse to the creek, which had been reduced to a few alkaline pools here and there along its normal course. Bill sniffed at the foul water but would not drink.

Hardy came down with his horse, and Pocket behind him.

"Alkali water here," Beck said, "Maybe they brought water up from the Yellowstone."

"So you and Simon are heroes now," chuckled Hardy, "mentioned in dispatches, no less."

"Surprised the hell out of me!" said Beck.

"Well I figure the lieutenant for a right smart feller. That was white of 'im!" Pocket said, quite pleased with his new found accolades.

"It do sorta cast him in a new light, I will admit that," said Hardy.

"We get any extra pay or such fer bein' heroes?" Pocket said.

"Nope," Beck said. "And since we are civilians working for the army, you don't even get a medal or nothing!"

"Well consarn it," Pocket chuckled, "this heroin' business ain't much of a benefit to a man's pocketbook, now is it! Think I'll go back to bein' a plain ol' scout fer a livin'."

"And I'll ride with you anytime, Simon. Us hero fellers have got to stick together, fer all that," Beck said. "We'll let Hardy tag along in a pinch, though."

He was leading the big horse back up to the camp when a cry went up. Bugles sounded. Men began scurrying about, saddling horses, cursing in the darkness.

"What's up?" Beck said to a trooper carrying a saddle by them in the dark.

"Not sure. Scouts came in, from what I gather the Nez Perce are just a few miles up the canyon, and Sturgis is bound and determined to close up and take 'em at dawn. Here we go again, brother!"

"Well Lige," Beck said as they reached the picket line and their gear, "You didn't need any sleep anyway, right?"

"Hell no! But I sure could use a shot of rye!" Hardy said.

"I'll second that!" said Pocket, saddling his horse on the other side of Hardy. They got the animals ready for the trail, and Beck found a water bucket with half its contents intact. He sniffed at it, and it smelled sweet. He took it back to the horses and let Bill get a few good slurps, then the other two horses. It was soon empty.

"Seen Fisher anywhere?" Beck said, as he swung up into the saddle.

"Nope, but I figure it might have been him coming in with the news," Hardy said.

"Well, let's see if we can't hunt him up and find out what he'd have us do, eh?"

"Shore 'nough," Hardy said. They turned the horses and urged them off toward the area where the command was forming up in the darkness. The cold of the night turned their breath to ghostly clouds in the starlight.

Chapter 23

The scouts rode their tired horses over to the columns of soldiers forming up. They sat in the dark, waiting, while the soldiers found their units by word of mouth and eased their horses into lines, jostling, nudging, the tired mounts putting up no fight. After twenty minutes, a group of officers and two civilians came out of the colonel's tent, spoke with other officers and sergeants waiting there, and then several forms came across the darkness, silhouetted by the light in the camp. They came up to the body of men and one of them announced, loudly, "All soldiers to stand down, picket your horses, return to your bed rolls, men. We will rise at 04:00 hours to prepare to move out before dawn! You are dismissed!"

The man muttered and grumbled, a soft curse or two rumbling up from the back ranks, and they rode their mounts back to the picket ropes. The scouts began to go, but were stopped.

"You men are the scouts who came in from down river?" said one of the men, unseen in the darkness.

"That would be us," Hardy said.

"Picket your animals and report to the colonel's tent, if you please," said the man. He and his unseen partner turned and headed back to the camp.

Beck heeled Bill into a walk back toward the picket ropes.

"Well at least we'll get a little sleep after all," he said.

They tied up the horses, stripped them of their gear, and went to the tent as ordered. Inside they found Sturgis and a civilian man pouring over the maps. Sturgis straightened, said, "Gentlemen, this is Mr. Fisher, my Chief of Scouts. Mr. Fisher, this is Beck, Hardy, and...I am afraid I have forgotten your name, sir?" he said to Simon.

"That would be Simon Pocket," Pocket said, as he shook hands with Fisher in turn.

"Pleasure to meet you, gents!" Fisher said loudly.

"Mr. Fisher has just come in with the news that the Nez Perce were seen to have begun erecting a fortification just up the canyon several miles," Sturgis went on, "And we undertook to go have a look. His scouts have since come in behind him with the news that this is not a permanent camp, as originally thought, but merely an impediment. So we have stood the men down for a rest, and we will pursue at first light. I must leave you now to make our arrangements for the morning. I would ask that you gentlemen work under Mr. Fisher in future, as we need all the scouts we can muster."

"Fine with us, colonel" Beck said.

"That's settled, then. I bid you gentlemen good night." Sturgis left the tent.

Fisher came around the table and leaned his butt against it, arms folded.

"You boys have a long pull of it?" he asked. His voice had a sharp edge to it that carried.

"'Bout like you'd expect," Beck said, "We came up through the Crow camps, scouted all that country south and west of Heart Mountain, then north to the Yellowstone. We had a little harassment from a few Nez Perce riders, them wantin' to keep us at arm's length from the main bunch. Made the Yellowstone about the time their raiders was hitting all the farms and towns down river from Canyon Creek, had us a little fight when they went by, then again when they drew back up river. They didn't make a real effort to wipe us out, which sort of surprised me, but I'm sure they had their reasons. We come up late in the day, found the camp here about dark."

"What shape are your animals in?" Fisher said.

"Pretty well played out, like most of the mounts here."

"That's been our biggest problem, finding fresh mounts," Fisher said. "We've had no time to search the surrounding country for horses or mules. The Nez Perce of course have hundreds of fresh mounts in their herd. The Crow got in among them today and cut out several hundred head, but it did not slow them down much. And now we find that the horses taken by the Crow are gone."

"Yes, we saw a couple of herds heading east, Crow warriors takin' 'em home, I would say," Hardy said. "Looked like they took a few scalps, too."

"Oh yes," Fisher spat, "Old men and boys mostly do the herding for the Nez Perce. The Crow killed a few, great warriors that they are."

"Well now," Hardy said, "they all do it. A scalp is a scalp to them, once it's on yer belt there ain't no telling how you got it."

"Not all of them," Fisher said. "The Nez Perce don't take scalps. Pretty much the only tribe I know of that don't."

"From what I hear they do enough killin' to make up for it," Hardy said.

"Seems to be the rule on both sides," Fisher said. "At any rate, here is what we are going to do. The Nez Perce have run up Canyon Creek. On either shoulder of the canyon is table land, cut up pretty roughly by gullies, side canyons and the like. I am certain they are running for the Canadian border. They will take whatever route is direct, and provides forage for their animals.

"I and my scouts will dog them on their main route. I need you and your people to take the eastern flank, and I will have another party out on the western flank. Do you have any Crow with you?"

"We did before we hit the Yellowstone," Beck said. "Ain't seen hide nor hair of 'em since we crossed the river. 'Cept to watch 'em drive their new horses by us on their way home."

"The red man has his own form of gold, you know," Fisher smirked.

"And we had half a dozen soldiers with us," Beck said. "They were Fifth Cavalry, part of Peachbow's outfit. Maybe we could get 'em along with us, if Sturgis don't have no use for 'em."

"I'll see what I can do," Fisher said. "Now, let's take a look at the map, then we can hit the saddle."

"You mean ride out tonight?" Hardy said.

"Of course!" Fisher grinned. "You think the Nez Perce are waiting around on our pleasure?"

Hardy swore as they moved around the table to examine the maps. There they found a way for the scouts to skirt the bluffs to the south and come up on the table lands to the east. It would mean a ten mile ride in the dark just to get to the top of the cliffs that could be seen from the camp in the east during the day.

Sturgis returned, and it was agreed that Lieutenant Morgan and his men would again accompany Beck and Hardy. The orderly was sent off to find the lieutenant and his men, and summon them to the tent. Sturgis had no supplies to give the scouts, but promised re-supply at the Musselshell River, a few dozen miles to the north. He proposed to move out in the morning, and thought perhaps General Howard and his troops might catch up by then. His orders were to pursue at all costs, and he did not intend to wait if they did not show up.

Beck, Hardy and Pocket left the tent and again went to their animals and began to saddle up. The horses were stolid, unmoving, exhausted. The scouts finished readying their animals, and awaited their army escort.

"You figure we can even catch up to them Nez Perce?" Pocket said. "By the time we go all the way around to get up on that table land, heck, they'll be in Canada!"

"We ain't goin' that way," Hardy said.

"You figure the east fork?" Beck said.

"I do," said Hardy, "Simon, you recall on that map there was a fork in Canyon Creek, couple of miles up?"

"Sure," said Pocket.

"Well, if we take that fork, we can get up on the table land about a mile out that way. Then all we have to do is move east another mile or so, then north, and 'fore you know it, we're back on the rim above the west fork, and we can shadow 'em easy." Hardy made it sound like child's play.

"Fisher don't know that way?" said Pocket.

"Most likely not," said Hardy. "Them maps is sort of general, like, don't show that the canyon wall is no more than a steep grade through a part of that east fork. I been through that country, and I know we can climb it."

"Why'nt you say something to Fisher?" Pocket said.

"Why hell, we's scouts, we don't need no maps and what not," Hardy chuckled. "This way we'll look like we earned our pay."

"Lige, you are a caution," Beck said.

Soon Lieutenant Morgan rode up in the dark, the breath of his horse puffing ghostly white in the crisp cold, his form looming dark in the saddle. He had two men trailing along behind him.

"Mr. Beck, I see we are to forge ahead after these renegades in your good company once again," he said. "Have you managed to secure any rations for your animals?"

"None, lieutenant," Beck said, swinging up onto Bill. "We'll only have what we can find on the land."

They moved out slowly in the dark, Beck leading, Hardy on his flank. The little column passed out of the camps and across the washed out valley to the creek bed, then up the canyon to the northwest. They moved slowly, the horses' heads low to the ground in fatigue and in peering at the footing ahead as they went. The canyon walls rose in screed slopes dotted with brush and timber, then abruptly up in sheer rock ramparts of several hundred feet high. After two hours, during which they had covered the same number of miles, they came to the fork and steered the horses in their plodding, short striding gait up the canyon branching off to the right. They had gone only a quarter of a mile when the lieutenant, riding behind Hardy, said quietly, "I think we are being followed!"

They all reined in, sat, listened. Behind them they heard the clicking and clattering of hooves on the rocks of the creek bed. The sound carried up the canyon for a time, then gradually faded away.

"That would most likely be Fisher and some of his scouts," Beck said. They all sat listening for a bit, and Beck added, "Sounds like they went on up the main canyon."

They started again, and several hours later began to find the light coming up, and shapes and shadows materializing out of the blackness of the night. Overhead the high sky paled, and on their left the vertical rock walls had given way to steep ramps of rock and earth. They drew up at the base of one of these slopes.

"Is that what you had in mind?" Beck said to Hardy, nodding at the steep bank just visible in the new light.

"That would be the place," Hardy said.

"On a fresh horse, maybe," Beck said. "Hell, that's a pretty good climb for a man on foot."

"It gets easier a mile or so up the canyon, if'n yer too scared o' this one," Hardy smirked.

"Well now, Lige," Beck said, "I'm always willing to learn. Show us the way, if you please," and he swung his arm in a broad gesture of acquiescence.

"Don't mind if I do!" Hardy said. He put the spurs to his horse and steered him onto the lower slope. The animal climbed across the face at an angle, going in great bounds for the first fifty yards, then slowing to a halfhearted leaping, pausing between lunges, then, about two thirds of the way to the top, came to a halt. Hardy's spurs got two more feeble jumps out of the exhausted mount, and then, no matter what he did, the animal just stood on the side of the slope, his head hanging, sides heaving. Finally Hardy turned him down the hill, and he came down tentatively, sliding on his haunches at times, rocks rattling down with him and then he was at the bottom and back with the other horses. He stood trembling, blowing hard.

"About a mile up the canyon, you say?" Beck grinned.

Hardy said nothing, just patted the horse's neck.

Beck led off up the canyon floor, following the flats left by the spring flooding creek water where it had scoured the rocks clean or left beds of sand. Another half hour and they found another place where the canyon wall was mostly scree and sloping dirt, with very low stone ramparts at the top. Several places showed where the ramp of dirt went all the way to the canyon rim. The canyon was not as deep there, and the slope not as steep.

"Looks like a possible, here," Beck said.

"Even easier further up," Hardy said.

"Let me show you how it's done," Beck said. He guided big Bill over to the base of the slope, and then started him up by going across the slope more than up it, gaining a yard up for every three he traveled. He walked the horse to the edge of the dirt, where a pile of fallen rock blocked his way, then turned him back across the slope the other way. They went two hundred yards angling gently up to another rock slide, then back again. In this way he got the horse, moving slowly to be sure, up to the rocky outcroppings at the top.

He walked Bill along the line of rocky teeth that jutted ten feet above him, looking for a space between them that would allow the horse to keep his footing in the soft earth and gravel. He found a likely place, and, turning Bill straight up the gully, spurred him on. The big horse lunged up the slope, and nearly made it to the top when he lost his footing and slid. They stayed together as the horse pawed at the yielding earth, going backwards as the bank gave way, coming to rest about where they had started.

Beck let the horse breathe, looking along the line of rocks for another way. He then walked Bill along the line of overhanging stones and found another slope of dirt through the rock outcroppings, this one broader. He dismounted, and, kicking the toes of his boots into the soft earth, made his way up the slope to the top. He looked around, and came back down to Bill. He took the reins and went back up on foot, leading the horse, which came slowly after, digging for purchase in the soft, sliding ground, and together they clawed their way to the top. With a scramble of hooves and flying dirt, Bill was over the edge and on flat ground.

Beck came back to the rim, looked down at the scouts.

"And that's the way it's done!" he called out softly. "Come on!"

Morgan started his horse on the trail left by Bill, and the others followed. Beck went back to his tired mount, the horse's breath fogging white in the first light of the new day. The horse was trembling.

"You know you're a magnificent sonovabitch, don'tcha?" he said, rubbing Bill's ears and scratching his neck. Bill nickered a bit.

Morgan reached the base of the final ramparts and dismounted, led his horse onto the final slope. It took them two tries to get the animal over the rim. The two soldiers came next, and the reluctant mounts just did not want to even try the final slope. With one man tugging the reins and another slapping the horses' rumps with a belt, they got the mounts to the top. Simon Pocket got his pony up in one scramble, rider in the saddle. Hardy finally reached the base of the rim rocks, his horse heaving and shaking. Nothing he could do would induce the animal to try the final slope. They finally got Simon's lariat tied to Hardy's saddle, two men behind slapping and pushing, and two more on the reins hauling the exhausted animal forward. Simon's cow pony backed hard on the other end of the lariat and Hardy's animal came, one trembling lurch at a time. Then it was over the top, skidding on its knees, and the men gave a little cheer.

The dawn was brightening in the east. The east fork canyon wound away to the northeast. The main fork canyon could be seen out to the north and west, winding through the mesa land, with smaller gullies, washes and canyons feeding into it. In the northern distance the land flattened under a purple morning sky, and seemed to roll like an unbroken prairie. They could see places scattered about the distance that appeared to be groves of trees and brush, thicker than that of the canyon walls, with grass lands predominating into the far north.

Morgan came to stand beside Beck.

"They're out in that canyon somewhere," Beck said, nodding toward the north fork.

"Out there," Morgan said, pointing to the table top lands that stretched before them to the north and east, "seems to be the easiest going. If we can make good time there, we can get to a point ahead of them, with luck."

"That's true," Beck said, "but without water and forage, these horses won't last the day. That's the first priority."

169

"The Nez Perce are the first priority!" Morgan said.

"How far do you think you'll get on foot?" Beck said.

Morgan just looked out over the rolling country. The wind was cold and cutting on the table lands, and Beck could feel it inch its icy fingers into every opening in his clothes as they stood. Finally Morgan said, "Water and forage it is. And don't pass up a chance at game, either," he said over his shoulder. "Shots may alert them we are here, but we can't hide up here in the open anyway. And we need food as badly as the horses do."

"Lieutenant, there's hope for you yet," Beck said.

While Morgan was assigning his men to sweep out across the rolling table lands in different directions, Beck got his moccasins out of his saddle kit and changed into them.

He then scanned the land ahead with his spyglass. He spotted a green swale, six or seven miles to the north, that looked to be more substantial than the tufts of green scattered here or there across the plain.

"Lieutenant, out there straight to the north, there's a grove of trees, some green stuff growing, might be water there," he said, handing the glass to Morgan. The lieutenant squinted into the eyepiece, wavering slightly in the direction Beck had pointed, then settled in and studied it.

"Could be," he said.

"Let's make our sweep along the Canyon Creek rim, and meet there about mid day. With luck, may be water for the horses, some grass," Beck said.

They scattered then, the tired horses walking at their own pace no matter how much their riders spurred or slapped them with reins. Beck set out at a walk, leading Bill who plodded along behind, eyes half lidded, head down. Pocket moved off to the northeast, the army men spread their forces to the northwest heading for the breaks above Canyon Creek, and Hardy trailed along behind big Bill. Soon he, too, dismounted and walked, coming up beside Beck as they trudged over the dry prairie grass. The sun lanced out its first rays of gold over the rim of the earth in the east. The wind came into their faces, an easy breeze but with the cold, stinging prick of cat's claws. Beck pulled his hat lower against the cold, fingered closed the top button of his fleece-lined coat.

"You know," Hardy said, "I figure them Nez Perce just might make it. Into Canada, I mean. They've got the edge in horses, and they ain't slowing down any. There ain't a fresh mount in the whole army command. I don't figure we have a prayer of stayin' with 'em, let alone headin' 'em."

"I figure Fisher's the only hope we got," Beck said. "If he and his scouts can slow 'em down somehow, we have a chance."

"What d'you know of Fisher?" Hardy said.

"Heard of him, never met him before last night. They say he can stick like pitch on a porcupine's ass to whatever he's chasing. Seems like a no nonsense sort of feller."

"Where you figure all our Crow went?"

"Home with the horses, most likely."

"Wish to hell they'd left a few for remounts. Even Injun-broke ponies would be better'n walking."

On and on they walked over the rolling country. They caught a glimpse of the army men over on the breaks, crossing a ridge here and there. They weren't moving fast. The wind brought the faint sound of gunfire several times. Late in the morning they came up to half a mile of the green oasis Beck had spied out on the brown prairie. Bill had perked up some, and his ears were working the wind, his nostrils flaring a bit. He nickered, and Beck noticed his interest.

"Something up ahead there's got Bill perked up," he said. "Probably water in those trees."

As they looked ahead again at the swale, two riders broke cover from among the brush, headed right at them at full gallop.

"Who the hell...?" Hardy said, squinting at the riders.

"May be some of Fisher's Crows coming in to report," Beck said. The two riders, crouched low over their mounts' necks, kept coming hard. "Look at the right foreleg of that one on the left!" he said, stepping back to the rifle on Bill flank and drawing it out of its leather. "That white band, cuttin' across the knee like that, that's Two Shirts pony or I'm a badger's butt!" He stepped up before Bill, went down on one knee and racked a round into the rifle's chamber.

"I do believe you are right!" Hardy said, going for his own rifle.

Beck steadied the long gun with his left elbow on his knee, palm up under the fore end of the rifle, nestled the butt stock against his cheek, lined up the sights on the left rider. The two horsemen were

171

two hundred yards out, and Beck squeezed the trigger. The big gun boomed and slapped back against his shoulder, the smoke instantly clearing on the wind past his face. Both approaching riders fired then, the smoke puffs in front of them also gone in an instant, and the bullets whizzed overhead. Beck racked in a new round, steadied the gun, and the two riders split suddenly, one going right and the other left, still coming but swinging wide of the scouts. Hardy fired, then Beck again, then the horsemen as they thundered down on the scouts, out about seventy or eighty yards, both now hanging onto the off-sides of their ponies, firing over their backs, passing by on the outside. Beck fired again, making no hits, as did Hardy. The bullets coming at the scouts whizzed high, then low, kicking up dust out in the flats in the dry prairie grass.

"Ah the hell with it!" Beck said, and drew a bead on the horse crossing before him, and squeezed off the shot. The animal went into the earth instantly, flipping over to skid to a halt rump first, and its rider rolled away over the grass a few yards. Beck rose and ran around the rear of their horses, and threw up his rifle at the second Nez Perce rider now receding quickly out of range. As they watched, the rider, now a quarter of a mile out, cut to his right and headed west, crossed the scout's back trail and quickly disappeared down a shallow gully.

Beck turned and took off at a run to the west, heading for the downed horse, his rifle held before him ready for instant action. He came up on the dead animal, but the rider was gone. A depression in the tableland about fifty yards away was the only cover at hand. Beck ran to it, arriving at the rim in time to see the second rider on the shallow grade below extend a hand to the running brave Beck had dismounted. They were a hundred yards out, and he thought of trying a shot, but knew it was hopeless. The runner caught the offered arm and swung up behind the rider as the horse hardly missed a stride. They were soon lost in the breaks of the north fork canyon.

Beck turned and walked back to the downed horse. It had been hit in the neck, breaking it, dead before it had hit the ground. He had been leading it at the head, and thought to himself that the bullet had traveled faster than he had reckoned. The big Winchester was teaching his new things every time he fired it.

.

He headed on back to their horses, and as he arrived he could see Simon Pocket coming across the grass from the east. Beck unloaded his rifle, then reloaded the magazine, leaving the chamber empty, and shoved the rifle back into the scabbard on Bill.

"Do any damage on your side?" he said to Hardy as he looked Bill over from stem to stern. A bullet had pierced the end of his rolled up ground tarp. Another had creased his saddle seat. Bill was untouched. He began picking up his spent cartridge casings.

"No harm here," Hardy said, looking over his own mount.

"That was Two Shirts for sure," Beck said, "that was his pony. Hated to have to shoot him, but what the hell, this is war."

Pocket came up and stopped before them.

"You boys havin' all the fun, as usual," he said with a small smile. "Saw the whole thing from over yonder, just comin' in to report. Ain't nothin' out thetaway," he said, jerking a thumb over his shoulder to the east.

"I figure there's something in those trees up there," Beck said, nodding at the tangle of green the Indians had come from.

"Funny the way those Injuns came at you like that," Pocket said, falling in beside the scouts as they took up their reins and started walking again for the copse of foliage just ahead.

"I figure they was usin' good tactics," Hardy said. "They seen the Crow and Bannock scouts all over the country, running around full tilt, I think they figured if they come right at us, they could get in close enough to shoot us down before we realized they was not our own scouts. If ol' Jon there hadn't recognized one of their horses for who it belonged to, they may have got away with it!"

"They ain't shy about a good fight, that's fer sure," Pocket said.

They soon reached the outer brush of the little knot of forest, and, tying their horses to the first bushes, they moving into the brush and tress, guns at the ready. They shouldered through the last of the bushes into a clearing.

"We'll I'll be go to hell," Hardy said, lowing his rifle. There before them was a spring, a small pool, and a rivulet trickling off toward the northwest. And beside the trickle of water was half of a buffalo carcass, the hind quarters missing.

"The mother lode!" said Hardy, laughing.

"Simon, you go over there in that flat and get a fire going," Beck said. "Lige, let's you and me take a quick scout around these trees, make sure we're not bothered. Then lets get some of that buffalo on the fire and eat up!"

They split up to accomplish these tasks, and the two scouts came in with the horses as the fire flared up before Simon. The horses went immediately to water, and Hardy and Beck drew their long knives and commenced to peeling back the thick, hairy hide still on the fore part of the buffalo. Soon they had slabs of shoulder steak suspended on pointed sticks over the flames.

They ate their fill, and set the horses to grazing in the brown grass just to the east of the trees. They took turns on sentry duty, and Simon was on lookout when he gave a low holler, "Riders comin' in. Army."

All three of the army men were coming, and Pocket waved them on when they could see him. They had dismounted and led their horses into the thicket, breaking through into the little meadow, when their tired, gaunt faces brightened instantly as they took in the riches before them, food and water for man and beast. Without a word they took the horses to the little pool, and turned to the meat the scouts had set over the fire in readiness for them.

They tore into the buffalo, burning their fingers in their haste, finally carving off chunks of the dripping meat with their knives and tenderly nibbling at it until their hunger conquered all fear of burns. Wolves would have considered them beasts, as they tore into the fat dripping meat.

As the horses slurped up all they could hold of the water, which nearly drained the little pool, Beck and Pocket led the horses to grass, turned them loose to eat. Pocket stayed with the animals to keep an eye on things.

"See anything down along the rim?" Beck asked Morgan.

"Not much," the lieutenant mumbled as he chewed. "Heard firing up on the table, later two Indians riding the same horse passed us up above. Too far out to make out who they were."

"Nez Perce," Beck said. "They came from this spot, made a run at us as we were coming up. I figure some of their people killed this buff, took off the hind quarters and lit out fer camp. Some of the others heard about it, came for the rest. Didn't have time to get anything afore we come along. They made a run right at us, we figure they hoped to get in close and shoot us down before we realized they weren't Crow. Didn't shoot our horses, though, I figure they meant to use 'em to take the meat back. I recognized one of their horses, belonged to one of my old Nez Perce friends, Two Shirts. Hadn't of been for that, they might have carried it off."

"You kill one of their horses?" Morgan said, wiping his chin of the grease.

"Had to. But they got by us anyway, and that's when you saw 'em."

"We also heard firing down the canyon," Morgan said. "Maybe Fisher and his scouts have got in among 'em."

"Could be. For sure they ain't coming this way," Beck said.

"Well, let's get mounted up and after 'em, then!" Morgan said, turning to look after the horses.

"If I might make a suggestion," Beck said. "The horses are played out. This is the first good feed they've had in days. The men, all of us, are hungry, or will be again soon, and you heard Sturgis say he has no rations. I say we take an hour or two, let the horses feed up, and take the time to cook some more of this meat, at least a pound of two for each man. I promise you, it will look like pure gold tomorrow if we don't find rations at the Musselshell."

"We have no time to waste!" said Morgan, "If that firing we heard was Sturgis catching the Nez Perce at last, we are missing out on the final battle. I want to be there when those devils are finally crushed!"

"Lieutenant," Beck said levelly, "think about it. One hour, give or take, will make all the different to our stock, and to our own bellies. One hour, give or take, will not mean a tinker's damn to your final battle. No one is going to run them Nez Perce to earth and beat 'em down in the time it takes to care for the stock properly! You've seen how the Nez Perce operate up to now. They're tough, and they can shoot. It won't be over by the time we get there, I know that, and you know that. So, let's take care of what needs to be done here, and then we can be on our way, in much better shape to carry out our duty."

Once again, Lieutenant Morgan looked off through the trees, his jaw working as he thought it out.

"I ain't trying to tell you what to do," Beck finally said. "It's your decision, and we'll go along. I promise you, from what I know of the Nez Perce, this is far from over."

Finally, Morgan said, "All right. Let's get all the meat on the fire we possibly can. When that spring gets the water in that puddle back up, get the canteens filled. Let the horses eat while we can. We'll water 'em again on the way out. If we must wait, we will wait. But only for an hour."

Chapter 24

The hour turned into two, then three. The horses worked steadily at the grass, and the men butchered the buffalo carcass, chopping sticks of green wood to pinion the pieces of meat over the flames and coals, gathering firewood, and eating some of the cooked meat as it came from the fire. Having had no decent food in days, it was difficult to ignore the sizzling, charred flesh as it came from the heat, even with bellies crammed painfully full. The salty taste of it was like an elixir, transfixing them with a brutish desire for more, more. At last they became torpid, slow, lazy, the warmth of the fire giving relief from the cut of the prairie wind, the trees of the little wood blocking the breeze. Morgan could see his men slow down, mired in warmth and full bellies and the desire for rest. He knew they wanted more than anything to sleep, as he himself battled to keep his eyelids from crashing down. As he detailed first one man, then another to relieve the first, each for an hour to stand watch over the horses, then a third, he realized they might not ever in his lifetime leave this place.

With a great effort he gave the order to break camp. The meat was wrapped in whatever each man could find and stowed in saddlebags, kits, sacks. Canteens were filled, and the horses brought in, saddled, turned into the last of the water in the little pond. They broke up the fire, and with Beck and Hardy leading the way, left the little forest of blessed shelter and struck out at a walk across the grassy plain toward the north.

The late afternoon wind still cut like a cold razor as they headed into it, heads down, coats wrapped tightly about them. The soldiers headed off to the front, left and right, and the riders spread out to cover as much ground as possible. They saw no single soul through the afternoon, working their tired mounts down the long slopes of the tablelands toward the valley of the Musselshell in the distance. The last of the light found them gathering at the base of a small bluff, where they camped in a draw out of the wind. The soldiers built a fire of the dead scrub wood rimming the draw, and they heated some of the buffalo meat and ate quickly. Once the stock had been picketed out in the dry, brown bottomland grass, a sentry was set and the men rolled into their blankets.

In the cold dawn they rolled out again, packed up, ate more buffalo, and headed north, following the creek bed toward the Musselshell. At noon they had the river in sight, and soon the horses were muzzle deep in the clear, cold water. Puddles and ponds along the river flats had a crust of ice, and calm backwaters on the river itself were iced. The wind held steady, biting, gnawing at any exposed flesh.

"Well, Mr. Beck" said Lieutenant Morgan, one mittened hand on a hip as the horses slurped up the river water, "which way do you think from here?"

"I would imagine west along the river will turn them up. The main command was chasing them up Canyon Creek, and they would have come out on the table lands to the west of us. If they've hit the river, that's where we'll find them." Beck leaned on his saddle horn with his forearms, then patted Bill's neck.

They turned westward, following the river, the wind held off by raised collars and bandanas wrapped around ears. The horses plodded steadily on, going at the only pace they had left. By mid afternoon they could see smoke on the river ahead, trailing low and thin to the south on the constant wind. Beck steered Bill up an easy slope to the left to gain a little vantage point, and stopping there put his glass on the smoke and its source. He then rejoined the scouting party.

"See lots of dark blue up there. Looks like Sturgis, probably going into camp on the north bank. Still a bunch of soldiers out to the south side, too."

Another hour of shuffling hooves brought them to the ford, where exhausted troopers were walking in from the southern hills in ones and twos, leading their drooping mounts, strung out for as far as the eye could see back into the hills. Across the river a camp was being set up, fires were flaring up, men were gathering wood, putting up the little tents of white canvas, unpacking mules. The scouts crossed the river with a party of the stragglers, as the stream was wide but barely wet the fetlocks of the horses. They climbed out on the steep but low northern bank, the horses hesitating in mid slope as if deciding to go on or not. The men finally climbed down off of their saddles in the midst of the camp.

Simon took hold of Bill's reins and Morgan's horse also, as Morgan and Beck walked to the largest tent on the flats. The south facing side had its flaps turned back, and Sturgis was inside talking to two of his captains. Morgan stepped in and came to attention, Beck just behind to his right.

"Ah, Morgan, isn't it?" Sturgis said, returning Morgan's salute and spitting tobacco juice into the dust of the tent floor just in front of his nearest captain, who made a small involuntary movement to avoid the sloppy missile.

"It is, sir, and Mr. Beck, one of our scouts."

"Yes, yes, I recall you, Mr. Peck. Did you detect any activity out on our eastern flank, Mr. Morgan?"

Morgan made his report, describing the action and lack thereof, noting the fine marksmanship of Mr. Beck, the excellent route selection of Mr. Beck, the good advice as to buffalo offered by Mr. Beck.

When he had finished, Sturgis said gruffly, "So it is Mr. Beck, not Peck, as you so persistently point out. At any rate, here is the situation. My command is spread out over ten miles, men worn out, horses done for, still no supplies to speak of. Howard is two days back, he has supplies, he is coming to meet us here.

"We know that the Nez Perce move when we move, camp when we camp. They seem to feel safe when they are about two days march ahead. They are somehow keeping an eye on us, just as we attempt to do the same to them. In coordination with General Howard, we are to wait here until the general comes up, and it is our concerted opinion that the Nez Perce will wait also. The Crow scouts fought a pitched battle with them yesterday, killed a few, but retired from the field when the Nez Perce made a determined attack. I believe most of them have retired all the way to the Stinking Water.

"Even though the strategy is to ease up on the pressure of our chase to get them to slow down, we are in no shape for a vigorous pursuit. Fisher and the last of his native scouts are ranged up toward Judith Gap even now, and we hope for positive news by tonight. So, for the time being, rest and feed your mounts, and rest and feed yourselves. It is my understanding that the river teems with fish, so we may in fact have something to eat tonight."

"Yes sir," Morgan said, saluting, and he and Beck left the tent.

They went back to Pocket and Hardy and the two troopers, and then moved west along the bank of the river, looking for a camp with flat ground and shelter from the wind. Half a mile up the stream they found a low bluff, cut sharply vertical by the river at spring runoff, with grass for the stock and good shelter. They had no sooner unsaddled the horses and turned them into the little meadow when an army corporal came up the river leading a string of drooping cavalry mounts. He turned them loose into the meadow also.

"Keep an eye on them ones, too, won't you?" he said, walking through the camp back toward the army's bivouac site. Pocket watched him go, shaking his head.

"Don't worry about it none," Beck said, "plenty of grass for all, there. What they really need is grain, though, the way we work 'em."

"I'm going down to the camp, get the lay of the land, see if I can find anything to eat," Morgan said.

"See if you can find any ammunition," Beck said, "and don't tell 'em we got buffalo meat left, otherwise we'll end up with empty bellies tonight."

Morgan nodded and walked off down river. The two soldiers were just getting a fire lit, using brushwood gathered from the riverbank.

"You know," Beck said, "We been riding together for days, and still don't know who you men are. Guess you know by now I'm Jon Beck, this here's Elijah Hardy, and that's Simon Pocket," he said, nodding to each of the others.

"Well I am William Ambrose Gander, sir, and always a pleasure to ride with a man who can find food!" said the tall, dark haired soldier, stepping forward and shaking Beck's hand with a grin. The other said, "I'm Gross, sir, Henry Talbot. Trooper." He was short, slim, and appeared to be about sixteen. He did not offer a hand, but looked down shyly.

"Either of you boys know how to fish?" Beck said.

"Why yes, sir, I do!" Gross said brightly.

"Lige, we got any fish line, hooks, anything?" Beck asked Hardy.

"I just might have," Hardy said, and went to his saddle pack.

"I hear tell this river's full of fish," Beck said. "Now, I know you boys would prefer three day old buffalo jerky, but fresh fish would add a nice little distraction, don't you figure?"

"Why I shore do, sir!" said Gross, and he and Gander went over to Hardy, who soon had fetched out some line and hooks from his kit. The troopers went off to cut willow poles and search out some bait.

The scouts dragged in weathered drift logs and branches, broke up what they could, rimmed the fire with stones, arranged saddles and packs and blankets around the camp below the bank in shelter from the wind. The sun broke a few golden rays free beneath the overcast in the west, then was gone below the crest of the distant mountains. They hunkered down around the fire to absorb some heat. They heard a whoop from up the river bank, then another. Laughter could be heard then, then more whooping.

As the late afternoon gloaming turned to dusk, the troopers brought in three large trout. Hardy quickly cleaned and split them, and got them into his cast iron pan. He unwrapped some of the buffalo meat, and trimmed a little fat from a few pieces, dropping it in the pan with the fish. He set the pan over some coals, and soon the smell of sizzling fat and frying fish wafted across the river on the wind. He got out the coffee pot, and fetched water from the river, then set the pot on the coals.

"How come you boys to soldierin'?" Beck said, as they all squatted at the fire or sat on driftwood logs.

"My pap was in the war," Gander said, "always telling stories and such. I figured to find out what it was all about."

"And have you? Found out, I mean."

"Mostly shoveling horseshit and shinin' boots, so far," Gander said. "Never thought I'd go hungry so often, nor freeze my butt off with such regularity."

"How 'bout you, Private Gross. Is the army your dream come true?"

"Not so's you'd notice," Gross said shyly, smiling a little. "I come west from Vermont with my family, lookin' fer a little land with more soil than rock. Pap settled in Illinois, right around Rexburg. But once we got to moving west, well, the momentum jest sort of caught me up, and I kept on goin', rolled clear out to Kansas City afore I bumped up against something solid enough to stop me."

"What would that have been?" Beck smiled.

"Army recruiting sergeant. Way he made it sound, a feller would be warm, dry, and well fed, and all he had to do for his pay was answer up when somebody called his name. And besides, I was all afire to fight them red devil Injun's, what with Custer's killin' and all."

"So how do you like fighting Indians?" Beck said. Hardy got the pan off of the fire, turned the fish, put it back on the coals. He got out the coffee sack and the knee grinder, and sat on a log with the grinder between his thighs and ground up the evening's coffee.

"Well, for nigh on the last year we been ridin' all over the country, sleepin' on the ground, eating whatever the mules could carry, mostly bacon and beans and biscuit, and we been roundin' up this little band and that little family, every damn one of 'em pitiful poor and no fight in 'em at all," Gross said. "Never fired a shot, just herded a lot of squaws and scrawny kids and hangdog warriors onto the reservations. I feel more like a dog catcher than a soldier."

"These Nez Perce, now, they's a different breed, ain't they Mr. Beck?" said Gander. "I mean, it looks like they're willing to fight, don't it?"

Beck looked at the flames in the deepening darkness. A faint glow over the mountains in the west was all that was left of the day. The wind had died somewhat, and the fire was a golden warmth. Hardy poked at the fish in the pan with his bowie knife.

"Yes, they are a different breed," Beck said. "And fight they will. You boys stick with me and I'll make sure you'll be right in the thick of it. The bullets will be buzzin' 'round your ears like angry bees, and if you so much as poke your nose out of cover, those Nez Perce'll sure as hell shoot it off! Why, I've lived with 'em for a time, and I've scouted with them when they were on our side. I've seen many of 'em knock a buzzard out of the sky with one shot. I've seen 'em drop a small deer at such a distance it took an hour to get to the carcass. I've seen 'em shoot a jumping salmon—"

181

"Oh fer the love a God!" Hardy blurted out, rolling his eyes. He dumped the freshly ground coffee into the pot beside the coals, and nudged the pot further into the heat.

"All right. Twern't a salmon, it was a carp, and anybody can hit a jumping carp. But if it's fightin' you boys is after, I figure the Nez Perce is just the ticket."

"Is it true that they've come all the way from Idaho?" Gander said.

"It is. Wives, kids, house and home, all atop horses and covering ground no sane man would have attempted, not sober, at least," Beck said.

"Wouldn't it have been better to just go on the reservation like the government wanted?" Gander said.

"More to it than that," Beck said. Hardy got the pan off the coals, set it on a flat rock, and they dug in, using their knives to piece out the chunks of fish and gingerly nibble at the hot, pink flesh.

"There was killing what started it," Beck went on. "Indians had been complaining that the whites had murdered some of their folk, and no one would do anything about it. So, when they began to gather to go on the reservation, some of the young bucks went out to the white farms and ranches where the killers were, and did a little killing of their own. They figured since they were leaving their country, they would settle some old scores before they went. Then of course all hell broke loose, and soldiers come up, and everybody was shooting at everybody. Soldiers got their asses kicked at Whitebird Canyon, and so more soldiers was brought up, and the Indians skidaddled into the mountains. At least the ones 'at couldn't abide being told what to do by the whites."

"But we've heard the Nez Perce have got the worst of it, and in spite of that they've treated prisoners well, and let people go sometimes, things like that," Gross said.

"I don't know about that," Beck said. "I will tell you this. I had a friend among them, name of Two Shirts. He and I scouted together during the army campaigns against the Cayuse and Yakima tribes in the Northwest. Got to know Two Shirts well, so well he asked me into his lodge to meet his family. Stayed with them for a time. He's got a wife and two or three kids, maybe more, so many of 'em runnin' around the place never did ferret out which were his own, which his neighbors'. But they were good folk, in their Indian way, just like you and me, only they come at things from a different side. Two Shirts took the time to learn me much of the language of his people, and I sat in the councils of their elders."

"Did you speak to their chief?" Gander said.

"They don't really have a chief, in the way we have a president," Beck said. "Sometimes a man of experience and proven bravery is elected by the band he travels with to speak for the band. Most Indians just speak for themselves. Elders are listened to simply because they've got more time on the earth than another, and wisdom is a product of experience, for most of us. Leaders are respected for doing, and followed for doing it right. Nobody gives anyone orders."

"How do they fight, then, if no one is in command?" Gander said.

"Well, it's like us, right here," Beck went on, finishing the last morsel of fish. Hardy laid the rest of the uncooked trout in the pan and put it back on the fire. "I have no authority to command you two troopers, nor Mr. Pocket there, he being an employee of the army like I am, nor can I tell Mr. Hardy what to do."

"But that don't keep you from trying, now do it?" Hardy snorted.

"But let's say the Nez Perce attacked the camp right at this moment. We'd all go for our guns and take cover. Then what? Well, havin' been shot at some in the past, I might holler at all of you to keep your asses low and follow me! I would of course have some brilliant strategy in mind and be acting on it. You fellers, on the other hand, would be open to whatever suggestion might keep a bullet out of your backside. So, you most likely would come along, thinking I might have some brilliant strategy in mind. You would probably come along as far as my brilliant strategy was working, and if you in fact found my brilliant strategy was to run at the enemy and get my ass shot full of holes, you most likely would abandon me somewhere along the way and devise a somewhat less brilliant but safer strategy of, say, ducking under cover. As long as I'm winning, you follow. If I get foolish about it, you go another way. And that is exactly how the Indian system of leadership works."

"Sort of different from the army," Gross said.

"Completely," Beck said. "You boys follow officers that may or may not have the ability to lead men. You do it because, by rank, you have to. The army is all about orders. Indians is all about bravery. If they fight, they have to fight as men, with bravery, with honor, or it's no good. But they are learning from us, the white man, that winning is sometimes more important than honor."

"Why don't we just let them go?" Gander said. "We hear they are heading for Canada, so why don't we just let them go?"

"Don't work like that," Beck said. "They have killed whites. They have to be punished. The government will have its pound of flesh. Can't let them set a bad example. Sitting Bull up in Canada is enough of a bad example as it is."

"But whites killed some of them, too, haven't they?" Gander said, "I think it's a shame we have to hunt them down and exterminate them, when they're only fighting back."

"Like I said, it's more complicated than that," Beck said.

"Was that the same Two Shirts you knew, back there at that little spring with the dead buffalo?" Gander said.

"Yep."

"Sort of odd, you running into him that way, way out here," Gander said.

"Oh, I think there's more to it," Beck said. "I seen him at the Crow camps, he was there with some of his people trying to talk the Crow into siding with the Nez Perce against us. Us whites. I think once he knew it was me 'at was scouting his eastern flank, and him knowing me and a little of how I operate, I figure he has made it his business to keep an eye on us, on me, actually, and it was him what got behind us at the Yellowstone, and had a run at us at the buffalo spring. Hated to kill his horse, but he might of got a lucky shot into one of our mounts, and I didn't want that to happen. He likes to play games when he's on the warpath, do things that will embarrass the enemy. Us being the enemy. Me in particular. Not that we ain't still friends, you understand, I figure if he killed me he'd still regret it some."

"Probably regret the loss of another cartridge more," Hardy growled.

"So you're saying that the Indians choose their leaders by the example they set, and we do it by rank and orders," Gander said. "What do you consider Custer to be, then? You figure him to be a real fighting man, or was he just another officer?"

"Never met the man," Beck said, "but the record speaks for him. In the war, he was a pistol! Fine cavalry officer, if you consider results. Never shirked a battle, and won most of them. Also had the highest casualty rate of any cavalry command in the war, so I am told. But you can't always be charging and not take casualties. Would you boys go to war with a man like that?"

"I would!" Gander said. Gloy just shrugged.

"And so would I!" said Lieutenant Morgan, approaching the fire out of the darkness. He had a sack slung over one shoulder, and carried a large square tin under his arm. "I have biscuit and bullets," he said, dropping his load to squat by the fire. "Now what's this about General Custer?"

"We were just comparing the military leadership style of the Noble Red Man to that of the U.S. Army," Beck said. "Custer seemed a fine example of the type, on the white side of things."

Hardy got the skillet off the coals and placed it again on the rock. After it had cooled for a short time, they dug in again with their knives, mostly deferring to Morgan who had not yet eaten. The biscuit tin was opened and hard tack shared out. Hardy poured out coffee into the cups brought out by each man.

"Anything new goin' on down in camp?" Beck asked Morgan.

"Things remain the same. General Howard is coming up. But I hear Fisher and his Crow and Bannock have come in, and they are heading south in the morning. They report the Nez Perce camped in the Judith Gap. Fisher says their enlistment is now up, and they're going home."

"Fisher quitting, then?"

"So it seems. That leaves us for scouting, I'll wager."

"I suppose the way is pretty clear, at any rate," Beck said. "They're heading directly north now, and if we can't catch 'em, they're in Canada for sure."

"Perhaps not. I also hear that Miles is on the march, to the east and north of us, and may in fact cut them off. One of the reasons we are to wait here for a day or two is to take the pressure off of the Nez Perce so that they will not move fast enough to elude Miles."

"And another reason would be that we are too beat out to run after them anyway," said Hardy. No one had much to say to this.

When the meal had been finished, Beck rinsed the long handled frying pan in the river, then put it back on the coals. The sack Lieutenant Morgan had brought back with him contained dozens of .45-70 cartridges, these for the full sized Springfield rifles that many of the troopers carried.

Beck retrieved a device very like a large pliers from his traveling kit, and, taking the cartridges out of the bag one at a time, used the pliers to twist the bullets out of their casings. He tossed the bullets into the frying pan. The powder he carefully poured out into a small canvas bag. The emptied cartridge cases went into a growing pile on the ground.

As he sat on his log working the cartridges apart one by one, Hardy watched him work. Pocket sat on the other side of the fire, nursing his coffee a sip at a time from the tin cup. Morgan and the two troopers had gone to the meadow to check on the horses.

The cold night breeze kept the fire burning strong, the coals glowing brightly. Soon the bullets in the skillet began to melt, and as they did the animal grease that lubricated them smoked off in a white streaming plume in the wind. Beck placed the end of the pliers on the coals, the end formed into a bullet mold, its two halves joined by the hinge holding the plier halves together. He spread a small piece of canvas on the ground, and taking the heated mold in his left hand, used a piece of buffalo hide to insulate his right hand, and lifted the skillet and carefully poured molten lead into the mold, allowing the excess to dribble over the top and plop on the canvas. He set the skillet back on the coals, took a piece of wood and knocked the sprue plate on the mold top aside, opened the mold, and out dropped a shining bullet. It lay on the canvas like a silver nugget.

"How many of those are you fixing to make?" Hardy said.

"Oh, fifty or sixty, I guess."

"That's what you get for shootin' a gun that nobody else does," Hardy said with a superior tone.

"You in a hurry to be someplace?" Beck said.

"Nope. Matter of fact, I may as well clean my own guns, seein' as how we might be out of action for a spell." He rose to fetch his rifle to the fire.

"That little paint of yours is a real comer!" Beck said to Simon as he worked. "She ever get tired?"

"Nope. Only pony I ever had that just loves to run. Good cow horse too, has a lot of sense, and she's quick. Been workin' her on cows fer a couple of years now, and she picks it up real quick."

"How'd you wind up in Quandry?"

"Oh just luck, I guess. Me'n Zak worked cattle in Texas, just coming up to full growed about the time the first drives started. We was wet behind the ears pups on our first trip north, but since then we made half a dozen drives, in all. Then couple years ago, we helped drive a small seed herd up through Cheyenne, heard about ranches up on the Crazy Woman, then over to Quandry. Went for a look see, stayed."

"That a good spread you were working for?"

"Yes it was. Treated us decent. But damn the winters is cold up here! I thought a Texas blue norther was a real chicken killer, but up here it's like that for six months solid!"

"So how you like scouting, Injun fighting?"

"Well, I don't understand it much. I mean the scoutin' is pretty plain, you go and have a look everywhere, report that you didn't see nothing. Only job I ever been paid fer seeing nothing. But like them troopers was a'sayin', I don't see why we just don't let them Injuns go on to Canada, be done with 'em."

"As I said before, government has a sense of justice. Can't let folks just run roughshod over the country killin' folk. Even if they have it coming. And a lot of the people killed in this war, on both sides, didn't. Have it comin', I mean."

"Mebby so. Seems like a gawd awful waste, runnin' 'em down like this."

"Well, there's always the possibility that once they get to Canada, they might come back at any time, and start it all over again. Like Sitting Bull and his Sioux, no one knows if he's ever coming back, and if he does, well, what then?"

Pocket said nothing to this. Morgan and Gross came back, and joined them at the fire. Gander had been left with the horses as a sentry. They all got out their firearms and commenced a general cleaning of steel. Beck kept up the molding of his bullets, one at a time. He was still at it long after the others had finished cleaning their guns and rolled up into their bedding.

Chapter 25

After Beck finished up the casting of his bullets, he put away the tools, scoured out the frying pan with sand, and cleaned his own rifle by the firelight. The wind had dropped, and the warm glow of the fire was satisfying, soaking him deeply in its gentle heat. He was very tired, yet he did not feel the need to sleep. The sympathy he had heard from the soldiers and Simon toward the Nez Perce rumbled about in his skull, wearing thin his indifference and his purposely ignoring of the fact that he liked Two Shirts, and his family. He tried not to think about what the children must be going through on this wild, cold, frantic chase across what seemed like half of the United States. In his visits to the Crow camps with Hardy, he had always made it a habit to bring candy if he could, for he loved the unfeigned joy in the children's faces when he had produced it for them. Even when he made them wrestle the Great Red Bear in order to get the treats, he growled on the outside and laughed within, and it felt like tussling with a great pile of puppies. One day he hoped to have little ones of his own, but this thought led to other sadnesses, and he quickly put it out of his mind.

With a sigh, he rose and slipped out of his riding jacket, sheepskin lined and warm, and put on his full length buffalo robe coat. Taking his rifle, he walked west along the river to the rich grass meadow where the horses grazed as lumps of greater darkness in the darkness of the night. At first he did not know where the sentry was posted, but a soft word brought his attention to the north rim of the meadow, where a clump of hazel produced a moving shadow as he approached.

"How'd you know it was me?" he said to Gander in a soft tone.

"That big horse of yours nickered a bit. Smelled you I figure. He wasn't nervous, so I figured it was you."

"Why'nt you go on down to the fire, get some sleep. I'll look after things here 'till your relief arrives."

"Why thank you, Mr. Beck!" said Gander gratefully, "I shore could use the shuteye." He moved off across the meadow and was soon lost in the darkness.

Beck strolled slowly out into the grass, humming a little to himself, making just enough noise so that the horses would not be startled by his presence. He found Bill, who nickered and turned his head, lowering his nose for a rub. Beck rubbed.

"You're getting worse'n some ol' hound," he murmured into Bill's ear, "sorry I ain't got you a lump of sugar, wish I had some myself. Coffee's a mite brutal when Lige makes it up, that's certain." He rubbed Bill's ears, then patted his neck. He went back to the hazel thicket, found a rock in its deeper shadow, and settled in to sit and watch the meadow. His eyes slowly got better at seeing in the dark, and he could make out a dozen animals standing or down in the grass.

The overcast sky allowed no moonlight or the diamond sparkle of the stars to peek through. The cold breeze wafted just enough to creep in at any opening in coat or britches, so that Beck moved a bit from time to time to try and keep everything closed up and warmer. He had about given this up as a lost cause when his eye caught a shadow moving out on the grass. It soon became the form of a man, and was moving in his direction. Private Gross soon spoke up.

"Mr. Beck?" he said quietly.

"Here, son!" Beck said, stepping away from the hazel shadows.

"Oh, well, I'm to relieve you sir," Gross said.

"Thank you kindly, trooper," Beck said. "Things are pretty quiet out here, but durned if you won't freeze to death if you don't keep moving. Careful, though, that's what an Injun looks for, sneaking up on a man. Staying perfectly still, he'll never see you. But move just a little, and you're dead meat!"

"Yes sir, I'll keep that in mind. Can they see you shivering, sir?"

"Oh yes, that's for certain. Can't be no shivering, none at all. Well, do what you can, be alert. I'll see you come sunup."

Beck headed on back to camp, smiling a little to himself.

The fire was down to a few coals, so he fed it some bigger pieces of wood, then turned in. He used the buffalo robe coat as an outer cover, and his saddle for a pillow. Once he was burrowed down in his bedding under the coat, he quickly forgot the hard ground gouging his hip and was asleep in an instant.

And an instant later, or so it seemed, he was awakened in the dawn by shouting, and the thump of hooves making the earth shudder, and the screaming neigh of a horse.

He threw the covers from him, leapt up as he scooped up his rifle, and took off at a dead run for the meadow, for he could see no other

189

threat around him. The others were just then sitting up in their blankets. The cold light of dawn silvered the eastern sky.

Within a few frantic strides he was at the meadow, and there, held at the end of his picket rope by a burley army sergeant, was Bill, plunging against the rope as the sergeant was jerked this way and that, just barely keeping his feet and a hold on the rope. Two other army men were in the meadow, one holding the lead of an army mount, the other watching. Gross stood at the edge of the meadow, his Springfield rifle across his chest at port arms, his mouth gaping, confusion in his eyes. He saw Beck, and started to say something, but Jon looked back at the sergeant.

Bill bucked and reared, and the sergeant was jerked off of his feet, but still held the end of the rope. Bill seemed to catch sight of Beck, and his eye stayed on his master as Beck stepped over to the edge of the meadow and leaned is Winchester against a bush. He strode out to the sergeant and his horse, just as the sergeant reefed in some rope, and, paying out the end a little, began to swing the rope's end to lash Bill. He was cursing in a loud voice.

Beck caught his arm just as he started forward to lash the horse with the rope. He whirled around, flinging off Becks grasp angrily.

"What the hell you doin'!" the sergeant bellowed at Beck.

"I could ask the same thing," Beck said, "why are you—"

The sergeant shoved both his hands into Beck's chest, rocking him back.

"Get away from me!" he bellowed, "I got horses to catch, colonel's orders!"

"So go catch 'em," Beck said, "just leave MY horse alone!"

"I got orders to fetch along the two best mounts in this herd!" the sergeant spat loudly, "If they is in this herd they is army mounts and fetch 'em I will!" He turned back to grab the picket rope he had dropped to shove Beck.

"Perhaps you don't understand the situation," Beck said, laying his hand on the sergeant's arm, "that is my horse you're foolin' with, and you ain't taking him anywhere!"

The sergeant turned his head to look at Beck's face, then down at the hand on his arm. He whirled suddenly with a roundhouse left, a snarl on his face.

Beck ducked under it, and landed a solid right into the sergeant's midsection. The sergeant staggered back a step, then threw a hard right, which glanced off of Jon's temple. Beck came over the top with a straight right that connected solidly with the sergeant's nose, rocking his head back. The sergeant stepped back again to regain his balance, then came in with another right, that missed, then a left, that landed on Beck's cheek. Beck got in a left and right on the sergeant's torso, and the man grunted with the impact. He grabbed onto Beck, trying for a headlock, but Beck drove several more punches into his gut, and the steam went out of him. He hunched a bit and stepped back, still snarling, panting, and his eyes seemed to focus for the first time. Bill, standing behind him half a dozen paces away, snorted.

"You had enough?" Beck said, fists cocked before his chest.

"Go to hell!" snarled the sergeant.

"Well I have!" said a voice behind Beck. He looked over his shoulder, and Lieutenant Morgan strode up, buttoning his tunic. "What's going on here, sergeant?" he demanded.

"Sent to get the two best mounts from this here pasture, lieutenant," the sergeant said through clenched teeth. "Colonel's direct order, get the two best mounts! Dispatches going back to the general, and up to Colonel Miles. This here galloot won't let me take this horse!"

"That's because it is his horse, sergeant!" Morgan said.

"A horse is a horse, goddammit! Beggin' yer pardon, lieutenant. If'n it's in an army herd it's by God army property! I got orders—"

"Sergeant," Morgan said, "find a horse out here with an army brand on it."

"But I got dy-rect orders! The two best—"

"You have new orders, sergeant. Leave this horse, and in fact any horse that does not have an army brand, alone. Am I clear?"

"The colonel's gonna hear about this, lieutenant! I got orders—"

"For the last time, sergeant," Morgan said, "take your two best army branded mounts and get out! Or would you rather Mr. Beck here continue the conversation you two were having as I came up?"

The sergeant looked at Beck's eyes, and did not like what he saw.

"All right, lieutenant, we'll do it your way. But the colonel's gonna hear of it, and that's a fact!"

"See that he does, sergeant. I wouldn't have it any other way."

The three army men soon found another mount, and leading the two of them left the meadow. The sergeant was still hunched as he walked, holding one arm across his middle.

"Thanks, lieutenant," Beck said as he moved Bill's picket pin and tied the rope to it. He went and retrieved his rifle.

"You can bet your bottom dollar I will answer to the colonel for it," Morgan said.

Gross joined them.

"Mr. Beck, I am sorry I didn't stop him from doing it," he said, "it's just that he said he had orders, and he's a sergeant."

"Don't worry about it, trooper," Beck said, "We have seen this morning how command in the army works. Rank can get you into trouble, and it can get you out."

"I hope you are right about that last part," Morgan said, as they started back toward the camp.

They soon had the fire built up, and Hardy set about cooking up some of the buffalo meat. He put on coffee, and soon the aroma of frying fat and coffee permeated the camp. Gander ate his breakfast and was sent up to relieve Gross, who came to the fire gratefully, and spent some time warming his hands before he could take a plate of food. He was still shivering when he finally cradled his coffee cup and sipped with a sigh.

Beck had dressed and donned his buffalo robe coat, and got out his cartridge making tools again, along with the powder and bullets. He retrieved the fired cases he had been collecting after each fight, and took them to the fire. He sat on a log by the fire and began making cartridges. First he used a long pin like a six-penny nail and, using a small stone as a hammer, ran the pin into the mouth of the case, seated the case over a crack in the log, and tapped out the spent primer. From his kit he took a little bag of new primers, and using the tong like tool, seated the primers in the base of each case.

"They see you shiver last night?" he said to Private Gross as he worked.

"I'm afraid they did!" Gross chuckled, "I figure the Good Lord and all his angels saw me shakin' so bad, weren't no hiding it atall!"

"Well, you're not the first one. I recall back in the winter of '68, during the Cayuse war, I pulled guard duty over some prisoners we had. Wind a blowin' that night, musta got to thirty below. Didn't have this fine buffler robe coat like I do now. Teeth got to chatterin' so bad, why them prisoners, couple of which was of Spanish blood, thought they was hearing the castanets of some senorita and began to dance in the moonlight! I was thinking how handy a nice guitar would have been—"

"Oh fer the love of—" muttered Hardy, shaking his head.

"Lige, why is it I can't get goin' on a good story, and you bust in with some remark!" Beck said in mock sternness.

"I just get tired of shovellin', is all," Hardy said.

When he had the cases all primed, Beck found a tin of grease in his kit, and opened it on the log. He took a bullet, and using his fingers, spread grease over it into grooves in the body of the bullet. He set the bullet on the log, and reached for another.

"What you figure comes next, lieutenant?" Beck said.

"Not at all certain," Morgan said, sitting across the fire nursing his own cup of coffee. "Obviously the Fifth has not come north, not unless they are with General Howard. When Captain Peachbow ordered us out, he gave no indication of when we should come back, only that we were to follow the Nez Perce to the Crow Agency, then beyond as far and as long as it took. We have done that, but I do not believe he has. I would expect Sturgis, or perhaps General Howard, will send us home shortly."

"And you say the other scouts, Fisher and his bunch, have quit?"

"So I am told. Don't know who Sturgis will send out, I do believe contact of some sort must be maintained. We cannot afford to lose them now, I would say."

"Well, if he sends you and your troopers back south, the three of us will most likely be the ones going north," Hardy said. He was making up a fresh pot of coffee.

Beck finished greasing the bullets, then took a newly primed case and pressed it onto a tapered nipple on the pliers tool. The taper of the steel nipple caused the mouth of the case to flare slightly. He took up case after case and flared each one.

Then he took out the powder bag, opened its mouth wide. He fetched a small tin dipper like a little cup with a long handle, and dipped it into the powder, tapped the side with his finger to shake off the loose powder and level the amount in the cup, and carefully poured the powder into a primed cartridge case. He seated one of the bullets on the case mouth, and eased the assemblage into the chamber of the pliers tool. He closed the pliers on the case, driving it into its chamber where the bullet was pushed into the case and seated to the proper depth, and the case mouth crimped around the corresponding groove in the bullet. Opening the pliers tool drew the case back out. He dropped it into his hand.

"Lemme see," Hardy said. Beck tossed him the newly remanufactured cartridge. Hardy turned it in his hand, his lips pursed.

"Pretty neat," he said, tossing it back.

"One down, sixty to go," Beck said. He paused long enough to sip from his coffee cup. The tin had cooled the brew quickly, and it was tepid. Hardy fetched the coffee pot from the coals, using Beck's piece of buffalo hide to insulate the handle, and poured coffee into Beck's cup, then refilled the others as the men held them out.

Beck sipped hot coffee, felt the heat of it all the way down, put down the tin cup and went back to work.

"You do much fighting in your career, Mr. Beck?" Morgan said.

"How do you mean?"

"Fist fighting, that sort of thing. That sergeant this morning, he looked to be a little outclassed, I would say."

"Done some. When I was growing up in Pennsylvania, I was always a little bigger than most kids my age. My uncle ran the village blacksmithy, and he put me to work early. He's a large man, not so tall, but thick. He was the oldest of the four boys in his litter, and when my Pa died, he took me in. Anyway, he was the rough-n-tumble champion of the county, and every year at the county fair he'd defend his title. He was good. What made him good, was that he rarely got angry. Oh, he'd get his blood up all right, but he never got killin' mad. That way he could think while he was fightin', find the weaknesses in his opponent, exploit them. Sort of like a good unit commander in the army, eh, lieutenant?"

"Very much so," chuckled Morgan.

"Well, because I was a big kid for my age, he figured he didn't want me to turn out to be a bully. Not that I tended to that, just that he is a careful man, a feller who looks ahead. So he taught me to fight. With him, of course. When you learn to fight like that, you also learn that there is always somebody bigger, meaner, tougher out there, just waiting for the time you meet. And with that he taught me about fightin' smart, thinking, looking at a situation carefully, planning a course of action ahead of time. And as you know, lieutenant, no battle plan ever survives first contact with the enemy. So he taught me to think on my feet, so to speak. He was a great counter-puncher, my uncle, he'd let the other man make his move, then counter that with a move of his own. The only flaw with a system like that, is you take a lot of punishment letting the other fellow get his licks in first. It's the one place he and I never saw eye to eye. If'n I see an opening before the other man knows of it, and I know it's going to be a fight for sure, I have no harsh feelings about stepping right in and getting' the job done.

"And with all this teaching of his came his code. You don't stomp a man when he's down, in a fair fight. If he has the means and tries to kill you, kill him. Meet force with force, only to the extent of the offense given. And never use your power against a weaker man for no reason. Uncle Fredrick knew when to turn his cheek, but in the end he was not a particularly religious man."

"Are you a religious man, Mr. Beck?" Morgan said.

"Not much any more," Beck said. "During the war I used up all my credit with God. I prayed so often, most of it when the bullets was nippin' at my hat, I figure God and me was on a first name basis. I know I used His often enough. I lived, but most of my regiment didn't. And they were all God fearing men, too, for the most part. When we finally went home in '65, not one in ten was left of the bunch that marched out in '62. I lost a brother, and another uncle. And God and I, well, we ain't spoke since."

"Your uncle sounds like a man of principle," said Morgan.

"Oh he is that!" Beck said. "First time he ever took me to a rough-n-tumble as a fighter, I got whipped pretty bad. Other feller was quicker, and though I saw elements in his style that I could have turned to my advantage, I just didn't know how to do it, at least not quick enough to matter. Uncle Fred just chuckled a bit and said we had some work to do. But I didn't die, and I didn't quit, and I sorta liked it. I was fifteen at the time. We went to every fight we could find after that, up to the time I joined the regiment and we went off to fight in the war. I learned a lot about fighting in those two years, and it never ceased to amaze me as to the number of different styles, and tricks, and just plain orneryness you find in folks. By the time I was seventeen I was winning about half the fights I was in, but more important, I was getting hurt a lot less. And I came to likin' it a lot.

Still couldn't beat Uncle Fredrick when he got serious, but I could throw him some, and that took some doin'!" Beck chuckled.

"Did you fight in the war? With your fists, I mean."

"Yes, quite rightly so. Mostly with fists, bare knuckle, they called it. We had fights organized proper like, when the regiment was waiting for action near Washington. Had me a big first sergeant from New York, some sort of bare knuckle champ from a burrow or something, and he taught me a lot, too. I was his sparring partner, he called it, for a time, until the Wilderness. He was killed in the very first volley."

"You were at the Wilderness?" Morgan said.

"Yes. I was the company bugler. When I wasn't blowing on that tin horn, I was farrier and blacksmith for the regiment. Or one of 'em, anyway. Shoed so many mules I began to think I actually had a hoof growin' between my knees. Gave me nightmares a'times."

"Not doing much blacksmithing now, then?" Morgan said.

"No, not now, but did work at it after the war, for the army. I enjoyed the work, the heavy pull of it. But after the war, well, when I went home, things were...well, different. Folks had died, some gone, some...well, I just pointed my face west and here I am. Knew General Howard from the army, I was with him at Seven Pines when he lost his arm. Stray shot, that. A pity. But when he was campaigning against the Yakimas and the Cayuses, then down in Arizona when he was going after Cochise, I signed on, been scouting for the army ever since."

The pile of finished cartridges as Beck's feet was growing. He steadily worked at the loading as the sun rose and added its weak heat to that of the fire. A high, thin haze kept the sun a silvery disk, but the wind stayed light, and the fire kept the men toasted. After days in the saddle, the rest was welcome. Private Gross dozed against a log, Simon went up to the meadow to check on the horses. Hardy cleaned up the skillet and pans, kept the coffee pot just warm enough at the edge of the coals.

"What about you, lieutenant?" Beck said. "You had said back in Quandry that your folks were killed in the Sioux uprising of '62. How'd you end up in the army?" Beck said.

Morgan sat and looked at his cup. He sighed deeply.

"Yes, they were killed before my eyes. The bloody savages thought they had killed me, too. Beneath this head of splendid hair," he said, lifting his hat and patting his head, "is a long scar where an Indian ax left its mark. For some reason they did not scalp me, or any of my family. But I lived, and was taken in by a neighbor. I was seven at the time.

"It turned out that one of our state senators had known my father, and remembered me. When I graduated with honors from our local school, he was kind enough to recommend me to West Point. I had a vision of vengeance, and so I went eagerly. I excelled in the courses on tactics, strategy, artillery. Engineering, mathematics, the classics, well, they were an afterthought.

"The first post I had was with the Ordinance Board in Baltimore. No one would listen to my pleas for frontier duty, cavalry duty. But I finally became so obnoxious that they had no choice but to get rid of me, and I think the officer in charge of transfers thought he was punishing me when he assigned me to the Fifth Cavalry. I very nearly sent him a bottle of champagne in thanks."

"Seen much action before this?" Beck said.

"Routine patrols, rounding up the odd native family here and there, ushering them off to the reservation. Incessant squabbles with white squatters over their right to settle on those same reservations. Stolen horses, stolen cattle, whiskey running, gun running, tracking down deserters."

"This what you been waiting for, this war?" Beck said.

Morgan again took some time to answer, looking into his coffee cup.

"It's not what I expected, I will tell you that. Things are a bit more...fluid, if you like, than I had imagined. I am hoping that we will yet come to grips with the Nez Perce, and go at them directly! No more of this flitting about hunting ghosts, I should hope!"

They looked up as a corporal crunched up to them in the gravel, stopped and saluted the lieutenant.

"Beggin' yer pardon, sir, the colonel sends his compliments and requests your company at luncheon, sir, at 12:00 hours. And you are to bring your chief scout, sir, the one 'at beat Sergeant Mullany this morning." A brief shadow of a smile flickered across the corporal's lips.

"Please advise the colonel that I shall be happy to oblige him," said Morgan, "And I shall indeed bring Mr. Beck."

"Thank you, sir," said the corporal, who saluted, did an about face, and crunched away.

"Well Jon Beck," Lieutenant Morgan said, "We shall soon see how well our recent sins set with our local god. Let us hope his vision of hell is a kindly one."

Chapter 26

"So it is that because Mr. Fisher has seen fit to go home, taking most of his Crow and Bannocks with him, I must now rely on you, whether I like it or not!" said a red faced Colonel Sturgis to the braced Lieutenant Morgan before him, and a somewhat pink faced Jon Beck standing at the lieutenant's side.

"Begging your pardon, colonel—" began Beck.

"No sir! I'll have no excuses, no explanations, no folderol! There is no excuse for fighting in the ranks, and the punishments are clear. Were you an enlisted soldier in my command, I would send you down to the nearest post for summary punishment! You are a hired scout, and I have the authority to fire you, which I would do in an instant if not for Fisher!"

"Colonel, may I speak?" Morgan said.

"And you! You are not even a member of my command, not on my roles, and you presume to order my men about! You presume to countermand my direct order—"

"I did so to stop the fight, colonel!" blurted out Morgan, "Your sergeant was about to be utterly destroyed, and would be of no further use to you, I am sure. I was only trying—"

"Silence! At this point I do not care for your reasoning! You have already explained all I need to know about the situation. I cannot spare the men, or the horses, to replace Fisher in contact with the Nez Perce. That job will now fall to you! And God help you if you let them slip away!"

"Yes sir!" Morgan said, staring straight ahead.

"I will detail four men to go with you, to act as couriers. If you find any Crow in the vicinity who are willing to scout in cooperation with your party, enlist them as you can. We received a small train of supplies forwarded from Howard this morning, so that I can provision you with several days' rations, but that is all. And you may take one of the ARMY mules," Sturgis spit out, "And you don't have to maul anyone to get it!" He was nearly shouting this last.

"Yes sir!" said Morgan.

Sturgis stood fuming, his jaw working, but slowly he calmed, and finally said,

"Now, come over to the map table and let's go over the situation."

It did not take long to locate the Judith Gap on the maps, nor the Judith River itself. The Nez Perce were thought to be camped at the Gap, and Colonel Miles was thought to be somewhere to the northeast. The scouting party would travel directly to the gap, locate the main Indian body, and send back runners on a regular basis with news of any movement. The scouts were to make every effort to remain undetected. They were to take the rest of the day to gather their gear, ready the mule, horses and men, and leave before dawn the following morning.

"The key, gentlemen," said the somewhat mollified colonel, "is to remain invisible to the Indians. If they think we are making a move against them, they will of course resume their march. I am certain they have scouts watching us even now, for they flush and fly like quail the moment we make a move in their direction. If you can find a way in your travels to kill or capture their scouts, do so. If we can blind them to us in any way, we can better move when the time comes.

"As I noted, Miles is probably about here," Sturgis went on, indicating an area east of the Judith Mountains. "If we can take a few days off of their flight, he may in fact be in a position to head them at the Missouri. But, at all costs, we must know when they move, and which direction they travel. Are we clear on these points?"

"We are indeed, colonel," Morgan said, straightening from peering at the map.

"Then I will leave your scouts to their preparations," Sturgis said.

"Ah, colonel?" said Beck, "I believe luncheon was mentioned by your corporal?"

Sturgis scowled fiercely at Jon Beck.

199

"The lieutenant will remain and dine with me," Sturgis growled, "but you, sir, may get the hell out of my tent!"

Beck flushed red in the face, glanced at Morgan, turned and left.

"Sir, you misjudge the man," Morgan said, for the first time standing relaxed. "He only did what he did when attacked by your sergeant. He was defending himself. And the sergeant had no authority to take Mr. Beck's horse. It is, after all, not an army mount.

"I know that, lieutenant," Sturgis said irritably as his orderly cleared away the maps and began to set eating utensils on the little camp table. "But I have a sergeant who is stove up even so, and I have now lost a man when I cannot afford to do so."

"I think you will find that Beck will more than make up for the loss of your sergeant," Morgan said. "And that horse of his is worth three army mounts, I would say."

"We shall see. Please sit down, lieutenant," Sturgis said, seating himself on a small camp stool at the table. "So, just come out from West Point, is it?"

"Actually ordinance, at Baltimore, sir," said Morgan. And so the lunch began.

Jon Beck returned to his camp and the fire. Hardy and the two troopers were sitting at the fire, and Simon Pocket was up in the meadow with the horses. Beck spelled out the plan for them as Hardy fried up their lunch of buffalo meat and hard tack. The coffee was already hot, and he poured a cup for Beck.

"Thanks, Lige," Beck said, taking the cup and trying a sip. The hot liquid burned his lips and he flinched a bit.

"You think any of your Crow brothers are out there keeping an eye on things?" he asked Hardy.

"Oh they're out there," Hardy said, "More'n likely keeping an eye on what horses they can steal. Army gonna give us any supplies for this little jaunt?"

"Yep, and a mule to carry them. And four more troopers for runners."

"What about us?" trooper Gander said.

"Oh, you're comin' too, I reckon," Beck said. "The colonel ain't too particular who he orders about, you know. He just doesn't take to that trait in his lieutenants. Or anybody's lieutenants, for that matter."

"We was sort of hoping they'd send us back south to the Fifth," Gross said. "At least we had a barracks, and three meals a day."

"But boys, this is your chance for glory!" grinned Hardy, "Stories to tell yer grandkids all about what heroes you was in the Injun Wars. Why, I've knowed a dozen men would give a right arm fer this chance!"

"Speaking of which," Beck said, "General Howard is due up in a day or so. Looks like we'll miss him again. Like to see the old gent again, been years since we said howdy."

"Do you know the general?" Gander asked.

"I was standing beside him at Seven Pines, waiting to take a message from him to the colonel of the 81st, when he was hit. Musket bullet smashed his right arm. Damned Rebs snuck up on us, got in close before we could get set, let us have it. He went down, I helped carry him to the rear, then went back to the 81st on the run, found my colonel had been shot as well. I recall that Howard stayed cool in the thick of it, told the officers around him what to do even as they carried him off. Admired him for that. Went to see him in the hospital after the campaign had quieted down some, bearing a message from our new colonel. We got to talking some, he being pretty encouraging even though they had just taken off his arm. I was seventeen at the time. He remembered me, found out my name, told me to come to him at any time for whatever help he could give me. A generous man, and kindly, at bottom."

"Do you figure he'll send us back to the Fifth?" Gander said.

"Don't know. But you'll be with us up north by the time they catch up, and if all goes well we'll have our teeth firmly clamped on the tail of that renegade bunch and we ain't gonna turn loose for love nor money! You'll get to go south after we've done our job, I 'spect."

"More hardtack and hard weather, then," Gander said, gloomily poking a stick at a log on the fire.

"Like I said," Hardy grinned, "Glory all the way! You can't expect to be no hero without you sacrifice some fer it!"

"I'll settle for some spuds and gravy, and you can keep the glory!" Gander said.

Lieutenant Morgan returned in the middle of the afternoon, detailed Gander and Gross to go to the east pasture and pick out a mule, bring it back to their nearby pasture. When the mule came up, led by the troopers, Hardy laughed.

"You let that sergeant pick that one out fer ya?" he said. "That's the sorriest animal I seen yet on this trip."

"It's the best one of the bunch!" Gander said. Hardy just shook his head and sighed.

Morgan and Gross went back down to the camp to see about supplies. The mule was stripped of its pack saddle and taken up to the pasture. Simon came in for coffee, gratefully accepting a cup from Hardy as he warmed himself by the fire.

"Goin' to have to move the stock tomorrow," he said, "they 'bout done fer the grass in that little pasture. Almost like they ain't had a decent meal in days," he chuckled.

"We're leavin' before dawn anyway," Beck said. "Most of the scouts quit and went home, and the good colonel has seen fit to send us out to latch onto them renegades and keep him informed of their whereabouts."

"Don't cha know it, just found a decent spot to loaf and we got to move again," Simon said.

"'At's what they pay us fer," said Hardy.

"Yup," said Pocket, "I jes want to keep my hair long enough to spend some of that pay!"

"Well, if this goes right, they ain't even gonna know we're on to 'em," Beck said.

"That been the case so far?" Hardy said.

"Not exactly."

"Well then I would say it is a good thing you done made up all them new cartridges, pard, cause if it goes like it's been going, we're gonna need 'em!"

Gross came back to the camp carrying sacks of supplies. The troopers went fishing again for the evening meal, and though it took them a little longer, returned with four large trout for their trouble. Gross had caught three, and Gander one. Gross was proud of his catch, and though Hardy criticized his fish for being slightly smaller than the previous day's catch, he was not abashed but grinned under the harangue. Hardy kept it up as he cut the fish into pan-sized pieces, saying they were too tough, and then that they fried too slowly. Finally, with all about the fire holding their tin plates in

202

drooling anticipation, he shared out the first pan full, noting that he'd never seen a trout stick to the pan so tenaciously.

"Just a damned reluctant dinner from start to finish, that's for sure," he mumbled, "feller ought to yank out a couple of trout that wasn't so hard on the cook!"

"Mr. Hardy, I'll go back and get you all you want!" Gross said, still smiling, as he took the piece slid off the skillet by Hardy.

"Somebody else better go," Hardy said, "yer judgment in fish flesh is a mite sketchy. We need more cooperative food, if you ask me."

"Well now, Lige," Beck said, "since you find these trout so troublesome, why'nt you just slide that last piece off on my plate, and I'll save you the trouble of having to wrestle with it!"

"Like hell I will!" mumbled Hardy, claiming the last chunk as his own.

He had eaten and started a second skillet of fish when Morgan returned, also bearing several sacks of supplies. When the fish was ready, Morgan got the lion's share, and the rest was divvied up among the still hungry. Hardy then got the last of the fish onto the fire.

Gross was sent to the meadow for the first watch of the night, and the rest of them cleaned up the cooking utensils, then readied their own gear for the next morning. The new supplies were taken from the sacks, sorted, and Hardy and Pocket worked out what would be packed and how. They had enough bacon and hardtack for a week, and even some beans. They had enough buffalo meat for the morning meal. They gathered again at the fire in the crisp, cold night air, soaking up one more penetration of warmth before turning in.

"Got four troopers lined up to meet us at the colonel's tent at four in the morning," Morgan said. "One of 'em's a corporal. Same corporal that came to us with the message from Colonel Sturgis about that lunch."

"Look's like his love of that sergeant is being rewarded," Beck said.

"Oh the two of them were best of friends," Morgan said. "Or so he says. Odd how he takes a marked delight in noting the sergeant may have a couple of broken ribs."

"What are friends for, after all," Beck said.

As the coals burned low, they laid on some larger pieces of driftwood, then went to their blankets, the frost of their breath puffing white in the firelight. The weather seemed suddenly colder, and the blankets, Beck felt, seeming mighty good once they warmed to him. He thought again of Howard, the little one-winged banty rooster who had the tenacity of a bulldog with the single mindedness of a badger. If you threw in the religious stubbornness of a good army mule, thought Beck, you'd have enough critters to start your own zoo.

It was the last thing he remembered before opening his eyes to the clank of a pan. Hardy was at the newly fed fire, getting the coffee on again. Beck rolled out of his blankets into the cold bath of morning air, and sighed.

"That time?" he said to Hardy.

"That time," Hardy said.

Beck woke the others, and went up to the meadow to fetch down the mule. Gander was on watch, and told him all was quiet. At the fire the mule was saddled and loaded, Hardy and Pocket grumbling at each other about what should go where. Beck tended the skillet, where the last of the buffalo sizzled in its own grease. When the mule was mostly loaded, Beck went back to the meadow and he and Gander brought down the horses, and they saddled and loaded the mounts around the fire. The stars were bright, icy in the icy breeze, and their clouds of breath whisked away on the wind. Gander ate the last of the buffalo, Hardy cleaned the pan and pot, and the mule was topped up.

They swung up onto their mounts, and Morgan led the way down the river. The sentry outside of the camp, already alerted to their coming, greeted them.

"You might tell your sergeant to get a sentry on the upper meadow," Morgan said softly to the man standing at his stirrup with his rifle across his chest.

"Yes, sir," the sentry said in a whisper.

They moved on through the camp of small tents and sleeping men, some snoring, some coughing in their sleep, the dying embers of cook fires here and there sending up the occasional spark.

They drew up in front of Sturgis's tent. His orderly stepped through the flap, said quietly, "Colonel asked me to convey to you his compliments, and good luck."

"Thank you, lieutenant," Morgan said. "Are those men he promised—"

And as if on cue, the four troopers appeared in the darkness, coming from the east end of camp. The corporal stopped next to Morgan and saluted. Morgan returned it.

"Morning, lieutenant," the corporal said, "I'm Corporal Dodd, these here are Bishop, Woodecky and Jones."

"All right, Corporal Dodd. We are a scouting party, and will not travel in any particular formation. You will take your orders from me, and from Mr. Beck, here," Morgan said, nodding over his shoulder to Jon Beck.

"That would be my pleasure, sir!" the corporal beamed in the starlight.

"All right, then, let's move out."

They left the camp and climbed out of the valley of the Musselshell along the sandy base of a dry stream bed. They traveled slowly in the starlit darkness, and after several miles the stream bed gave way to rolling grassland, cut with ravines and shallow water courses, dry now in the fall. As the first light of dawn glimmered in the east, the army camp was well behind them.

Beck led the way, using the low ground when he could, keeping them off of the ridges and skylines, and out of the steady, icy wind. The pace was not hurried, for though the horses had rested and eaten grass for two days, they were not yet fully recovered from the weeks of rough travel behind them. Bill worked along solidly as he always did, walking quickly with the swaying rhythm of a sure footed animal no matter what ground he covered.

When the light had come up to full dawn, they sent outriders to the flanks, looking for the main Nez Perce trail, now several days old. In the long hours of the morning, they plodded steadily north and west, and then about noon, Jones came in with the news that he had cut the main trail. They worked their way to the north and found it directly, the earth plowed up by the passage of hundreds of horses. The wind had already begun to fold over the traces with blown earth, and the prints were blurry in appearance as a result.

They took a sighting of the far mountains, and the general direction of the trail, and decided to follow it generally, with the main body of scouts paralleling the trail about a mile to the south, and outriders further out on each side of it to make sure they were

205

traveling in the same direction and did not lose it. In this manner they moved northwest, and Beck frequently rode Bill to nearby hilltops and ridges, and glassed the country ahead, looking for any sign of the main Indian encampment. He saw individual riders in the distance several times, but they were moving south or east, and he could not make out who or what they were.

At mid afternoon they gathered in a dry wash out of the wind, and ate a cold meal of hardtack and water. The horses munched the dry, brown grass without enthusiasm.

"Seen a few riders out there," Beck said to Morgan, "May have been their scouts, or Crow."

"If we see any lone Nez Perce, we need to stop them if we can," Morgan said to the assembled men, "they most likely already know we're out here."

"Or maybe not," said Hardy, "by leavin' in the dark, we may have got past their watchers."

"You certain they had watchers back there at the Musselshell?" Morgan said.

"Yep. Or maybe a few miles north. I know I would."

"All right," Morgan said, "be alert, men."

They moved out again, and kept to the low ground, sending out the outriders as before. No contact was made, but they cut the trail twice more, as it wound through the country by the least laborious path. The afternoon wore away to dusk, and they found shelter in a little canyon next to a slowly meandering stream. The water was sluggish and alkali, and they could not drink it. They made a dry camp, and got a fire going only after the last light of day had drained out of the western sky. Hardy cooked bacon to go with the hard tack, and they ate and turned in immediately.

At dawn they were in the saddle again, pushing north to the Judith Gap. The Big Snowy Mountains rose on their right, low peaks with snow blanketing their cones, true to their name. They entered the basin between the Big Snowy and the Little Belt Mountains to the south. They came at dusk to the remains of a Nez Perce encampment, where a small stream came out of the mountains and across the basin floor, winding languidly to the north and northwest.

The riders dispersed to the various high points close to the encampment grounds, looking for any trace of the Nez Perce still in the area. Nothing could be detected moving in any direction. They returned to the campgrounds.

The Nez Perce had gathered buffalo chips for fuel, and some of them were still about near the blackened fire pits. The scouts moved to a depression in the basin floor a short distance away, and, after gathering in all of the chips they could find before the light faded, built a fire in the bottom of it. Once again, bacon was the fare, but Hardy found the trickling stream drinkable, and so made up beans and coffee to go with the hardtack and bacon. The horses were taken to tiny pools along the rivulet and watered. No grass of any real density was near, so the mounts had to go hungry.

The men attacked their food with real appetite, and not a word was spoken as they used knives and fingers to scoop the beans and bacon into their mouths.

"Mostly down hill from here," Hardy said, finally, sitting back and letting the small fire warm what parts of him it could.

"Judith Basin ahead, and that's where we'll find 'em, I'll bet even money," Beck said. "Probably on the river directly north by west. Maybe buffalo in the basin, too. Used to be thick with 'em, this time of year."

"If they stop to do any hunting, we'll be up on 'em in no time," Hardy agreed.

The next day was overcast and the light rose from grey to brighter grey, as the scouts moved into the Judith basin. Rolling hills cut by the breaks of the various streams and rivulets filled the countryside. The Nez Perce trail began to diminish as they moved toward the river, with smaller trails showing groups going off this way and that. Beck kept them to the low ground once again, and at every crest or ridge they had to cross, he dismounted and walked to the skyline to glass the country in advance. He spotted a herd of buffalo far off to the northeast, but no other movement. The men took turns riding on the flanks, and they, too, kept to the low spots and used caution on the hilltops.

By mid afternoon they had come to a major stream feeding the Judith, and turned down that toward the river. They were on a smaller Nez Perce track now, but as they neared the Judith it swelled with the tracks of more riders. The stream they followed was brackish and somewhat alkali in the pools and sluggish rivulets it offered, and the horses could smell the water of the river and eagerly moved ahead when guided in that direction. Beck had just come down off the nearest hill, where again he had seen only grassland and gullies and a hint of trees on the river some miles away, when Lieutenant Morgan pulled his mount to a halt and, raising his hand, said "Halt!"

The scouts stopped. They looked at Morgan. He sat his horse, gazing off into the distance.

"Hear that?" he said.

The others paused, listening. The wind, even in the hollow where they sat, rustled the dry bunchgrass, the horses stamped a bit and snorted, impatient to be on to the water, and there, faint as distant thunder, the sound of gunfire.

Both Morgan and Beck wheeled their mounts and galloped to the crest of the hill Beck had just descended. They dismounted and left the horses below the crest, and moving carefully, worked up to the top and lay in the grass. At first they could hear nothing, and the landscape lay as before, rolling breaks and the river far off, marked by the darker line of trees along its course. Then, as they watched, a pillar of smoke rose up and canted on the wind, streamed away to the east. The just discernable popping of gunfire came down on the wind. Beck got his field glasses on the smoke, as did Morgan.

"What do you make of it?" Morgan said.

"I'd say our pet Injuns have run up against somethin' they don't like," Beck said.

Hardy came up and lay beside them, panting a little.

"How far you figure that is?" Morgan said, lowering his glass.

"Maybe five, six miles," Beck said.

"Amazing we can hear it," Morgan said.

"Sometimes the wind'll do strange things," Hardy said.

Beck handed his glasses to Hardy, who took his turn examining the smoke column. It was coming steadily, bending with the wind and streaming off to the east.

"I don't like it," Hardy said. "Don't figure there's miners on the Judith. Most likely hide hunters, or maybe squatters. Don't recall no squatters, last time I was through here. What I do recall is kin. No hide hunters this far north, no sir. My recollection is kin down there."

"What do you mean, kin?" Morgan said.

"Maggie's people," Hardy said. "River Crow. My wife, she's actually River Crow. They been on the Judith in years past, and I'll lay you even odds…."

He lowered the glass, pursing his lips.

"Well, we're beyond helping them, whoever it is," Beck said.

"And, we have our orders to remain concealed if at all possible," Morgan said.

"It don't make no never mind," Hardy said. He handed the glass back to Beck, and left the ridge top.

"With all that firing, I would say whoever is down there ain't done so well," Beck said. He put the glass back to his eyes. The smoke plume seemed to be swelling, moving out to the east.

"Let's move on down to the river, water the horses, and we can follow the Judith on down from there. We should get there while there's still light," Morgan said.

They returned to the horses, and moving down the course of the stream gully, made their way to the Judith. At that point the river was only a few inches deep, but was wide and rippled over a gravel bed. The horses drank deeply, the men refilled their canteens, and after a short rest during which the horses munched grass in the river flats, they moved out down river, toward the smoke that still piled into the sky in the distance.

As they moved along the slopes of the river valley, Beck sent riders in turn out to each shoulder of the hill or ridge or gully rim ahead, where they dismounted and scanned the country before them. They could not risk coming up on the main body of the Nez Perce suddenly, so the caution of their travel slowed them. It was late in the afternoon when the source of the smoke came into sight. It was an Indian camp, and as they glassed it from the crest of a little knoll half a mile from the river, several of the tepees were still burning. They could see bodies lying in the open. The fire from the encampment had spread to the downwind grass, and a black swath of burned-over grassland stretched away to the east and southeast. The sky was full of smoke in that direction, though the burning remains of the camp gave off little smoke. That was dark, oily where the flames still flared, and white in many places where the fire had given way to the smoldering of ashes.

No living thing moved in the camp or anywhere they could see.

Beck went down alone, walking Bill slowly toward the ruins. He kept his eyes moving, looking for any sign of the Nez Perce. He had taken his rifle out of its scabbard and held it across his saddle pommel. As they came up on the ashes, Bill caught wind of the stench of the burning, and snorted. Beck halted the big horse at the edge of the camp. He waved his hand without looking back, keeping his eyes searching for any movement. The others plodded their horses up to join him.

"Let's get some scouts out to the north, and up there on that hill," he said, pointing to a nearby knob. Morgan sent out Gander and Bishop. Hardy climbed down off of his horse and walked out into the camp, looking at the bodies, turning this one over, then that one, looking into the blackened remains of the several tepees still offering some structure. Beck could see eight dead from where he sat. Four dogs. One horse. Eleven tepees, all destroyed. Then he looked back at Hardy, who was on the far side of the camp near the brush along the river. Hardy had spoken what sounded like Crow.

He was looking at the brush, and spoke again. After a moment, an Indian came out of the brush, and hesitantly walked toward him. It was a young girl, and she was reluctant to get very far from her cover. Hardy spoke to her, and she to him, and then she came a little closer to him. He dropped to one knee, held out his hand, resting is rifle butt in the dirt with the other hand. She did not come right away, but then little by little, edged toward him. Finally she came within his grasp, and he folded her into his arm and stood up with her. He came back across the camp, carrying the child. She clung to his neck.

"Dumb Bull's camp," he said as he came up. "River Crow. Nez Perce came in at dawn, wanted food, ammunition. Dumb Bull said no, he would be happy to share the morning meal, but they did not have enough food to last through the winter. Buffalo scarce, no elk to be found, the usual thing for these people 'round this country. Nez Perce sat a spell, had some food, left for a time. Then a party of warriors came back, wiped 'em out. She says no warning, no palaver, just wiped 'em out. Some of them got into the brush around the river, the rest killed or run off into the hills. This one," Hardy said, hefting the child, "was coming back to see if anyone was still alive. She says her grandmother and brother are in the bushes, but they will not come out."

"How many were here?" Morgan said.

Hardy spoke to the child. She replied.

"Maybe sixty or so. She says the lodges were as her fingers, and a toe. She says…" and Hardy listened as the child spoke again, "She says the warriors of the camp were as her fingers also, and the old men fought, too. She thinks they are all wiped out."

Across the camp Beck saw a woman emerge from the brush, then a boy. Further to the north two more figures came out, a woman and another girl. Hardy saw Beck's eyes and turned. He called out in Crow, and set the child he carried on the ground. She scurried across the charred ground to the old woman, chattering as she went. She grabbed the old one's hand and half led, half dragged her back to the scouts. The other survivors came hesitantly further out into the open. They wanted to hear what the strangers said, but they did not want to lose the option of a safe retreat into the brush.

The old woman halted before Hardy, grief twisting her face. Hardy spoke, then listened as she replied. The bitterness was evident in her tone and her face as she spat out the words, even though Beck could not understand the language.

Finally Hardy said, "As the little one said, the Nez Perce came into the camp at first light, and at first were friendly. The old one said they have hunted buffalo with the Nez Perce for many seasons, they were not enemies. Some of them were cousins. They ate the morning meal, and the Nez Perce left, going down the river. Later, warriors came back, demanded what food the camp had. Dumb Bull would not give it. They shot him down, then opened fire on all the rest. The men of the camp were caught without guns in their hands, for the Nez Perce were cousins. They all died. The women and children ran into the brush. The old one said there are maybe twenty…?" and he turned to the woman and made signs. She held up her splayed fingers, twice. "Maybe twenty left, most of them hiding out there," he said, nodding toward the river and its brushy banks.

"So it would seem the Nez Perce are not far away," Morgan said.

The pounding of hooves announced the approach of Bishop, who came into view from down the river. He galloped across the camp, raising black dust from the ashes, and skidded to a halt before the party. The Indians jumped out of the way of his horse.

211

"I seen 'em, lieutenant!" he blurted out, "From up on that knob! They ain't five miles away from here, headin' northeast!"

"Good work, Bishop. Take Mr. Beck back up there and show him, if you please."

Beck followed Bishop across the blackened grass of the burned out camp, then through some scrub trees and brush, then up the slope to the knob. They left the horses below the crest, and scrambled up to the top. Bishop pointed to the northeast, away from the river bottom. Beck put his field glasses to his eyes, following a plume of dust that rose and trailed away on the wind. He could see color at the base of the dust cloud, bits of white, and red, a speck of blue. It was the hundreds of horses and people that made up the fleeing Nez Perce band. As he watched, they topped a rise and disappeared from view, the dust moving away in the distance over them

"That's them, all right," Beck said, lowering his glasses. "Good eye, Bishop. Let's get on back."

They returned to the horses, mounted, and rode down the slope to the burned out camp and the waiting scouting party.

"They're maybe ten miles out," Beck said to Morgan, "The main bunch, this time. We finally hit pay dirt."

"Heading?"

"Northeast. Gonna strike the Missouri for sure. What fords are up there in that direction, Lige?" Beck said.

"I would say Cow Island would be the surest bet. They ain't gonna want to go to the north west, too close to Fort Benton, might be troops out patrolling from there. Naw, I'd say Cow Island, if it was me."

"We have any troops up there?" Beck said.

"Not that I am aware of. But in this situation, surely the army will have alerted all available troops in the area, and the ford will be heavily guarded," Morgan said.

"They got a freight station there," Hardy said, "in low water the steamboats unload there, and the wagons freight the goods on north and west. High water they can get all the way to Ft. Benton, but this time of year they'll have freight at Cow Island. All the more reason to believe the place will be manned by the army."

"Then what we must do is hurry Sturgis along, so that he can catch them as they run up against our forces at the ford," Morgan said. He stepped to his saddle bag, took out paper and pencil, and knelt to write a message using his knee as a desk. Then he rose, folded the paper, and handed it up to Bishop.

"Think you can find Sturgis?" Morgan said to the mounted man.

"Without a doubt, sir!" Bishop said, and saluted his lieutenant.

"Well go to it, man!" Morgan said, returning the salute. Bishop spurred his mount, and was soon lost to sight in the scrub brush along the river to the south.

"If Sturgis comes up quickly, we will have them!" Morgan said, turning from watching after his departing trooper. "We will have them and we will crush them!"

"And us?" Beck said. "What would you have us do?"

"We now have them in sight, and we must not lose them," Morgan said.

"Got our teeth in the badger's tail," Beck said, and smiled.

More of the scattered Crow came out of the brush, and as they began to move among the dead, the wailing of the women began.

Chapter 27

The scouts headed out down the Judith and then after a few miles up over the folded canyon ridges to the northeast, where they cut the Nez Perce trail and paralleled it. They moved as quickly as their tired mounts would plod, again riding to the crests and carefully peering into the distance from every height they had to cross. The light left quickly, and they found themselves in yet another creek bottom as the darkness closed in. Beck took his glass to the highest point nearby, a rocky knoll half a mile from their camp. He could see a few cook fires on the slopes of a little valley several miles away. He studied these with his glass, but could determine nothing from the points of light.

Back at the camp, Hardy had food on the fire, and Beck accepted a cup of coffee as he sat among the men about the fire.

"I could see 'em out there, maybe five, ten miles out. Fires in plain sight. They don't figure we're here, or don't care," he said.

"Probably don't care," Morgan said.

"Or they don't know," Hardy said. "Way I figure it, they missed us getting out of the Musselshell camp, and their people know Sturgis and Howard are several days back. They ain't worried, so long as they know where the army is. They ain't looking for us, and what Crows is around 're layin' mighty low."

"We will steal a march on them tonight!" Morgan said with sudden conviction. "If we can close the gap, maybe come up even with them, it would be easier to keep an eye on them. I think if we stay in the area between the Judith and their line of travel, we'd have a place to fall back on if they discover us and come to fight. We could fall back on the river, maybe lose them in the brush, just as the Crow of Dumb Bull's camp did."

"We could do that," Beck said, "if you want to make a cold camp every night. We get a fire going upwind, they'll sure as hell smell it. Better to head for the open country to the east. We can skirt the Judith Mountains, or even head through them if need be."

"Better yet," Hardy said, "Why not go to the northwest, get upwind of 'em, and fire the prairie like what happened out of Dumb Bull's camp? If we can get a blaze goin' across their front, we can slow 'em down, or even stop 'em for a time. And once we burned the place out, we can cook all we want and nobody's goin' to smell nothing!"

"I like that, Lige," Beck said.

"Yes. Indeed. We may be able to actually stop them for a time at that!" Morgan said.

They ate and rested the horses, the men catching a little sleep, then after midnight saddled up and pushed on. Beck led the way on the sure-footed Bill, moving slowly in the darkness. They did not have to stick to the valleys and low spots, and so took a direct route over the folded hills toward the northwest. Bill moved steadily in the dark, but not quickly, feeling his way under a cloud-darkened sky. The rest of the scouts trailed out behind, no one speaking, all wrapped against the cold wind that never seemed to slacken. They could see the tiny points of light of the Nez Perce cooking fires off in the distance from time to time, but by the time they had covered several miles, the fires had all but disappeared. Several times as they traveled, deer or elk crashed out of the close cover in which they were bedded down, startled by the approaching horsemen. The scouts could hear them charging through the brush, then the thump

214

of hooves as they scampered away. They could not see the animals but for an occasional lighter blur in the dark of the night.

Dawn was graying the eastern sky, silhouetting the low peaks of the Judith Mountains when Beck finally called a halt. Morgan and Hardy came up to stop their mounts next to Bill.

"I figure we need to wait for first light, get up on the high spots, and pinpoint the Nez Perce from here. If we keep goin' blind like we been, we may run into the main bunch or part of 'em. They can't be far away by now," Beck said.

"All right," Morgan said, "let's get the men into camp, get some of us up on the hills."

This they did, the troopers and the pack mule filing into a small sink at the base of a butte, while Beck, Hardy, Corporal Dodd and Trooper Woodecky each chose a hill and went off to climb it. As Beck was guiding Bill toward a long nearby slope, Simon Pocket came up alongside.

"Mind if I join you up there?" Pocket said.

"Not at all, come on!" and they spurred their mounts for the top of the hill. It turned into a bit of a contest, as the slope steepened near its crest, and Bill's great leaps were matched by the spotted pony under Pocket with quicker lunges but shorter in stride. They reached the curve of the crest together, and stopped just before sky-lining themselves. The horses blew as the men swung down and edged on up to the top. Beck got down and crawled through the sparse grass, coming to a rest on his belly, field glass in hand. Simon wormed up to his side.

Beck swept the panorama of the country before him. The northern peaks of the Judith Mountains lay off to his right in the golden light of the morning sun. The overcast sky reflected the gold, added pink to it, so that the dark mass of the mountains seemed to be on fire. Out to the north the land lay broken up by rolling hills, gullies, some of the buttes topped by clumps of brush, small trees. Off to the left in the distance, the course of the Judith River was marked by the dark clothing of trees and brush along its course.

And then his glass found the quarry, movement on a slope six or seven miles out. He could see the distinct mass of traveling animals traversing the slope, moving away from the Judith River, bits of color in the mass indicating people and their possessions.

"Well dammit to hell!" Beck said disgustedly, handing the glass to Simon. "We worked all night to close the gap and they're already running five miles ahead! Don't them people never sleep?"

"Don't reckon so," Pocket said, peering through the glass. "I'll wager you a days pay they don't have to worry about tired ponies, neither, what with all them spare horses they got. But wait just a minute, what's that?" He had shifted the glass to the left, lower down. "Looks like we may have company a'comin',"

"What?" Beck said, taking the glass and peering in the direction Simon pointed.

At first he saw only the rolling hills, chopped-up gullies and lone stands of pine, but then, in the valley where he had left the soldiers only minutes before, less than a mile north and coming fast, a dozen riders. He stared intently at them.

"They Nez Perce?" Pocket said

"I can't tell," Beck said, "Seem to be Injuns right enough, but which Injuns I can't say. Might be some of the Crow that's been hangin' around. One thing is sure, they keep goin' the way they're goin', they'll run right over our boys down there. Question is, can we get down there in time to warn 'em! Come on!" and he rolled off the top of the hill, then took to his feet and ran for the horses. Simon was right behind him.

They got to the horses and scrambled aboard, spurred the mounts down the hillside toward the camp a mile away. They had the downward slope and the knowledge of the other party, and so drove their horses as fast as the steep slope would allow. Bill used his length to bound down the grade in great lumbering leaps, while Simon's pony skittered along at his side, taking shorter strides but keeping up, even pulling ahead with its quickness. They came off the steeper part of the hill and the horses stretched out their strides, running now full out. Beck could hear his big stallion blowing hard as they entered into the smaller hills and knolls that concealed the soldier's camp. Just a little further down a gully and they would be within sight of the soldiers.

A shrieking war whoop split the air, followed by a shot. The bullet whined over Beck's head. Then more shots came, and Beck glanced over his right shoulder to see a line of Indians coming down the near slope, the white puff of rifle smoke billowing out here and there as they fired.

"Don't think them boys is Crows!" Simon hollered as they came in sight of the soldiers' position. A bullet smacked into Bill's right side and the horse twitched in mid stride. The bottom dropped out of Beck's gut, and he swore loudly. But Bill kept pounding along, and then they were into the hollow with the troopers and a responding volley crashed out from the soldiers at the pursuing warriors.

Beck jumped off of Bill and leapt around to the right side of the horse and grabbed the butt stock of his rifle to pull it out of the scabbard. The stock came out, but the rifle did not. He looked at the shattered wood in his hand, stunned for a moment, then stepped over to the low earth bank serving as a breastwork for the soldiers. The firing had become general, now, and the white smoke from the rifles hung thick in the air. Down in their hollow, the wind was only slowly dissipating the gun smoke. The men loaded and fired their Springfields deliberately, looking for targets to get a good bead on. Lieutenant Morgan walked among them, a grin on his face.

"That's it, men, don't waste your ammunition, find a target, careful aim, now, make it count, that's it boys, keep it up...."

The Nez Perce had retreated after the first volley, but only so far as to hide their horses and find cover. Now they were returning a deliberate fire of their own, and the bullets started to score. The troopers hunkered down into the basin, only rising far enough for a shot each time. Morgan crouched lower, then lower still as a bullet clipped his shoulder. Beck sat against the base of the dirt bank, looked again at the stock of his rifle in his hand. He swore again, shaking his head, thinking of a bag of ammunition freshly made, now useless.

The Nez Perce were firing from a ridge top and a gulley on two sides to the north and east. Their closest warrior was eighty yards out, with most of them fifty yards further away. They had a slight elevation advantage, but could not see the horses which were in the bottom of the sink, where a rise of ground kept them out of sight.

Beck moved at a crouch back to the horses, and went to examine Bill's side. The bullet which had hit the wrist of the rifle had passed through the rifle scabbard to do so, but the leather of the scabbard on the horse side prevented it from going further, after its force had been absorbed in smashing the rifle. However, a splinter of wood had pierced the leather, and Bill. Beck carefully pulled it out, and Bill's side twitched in response. Its sharp tip had only penetrated an inch or so into Bill. Beck patted Bill's flank and then walked to his head. He patted the big horse's neck.

"We got lucky again, big fellah," Beck said.

He went back to the scabbard and drew out the rifle, looked it over. When the bullet shattered the stock, it also mangled the mainspring which was housed in the wrist of the stock. The rifle was useless. Beck shoved it back into the scabbard.

Beck moved back to the earth bank at a crouch, and found that one of the troopers, Jones, had been hit high up on one shoulder, and was lying at the base of the bank. Morgan turned from talking to him.

"Not serious," Morgan said, speaking loudly over the thunder of the rifles.

"My rifle was hit in the chase, ruined it," Beck said, "I'll need his."

"Welcome to it!" Morgan said, and moved away so that Beck could get the Mills cartridge belt from Jones. The belt still held two dozen cartridges. Beck tried to buckle it on, but Jones was a much slimmer man, and it would not fit. He finally fastened its ends together and put one arm and his head through it as a bandolier. He took up Jones' Springfield, half-cocked the hammer, lifted the breach block, found it loaded with a fresh cartridge.

"Had me one o' them devils in my sights," Jones grinned, a little pale. "He was a mite quicker."

"I'll see if I can't get a couple for you, trooper!" Beck said, patting Jones' unwounded shoulder.

Beck moved over to Morgan, who was popping his head up from time to time, encouraging his men, spotting targets, trying to puzzle out their situation. The men were firing less, as their quarry was well concealed and not many clear shots offered themselves. The Indians were sure to send a bullet after any part of a trooper that was shown.

"Where'd this bunch come from?" Morgan said as Beck crouched beside him.

"We spotted 'em coming down the valley, way I figure it, they was going out along their back trail, probably the rear guard or some such. By their line of march I figured they would run right over the top of you if we didn't warn you. They seen us comin' down off the hill and here we are."

"Where is the main body?" Morgan said.

"Caught a glimpse of them about six or eight miles out. All that work we did last night was for nothing. They must have broke camp about the time we did, or shortly thereafter."

"Do you think they were aware of us?"

"Don't know. This bunch here, now, I think they was just heading out on a scout. If we can prevent them from going back...."

"Looks like they're doing all the preventing at the moment," Morgan said dryly. Then loudly, "Men, save your ammunition. We're doing no good at this range."

"Lieutenant, how about a flank attack?" Beck said. "So far they haven't got us surrounded. I could take a couple of men, maybe Pocket and Gander, out to the west, and we could try to get behind 'em."

"Getting the horses out of that sink would be the hard part," Morgan said. "Where they are they're protected, but for a hundred yards or so down that gulley you'll come under fire."

"Yep, I figure. But what else you got in mind?"

Just then a yelp from the firing line, and Gross slid backward to the base of the bank, his hat tumbling with him. He put his hand to his head, and it came away bloody. Morgan scrabbled over to him.

"You hit bad?" he said to Gross.

"Don't think so, sir," Gross said, fetching his hat. Blood dribbled down the side of his head. "But I think they've definitely found the range."

Beck's head came up, and he was listening.

"Hey, listen to that!" he said. They heard war whoops, shots fired. But no bullets zinged overhead. Several of them risked a look over the earthen bank. They could see a brave here or there rise and run away from them. Some were firing, but in the opposite direction.

"It's Hardy!" Beck said, jumping up. "Come on!" He sprinted for the horses, and clambered up on Bill. Simon Pocket was there, and two of the troopers. They all galloped out of the sink, down the dry wash to the west, and then Beck led the way up a long side slope to the north, looking to gain high ground. They galloped up the slope and curved around to the right, and topped a shoulder of the hill. There below they could see a small herd of horses being run by two mounted men, and a third mounted man hanging back, firing at

Indians who pursed on foot. As they watched four mounted Indians emerged from a draw and headed for the herd.

"Come on!" Beck shouted and drove his spurs into Bill's flanks. He charged down the slope toward the escaping herd. Somehow Hardy had linked up with Corporal Dodd and Trooper Woodecky, and they had managed to drive off most of the Nez Perce horses. But they did not get them all, and the four remaining mounted Indians could easily overwhelm the scouts, who had their hands full with the herd. Beck knew that if they could get there in time, the attack would be broken, the Nez Perce mostly afoot could not report back to the main body even if they escaped. It all depended on whether they could get to the mounted Indians and head them off or kill or capture them.

They swept down off of the slope and pounded through the scattered warriors on foot, shooting at them as they passed. Several fell, but most dodged into whatever cover they could find and returned fire. Then the scouts were in the clear and bearing down on the four mounted enemy, who looked behind them at the sound of gunfire. As a group they broke to the north, heading up a long grade covered in short, brown prairie grass. At the same time, the three scouts with the stolen ponies broke from the horses and galloped across the slope to try and head off the four Nez Perce horsemen.

The four Indians suddenly split up, two of them wheeling their mounts and heading for the abandoned horses, one more going straight up the hill toward the three scouts, the last pulling left and heading back to the west across the slope.

"The herd!" Beck called, "Don't let them get to those horses!" The three riders with him pounded on across the slope, and one of the scouts who had been with the herd wheeled his horse and headed back toward it. The other two scouts charged down on the lone brave coming their way. Beck veered off to the west in pursuit of the lone rider heading in that direction, and as he did so that rider fired a shot at him. The bullet whined harmlessly by overhead. Behind him, Beck could hear firing from further down the slope.

Bill was blowing hard with every stride, gaining ground up the slope in the long, lunging gait that Beck had always counted on to eat up the ground. He could not head the rider, but found himself following the Nez Perce across the slope at about forty yards back. He had the Springfield rifle in his hand, but the rough pounding of the horses made a shot too chancy. But not for the Nez Perce, who fired a shot by twisting in his saddle. The bullet went wide.

The chase took them around the hill, and soon they were out of sight and sound of the battle they had left. Bill was running smoothly, but he was not gaining. They pounded down a long slope, through the wash at the bottom, up and across the next slope. Bill began to slow bit by bit, and the distance between pursued and pursuer stretched to fifty yards, then sixty. The Nez Perce broke suddenly down hill, heading for a table of land that sloped off gradually toward the Judith. Beck cut the corner, picking up a little ground, but soon the Indian pony was as far ahead again and gaining. Then they were racing across the table, and up ahead Beck saw the Nez Perce suddenly slide his horse to a halt and wheel to face him. His rifle came up, the white smoke of his shot billowed out, and the bullet jerked at the sleeve of Beck's coat.

The Indian warrior then heeled his horse for a run straight at Beck, who brought the long Springfield up and tried to sight it, but the shot when it broke was clumsy and had no effect. As the two horses closed, the Indian screeched out his war cry and swung his rifle like a club, while Beck yanked Bill directly into the shoulder of the oncoming Indian pony. Reflexively he threw his own rifle up to ward off the blow of the Nez Perce as the horses collided and the Indian pony went down. Its rider had broken his rifle over Beck's Springfield and had gone sprawling as his horse tumbled. Bill was knocked staggering, but kept his feet and his stride, and Beck hauled him in, and around, and there the warrior was, on his feet.

Beck half cocked the hammer of the rifle, levered open the breechblock, sending the spent cartridge casing spinning into the grass. He grabbed a fresh cartridge from his bandolier, thumbed it into the breech, slammed home the block, and cocked the rifle. The Nez Perce had got his horse up, and swung up into the blanket covered saddle just as Beck lined up the sights and fired. The warrior screamed and tumbled back into the grass. His horse stood, head down, trembling.

Jon reloaded the Springfield and walked Bill over to the fallen brave. The Indian lay on his back, spread eagled, eyes open. The front of his buckskin shirt turned red from the spout of blood pumping out of a hole in his chest. The blood stopped flowing. The man did not move.

Beck swung down from Bill, and retrieved the Nez Perce's rifle. The stock had been broken off, just like his own. He worked the lever awkwardly, saw that the rifle was empty. He went to the body and searched it. The man had no more ammunition. He went to the pony and stripped away its bridle and saddle, slapped its rump. It moved a few paces and stood, drooping.

Jon swung wearily back up into the saddle, and walked Bill over to the edge of the table. A cliff dropped straight down for about thirty feet. Now it was obvious why the warrior had turned on him. He turned Bill and started back the way they had come. After a mile or so, he got down and walked, leading a worn out Bill who just didn't want to move at all. Near mid morning, Simon Pocket came along the trail, tracking Beck and his quarry by the gouges in the prairie grass they had left. He turned his horse and fell in beside the trudging Jon Beck.

"That pony of yours ever get tired?" Beck said.

"Not so's you'd notice," Pocket grinned.

"So, how'd it come out, back there?"

"We got the mounted ones, every one, and we got the horses. Half a dozen redskins a'foot got away. They was ready to fight, that's fer certain, no quit in that bunch."

"Anyone of our folk hit?"

"Yep, Hardy and Gross got nicked—"

"Hardy? How bad?"

"Oh, he'll be okay, just hit him in the foot, just a nick, really. Gross took a spent bullet in the hip, looks like he'll make it, too. They got a couple of our horses, but we got theirs, entire, so we're in good shape there."

"By "got," do you mean stole, or kilt?"

"Oh, kilt, for sure. None of them got away on a horse."

"I heard firing in the valley as I was going after my man. What was that?"

"Well that Morgan, he put on a charge into that bunch on foot, scattered 'em like rabbits. Once that was done, the rest was easy. Well, at least as easy as killin' a man ever gets. How 'bout you, that Injun get away?"

"No. Got him boxed in on top of a mesa. He turned around and come at me, full of fight to the end. Had no more cartridges, but he wasn't about to give up. Bill, here, knocked his pony down, and I shot him."

"Knocked his pony down? How'd that happen?"

"He got up to the edge of the mesa, saw he was penned, turned and came right at me. The horses collided, and Bill knocked that little Injun pony ass over teakettle. If he'd got past me, that would have been the last of him I'd 'a seen. Bill's got bottom, hell if he don't, but he's just plain wore out, like all our mounts. I was surprised he could stay with that Nez Perce nag for so long. Last couple of miles he was steamin' along on heart alone."

"He's a fine one, I'll say that," Pocket said, grinning. "Ever think to sell him?"

Beck looked over at Pocket as if the man had suggested some unnatural act.

"Would you sell your mother?" he said finally.

Simon laughed. "Just funnin' you, Jon, I know you're married to that beast! Hey, but I'll tell you what, wouldn't it be some horse if we was to mate your great big charger and my tough little mare? Now, that might be something," he said, leaning forward to pat his paint on the neck.

"It would at that," Beck said.

"Why, we could go inta the horse raisin' bidness together!" Simon laughed. "That is, if'n we have any horses left after all this is over!"

"Yep," Beck said glumly, "assuming that."

They came down the long hill into the soldier's camp near mid day. The wounded were lying on the base of the bank.

"Get your man?" Morgan said as Beck came up. Simon took Bill's reins and led the horse away toward the herd.

"He won't be tellin' no tales around the camp fire tonight," Beck said. "What's the damage here?"

"Three wounded, none too seriously," Morgan said.

"Do I count as two, since I been shot twice?" Gross said with a grin.

"Sure, trooper, you can count as two," Morgan said, shaking his head.

"That mean I get double rations and twice the pay?" grinned Gross.

"Don't push your luck," Morgan said.

Beck went over to kneel before Hardy, who lay with the others against the bank of the sinkhole. Beck turned up the corner of the bloody bandage that was wrapped around Hardy's right foot. He shook his head. He reached around his right hip, and pulled out his bowie knife.

"Looks like it'll have to come off," he said, "Here, Dodd, Woodecky, you grab his arms, Lieutenant Morgan, if you will be kind enough to sit on his chest, and Simon, you lay across his legs," said Beck, turning to each of them in turn.

As he turned back to Hardy, he found himself looking down the bore of a .44 revolver.

"Now Lige—"

"Don't "Now Lige" me!" Hardy said, "You ain't touching that foot while I'm alive, and that's a fact!"

"Oh come on, Lige!" Beck grinned, "What's a little cuttin' among friends? I'll let you keep the foot, you'll just have to carry it in your saddlebag!"

"Like hell!" Hardy said, glowering.

"Oh all right," Beck said, sheathing his knife, "Have it your way. We'll just wait until you're asleep, and then—"

Hardy cocked the revolver. Beck's eyes widened.

"Now Lige, you know it's a fact certain that I is only funnin' you, don't you!" Beck said, his palms held before him in a mock surrender.

"What I know for certain is that I don't particularly care for your sense of funnin' right at the moment," Hardy said, lowering the revolver hammer to half cock. He opened the loading gate, shucked out the empties, and reloaded the revolver before sliding it back into his holster.

Beck just shook his head and rose to his feet.

"Well, lieutenant," he said to Morgan, "If our stock wasn't beat out before, they sure are now. Them Nez Perce ponies any good?"

"Some of them seem to be," Morgan said. "We lost Hardy's mount, and one of the army horses. Those we can replace from the Indian horses. Two more of ours have suffered bullet wounds, which, though not immediately fatal, may prove so in the long run. Again, the Indian ponies will have to suffice for them."

"If I might suggest it," Beck said, "We should head for the river, then follow it north. We won't be on the trail of the main body of

224

Indians, but the traveling will be faster and easier over flatter ground. It will give the horses good feed and water for a day or so. Then, when we reach the Missouri we can head east to pick up the Nez Perce trail. Lige seems to think they're making for the crossing at Cow Island, and if the army has troops there, they may be bottled up for a time."

"My orders are to find the main body of renegades and hang on. If we take the river route we lose them entirely."

"Maybe not. We could send out one or two men at a time to keep an eye on 'em. The rest of us get to rest, and more importantly, go easier on the horses. If we rotate the hard riding among our own horses and the Nez Perce mounts, they will last longer, and be fresher."

Morgan said nothing for a time, thinking it over. "That makes sense," he said.

"And, we must take the horses with us in any case," Beck went on. "We cannot risk them being recovered by the Nez Perce that escaped us here on foot. They may strike out after their kinsmen afoot, or they may follow us and attempt to steal back their mounts. Either way, we've bought a little time, during which the main body will not feel threatened enough to run faster. And, on the river we'll be better able to care for our wounded, with plenty of clean water, and willow bark for tea."

"You have convinced me, Mr. Beck. First things first. I will write a dispatch advising Colonel Sturgis of our position, and the action in which we fought today. Then we will head for the river and see what time can be made."

As Morgan got out his dispatch case, Woodecky and Dodd went to advantageous spots above the camp to act as sentries. Gander gathered buffalo chips and dry wood from a nearby clump of scrubwood, and got a fire going. Beck went to the mule and fetched back the coffee pot and pan, along with hardtack and bacon. A fire was soon going, the canteens used to fill the coffee pot, and bacon and the coffee were set to cooking over the flames.

"Like I was telling you, son," Hardy said to Gross, "you'll have stories aplenty to tell your grandpups, how you suffered terrible wounds at the hands of the hostiles, while saving the civilized world from the ravages of the redskin!"

"My head hurts, Mr. Hardy. And my hip is no better. So far glory has been far too costly for my taste," Gross said.

"So you say now," Hardy said, "But with the passing of time, you will remember the pain less, and the glory will flame brighter! It may even come to pass, in some candle-lit kitchen in the distant future, the stove giving off warmth on a winter's night, the smell of biscuits in the air, the little ones gathered at your feet, it may come to pass that you, Trooper Gross, won the Nez Perce war single handed! And you have the scars to prove it!"

"Will there be gravy with those biscuits, there in the future?" Gross said.

"I would expect so," Hardy said.

"Then it's a scene I will certainly aspire to, Mr. Hardy," Gross said.

Chapter 28

Woodecky left with a dispatch for Sturgis on one of the Indian ponies, which had to be broken to the army saddle and the strange smell of an unwashed trooper before it would allow itself to be ridden. It was early afternoon when the rest of the scouts, the wounded mounting up with the assistance of the others, started their trek down the valley toward the Judith River bottoms. Each of the unwounded led a spare horse or two, or the pack mule, and Hardy also led a horse. Jones and Gross had their hands full just hanging on to the horses they rode.

Corporal Dodd volunteered to head off after the main body of the Nez Perce, and, after an evening rendezvous point had been agreed to by picking out a distant butte to the north, he rode another of the Indian ponies off to the northeast.

Hardy was having a hard time keeping control of his own Indian horse, as well as leading a spare, because he could not use the stirrup on his right side. Beck called a halt, and the grumbling Hardy was put aboard Bill, and Beck mounted the Indian pony and took the led horse as well. Bill knew Hardy and accepted his touch on the reins with placid cooperation, and they started again for the Judith.

At the river they dismounted, watered the horses, then turned them into a flat of rich grass within a narrow bend in the watercourse. The wounded were stretched out on the river bank, and Beck and Morgan removed the makeshift dressings and examined and cleaned the wounds. Jones's shoulder was in good shape, as the bullet had passed clean through and the blood only seeped a bit now. They cleaned and dressed the wound, fitted a makeshift sling for his arm, and went to look at Gross.

His head was furrowed where the bullet had passed along the skull, but after washing the dried blood away the scrape did not appear to be serious. The bullet which had hit him in the left hip had penetrated but not exited. They cleaned the wound and Morgan dug the bullet out with the tip of his knife. Gross grinned sickly through it all, and chuckled a bit when the rinsed bullet was handed to him.

"Something to show those grandkids, eh, Mr. Hardy?" he said to Lige.

"Glory, son, glory," Hardy said tiredly.

"Lieutenant, I hate to say it," Gross said, "but just getting down here to the river was a pure hell on that hip. Maybe I could stay behind for a few days, until it heals a bit."

"We'll not leave you, trooper, and I can't spare the men to stay with you," Morgan said.

"We could rig up a travois for him," Beck said. "At least get him to the Missouri, where I'm sure we could put him aboard a boat."

Morgan agreed to this, and Gander went off to cut a pair of travois poles.

"And now," Beck said, kneeling at Hardy's bandaged foot, "let's have a look at this one." He unwound the crimsoned cloth from Hardy's foot, and they cleaned away the dried blood with river water. The bullet had passed through the foot, entering just to the left of the instep peak and punching out though the sole. A small bone fragment protruded from the ragged hole in the bottom of Hardy's foot. Fresh blood oozed from the wound as they examined it.

Beck reached behind his hip and once more pulled forth his bowie knife.

"I told you before and I'll say it again," Hardy said, laying a hand on one of his pistols.

"Shut up, Lige," Beck said quietly, "no foolin' this time. You have a piece of bone sticking out the bottom of your foot. If we stuff it back in, it's sure to infect the wound, and you will lose your foot, maybe even your leg! I'm going to get that bone out of there, but that's all I'm going to do. It's goin' to hurt, so you save all your guts for the cuttin'!"

"Well, if'n you gotta do it, do it!" Hardy said gruffly.

"Simon!" Beck called to Pocket, who sat his pony near the meadow watching the horses. Pocket rode over and swung down.

"Lieutenant, if you will grab on to his leg, wrap it up in your arms so's he can't move it. Simon, you lay yourself across his lap," Beck said.

"I ain't a gonna struggle none," Hardy said, "I know you got to do this."

"You won't have a say in it," Beck said, "When I start working, you're leg'll kick out like it's got a mind of its own."

They all took position and draped themselves all over Hardy. Simon grinned in his face. "I don't have to kiss him, do I?" he said.

"Why you pissant little jackass---Yeow!!" Hardy started and then jerked violently as Beck applied the knife. He gritted his teeth and grunted, holding his breath. Beck whittled away at what needed removal, and Hardy ground his teeth and cursed and his leg jerked and jerked again. Gander came up dragging two long poles, freshly cut from riverbank trees, and stopped as he saw what was being done to Hardy's foot. His mouth dropped open, and he stared, his face draining white.

"Gander, you got a needle, some thread maybe?" Beck said, glancing up at him.

Gander could not take his eyes off of the bloody foot.

"Gander!" Beck said sharply.

"Oh, ah, yes sir, I believe I do!" Gander said, as if waking from a dream. He went to the meadow to find his horse and saddlebags.

Beck finished with his knife, and bathed the wound again in clean water.

"Best I could do, Lige," he said, glancing at Hardy. "We'll sew her up, and hope for the best."

Gander returned with the needle and thread, and Beck commenced to sew the wound closed as Hardy again gritted his teeth and muttered curses as Beck worked. The sewing completed, he bound the foot in one of Hardy's shirts.

Beck rinsed his knife in the river, wiped it on his leg, and slipped it back into its sheath.

"We may need another travois," he said to Morgan.

"Not on my account," Hardy said. "I can sit a horse just fine."

Morgan took Beck's arm and nodded toward the river bank upstream. They walked a bit and then stood, looking out over the shallows. The water was clear and bright, and burbled around the stones and rocks it flowed among.

"This is shaping up to be a complete disaster," Morgan said. "The wounded will slow us to the point of losing the Nez Perce altogether. Furthermore, I'm fast running out of men to send out as couriers. The horses are worn out, the Indian ponies are half wild, and there's a good chance those Nez Perce we set afoot this morning are watching us right now, looking for an opening to get at their horses. I will confess to you, Mr. Beck, that I am confounded and somewhat perplexed as to what to do to save the situation."

Jon Beck pursed his lips and rubbed the red beard stubble on his cheek. He sighed.

"Lieutenant, you spooned 'er all into a nutshell and tamped 'er down tight!" Beck said, shaking his head. "But you got to realize one thing. We do what we can do, and what we can't do we don't fret about. Now, the way I see it is this. You and I know we can't leave the wounded behind. The travois will slow us some, but all we got to do is make the Missouri, and we can leave the wounded with one man. A boat will be along one way or t'other, I s'pect. We have five good men left, or at least five unwounded men left, and we can still keep an eye on the Nez Perce if we split the command. Gander, Dodd, Simon and I can tend to that chore. Or, keep either Dodd or Gander with you, and the three of us will do the scouting. When we have definite news that needs to get back to Sturgis, send either Dodd or Gander. I need Pocket with me, and you will need to be with the wounded.

"But it may not be as bad as all that. There are settlements on the Missouri, steamboats up to Cow Island at least, for this time of year. The Nez Perce seem to be heading for the Cow Island crossing, and with luck there will be army folk there to give them a welcome. If they are stopped at the Missouri, our job is done. If they slip through, there is bound to be army folk about to give chase. After all, Miles was coming up from the east and south, and for all we know he's at Cow Island now.

"What I'm getting at, is that we just have to keep heading on down that trail up ahead, and do what we can."

"Of course," Morgan said. "It's just that I feel we must be doing more, somehow. There's got to be a way—"

"Lieutenant, we are doing all we can. Sometimes you just have to settle in, take the long view, and let things play out as they will."

Morgan sighed, and pursed his lips, and thought. Finally he said, "All right, then. The first goal is to reach that rendezvous butte by nightfall and, with luck, meet up with Corporal Dodd. Depending on what he has to say, we'll make our plans from there."

"Fair enough, lieutenant," Beck said.

But the butte was further than they had guessed, and their river bottom travel slowed by the use of the travois. Gross was strapped aboard it, and Hardy mounted once more on Bill, though he protested this at first. Jones was helped up onto one of the army mounts, and off they went. They kept to the flats and the shallows, traveling in the river bed where the horses had easy footing. The Indian pony dragging the travois would only walk at a steady pace, and thus they all did the same. The casualties felt their wounds begin to tighten up, and the steady ache of pierced flesh rose in each of them like a tide of pain. The autumn drought had lowered the river level to a mere stream in places, and the column of riders could travel in a nearly straight line down the river bottoms.

Early evening found them still several miles from the butte. Beck spurred his mount from his position next to Hardy up to the lead rider, Lieutenant Morgan.

"We'll not make the butte by nightfall at this rate," Beck said. "I'd like to ride on ahead and try and link up with Dodd, if he makes it. If you just keep on going down the river, we'll find you. Don't go further than due west of the butte."

"Consider it done, Mr. Beck, and good luck to you," Morgan said.

Beck spurred his horse on down the river, cantering through the shallows in a splash of hooves in the clear water. Half a mile downstream his steered the horse up the low bank, through the trees and brush bordering the river, and then he was in the clear and climbing across the face of a long mound of a hill. He kept the horse cantering along, and the butte, which was several miles east of the river, loomed closer and closer as the light of evening began to fade.

An hour later, in the last glow of the sunset in the western sky, Jon Beck was at the western base of the butte. He worked the horse through gullies and around rockfalls, gradually traveling to the north and then east. As the last of the light went, he spurred the exhausted horse to the top of a low bluff, and found a little wash filled with scrub oak and brush. He swung down and tethered the horse, gathered wood into a heap on the top of the bluff, and started a fire. Just as the flames began to lick up into the wood pile and thrive in the light wind, the last of the light disappeared in the west. The darkness was complete.

Beck settled the sticks and small logs of the fire a bit, tamping them down on the already glowing coals, added more fuel. He went to his horse, and moved the animal into the thicket where he had been getting the wood, and tethered the animal out of the firelight. He slipped the Springfield rifle from it scabbard, and went to find a place among the nearby rocks. He would wait there for Dodd, but he did not know who else might see the fire and come to investigate.

He hunkered down out of the wind as best he could. The night was silent but for the soughing of the wind over the hills and scrub forests. The horse stamped from time to time, and nickered a bit. It wanted water and the grass they had left earlier in the evening. Beck could feel the need for the warmth of the fire, for food in his belly. He reflected that his pants did not fill out the waistband as they did a few short weeks ago, and his shirt hung more loosely about his middle. He was not a fat man, but he had always had the shape of a barrel, more or less, and that shape was bound in muscle. Now he felt his spare frame was shrinking, and like a bear in autumn, he wanted food almost desperately at times. Anything with fat on it was mouthwatering to him. He was thinking of the last turkey he had shot, years ago before the war, and how it had baked up in his mother's great cast iron oven, dripping in fat, when his horse nickered. And nickered again.

He froze among the rocks, listening. He could hear the wind, and the cracking and popping of the fire. Then, from down the slope in the darkness, a voice.

"Halloo the fire!" came the call.

It was Dodd. "Up here!" Beck called back. But he did not leave the rocks.

After a moment Dodd came into the firelight, leading his horse. Beck rose and joined him. They both warmed themselves over the blaze.

"Any trouble finding me?" Beck said.

"Naw, you's right about where I figured you'd be. Where's the rest of 'em?"

"Down on the river. We had to put Gross on a travois, slowed us down. I came ahead to find you. Now we've got another hour of two of ridin' to find the camp."

"Well, I did sign up for the cavalry," Dodd said, tiredly. Beck tamped down the fire, then heaped it with dirt. He went to his horse, slid the rifle into its scabbard, and led him out to Dodd. They mounted, and Beck leading the way, turned toward the west, downhill, and the river.

It was after midnight when Beck and Dodd spotted the small fire of the soldier's camp. It was in the trees on the west side of the river, and as they splashed across the shallows, a voice called out, "Who is it!"

"Beck and Dodd," Beck called back, and then they passed Gander on the west bank and came up to the camp. They unsaddled the horses and took them to a meadow nearby with the other mounts. They picketed the horses there, and returned to the fire.

Simon Pocket had materialized from the darkness and was tending a pan on the fire. He poured out coffee into two cups, and handed them to Beck and Dodd. Morgan then stepped up, pulling on his uniform blouse.

"What'd you find, corporal?" Morgan said.

"Well Sir, I latched on to them Injuns pretty quick, they wasn't in no big hurry. I think you were right, in that they've headed the main bunch toward the Cow Island crossing. They got parties out all over the country, though, 'ceptin' back the way they come. They must be figuring on that bunch we ran into this morning watching their back trail. Anyway, they're camped about a dozen miles off to the northeast, and I figure they'll hit the Missouri tomorrow."

"Then we must do the same!" Morgan stated. "If they get bottled up there by army units, we can come on their rear and maybe do some good!"

"Lieutenant," Beck said, "I thought we decided—"

"Change of plan, Mr. Beck!" Morgan declared. "This will be our chance to go on the offensive for a change, help put an end to this cat and mouse game. And after all, our job is to find them and not lose them. I want to be there when the army finds them as well."

"Offensive?" Beck said, "We have three wounded and horses barely able to get out of their own way, what good do you think we're going to do against a force at least a hundred times our size?"

"Well, we must try!" Morgan barked. "We must try. I am sick to death of hanging back and waiting for them to make their move. We can take the initiative at the river, and we can make a difference in the outcome. Is that too much to aspire to, Mr. Beck?"

"Suicide ain't too much to aspire to, but it's a solitary occupation," Beck growled.

"Are you saying you won't fight?" Morgan snapped.

Beck looked into Morgan's eyes and his face reddened a little.

"Lieutenant," he said into the stillness, "you hired me, or the army did, for a job of work. Part of that job is obeying the wishes of my commander, in this case, you. So far, you have seen whether I will fight or not. If there is some question about that, then you had best ask it now. If not, I will be with you and taking your orders for the duration. But I will also give you my opinion of the situation, whether you agree with that opinion or not, because that is what you are paying me for."

Morgan in his turn did not speak immediately, but looked at Beck, then at the fire. Finally he said, "All right then. We leave at first light. Get what sleep you can. And Mr. Pocket, when you are done there, would you please relieve Trooper Gander."

"Shore 'nuff, lieutenant," Pocket said. He dished up grub from the pan and handed a plate to Beck and Dodd. "More coffee?" he said, reaching for their cups.

Morgan left the firelight, heading back to his bedroll. Beck and Dodd squatted by the fire, using fingers and knives to shovel in the food. The bacon grease was sopped up by hardtack, and the beans were hot and went down quickly. They washed it all down with coffee that Pocket handed over one cup at a time.

"Simon, you want to go relieve Gander, I'll clean up the dishes," Beck said.

"Thanks, Jon," Pocket said. He wiped his hands on his britches and went to fetch his rifle.

"Wind ain't so bad, down here in the trees," Dodd said.

"Yep. Feels good to have a fire you can relax at."

They ate for a time, and when the plates were licked clean, Beck set about cleaning up the pan and the plates.

"That sergeant back at the Musselshell," he said over his shoulder as he scoured the tin with wet sand in the river, "he really a friend of yours?"

Dodd rose from the fire and came to squat beside Beck. In a low voice, he said, "That bastard? By God I'd like to see him shot, and me given the task of diggin' the bullet outa him! The sonuvabitch has been making my like a misery nigh onto three years! He found out I was a…a Reb in a former life, don'tcha know, and he hain't let up on me for a second. Hopin' to run me out of the army, I figure."

"A Reb? And you're now in the Union Army?"

"Feller's gotta eat," Dodd said, chuckling, "though we didn't eat near often enough when I was with Jackson. Got used to soldierin' though, and I figured if'n I had a horse to ride, well, life could be right comfy!"

"And is it?"

"Oh, it'll do. But you know, when you busted up that sergeant, it was like somebody gave me the biggest Christmas present I ever got! I can't tell you how much I enjoyed that!"

"Glad to be of help," Beck chuckled. "What got you into the War of Southern Secession?"

Dodd laughed a bit. "Oh, you mean the War of Northern Aggression?" he chuckled.

"Yes, that war."

"Aw, you know how it is. Yer kin all goes, and yer neighbors go, and yer best friends get to jawin' on ya, and 'fore ya know it, yer totin' a rifle and listenin' to some jughead sergeant bellow all day long. Never did really figure it out, ceptin' only I shore as hell didn't take kindly to other folks tellin' me what to do."

"You mean the sergeant?"

234

"I meant the damned yankees."

"And you're in the Union Army," Beck said again. He rinsed the plates and pan and turned back to the fire, Dodd coming with him.

"That's a fact," Dodd said, chuckling, "it purely is."

Beck added fuel to the fire, got his bedroll, and found a spot along the river bank to turn in. He had just closed his eyes when he was nudged awake by Simon Pocket. He grunted, said nothing, rose and rolled up the bedding. Pocket went about the camp waking the others, and then started up a new pot of coffee.

They saddled and packed the horses and the mule, and had coffee just before dousing the fire with river water. They were in the saddle and moving across the river by first light.

Corporal Dodd led them out in the direction he had last left the Nez Perce, and they moved slowly across country from the river in the growing light. They skirted the slopes of the butte and as they rounded its northern flank the pink dawn shown in their faces. The horses plodded up the slopes and down the grades and through the ravines without enthusiasm. By mid day they had cut the Nez Perce trail, and passed through the camp they had made the previous night.

Beck sent out one rider or another to scout the ridges and hills ahead of them, always with a cautious approach to the skyline, always waving on the scouts from the heights. In the early afternoon they found a small stream, brackish, but with some grass, and stopped to let the horses graze and the men eat a bite. Morgan and Dodd went to nearby hills to scan the country ahead.

Beck went to the travois and knelt beside Gross. He was resting with his eyes closed, as the horse he was attached to munched grass.

"Ain't no picnic, is it," Beck said.

"No sir, it is not!" Gross smiled, but did not open his eyes. "But it beats sittin' in a saddle by a long shot," he added.

"I figure we'll be at the river by tonight," Beck said. "Most likely get you on a boat and down the river to a proper doctor. No more of this bouncin' all over hell for you."

"That would be joy, Mr. Beck, it purely would."

"You warm enough?"

"I am, sir, and thank you for asking."

"All right, then," Beck said, patting Gross's arm and rising.

He went to sit beside Hardy, who was resting against a bank of the stream with his wounded leg straight out before him. The bandage was stained red where the blood had seeped through it, but most of it appeared dried, and Beck did not unwrap it.

"How's that hind paw doin'?" he said.

"Feel's like a badger's gnawin' on it," Hardy said.

"Should be at the river by sundown," Beck said.

"You figure the army will stop 'em there?"

"Nope. I figure if the army is there in force, the Nez Perce will simply head up river or down, or both, and cross where they can. I don't think they will stand and fight until they can get their families across. Besides, they ain't trying to conquer the country, they're on the run. Morgan's thinkin' too much like a military man, not like an Indian. No, they'll slip by one way or t'other, just like they been doin' since Idaho."

"Well, it ain't no secret I'm done," Hardy said disgustedly.

"Lige, you done your part. With luck that foot'll heal up just fine, you'll be fit as a fiddle in no time!"

"I'm thinkin' maybe my Injun fightin' days is done," Hardy said. "Sometimes all I think about is Maggie and the kids, maybe takin' up a little piece of Crow land and puttin' in a crop. Others have done it, I could too."

"You never was a farmer, Lige. You been huntin' and trappin' this country for most of your life. You think farmin' and you'd get along?"

"Don't know fer sure," Hardy said. "But times is changin', that I do know." He shook his head tiredly, and sighed. "One way or t'other, Jon, I figure I'm a mite tired of shootin' at folk."

"I think you're already tired of bein' shot, that's what I think!" Beck said, and laughed. "You just wait it out, Lige, you'll get all healed up and be rarin' to go at it again in no time! Why, I've seen men I soldiered with hit worse than you, and right away they get down and gloomy and just want to crawl in a hole and die. And it ain't the hurt so much as does it, it's the fact they is down and out and can't go to fightin' 'long side their pards no more! That's all it is, you're just gloomy about the fact you been taken out of the fight! Well, that's just the way it goes. I know you'll heal up and get back in it, I seen it a hundred times during the war."

"Maybe," Hardy mumbled.

"I know it sure as I'm sittin' here!" Beck said, slapping Hardy on his outstretched leg. The leg spasmed in reaction, causing his foot to jolt. "Ow!" Hardy yelped, and began to curse at Beck violently.

"Now that's the Elijah Hardy I know!" Beck laughed, dodging out of the reach of Hardy's punch. Beck rolled to his feet as Morgan rode to a stop at the creek.

"See anything up there, Lieutenant?" Beck said.

"Yes. Missouri in sight. And I do believe I saw the Nez Perce, although they are too far out to be sure. Let's mount up and get moving."

They did. The little column moved as quickly as it could, held back by the travois, which began to lag behind. The men did not use as much caution on the ridge tops as before, knowing that the Indians were so far ahead they would most likely not be seen at this distance. They worked down through the table lands to the Missouri River breaks, then through that broken country to the bluffs overlooking the south side of the river. Later afternoon found them two miles from the Missouri. They topped a gentle ridge and waited for the travois to come up.

Beck glassed the valley, as did Morgan.

"That would be the army post," Beck said, "where the smoke streams out. Must be cooking about now." He could see the white of tents in a cluster on the north bank flats near the river, and a few hundred yards downriver near the mouth of Cow Creek, white canvas covered piles of freighted supplies.

"Nez Perce are across and camped to the west," Morgan said. Beck turned his field glasses to the direction Morgan was looking, and could see more cook fire smoke, lodges in place, some color of the horses and people moving about the camp. They were about a mile or two up the river from the settlement.

"So much for the army stopping them here," Beck said.

"All right," Morgan said, "when the wounded come up, we'll ride on down to the river, and find the ford. We can cross in the darkness, and come up on them before dawn."

Beck looked at Morgan as he leaned on the pommel of his saddle.

"Attack at dawn, then?" he said wryly. He looked away and shook his head.

"We shall see. Trooper Gander, come here," Morgan said, reaching his dispatch pouch out of his saddle bag. Gander walked his horse over to the Lieutenant. Morgan placed a piece of paper on his saddle and wrote out a dispatch, and handed it to Gander.

"Take a fresh horse, and get this message to Sturgis," Morgan said.

Gander tucked the paper into his shirt, then transferred his saddle and bridle to the horse he had been leading. He mounted up, and saluting Morgan, who returned the salute without a word, he urged his horse into a canter back down the trail they had just come up. He passed Pocket leading the pony pulling the travois as they came up to join the scouts.

"Let's get down to the river," Morgan said.

The horses had a better time of it going down the gullies and ravines of the river breaks, and they seemed to sense they were going to water, or they smelled the water, for they moved at a quicker pace. The sun was setting in the west, and the deep shadows of the cuts and slopes hid their presence from the Indians across the river. The evening had deepened to a purple gloaming as they came out in the flats of the river bottom itself. The azure blue of the western sky reflected off the curve of the wide Missouri, like a bright mirror of moving blue silver. When they were half a mile from the water, they heard the echo of rifle fire from across the river.

Morgan drew the column to a halt at the first crescendo of a volley. They sat and listened as the firing became intermittent, rising and falling in intensity. They could see the muzzle flashes of the rifles at the army camp, and from the brush and willows out on the sloping ground above the camp to the north.

"Well lieutenant, here we are at last!" Beck said. "Looks like the army is holding its own, for the moment. Would you suggest a flank attack, or go straight at 'em?"

"Mr. Beck, your sarcasm is unwarranted," Morgan said bitterly. "Unless we can locate the ford with accuracy, we cannot attempt the river tonight. Would you be willing to do that for us, find the ford in the dark?"

"If that would be your pleasure, lieutenant," Beck said.

As they watched in the deepening light of dusk, flames leapt up from the tarpaulin covered freight piles downriver from the army camp. The scouts started for the river in the dark, moving slowly and keeping careful watch for any man or beast on their side of the river. They reached the banks of the Missouri, nearly a half mile wide at this point, where the light of the fire, now burning fiercely, glinted off of the rushing water. In the darkness they watered the horses, then moved them back into a willow thicket near the river.

"No fire tonight," Morgan said, "We can't risk being spotted. Mr. Beck, as you promised, please see what you can do about finding us a ford for first light."

"My pleasure, lieutenant." Beck reclaimed Bill after Hardy deposited himself in the long, course grass growing up in the willow thicket. He rode out of the camp toward the west, moving along the river bank carefully. The glare of the blaze in the north bank lit up the countryside for miles, and he moved the big, tired horse from clump to clump of willows or bushes or boulders, trying to keep as much as possible to the shadows of the firelight. The rifle fire from the army camp popped along steadily, for it appeared that the Indians found there a tougher nut to crack than they had anticipated.

Beck dared not take his horse out into the water, for the light of the fire would make him perfectly visible to any watcher on the north bank. He found the spot where the Nez Perce had crossed, for the bank was well chewed up by the passing horse herd and pack animals. From there he turned east, skirted his own camp by a wide margin, and then came near the water again and found a second set of tracks, indicating part of the Nez Perce had crossed at that point, also. Half a mile further east showed no further tracks, so he turned Bill west again and returned to the camp.

The horses were tethered in the thicket, and he tied Bill there too. Then he eased through the thin trunks of the willows to the party of scouts. They were crouched just inside the edge of the thicket, watching the fire across the river. As Beck sat among them, the rifle fire suddenly increased, the echo of it coming across the water like a string of firecrackers on the Fourth of July. The heavy popping went on for five minutes, then died back to the intermittent firing as before.

"Sounds like they rushed the camp," Beck said.

"And didn't succeed," added Morgan hastily. "What did you find for fords?"

"At least two places where the Nez Perce crossed, one about a mile up river, another half a mile down. With that fire goin' over there, I didn't take Bill out into the river, as I would have been jack lighted like a 'coon in a henhouse. But the river is pretty shallow all along here this time of year, we just have to watch out for quicksand, and the main channel. I might say, though, that whatever's going on over there, we can't do much to help, what with four able men and played-out horses."

Morgan thought for a time and sighed. "You are right. We'll camp here for the night, and cross at first light. Or at such a time as we can, and not get shot to pieces. We are finally within a good rifle shot of the enemy, and we cannot fight him."

"We ain't supposed to fight him," Beck said. "We're scouts, we're supposed to keep an eye on 'im, so others can fight him."

"I know that," Morgan said tiredly. "God help me, I do know that."

The fire blazed through the night, flaring up even brighter as it ate its way into the piles of freight. The firing in and around the Army camp popped its way along in the darkness, never ceasing completely, and flaring into a furious flurry twice more as the night wore on. Each time the shots kept coming sporadically afterwards, indicating the defenders were still defending. Beck could see that Morgan was positively jumping to get across the river and enter the fray, but his duty, when it came down to it, held him in check. They watched through the dark hours, some of them dozing out of sheer exhaustion, but Morgan, bright eyed and busily scanning the flames and the camp with his glass, rested his attention not at all.

Chapter 29

Through the long hours of the night the fire on the north bank blazed and the scouts listened to the popping of the battle just across the water. The men dozed among the willows, bundled in their coats, the horses browsing on the long grass or sleeping behind them. As the first grey light of dawn crept up in the east, a light snow began to fall. The wind shifted slightly west of south, and the smoke of the fire wafted over the waters to them. The smell of burning tar and bacon tainted the wind.

Beck had found a soft spot in the grass and was nestled in like a sitting prairie hen, his buffalo coat collar turned up against the cold. He nodded off again and again, only to jerk awake repeatedly. He was exhausted, as were they all, but he could not relax with the Nez Perce half a mile away and popping away at soldiers.

Lieutenant Morgan never ceased to watch the fire and the soldier's camp as the dawn brought it all into milky twilight. The firing died away as the world brightened. The low overcast that brought the snow kept the sun from appearing. The sky simply became a lighter shade of pale.

"Well lieutenant, what say you?" Beck said. "I could go over and have a look, see if anyone made it out alive."

"Do that," Morgan said, "we'll get the wounded fed and mounted, and await your signal."

Beck thought for a second, then rose and took his rifle to Bill, who was chewing a mouthful of grass. He untied Bill, swung up onto his back, and headed the horse down the river to the east. He soon found the trail he had discovered the night before, and, after Bill drank his fill, started the big horse across the river. The water was shallow, but dipped into deeper channels here and there, and the main channel was swiftly moving but only belly deep on Bill. Beck scanned the approaching bank carefully, looking for any sign of an Indian welcoming party. Then he was at the steep, little slope of the river bank itself, and spurred Bill up into and through the scrub brush and onto the flats of the river bottoms. He turned toward the fire still blazing at the confluence of Cow Creek and the Missouri. The roar of the flames was like the breath of a huge beast as he passed between the burning freight piles and the river. Ahead a hundred yards was a low bank surrounding the tents of the soldier's camp. Bill plodded the distance steadily, and Beck drew up at the base of the riverside bank.

As he came up, several soldiers stepped up atop the bank.

"Howdy," Beck said, "heard you boys shooting all night. Take many casualties?"

"None, by the grace of God!" said a soldier wearing sergeant's stripes. "Although two of the civilians here were hit in the beginning. Who are you?"

"Jon Beck, chief scout of the Fifth Cavalry. We come up from the Yellowstone, been on the track of these Injuns for a month now."

241

"We? You have troops with you?" the sergeant said.

"Four of us, still standing."

"Four. From the Fifth Cavalry? You are a long way from home, sir!"

"That we are. You have any food here?"

"Certainly! Although the bulk of it is now rather well cooked!" said the sergeant, nodding at the bonfire down the river.

"We have wounded with us, and we're powerful hungry. Think you could spare a bite for us?"

"Most certainly! But I caution you, the Nez Perce broke off the fight at dawn, and we have no assurance they will not be back. I would advise you to come over quickly, before they decide to take another poke at us."

"We'll do that," Beck said. He turned in his saddle, removed his hat, and waived it slowly back and forth, knowing that Lieutenant Morgan would be watching through his field glass. Even before the hat was back on his head, a horse and rider broke from cover at the place he had crossed the river, and walked down the bank into the water. The rest came on his heels, and Beck could see that they were all mounted, now, and the travois had been abandoned. He turned back to the men on the breastwork.

"So, you boys fought all night and none of you hit," he said.

"Correct, Mr. Beck, and I do believe it was the light of the fire that saved us. They rushed us several times, but we could see them coming, to some degree, because of the fire. Without that, they would have been able to get close enough to do real damage."

"How many men have you here?"

"Twelve, and myself. And four civilians, men with the freight company."

"Well, sergeant…what is your name?"

"I am William Molchert, Company B, Seventh Infantry."

"Sergeant Molchert, it would seem you have done right well. I am sure my lieutenant will be mentioning you in his dispatches. Any other troops about?"

"There is a body of engineers on the river to the west of us. Beyond that, I believe Fort Benton would be the nearest troop."

"Anyone warn you that the Nez Perce might be coming this way?"

242

"Why, no sir, not exactly. We had heard rumors of the war, but all assumed the cavalry would have them run down in short order."

"Apparently not," Beck said dryly.

"Yes sir. Apparently not," Molchert said tiredly.

Morgan led the scout party in, and they all tethered the horses in a shallow wash-out of a ravine between the river and the camp. The wounded were carried and helped over the embankment into the camp, and laid in two of the tents. The white canvas of the four-man army tents was holed in many places by the incoming bullets of the fight.

Molchert made a formal report to Lieutenant Morgan. His command had been sent down the river from the engineering party to the west, with the purpose of guarding the supplies. Molchert himself had just arrived the day before to carry back supplies for the engineers. When the Nez Perce appeared on the south bank of the Missouri, Molchert gathered all the men in the little camp, as the only defensible position near the piled freight. The Nez Perce had sent a few warriors to ask for food, and they had been given some bacon and flour, but only enough to fill one sack. The Indians had left, and Molchert had followed them, at a distance, going far enough up the river to spot their camp about a mile to the west. Just after he returned that evening, Indians were seen sneaking into position on the low bluffs to the north. Molchert got the men down behind the low ramparts surrounding the tents. He thought for sure they would be overrun in the first charge of the warriors, but nothing happened. Just as the light was finally going, the Indians fired a volley and the fight was on. They did not charge at once, but stayed in cover on the north slope, among the brush and willows and rocks.

In the semi darkness the soldiers could see Indians at the supply depot, but they could not see how they got there. The Indians made a rush just after full dark, but the soldiers drove them back, most of the time firing at the rifle flashes made by the Indians' shots. Then the Indians fired the freight, and the light quickly grew with the blaze. By that glow the soldiers could see movement in the brush, catch glimpses of warriors, see the glint of the firelight off of rifle barrels. Their fire became more accurate, and the Indians withdrew, but kept up the fight at longer range.

Twice more during the night the Nez Perce rushed the camp, but each time accurate rifle fire drove them back. Sniping by both sides continued through the night, and finally in the dim light of dawn the Indians ceased firing and moved out.

"If it had not been for the light of the burning freight, lieutenant, I do believe they would have overwhelmed us," Molchert said at last.

"Thank you, sergeant, I shall pass along your excellent action report to your superiors. We were on the south bank during the night, and know that you fought long and well. Well done," Morgan said tiredly.

"I'm Mike Foley," said a civilian who had been standing by during the report, "I was in charge of the depot here, for the Josephine Line. They wiped us out, lock stock and barrel! How come the army didn't have no troops here to head 'em off? You could have had 'em plum boxed if'n you'da wanted to! Now they've gone and burned more'n forty tons of Josephine Line goods, and who's gonna pay for all that?"

Morgan looked at the man, who was dark haired, slender, a large mustache crawling across his upper lip. His face was spattered with flecks of mud, and his Derby hat sported a fresh bullet hole.

"Well Mr. Foley," Morgan said, "as to who is going to pay for your destroyed property is not for me to guess. And though the army did not have sufficient men on hand to "head 'em off," as you say, the men that were here did a heroic job of keeping your ass from being perforated by Indian bullets for all that. We have been chasing these renegades for weeks, and they have not seen fit to inform us of their ultimate destination nor their route of travel. When they do, we'll be more than happy to "head 'em off" just as neat as you please, I assure you."

"You and who else? You ain't got enough men to head off a sick jackrabbit, from what I can see!" Foley said hotly.

"That could be true," Morgan said, "but you're just the man who can remedy that situation. We will have to leave our wounded here, but we have extra horses, and we must go on after the Nez Perce. You, Mr. Foley, can volunteer your services and come with us to act as scout, courier, mule skinner, and, of course, Indian fighter. All of you can, for that matter," Morgan said, sweeping his gaze over the soldiers standing around the camp, and the two civilians with them. No one said a word, nor moved a muscle.

"Well, Mr. Foley?" Morgan went on, leveling his gaze once more at the steaming freight clerk. "Your freight is gone, your camp is gone, you are now, for the moment, dependent on the army for your food and shelter. Care to earn your keep, as it were? As one of my scouts has so often mentioned, there is great glory in Indian fighting. Just ask any of those men over there in the tents, the ones with Nez Perce bullet holes in them."

Foley looked at the ground. Still no one spoke. "Well consarn it, I'm a clerk for god's sake!" he finally said. "I'll stand and fight 'long side any man, when the chips is down, but I an't about to go off lookin' fer trouble, glory be damned!"

From one of the tents, Hardy was heard laughing out loud.

"Very well then," Morgan said, "the army will proceed to do what the army does. And this part of the army is going on after the Nez Perce. Sergeant Molchert, can you spare any men to go with us? I cannot order you to do so, as you are under a different command and have your orders."

"I must turn you down on that, lieutenant, since you is askin' and not tellin'," Molchert said. "What with the supplies being wiped out, I figure to march the men back up the river and see about warning and defending the engineering party up there. None of us is cavalry, anyway, and though most of us might be able to ride, we ain't used to horses much, and we probably wouldn't be of much help."

"If you go back up river, what of the civilians here?" Morgan said.

"We'll make do," Foley put in eagerly. "When them Injuns showed up last night we sent a message down river to the colonel, he'll most likely get a boat up here right quick."

"Colonel?" Morgan said. "Are there troops just down river?"

"Well no, lieutenant, that would be Colonel George Clendenin, the freight agent for the Josephine."

"I see," Morgan said. He looked about the country and river for a moment, then at the smoke column leaning off in the wind to the south east. Light snow flakes sailed past on the breeze.

He brought his attention back to the assembled soldiers and freighters. "General Howard with Colonel Sturgis is one day back of us, and should be arriving by nightfall tomorrow. Or so we estimate. Mr. Foley, if you intend to remain, will you be able to tend to my wounded until a steamboat arrives?"

"Certainly, lieutenant!" Foley said brightly, now that talk of his volunteering had ceased.

"Sergeant Molchert, may I have a word with you?" Morgan said, and stepped off the rampart toward the river. "Mr. Beck, please," he said, nodding toward the water. The three of them walked a short way from the camp.

"Sergeant, I do believe the Nez Perce are intent on reaching Sitting Bull in Canada, and will pose no further threat to you here," Morgan said. "Do you agree, Jon?"

"Yes. But you saw what happened at Dumb Bull's camp, lieutenant," Beck said, "there's no predicting what they'll actually do."

"And that is why I have a suggestion for you, sergeant," Morgan said. "We came across a Crow camp on the Judith, wiped out. The Nez Perce had stopped there asking for food, and when it wasn't given to them, they went on. But a small party of warriors came back and wiped out the camp, in vengeance I believe. Now, you and your men put up a valiant fight against these same Nez Perce, and held your ground. An excellent piece of soldering, sergeant, and I commend you."

"Thank you, lieutenant!" the sergeant said, grinning.

"But I suggest," Morgan went on, "that you stay put, do not leave your position for at least a day or two. It's a long shot, but if the hotheads among the Nez Perce take it as a wound to their pride, they may attempt a parting raid just for spite. You now have my wounded and the civilian wounded to think about, and I do not want to see them abandoned. I do not believe your engineers up river are in any danger, as I have said the Nez Perce are heading north, not west. Will you stay with the wounded for at least a day, so that no harm comes to them?"

"Well, lieutenant, I was told to get supplies and get back up river. But since there are no longer any supplies, well, another day ain't gonna matter much."

"Good. If you need authority for your delay, I can give you an order in writing. It would not amount to much in official channels, but it would at least give you some excuse for your actions.

"And I am thinking not only of the wounded, sergeant," Morgan said, glancing at the redoubt and the half dozen men perched atop its wall like buzzards over a still struggling carcass, "I am thinking that if we are driven back and must put our backs to something, then we will need your little fort and you men something fierce, I'll warrant."

"Driven back?" Molchert said inquisitively.

"Yes. We're going after them immediately," Morgan said.

"But there's only a handful of ya!" Molchert said.

"We're scouts, it's what we do," Morgan said. "Right, Mr. Beck?"

"It's what we do," Beck said with a grin.

"Well there's more white men up the canyon, you might get to them afore the Injuns do," Molchert said.

"What white men?" Morgan said.

"Wagon train, freighters, left yesterday morning, eight, maybe ten wagons. Headed up Cow Creek Canyon, bound for the mining camps."

"Were they armed?" Beck said.

"Don't know for sure. Maybe a rifle here and there."

"Did they know of the Nez Perce?" Morgan said.

"Only the same rumors the rest of us had heard," Molchert said, "they left afore the Injuns showed up."

Morgan looked at Beck. "If the Nez Perce have not broken camp as yet, we may have a chance to get out ahead of them and warn those teamsters," Morgan said.

"Well, I'll just go get my horse and go find out," Beck said. He walked off toward the picketed animals.

"Sergeant, can you rustle us up some grub from what supplies you have? I will write you that order as I promised. I only need twenty four hours, for by then you should be reinforced one way or the other."

"Sure thing, lieutenant."

Beck unpicketed his big horse and swung once more into the saddle. He sighed, thought for a second, then heeled big Bill up out of the shallow ravine and west along the river. He followed the river flats but kept to the edge of the bluffs on the north, easing around each shoulder of ground or over each low ridge carefully, scanning for the Nez Perce encampment they had seen on the high ground to the west. The blowing snow was light, and came in flurries. The cold had hardened the ground, and where it was bare the wind blew the snow off the heights and toward the river.

At last he walked Bill up a low slope and caught sight of movement. Just to the west of Cow Creek Canyon, a long sloping shoulder carried from the river to the table lands to the north. He

247

could see movement on the upper part of the slope, and pulled his field glass from his saddle pack. He was just in time to watch the last of the Nez Perce band top the ridge and disappear from sight. He turned Bill and walked him the mile or so back to the soldiers camp.

Morgan, Dodd and Pocket were in the ravine with the horses, saddling them and packing the gear on them as well as the mule. Beck walked Bill up to them and halted, leaned on his crossed arms on the saddle pommel.

"They just pulled out," he said to Morgan, who halted in packing his horse and leaned against the saddle. Morgan pursed his lips, thinking.

"We at least have to try for that wagon train," Beck said, "if they're attacked, we're the only help around."

"All right," Morgan finally said. As they finished loading the animals, Beck climbed down off of Bill, pulled his Winchester from its saddle scabbard and slipped the long Springfield in its place. He fetched out the broken stock from his saddle pack, climbed the rampart to the camp, and went to Hardy in his tent, who lay on a cot, covered with a buffalo robe. Beck knelt beside him.

"Well Lige," he grinned, leaning on the broken rifle, "while I'm gone after them murdering savages, I have a little job for you to do. I want you to fix this here rifle, whittle me a new stock, and get this mainspring straightened out. We'll be back in a day or so, and I surely do need this here repeater back in shootin' condition."

Hardy eyed him and the rifle. Beck laid the stock on his belly, leaned the rifle against the cot. "Two days at the most," Beck said, still grinning. "Now I know you are right handy with a whittlin' knife, and I figure you won't have no trouble atall getting' 'er done, right, pard?"

"I'll tell you what you can do with that rifle, you lop eared pole cat!" Hard growled, sitting up and grabbing the stock piece by the wrist and taking a swipe at Beck, who ducked and darted back.

"Hah!" Beck said, "You always was too slow to—OW!"

Hardy had swung a low blow and barked Beck's shin with the stock. With a look of triumph, he settled back on the cot, the stock firmly gripped in one hand to his chest.

"Take care, Lige," Beck said, turning to go.

"Jon," Hardy said, and Beck paused. "Don't forget to duck."
Beck chuckled and went out.

Chapter 30

The four scouts moved out at mid day through the lightly blowing snow, Corporal Dodd trailing last and leading the mule. Soon they were in Cow Creek Canyon, where Cow Creek still rushed and burbled along its rocky bed. The wagon road, which was little more than a twin tracked trail, led them along the canyon bottom, which was occupied by the creek, and so they crossed, crossed again and yet again through icy water as they traveled. The snow stopped as the afternoon wore on, but the sky stayed solid and gray, and the wind found them even in the canyon depths.

The horses had taken a little rest on the south side of the Missouri, and some grass, but would not be pushed. The scouts carefully peered around every shoulder of the canyon wall that sloped down to the water, looking for the first sign of the Nez Perce they knew to be before them.

By late afternoon they had come to an area where the canyon opened out, the land was flatter and the canyon bottom wide. Brush and trees grew along the water, and in bunches closer to the round-shouldered hills hemming in the canyon walls. Beck was in the lead, and paused as he usually did in the last cluster of bare limbed trees and brush before breaking into the open of the creek flats. He held up his arm. The others halted as well. Morgan eased his horse up beside big Bill.

"What do you make of that?" Beck said. Morgan got out his glass and peered at several white shapes that could be seen half a mile away up the valley.

"It's the freight train!" he said. "I can see the teamsters about, they've got cooking fires going. Thank God we've reached them in time!" He put away his field glass and was about to spur his horse forward, when Beck stopped him with a hand on his arm.

249

"Hold on, lieutenant," Beck said. "You recall back there at the Missouri, the Nez Perce seemed right friendly, according to the sergeant, until evening. That's when they attacked. What if they're sittin' on them bluffs above the train right now, getting ready to swoop down on those teamsters?"

"Well, then we've got to warn them!" Morgan said angrily, "I'll not sit by and watch a surprise attack without doing something to prevent it!"

"I'm with you on that, lieutenant, don't mistake me. But how about if we get ourselves into a defensible position, then send one man down to the teamsters and let 'em know what's what. If we're to get word back to the general, we can't be caught in the open."

"All right, all right, what do you suggest?" Morgan said.

Beck scanned the valley, then pointed to a low hill to the east.

"Up there, we can dig in if need be, and with the high ground we can see what's going on, and make a stand of it if things go sour. We need to camp for the night anyway, and that's as good a place as any."

"No water up there, and most likely no grass," Morgan said.

"But a good field of fire and a good chance we'll keep our hair."

Morgan looked the valley over himself. "All right, all right, we'll retire to the heights."

"So which of us should go tell them teamsters they're sittin' on a powder keg?" Beck said.

"I'll go!" Simon said, nudging his pony up to the others.

"All right," Morgan said yet again. "Just let them know the Nez Perce are in the area, and they should be ready. They ought to fort up those wagons and post guards. But they'll know that, if they've any brains. In the mean time, we'll take possession of that hilltop yonder, and wait for your return."

"Yes sir!" Simon snapped and turned his paint for the teamster's camp. As the light faded, the camp's cooking fires began to stand out. The white spots of Pocket's paint horse made it easy tracking Simon as he rode across the flats, and then were lost as he descended into the creek bottom.

Beck led the way down a side draw, then up over a low saddle and across the small valley, then up the slopes of the chosen hill. The last of the light was going when they reached the top. They could see three fires in the teamster's camp from the hill. And in the distance up the valley, a dozen more.

"There's your Indians," Beck said as he swung down from the saddle. Morgan sat his horse and stared off into the deepening darkness at the points of light.

"Looks like they just missed that freight train," Morgan finally said, dismounting.

"Or they're waiting for it," Beck said. He unloaded Bill, and staked him out in a small table of sparse grass just behind the hill. The other horses and the mule soon joined him, and they all began snuffling out what course grass they could.

The men settled down to wait in their blankets on the brow of the hill, glassing the lights of the fires up the valley from time to time, but seeing nothing but the tiny gleams of yellow light. An hour passed, and then another. Then they heard Simon coming, his pony's hooves thumping hard as the animal climbed the slope. He nearly ran over them as he crested the ridge and the pony shied a bit at the sudden forms almost underneath him. Simon laughed a little and climbed down.

"They going to fort up those wagons and keep a lookout?" Morgan asked.

"Nope, none of it," Simon said, as he stripped the gear from his horse.

"What? Are they mad?" Morgan spat.

"None of that neither!" Simon said. "They said the Nez Perce came to the camp just before we got to the valley, or thereabouts. They was friendly enough, looking for food. Teamsters gave 'em some coffee, but that was it. Told 'em that even they were not allowed to disturb the freight in the wagons, as it all belonged to someone else, wasn't theirs to give away. Injuns took that to heart, they said, and went on up the valley. Them wagon drivers also got a herd of beeves just up the valley a bit, but the Injuns ain't bothered them none, either. Bottom of it is, those boys ain't worried none atall!"

"Do they have arms?" Morgan said.

"I saw a rifle or two, couple of revolvers. Not much else."

"Why did it take you so long to get back up here?" Morgan said.

"Well they did ask me to supper, and being a polite Texas boy I just couldn't turn 'em down!" Simon grinned, his teeth showing white in the darkness.

"Who's in charge of the train?" Beck said.

"Feller by the name of Barker," Simon said, "right large feller, and don't brook no nonsense from none o' the rest. When I told him the Injuns might come after dark, he just laughed and said he like to see 'em try."

"Brave fellow," Morgan said ironically, "or a complete fool."

"I do believe there was whiskey somewhere about the place," Simon chuckled, "some of 'at may have tainted his judgment a mite, as my grandmomma used to say."

"Taint any of yours?" Beck said.

"Maybe, don't rightly recall," Simon said, leading his pony to the little table with the other horses.

"Think we ought to join them, Mr. Beck?" Morgan said. "They might listen to you or I, take a more defensible position."

"I don't figure they would," Beck said. "Injuns have come and gone, they see no harm in what they done so far, they figure the Nez Perce is reasonable folk and intendin' to be peaceful. And if they got into the whisky, there's gonna be no talkin' to 'em, whether we're right or wrong. No, I figure we may as well stay put, get some sleep, and when we can see at first light, we'll just head on up the valley after the Nez Perce. Who knows, maybe nothing will come it. But, I got me a feelin'...."

They bedded down below the brow of the hill, trying for a little relief from the wind. No one slept well, and Jon Beck was up checking on the horses at the first hint of dawn in the east. A mist had come over the hills, and the wind had died. Frost silvered the grass, which crunched under the hide of his moccasin soles. As he walked back to the gear on the hillside, Morgan slipped out of his blankets and went to sit on the brow, his glass trained on the valley below. Dodd sat up in his blankets.

"Corporal, think you could rustle us up some breakfast? Enough buffalo chips about for a fire."

"Sure thing, Mr. Beck," the corporal drawled, and stretched and yawned. Simon still snored beneath his canvas bedroll cover.

Beck got his glass from his gear and went to sit beside Morgan. The mist blotched much of the valley below them, but it was in patches here and there.

Without the wind, the air was like a palpable mass of cold. Remaining still, it would hover just beyond discomfort, but any movement was like moving through an unseen mountain stream, the air stinging cold, almost drinkable. Their breaths came in clouds that quickly crystallized in the frigid air. Simon came up behind them, knelt.

"Mornin' gents," he said. "Anything going on down there?"

"Hard to tell," Beck said. "How's about you ridin' down there to those teamster fellers and lettin' 'em know we're pullin' out. Grab a bit of breakfast, first."

Dodd had the bacon sizzling soon, and that and hardtack and coffee warmed them all. Simon saddled and packed the paint, and eased off down the slope toward the creek bottoms. The mists had thinned, and the sun was splashing gold on the low clouds in the east. Beck saddled up Bill, rubbing ice crystals off of his broad back before settling in the saddle blanket. He finished with the saddle, leaving the cinch slightly loose. At the fire, he took up his cup and held it out as Dodd filled it from the steaming pot. The buffalo chip fire gave off little smoke in the still air.

Beck took his coffee cup over to Morgan, who sat watching the freighter's camp through his field glass. He would turn the glass on the northern end of the valley from time to time, but the mists obscured any sign of the Nez Perce camp.

"Well, lieutenant," Beck said, seating himself beside Morgan and taking up his own field glass, "what now? We go directly after the Nez Perce? Send a message back to the river? Join the teamsters? Stay put?"

"Mr. Beck, for the love of heaven will you cease!" Morgan said irritably.

"All I'm sayin' is we could talk about it," Beck said with a small smile. "Ain't nobody around much to impress at the moment, 'cept me 'n Dodd, so what's the harm in a little discussion? Just like to know how yer thinking on this one."

"And me too," Dodd said, coming up to kneel beside them and scan the valley.

"Shut up, Dodd," Morgan said dryly.

"Yes sir!" Dodd said emphatically. He smiled a bit too.

Morgan sighed.

"All right," he said, "what I don't figure is why they would attack dug-in soldiers at the river, but leave these wagons with their lightly armed drivers alone. They're camped not two miles away, and they come in to talk to the teamsters all polite and obliging as a maiden aunt. Then nothing. I don't understand it."

"Well, consider this," Beck said. "The first visit was a reconnaissance, they sent a couple of men in to see who they have to kill, where the guns are, whether the drivers are fighting men or not. Same thing at the river, they sent someone in to talk, ask for food. They wasn't looking for food so much as they was scouting out their enemy. But, saying all that, I figured they would have attacked last night."

"I would agree," Morgan said. "Why didn't they?"

"Them cows!" Dodd said. "I betcha they want them cows up the valley, that's what! You ever try pushin' a herd of cows at night?"

"My God!" Morgan said, stiffening. "You are exactly right, corporal! Look, Jon, coming out of the brush along the creek!"

Beck quickly peered through his field glass, and though the mist sill lay in patches in the valley, he could make out a dozen riders emerging from the trees and brush a short distance across the valley from the teamster's camp. They came across a grass swale toward the wagons. As Beck watched, a solitary figure left the freighter's camp and walked out to meet them. Then another line of horsemen emerged from the brush across the valley, backing up the first. The riders approached the solitary man who had come out from the camp.

The scouts watched intently, not a man taking a breath. On the south end of the line of horsemen, the last rider suddenly whirled his mount and charged up the line toward the lone teamster and two of the Indians who appeared to be talking to him. Then a puff of rifle smoke billowed out from one of the Indians, then another and another. The teamster threw up his arms and collapsed. The line of Indians broke for the wagons, and several more puffs of smoke billowed out from this rider, then that. Several shots answered from the camp, but then the scouts could see the teamsters scattering, running from the wagons and disappearing into the brush along the edges of the valley bottom. The sound of the gunfire rolled up to meet them, muted in the cold, dawn air.

A lone horse erupted from the camp, fleeing at a dead run as the rider clung to the saddle horn and then hopped aboard the saddle. It was Simon Pocket's paint pony, and it was quickly pursued by three Nez Perce riders who streaked straight through the wagon line and pounded after him. Simon was into the brush then, but headed south along the edge of the flats. He did not turn up the long slope toward the scouts on the hill.

"Where the hell's he going to" muttered Beck.

"The army, that's where!" said Morgan excitedly, pointing down the valley toward the constricted hills where the creek entered its canyon. Beck swung his glass, and could pick up spots of color and movement, several horsemen a mile away. "They've finally caught up, God bless 'em!" Morgan said.

"Maybe not," Beck said, studying the tiny figures dancing in the magnified image of his field glass. "Them ain't uniforms I'm seein', least not the good old cavalry blue."

Both men remained quiet for a few seconds studying the riders.

"Maybe they're scouts," Morgan said.

"Maybe they're Nez Perce," Beck said. He then swung his glass back up the valley, and found the running paint pony with Simon Pocket laying along its neck. The three pursuers had spread out, and they were shooting. As Beck watched, the paint zigzagged through a swath of brush and dropped into a wash off its steep side, and Beck could see the horse go down and roll, dust hiding Pocket from view. Then the pony was up, moving, limping. Then Pocket was up, and Beck could see him retrieve his rifle from the ground and leap to the edge of the wash, and a puff of smoke billowed out toward the three approaching horsemen. Then another. The Nez Perce stopped, then the center man dismounted, and the other two cut east and west, moving to flank Pocket.

"God dammit to hell!" Beck growled, and jumped to his feet and ran to Bill. He dropped the field glass into his saddlebag, and with fumbling fingers tightened the cinch. He grabbed the reins, and with his hat slapped Bill on the rump and grabbed the saddle horn as the big horse startled into a run down the back slope of the hill, Beck heaving himself aboard the saddle with a kick in the earth to jolt him up. Then they were pounding down the hill, and Beck guided the horse in a long arc out to the south and then west. He could see the rifle smoke in the valley half a mile away, and from the dispersal of the clouds knew that they had Pocket boxed.

As he crouched in the saddle and spurred Bill on, he looked at the empty rifle scabbard under his right stirrup leg and realized his Springfield was laying next to his bedroll back at the hilltop camp. He cursed to himself and unbuttoned his heavy coat, and slid the holstered army Colt forward on his belt to the front of his hip. He gritted his teeth, shook his head, and cursed again.

Up the valley, gunfire could be faintly heard at the freighter's camp, but it was random, occasional, almost casual. Beck steered Bill into the head of the draw that he had seen Pocket fall in, and then he was past the point where one of the Nez Perce was concealed in the brush and firing. As he went by, he drew the big Colt and fired a round at the smoke that was sitting like a neat little cloud along the top of the brush. Then he was under the rim of the draw and Simon was there, looking over his shoulder as he crouched just under the edge of the bank.

Beck holstered the revolver as Bill pounded down the draw and Simon came bounding down the steep side with his rifle. "Come on!" Beck hollered, holding out his arm. The big horse hardly missed a beat as Pocket grabbed the arm and leapt down and onto the back of the saddle, his rifle waving in his free hand. Pocket's horse was standing just ahead, and as they plunged past it, the paint pony fell in behind, running with a hobbling, bounding gait, favoring its right foreleg.

As long as they were in the bottom of the draw, the Nez Perce could not get a shot down at them without coming to the rim of the gully. Beck had gambled that he could get them to cover before the Indians realized this and ran forward through the brush. He had no idea where a safe spot would be, but anything was better than the position Pocket was in to begin with.

The wash wound about a bit, and then they entered a section where the banks were less steep, but covered in low brush. Then up ahead he could see what appeared to be a wall, an end to the wash. He swore again, but spurred the horse urgently. Then they had reached the wall, and found that the gully took a sharp left, which they took, the then a sharp right. The banks above them were thickly covered with scrub oak, stripped bare in the cold autumn wind, and low brambles amid tufts of coarse brown grass. Beck hauled in Bill, who skidded to a stop on his haunches. Simon leapt to the ground, and immediately scrambled up to the inside corner of the bank they had just come round. Beck jumped down too, as the paint pony came around the tight bend and stopped next to Bill. Beck climbed the bank opposite of Pocket, drawing his Colt, and at the crest peered into the brush. He could hear someone moving through the thicket, and thought he saw movement several dozen yards out. He leveled the .45 and fired a shot, the gun jumping in his hand with the recoil. White smoke filled the brush before him. He crabbed sideways along the rim of the wash, trying to see around the gun smoke.

Behind him he heard Simon fire, then again. An answering shot was fired, and the bullet thwacked into the brush off to Beck's right. Both men paused, watched, listened. Beck reloaded the spent rounds in his revolver, all the while looking intently into the brush land before him. He glanced over at Simon.

"You hit?" he said in a low voice, just enough to carry to the other rim of the draw.

"No. Pony got hurt, though. May of broke her leg."

"Hardly. She limps along about as fast as Bill can run!"

Pocket glanced down at the two horses. He grinned.

"Don't that beat all!" he said, looking back to his side of the wash.

"What happened at the camp?"

"Havin' a nice breakfast, ham and biscuits, gravy, coffee, man I tell you, one o' them mule skinners can surely cook—"

"So what happened?" Beck said sternly.

"Injuns came up out of the brush near the creek. Couple dozen, maybe. I told them drivers they better get ready to dance or run, we was in for it! I got my hawse untied and shore 'nough, one of them braves come high tailin' it up from the south end of the line yellin' to beat all, and they just shot the boss teamster down like a dog! He done nothing to 'em, wasn't even carryin' no gun. Just shot 'im down. Rest of 'em mule skinners hid behind the wagons, fired off a shot or two, but they scattered like rabbits when the Injuns come on. I did too!"

"Why didn't you try and make the hill, get back to us?"

"What chance you think you'd a had against thirty of 'em? Hell, no, I figured I'd head on down the valley, lose 'em in the brush. I figured they'd give up right soon and go loot them wagons, 'at's what they was after."

A shot rang out from the brush away in the front of Simon, and he hunched his shoulders instinctively. The bullet whined away into the air after slapping a twig or two off to the left.

"Well now they're after us," Beck said.

They heard a flurry of war whoops off to the west, most likely near the creek itself. Beck peered ever more closely at the tangle of undergrowth in front of him. He glanced to his left. The gulley flowed that way another fifteen yards, then banked a hard right, disappearing around the corner. To his right, the gully banked right again, disappearing to the east. Pocket was perched on the inside wall of the angle, at the top. He had cover from the east the north, thanks to a shoulder of the bank that jutted out on his left. Beck was exposed to his left. It made him uneasy to think that an enemy could creep up in the heavy scrub on that outside corner of the bend, and line up a shot at him without his even being able to see the foe. He scrambled along the bank to his left, until he had reached the inside angle of the bank. He peered around the corner, looking along the gully to the west. As he looked, an Indian broke cover on the north bank, ran down into the gully and started up the south wall. Beck brought up the revolver and snapped off a shot at the running Nez Perce. When the smoke had cleared, the gully was empty. And off in the distance, at about a quarter mile away, a dozen Indian horsemen were also crossing the wash, headed south.

Now he knew he had an enemy on the south bank, and he could not wait. He ran down the slope, crossed the bottom, and up the south slope. At the rim, he stopped, panting, looking again into a tangle of small, naked trees, scrub brush, tufted grass. He could see nothing. Carefully, gritting his teeth, he crawled forward into the brush, making every effort to make no sound. Soon he was out of sight of the gully, and surrounded entirely by winter-dead foliage. He lay still.

As a boy in the Pennsylvania woods he had played at Indian fighting with the other boys, using homemade bows and whittled arrows. He had learned to track and to move silently in the woods, for he knew that the first fighter to give away his position was the first to die. Movement in the woods was the deciding factor, for it was movement, however slight, that signaled the presences of any living thing. Or an enemy. So he waited, knowing he was unseen from anyone in the gully, or on its rim. And hoping he was unseen from anyone on the south bank.

He had opened his coat lapel, and breathed into the space created between the coat and his body, so that the frosty cloud of his breath would dissipate there and not form a beacon for his enemy to see. Each breath was drawn and exhaled slowly, carefully, and gradually his thumping heart settled. In the dead silence he could hear a distant Indian yelp, the cry of a hawk, then a far off rifle shot. Then a flurry of shots in the distance to the south. Whoever that party of horsemen at the south end of the valley had been, they were no friends to the Nez Perce.

Still he waited. It gnawed at him that the bank he had left, at the back of Simon Pocket, was unprotected. But he knew at least one warrior was with him in this thicket, and he had to face that threat first. He wanted in the worst way to do something, to move, to shoot, to run forward, to attack, anything. But he also knew that he must wait, and hope that the brown of his buffalo coat would be enough to blend into the grey, dead foliage of the grappling pile in which he lay. His revolver was held in his hands before his face, his eyes darting here, there, his chin low, breathing frost into his clothing.

The firing in the south went on and on. He heard Simon's rifle bark again. Once the nicker of a horse came to his ears from the wash bottom. He heard the snap of a twig off to his right. An enemy? Frozen wood popping? His eyes flickered everywhere, and he hardly dared to breathe.

Then he saw it. Or thought he did. Movement. Brown on brown, something. He froze, not daring to breathe at all. Nothing. His eyes had betrayed him. He was about to exhale when it saw it again. No mistake. Something, or someone moving toward the gulch off to his right. He stared, blinked, stared. Then he saw what looked like a moccasin clad foot. It disappeared. A bit further along, a shoulder and arm, its owner on his belly inching toward the gulch. It could only be a Nez Perce. Ever so slowly Beck rolled slightly on his left side, curled up a bit to allow his arms to swing the revolver toward the Indian. As he finally lined up the barrel with where he thought the body of the man might lie, he realized he could not see any portion of the man at all. He had moved behind more blocking brush.

To take the shot and hope for luck? If he missed, he had given away his position. He would not get another shot, and might be shot in return. He could not do it. All his life, Jon Beck had been a planner, a calculator, and he never went into a situation without an edge, if he could help it. He was not the stuff of wild charges and condemned torpedoes, he was a man of the siege, the trap, the planned campaign. When cornered by unexpected circumstance, his reaction had always been to smash his way out with bear-like strength. And he hated to be cornered, for it meant he had failed at what he did best.

So he waited. The crawling Indian was somewhere directly to his right, about twenty or thirty yards off in the brush. Beck was now curled up on his side, revolver held in both hands, looking through the tangle with the intensity of life itself. He could feel the cold air like fire on his face, made wet with sweat and the breath he had been hoarding like gold at his bosom.

A head eased out from behind a clump of brown grass. Black hair, tied back with a thong. A brown, Roman nose, full lips. A strong profile, Beck thought, as his sights lined up on the ear. But the gun was not cocked, and he suddenly realized to do so would be to make noise. And to do so would also require losing his sight picture as he thumbed back the hammer. He would have to cock and shoot in an instant, and the only sure target was the head of his enemy. He licked his lips. As he set himself for the try, the Nez Perce turned his head, and looked him in the eye.

He went for the hammer, snapped it back and pulled the trigger. The gun bucked, the air was instantly full of white smoke. He rolled to his hands and knees, then lurched to his feet as an answering shot ripped the ground where his head had been. He fired twice more through the white smoke in the direction of the sound and scrambled through the brush toward the gully. Then he was over the rim and sliding down the bank. He immediately turned and clawed his way back up to the top, and peered over the rim into the tangle once more. He could see white smoke like a cloud throughout the brush before him.

He looked over at Simon, who was looking over his shoulder at him, his eyebrows raised in a question. Beck held up one finger, then two, shrugged. Pocket made a slicing motion across his throat, asking if they were dead. Beck shook his head. He turned back to looking into the underbrush. He reloaded the revolver once again, glancing at the cylinder as he rotated the spent shells into the gate and ejected them out, his eyes darting from gun to brush and back. With the gun fully loaded again, he took stock.

Their position was untenable, and he knew it. With heavy cover all around them, and only the two of them to guard all sides, it would only be a matter of time until some enemy crept close enough to get a shot into one or both of them before they could react. They would have to run.

The sound of the firing to the south had taken on the sporadic, deliberate beat of a set battle, but one of distance and cover. He had seen many Indians down the gully to the west. Were they still in the vicinity? Or were they in the battle to the south? He had shot at and most likely missed at least one Nez Perce just to the south. That left two others of the three originally chasing Simon. One he had passed on his way down the gully to rescue his friend. Where was the other?

The urge to move gripped his guts ever tighter. Simon's pony was an unknown factor. Was it hurt badly? Could it be ridden? The answer was no. They would have to trust to Bill. Which way to run? It would have to be to the east, back up the gully down which he had come. In that direction was at least the possibility of Morgan and Dodd. He would have to rely on Bill to carry the two of them, up hill for more than a half mile, at a dead run. Or the nearest thing to a run the tired beast could manage. They had to move now!

Beck holstered his Colt, and slid down the bank to the gully bottom. "Simon, come on! We've got to run for it," he called softly, moving to Bill, catching the reins and swinging into the saddle. Simon came off the bank in a hurry.

"Swing your rifle into the scabbard," Beck said. Simon took a step toward the paint, and Beck said, "No! My scabbard! My horse will have to do, we can't rely on yours!" Simon hesitated. "Now, man!"

Simon stepped over the slipped his Winchester into the scabbard on Bill.

"I ain't leaving my pony," Pocket said, stepping back.

"Ain't asking ya to! We'll lead her, now come on, get up here!"

Pocket caught the reins of the paint and grabbed Beck's arm, who swung him up onto the cantle. Beck put the spurs to Bill, and they headed out and around the sharp bend and up the gully the way they had come. Behind them they heard a screeching Indian yell.

Beck hunched over Bill's neck, expecting at any time to feel the slamming bite of a bullet from the brushy rims of the gully. The big horse chuffed along the rising grade of the gully following the tracks he had left a short time before. They neared and passed the place where Beck had taken a shot at one of the Nez Perce on the way in. No shot came from that area. Beck nearly shouted with relief as Bill hammered on up the slope, thinking they had made it after all.

Then shots began to pop off from behind them, and the bullets whined overhead and smacked the ground out in front of them, raising puffs of dust in places. Half a dozen shots and then they rounded a gentle curve and were screened from the enemy by a low bank.

Bill slowed too, for the grade steepened, and then they were in another small table land of sage and tall grass. They heard a shout, and looking up the slope to the south east, saw Lieutenant Morgan waving his arm in the distance. He was at the head of a shallow saddle, standing, holding his horse. Dodd was there as well, with the mule.

Beck's big horse labored on up the slope, and Beck eased him back a bit to a lurching lope as he fought his way, sides heaving, up to the Lieutenant and Dodd. There they halted, and Pocket slid off the back, then Beck swung down.

Beck turned to Pocket, who still had his pony's reins in hand, and grinned.

"Ain't he some horse!" Beck said, patting Bill's shoulder. Pocket grinned back.

"I owe him my life," Simon said, "And you." He held out a hand to Beck.

"Any time," Jon said, taking Pocket's hand, "I figure you'd do the same."

"While you two were down there sweet talking those renegades," Morgan said, "I think I found a way we can finally be of some use. Come on up here." He turned and moved up to the brow of the saddle. Beck fetched out his field glass and he and Pocket followed.

They had a good view of the valley, and the freighter's camp was blazing with several fires. The Indians had looted and fired the wagons. On the south end of the valley, white smoke billowed from dozens of spots in the brush and trees, from low hills, from along the creek bottom.

"So who are those folks down there?" Beck said, glassing the battle.

"Appears to be irregular troops, maybe scouts, don't think it's army," Morgan said. "They have enough manpower and nerve to put up a good fight. From what I've seen of the freight train and the camp to the north, this action in the south is most likely to keep whoever they are from interfering with the looting of the train. Judging from the fires, they've apparently got whatever they came to get, and burned the rest. Now I calculate they are just waiting for the main body to pack up and begin their withdrawal, then we'll see them break off the fight and disappear up the valley."

"At which point we take to trailin' 'em again, I take it," Beck said.

"Not exactly," Morgan said. "Do you see that low ridge down there, about a quarter mile up slope from the battle? As you can see," and Beck glassed the area indicated, "the Nez Perce have taken up positions on the first heights above the creek. But their back is exposed to that ridge. If we could get a troop of men onto that ridge, we could take them from the rear, and make it damned hot for 'em to hold out against the men in the valley. We could catch them between two fires, and we could hammer them severely!"

"All we need is that troop of men," Beck said.

"That would be us," Morgan said, a small smile on his lips.

Beck lowered his glass and looked over at the lieutenant. "The four of us," he said at last.

"Yes, but here's the hole card," Morgan said excitedly. "You can see that the ridge is heavily foliated with brush, and a crest of boulders in one spot. If we space the four of us out, and each of us fires and moves and fires and moves again, we can seem like a troop! We will have surprise on our side, we will have position on the enemy, and how are they to know that we are only four men?"

Beck pursed his lips, thought about it. "Lieutenant," he finally said, "I do believe I like your style!" He smiled.

"All right then!" Morgan said, grinning. "Here is what I propose. If we leave the horses up here behind this saddle, we can take that gulley over there where the route is down hill all the way, so the march should not be hard. We take only water, the guns and ammunition. We can be in position within the hour, and if the Nez Perce should send a force against us, we can retire into that forest of scrub and tangle there on the left."

"No horses?" Dodd said.

"I hardly think they will do us much good if we had to run for it," Morgan said, looking at the exhausted Bill, the paint standing on three legs, his own mount. "No, we go afoot, and if we do it right, the Indians will pull out. We haven't the manpower to chase them anyway. We'll have to do all the damage we can while we have the superior position."

"Fair enough," Beck said, "I been looking for a superior position all day!"

Chapter 31

Morgan and Dodd had brought over all of the camp equipment and Beck's Springfield. They unsaddled and staked out the horses, gathered up canteens and all of the ammunition, and, taking their rifles, hurried on down the back slope of the saddle to the shallow gulley that emptied out behind the brush covered ridge. Half an hour later they were behind the boulder pile just to the south of its center.

"Now here's what we are to do," Morgan said as they paused, panting from the scurry down the wash. "We'll space out about twenty yards apart. Each man find several firing points, four or five if you can. When I give the signal, have at 'em! Never fire from the same spot twice, move a lot, don't worry about hitting much. The range is too long for accurate rifle fire, and the object is to make the Nez Perce think they have a troop of cavalry at their rear. If you can hit 'em, fine, but the goal is rapidity of fire. Understood?"

The three men nodded, and Morgan said, "Good, now go find a few good spots. Wait for my signal."

Beck moved off to the south along the ridge, and looking back to judge where the others were, and where he would be moving back and forth, he quickly found several openings in the rocks and brush that allowed a good field of fire onto the ridge below. As he looked, he could see the puffs of smoke from the Nez Perce guns, and in several places the warriors were in plain sight behind rocks, bushes, or lying on the grass at the brow of their hill.

He judged the distance to be about four hundred yards, and set the ladder sight on his rifle accordingly. He found a good rest for the rifle on a low mound of earth under a thick tangle of greasewood, and selected a target, a warrior standing next to another man, who was prone and firing around a rock. He stood back, looked down the line at Morgan, who also stepped back, looked both up and down the line of his meager troop, and waved his hat. Beck turned back to the rifle, cocked the hammer, and drew a fine bead on the standing warrior. His finger tightened on the trigger as his front sight blade settled into the rear sight notch, centered on the enemy. Off to his right a shot boomed out, then another. His target turned and looked, then his own shot broke.

White smoke billowed as the musket bucked into his shoulder. He scrambled up and ran a few yards to his left, loading the Springfield as he moved. He found an opening in the scrub, cocked the rifle and threw it to his shoulder and cheek, lined the sights on an Indian who was sitting on the ridge looking up in his direction. Again the rifle bucked and belched white, and he ran to the right, loaded, cocked, lined up and fired. Then still right again, loading and firing as the others along the line did the same.

When he had made the full cycle back to his first firing position for the second time, the readied rifle cocked and aimed, he found nothing to shoot at. Not a single enemy occupied the ridge. He saw two bodies lying on the far slope, but as he squinted along the line looking for anything moving, the two prone figures slid down from view and were hidden by the trees and brush at the base of the low slope. He lowered the rifle. Either they had not been killed, or their comrades had dragged them to cover. He watched for a time, but nothing else moved.

Other shots were still being fired deeper in the valley, but gradually they became fewer and fewer. After about ten minutes, silence. Beck lowered the hammer on the rifle and hiked along the ridge toward Morgan's position. Simon joined him as they came up to the lieutenant. Then Dodd came in. He took up a post at the top of the ridge, keeping an eye on the enemy position below.

"Looks like you did it, lieutenant!" Beck said. "Troop P of the Fifth Cavalry carries the day!"

"Troop P?" Pocket said.

"P for paltry," Beck grinned. Morgan smiled.

"Hey lieutenant!" Dodd said, "Look at this!"

They all stepped up beside Dodd, who pointed to the west and north below them. A line of Indian ponies filed out of the brush, heading up the valley to the north. Then, further out near the bed of the creek, another group of Indians materialized out of the scrub, also traveling north.

"Yes, sir!" Dodd said, "They're pullin' out all right! We done it, we surely did!"

"We're just lucky they didn't come this way," Pocket muttered.

"All right then," Morgan said, "let's get back up to the horses and go find out who was taking all that fire."

"Now if we had o' ridden them nags down here to begin with—" Dodd said.

"Shut up, Dodd," Morgan said. "And well done, all of you."

They trekked back up the gully, trudging with rifles over their shoulders, using the last of their water on the hour long climb. The cold air felt good as they worked up the rising slope, and by the time they had reached the saddleback, Beck had shed his buffalo coat and was carrying it like a great hairy body over one shoulder. At the top, they all sat and rested for a time, letting the heat of their bodies bleed off into the cold crisp breeze that had come up. Soon the wind began to cut into clothing wet with sweat, and they began to move again, buttoning up to keep warm.

The gear was sorted out, the animals packed again, and by mid afternoon they started back down the gully toward the valley. Simon walked, leading his pony, and Dodd brought the mule along.

They cut around one end of the ridge they had occupied, and then over the ridge that had been covered with Nez Perce warriors. They saw no dead or wounded there, but several bright patches of blood showed on rocks or grass. Then they were on the flats and came up on the low hills where the broader canyon narrowed between sharp bluffs. They could see men moving about, horses, and a wagon. As they came up, it was clear that all of the men were civilians, save one. An army major rode out to meet them.

Morgan came to attention as the major rode up, and saluted. "Lieutenant Morgan, Fifth Cavalry," he said.

The major halted, returned the salute. "I am Major Ilges, Seventh Infantry, commanding Fort Benton. Are the rest of your men still in the hills?"

"No, sir," Morgan said. "This is it."

The major looked at him for a long moment, then at the others. "That was you, up on the bluff, behind the Nez Perce?" he said, disbelievingly.

"It was, major. The four of us. Trying as hard as we could to resemble a full troop of cavalry."

"Well bless my soul," the major said, smiling, "You did a damned fine job of it."

"What is your force here?" Morgan said.

"These are all civilian volunteers from Fort Benton," Ilges said, "thirty some in all. I had one soldier in the lot, and he has been sent back to the Missouri to bring up the infantry. Where have the Indians gone?"

"We saw most of them heading north," Morgan said. "We figure they're pulling out. They burned the wagon train up ahead."

"Yes, we could see the smoke. Did they kill many there?"

"We know of one man shot down, not sure about the rest."

"What if they regroup and come back?" Ilges said.

"I don't think—" Morgan began.

"I am exposed on my left, as you can see, the over hanging heights offer the enemy too much of an advantage. They can fire from those bluffs right down into my position. If they circle around the take those heights, I must withdraw. And I cannot advance across the open plain ahead, as they have several times the warriors I do. I had thought your party might have been Miles come at last, but with only four of you, well, I am badly outgunned."

"I don't think—" Morgan tried again.

"We've had only one man killed so far, but the volunteers are not cavalry, and I can only ask them to proceed and not order it. Therefore I must withdraw for the time being, and if my infantry come up, then so shall I. In the mean time, come with us, I could use the extra manpower."

"You'll not need extra men to withdraw," Beck said.

"And who are you?" Ilges said, glaring at Beck.

"Jon Beck, chief scout for the Fifth Cavalry."

"Well Mr. Beck, there is greater safety in greater numbers. We had hoped to overtake the freight wagons before the Indians found them, but we have failed in that. I do not see the point in chasing and possibly attacking a superior force with troops who are not troops at all. No, I will withdraw, at least to the point of finding my infantry. Then we shall see. You are welcome to join us, or not, as you see fit."

"We have orders to stick with the Nez Perce, major," Morgan said. Then firmly, "I don't think they will be coming back this way. We have been trailing them for weeks, and we know how they operate. They are making a run for the Canadian border and Sitting Bull's camp, and we are to follow and report their position back to the pursuing army command as warranted. Can you spare me any men to act as couriers, major?"

"That is beyond my authority to command. But I will certainly inquire of the men." The major wheeled his horse and rode back to the creek bed where the men were standing and sitting around, watching the parley. He rode among them and began to speak to them.

"He's right, I suppose," Morgan said. "If he's leading volunteers, he has no real command. Looks like they gave a pretty good account of themselves so far, I guess a man couldn't ask them to chase after a superior force, knowing they would most likely catch hell if they actually caught up with them."

"Ain't that what we're doing?" Beck said with a chuckle.

"Some. Some not. We aren't supposed to actually catch them, we are supposed to keep them in sight and report on that fact."

"You know, lieutenant, you and I are finally coming to think some 'at alike," Beck said.

Ilges rode back out to the party of scouts, drew rein before Morgan.

"No volunteer couriers, I am afraid," he said. "I will report your position and condition to the forces coming up behind us. And I will certainly relate your heroic action in driving off the enemy today! My compliments to you, sir, and good luck!" And the major saluted the lieutenant, who returned the salute with a surprised expression on his face. The major turned his horse and walked it back toward his command.

The scouts turned their own mounts up the valley toward the north, toward the column of black smoke that marked the remains of the wagon train. Pocket swung up aboard his paint pony, and let the animal try a few steps. Though it favored its right front leg, the animal did not balk, but limped along with the others. But Pocket soon slipped from the saddle and took to leading the horse, watching how she favored her foreleg as they went.

They reached the train at dusk, moving only as fast as the little paint would go. As they came up, the light of the eight burning wagons cast a warm glow over the grey of the sky and the grey brown of the surrounding land. Bits and pieces of the freight from the wagons were littered all about, where the Indians had rummaged through the goods and flung things everywhere, split grain sacks, smashed barrels, scattered bolts of cloth, broken tools and bottles and jugs. The scouts sat and looked at it all, and one of the teamsters came from around one of the wagons.

"They gone?" he said, his eyes darting about nervously.

"We think so," Morgan said. "How many of you are hurt?'

"Don't know. I'm the first to come out of the brush, three or four others with me. They shot down ol' Barker, he's still lyin' out thar. We're lucky they was after the wagons and not our hair."

"Call the others in," Morgan said. The teamster went back around the end wagon and they could hear him hollering into the brush. Soon a dozen men had gathered. Two were carrying rifles. Two had revolvers stuck in their belts. The rest had belt knives, and one carried a coiled whip.

"I know you men have had it rough today, but I would ask a little more of you," Morgan said. "I would like you all to spread out and see what can be found to get us up a supper for tonight. And, you will need to bring in the body of your fellow, there," and he gestured toward the corpse that lay fifty yards away on the grass of the meadow.

"The troops at the other end of the valley have withdrawn back toward the Missouri," he went on.

"Then we ought to be goin' with 'em!" one of the teamsters blurted out. "Them redskins come back, they'll have our hair for sure!"

269

"I don't believe they will be coming back," Morgan said.

"How d'ya know?" another teamster cried. "If they do come back are you gonna stop 'em?" he finished with a sneer.

"I don't believe they'll be coming back because they've already got what they wanted from you," Morgan went on firmly. "If they were after blood and scalps, they would have chased you down like rabbits in the brush! But they did not, because they wanted the wagons, not you. Same with the fight down there," Morgan said, waving his arm at the south end of the valley, "they didn't want to defeat the soldiers so much as hold them up while their main body packed up and pulled out. Once that was done, the warriors pulled out too."

The teamsters looked at one another, one of them muttering.

"What I propose is this," Morgan said. "Let's make our camp here tonight, see what we can salvage to eat, and take care of the body of your friend. If you leave now, you will have a rough go of it in the dark, and remember that the road crosses Cow Creek dozens of times. You won't be perched on a wagon box this trip, you will be wading the creek and walking ten or fifteen miles in wet boots. If you wait until morning, you will at least be able to see where you are going, and maybe get across the creek without soaking your shoes. I make no promises to you, men, but if we stick together, we will be a tougher nut to crack in case of trouble."

The teamsters talked it over the agreed to stay. They spread out among the still burning or smoldering wagon to search for anything still useful, and four of them brought in the body of their fallen comrade. They found a piece of canvas and covered him over.

Pots and pans turned up, bacon and beans salvaged from the grass, a half sack of flour rescued, and they even found an unbroken bag of coffee under one of the wagons. Soon their designated cook was busy putting together a supper. The horses were watered and picketed in good grass. Several of the men went up the valley to see if the cow herd was to be found, and came back with two mules they had discovered in the brush. The cattle had been scattered, and they reported seeing small bunches and single animals on the surrounding hills.

The men gathered in the fire light from the last two burning wagons, where the cook had his own fire going and the biscuits browning in his Dutch oven. They had only found five tin plates and three cups, so they had to eat in shifts. Beck and Morgan let the others go first, along with several of the mule skinners. The men ate hungrily, and it did not take long for the plates to be emptied and washed and filled again for the second round. Simon had been right, the camp cook knew his trade, and the hot food was the best that Beck had tasted in weeks.

The teamsters settled in around the fire with their coffee, the men sharing the cups as they watched the flames. The presence of their fallen comrade, lying a few yards away under the canvas, placed a pall over their mood, and they spoke little. Their freight was gone, their wagons done, most of their mules gone, and they faced a long trek back to the river. They had a little food, the clothes on their backs, and not much else.

Morgan asked Beck, Pocket and Dodd to come with him to check on the horses. They moved out to the meadow where the haltered animals could be heard cropping the course grass as they came up in the darkness. Simon went to his pony, and, after patting it on the neck, ran his hands down its right foreleg and felt of the tendons and muscles. The animal tensed and shied slightly to his touch of the swollen foreleg, but let him feel of it.

"She ain't gonna be carryin' much for a few days," Pocket said, stepping over to the other men.

"Maybe we could get those freighters to turn loose of one of those mules they recovered," Beck said. "You wouldn't mind a mule under you, now would you, Simon? You might even break 'im in to working cattle, given time and a little effort." Simon could not see Beck's grin in the dark.

"Work cattle with a mule? Why, I'd as soon saddle a porcupine as work cattle with a mule!" Simon said disgustedly.

"Well t'ain't no never mind," Beck said, chuckling. "Those teamster mules is most likely only good for haulin', I don't figure they would be broke for ridin', but then, you never can tell. In the morning, let's get a saddle up on one of 'em and you can give her a go!"

"You really think a mule like that is gonna be fit to ride?" Simon protested.

"Now, you ain't scared of a little ol' mule, are you? I thought a Texan could ride anything with four legs!" Beck chided.

Simon snorted in the darkness.

271

"Why, I can ride anything you can get a saddle lashed to, and that's a fact!" he drawled. "Why, one time me and the boys roped a grizzly bar up on the divide, just funnin' with 'em, and ol' Johnny Buck bet me two dollars I couldn't ride 'em. Now that was a sucker bet, for certain, 'cause I done cut my teeth ridin' bars down in Texas. I told Johnny if he could get his saddle cinched down tight on that ol' grizzly, I'd jump aboard and stick 'till I'd tamed him down to a circus bear, hoops and all! Well, now Johnny Buck was a little slow on the obvious, but he was game for anything, and besides, two dollars is two dollars. He humped that saddle right off'n his bronc and while we had that bear stretched betwixt two ropes, he went in to saddle 'im up. Got 'er just about cinched tight when that bar slipped one of the ropes and came up spittin' fire! Knocked poor old Buck thirty feet with one paw, then commenced to disrobin' hisself of that saddle. I had to hand it to Johnny Buck, that durned fool was the only man I ever knowed 'at was game enough to try and saddle a grizzly bar!"

"Did you ride him?" Morgan said. "The bear, I mean."

"Hell no!" Pocket said, "Once he ate that saddle, how was I to hang on?" And then he let go with a laugh, and finally Morgan chuckled along as well.

"So, lieutenant," Beck said after a bit, "We go after those Nez Perce again in the morning?"

"Yes, just as before. I am afraid they are going to make the border after all. If all we have for pursuit is a civilian…posse, as it were, out of Fort Benton, then nothing will stop the Nez Perce from eluding us. Although I do note that they are not moving as fast as they once did. Perhaps they know just how weak we are, and how far away we are from heading them."

"I'd wager they do," Beck said, and sighed. "I don't know about you, but I'll be mighty glad when this finally comes to an end, one way or another. I am tired to the bone, and the horses are too. If those renegades get into Sitting Bull's camp, well, that's just the way it goes."

"But in the mean time, we have our job to do," Morgan said.

"That we do, lieutenant, that we do."

"Dodd, if you will take the first watch, I will spell you in two hours," Morgan said. Dodd took up his rifle and walked over to a log silvered in the darkness, and sat. The others returned to the teamster's camp.

Most of the teamsters' bedding had been destroyed by the Nez Perce, so the scouts shared what blankets and bedroll covers they could spare, so that some of the men could sleep while the others crowded the fire for warmth. During the night, they traded places, and by the first crisply cold light of dawn most of the men had managed at least two or three hours of sleep.

The magical cook worked up a splendid breakfast for them, using up the last of the food, the menu duplicating exactly the fare of the night before, but hot food in the cold light of a grey dawn was delicious by virtue of its mere presence. Once finished eating, the teamsters were ready to depart for the Missouri. They could not bury their dead leader, for all the shovels in the train had been burned in the wagon fires. They would not even let Pocket try one of the mules, claiming they needed them both to transport what little gear they had left back to the Missouri. Morgan was about to attempt to requisition the mule as an army emergency, using force if necessary, but thought better of it. The scouts brought in the horses and their own mule, and by packing most of the mule's burden on the other animals, they had the mule left to carry Pocket's saddle, which they flopped atop the mule and cinched down. Simon tried getting his pony's bridle on the mule, and it was fight. The mule finally accepted it, but was not at all placid about it. Simon went to the mule's side, reins in hand.

"Well, it ain't no bar, but I guess he'll do," he said wryly, and stepped aboard. The mule stood quietly, head down, trembling. Pocket dug in, hunkered down, and set his spurs into the mule's belly. The animal exploded, stiff-legging it with a humped back around the camp like a maddened bar stool, then bolted in a dead run for the creek. After fifty yards he dug in all fours, lifted his rump to the clouds and danced around on his forefeet with his head appearing to be examining some minute insect in the grass. Simon's stirrups were straight down along the animal's neck, but he leaned into it and felt his hat knocked off by the mule's rump coming up behind. He let out a war whoop and hauled on the reins to get the mule's head up.

And up he came on the other end, now dancing on his hind legs and pawing the air with his front hooves, his muzzle snapping side to

273

side as if trying to fling the bit from his mouth. Simon was now hugging his neck, his stirrups slapping the mule's flanks. Another war whoop and the animal came back to earth scrambling around and around in a circle like a whirlwind, seeming desperate to see where he's just been. Then he lined out for the creek again, his hooves churning up clods of earth and grass as he tore for the water. At the creek's edge a sandbar stretched out into the flowing water, and the mule dove out over the bar, his head down and all four hooves planted stiff legged in the sand, skidding to a halt at the water's edge. Simon sat there, panting. The mule stood there, panting. The he lowered his head and drank.

"Well I'll be damned!" Beck said, chuckling. "He was right."

After the mule had a belly full of water, Simon turned him and walked him back to the camp. The teamsters laughed and said, "Good ride!" and "That was a thing of beauty!"

Pocket swung down, and the mule turned his head to look at him.

"Well, you ain't as much fun as a bar, but you'll do," Pocket said to the mule. The animal looked away, and snorted.

"All right, then, let's get on with it," Morgan said. They transferred the pack saddle to Pocket's little paint, and packed it light. The teamsters set off down the valley toward the Missouri, leaving the body of their fellow rolled and bound in the canvas. They would find the proper tools, and reinforcements, and come back to bury him.

The scouts moved up the valley to the north, Simon's mule giving a jump or two when spurred, but settling down to a reluctant servitude as they traveled. They soon found the site of the main Nez Perce camp, and the remains of several head of cattle. They also counted over twenty head of horses, most of them dead, up and down the creek, several still standing. They were in poor shape, and had been abandoned as unfit by the Nez Perce. By mid day they had spotted the Indians miles ahead topping a ridge. Off to the northwest the brown cones of the Bear's Paw Mountains rose in the grey sky, and to the east the low peaks of the Little Rockies loomed. The country was broken up into low, round hills and ravines cutting up the country everywhere, and their travel was slow. They either labored up the slopes or slid down them, and the horses were soon moving at that deliberate, dogged pace that no rider could quicken for long. Pocket's little mare fared well, limping along but eager to keep up. They camped in the failing light in a hollow brown with grass, a trickle of a stream running along its bottom. The wind had picked up, and they built a buffalo chip fire in the bottom of the hollow, out of sight. Dodd cooked up warm food for supper. They ate without speaking much. The fatigue of the constant slopes had seeped deep into them, and when it was time to turn in, Beck took the first watch.

He carried the long Springfield rifle to a little table of rock on a knoll a few yards from camp. He had a view of the horses, dark shapes in a semi dark world, some soft light coming from the clouds that lowered overhead. He hunkered down below the edge of the rock atop the knoll, trying for some shelter from the wind.

The Nez Perce were close, now, to the border and safety. He had a job to do, and it had settled into his awareness like a steel cage, a thing he could neither discard nor ignore. But he was fed up with it, with the chase, with the frustration of it. The Indians had won, even though they were not yet over the border. Time and again he had seen them turn aside pursuit, delay their enemies, slip away one more time. They were killers, he knew, reacting to their pursuit with a ruthless determination to survive. He thought of them as wolves in a long winter, doing what they must do. But no, wolves had little choice. The Nez Perce had choice. They killed here, they spared there. Why? What drove them to take one life but spare another? They were men, like he was, and they made a decision in each case. He could not think of them as savages, reacting to each threat with only violence.

He thought of Two Shirts, and his squaw and children. What did he have now, three of them? Were they still alive? What was it like for them, constantly running, every day, every moment a question, a threat, where to next, who is waiting to kill you tomorrow, today, in the next minute. He had lived in the lodge of Two Shirts, he had hunted deer with the man. And he had hunted men with him. He had seen the wife of Two Shirts smile at her husband, shyly in the presence of a stranger. He was the stranger. He had lived in their world for a time but was not a part of it. He had walked through it and not truly known it. Otherwise he would know why they had killed some and spared others. He felt a regret, a loss, that he had something good in his grasp and had let it slip away without coming to understand it.

He knew that Hardy could understand it. Hardy had lived, still lived, in the Indian world. Hardy would know. He wished at that moment that Hardy were with them now, because at that moment he needed to know. He needed a reason to go on. He needed some chink of light in the darkness and fatigue that bore down on his great shoulders like the anvil he had carried from spot to spot for his uncle, back in Pennsylvania, so long ago. That hunk of iron was dead weight, and the first time his uncle asked him to move it "to better light," he had gladly agreed. And found it immovable. It angered him. He tried again, harder. It would not budge. It was not going to yield to half measures, it would take all he had. So he had gone after it full bore, red faced, the bear-like strength of his great chest and arms and shoulders taxed to the fullest. And he had moved it, picked it up, carried it to the designated spot and set it down.

He felt the weight of it in his memory, and every time he had moved that chunk of iron it had taken a complete effort. His uncle asked him to move it regularly, and he knew after the first time it was his uncle's way of training him. And now, without the iron present, he felt the weight of his fatigue, of his reluctance to go on, of his will to let the Nez Perce have their victory, for they had earned it and they had earned his admiration in the process. And he knew that to go on now would require a maximum effort, all that he had, not because he was too tired to move, but because his soul was too tired to care. The steel cage of his responsibility hemmed him in, bound him, and he sighed deeply with the burden of it.

"My God, I am tired to death," he muttered. He fought to keep his eyes open, to stay aware of his surroundings. When Morgan came to relieve him in the middle of the night, Jon Beck was only half aware of it, and just awake enough to stumble to his kit and roll in. He was asleep before his head rested on his saddle.

Chapter 32

Steadily north they dogged the Nez Perce, staying in distant sight but well out of the range of foraging parties. Twice they spotted other scouts watching the fleeing tribe, but were never close enough to determine who they were. The Nez Perce seemed almost languid about their flight, and Beck chalked it up to fatigue, or in their confidence that they had won through, that the border only fifty miles away was easily attained. On the third day, Morgan wrote up another dispatch and sent Dodd off to the south with it. It mostly said, "Border nearly in sight. Nez Perce moving more slowly. Come at once."

That last phrase was the lieutenant's attempt at wry humor. He, also, seemed to have accepted the possibility that the Indians would travel through to Canada without the least amount of opposition before them. His duty now lay in simply watching them do so.

He had no one to command, now that Dodd had departed south with dispatches. Beck and Pocket worked for the army, but as scouts and not as soldiers. He had no direct command over them, although he could ask them to do what he wished. He could not order it done.

But they worked as a team, now, and shared the work equally. All of them were tired, as they had to share the night watches as well, so that no one got a full night's sleep. And they stayed in the saddle from before dawn to last light, urging their exhausted mounts to go and go further. Simon continued to lead his pony, whose footing seemed to get stronger as the days passed. The mule was a handful, and he had to wrestle it strongly all day long. It would not go forward without constant urging, and it would not steer without rough handling on the reins. It was an animal used to being led along, bred to a guide rope and not a bridle. The bridle itself was a constant irritant to the animal, and it would not accept its insertion into its mouth each day without a struggle. And, each day, when Simon mounted up, the mule would kick up its heels a bit just to show that it was still in the fight.

The overcast skies and the wind never ceased, but the temperature rose a bit, and the frost let up. At dawn on the fourth day the cold hit again, and with it snow. The three scouts had just packed the animals and were preparing to move out when Dodd came riding in through the blowing flakes, and with him three Indians.

"Morning, lieutenant!" Dodd said, drawing up his horse as the braves came up. He saluted his officer, who returned the salute.

"Dodd!" Morgan said, "Did you find Howard and Sturgis close behind us?"

"Not exactly, lieutenant," Dodd said, "ran into a party of scouts, these here are Cheyennes," he said, nodding sideways at the Indians. "Colonel Miles is just to the east of us, maybe a bit south as well, and he's got men out all over the territory, from what these people tell me."

"Miles!" Morgan said, "At last! How far away is he?"

"Not sure," Dodd said. "They had a white man with 'em, I gave him your message, if you don't mind. He headed on back to the command, these three came on ahead with me."

"Let me try to palaver with 'em," Beck said. Hardy had taught him some sign, and he had used it with other tribes, although never with the Cheyenne. He spoke the words he was signing as his hands and arms moved, so that Morgan would understand what he was saying. To the three warriors before him, he signed, "Greetings." They nodded.

"Who sent you?"

" Red Shirt," signed the central Indian of the three.

"Blue Coat?"

"Sometimes. Today Red Shirt. Pony Soldier Chief."

"Where are the Nez Perce?"

"Over the hill."

"Where is Pony Soldier Chief?'

"Over three hills," the warrior signed, gesturing to the east.

"Where do you go now?"

"We see Nez Perce, go Pony Soldier Chief."

Beck turned to Dodd. "What did the white scout tell you?" he asked.

"Only that Miles was away to the south and east, and that they were looking for the Nez Perce camp. When I told him we were on their trail, just behind them, he said he would take that message to Miles, and that these three would come on ahead and locate the camp for sure. And here we are."

"Did he say how far away was Miles?" asked Morgan again.

"No sir, not exactly," Dodd said.

"According to this here Cheyenne dog soldier, Miles would be about ten, maybe fifteen miles out," Beck said. "Over one hill usually means just within sight, or four or five miles or so, in this country. Over three hills, well, half a day's ride."

Beck made sign to the Cheyenne that the Nez Perce were to the north of them about five miles. The warriors spoke among themselves briefly, and then signed, "We go now." They rode away to the north, and soon were lost over the brow of the next rise, the thinly blowing snow blurring the horizon.

"Well, we may as well mount up and follow them," Morgan said. "If Miles is within striking distance, he will strike, I am sure of it! It is a matter of whether he will be able to close in time." He mounted his horse, and Beck swung up onto Bill. Pocket climbed onto the mule, which jerked his head against the bit and jumped sideways a few steps.

"Lieutenant, it seems to me that the army is fast coming to grips with its enemy," Beck said, "and they may just stop them after all. Where do we go from here?"

"We'll follow those Cheyenne," Morgan said, "I don't want to miss this!" He led the scouts up the slope to the north.

The horses plodded into the wind and the finely blowing snow, the men hunched in their coats against the cold. By mid day, the snow had stopped, but the wind continued. A thin blanket of white lay on the landscape, and low clouds caught in the gullies and ravines of the Bear's Paw peaks and streamed away in the wind. By early afternoon they topped a long shoulder of the mountains, and Beck held up his hand.

"Looks like a herd of something out there, the little table land on the bank above that little creek bottom," he said, digging out his field glass from his saddle pack. Morgan did likewise, and they glassed the land ahead. Beck could see the horse herd then, and several outriders around it. No camp was in sight.

"Where do you figure they are?" Morgan said.

"Have to be that creek bottom. See how that darker area snakes through there just to the north? Look hard there, you may see smoke, but the wind wipes it out pretty quick."

"I see nothing there. But if their horses are there, so are they."

"How far you figure?" Beck said, peering at the country surrounding the herd through his glass.

"Four or five miles," Morgan said.

"Look up there to your left on the heights," Beck said. He had pinpointed three horsemen on a knoll, sitting, watching.

"I see 'em!" Morgan said. "Ours or theirs?"

"Theirs. Ours would be out of sight."

All right," Morgan said, lowering his glass. "Let's find a way to close with that herd, and maybe go around it to the west. That would take us between the herd and those sentries up on the hill. If we can locate the camp for sure, we can send Dodd back with the news of its precise location. Miles will be up in the morning, and he will need that information."

"His Cheyenne might get it to him sooner," Beck said.

"I think he would prefer to hear it from a reliable source," Morgan said.

Beck shrugged. "Well, do you see that ravine traversing the slope there below the first bluff?" he said, pointing off to the left. "If we use that, we can get within a mile of the herd without being seen. Then we'll have to wait for dark, before we can skirt them and make any kind of approach to that creek bottom. It'll be risky, since they'll have hunters out, and scouts of their own, and we may be seen at any time. If they catch us, they just might stay and finish the job this time."

"So be it. Mr. Pocket, I want you and Dodd to circle back off of this ridge, take that little valley over there," Morgan said, point to his left, "and hole up at the base of that butte, the little one with that chimney rock sticking up. Do you see that, the little hollow there on the south side?"

"Yep, shore do, lieutenant," Pocket said.

"You will be our ace in the hole," Morgan said. "If we do not come back by mid day tomorrow, and if Miles does not come up by then, you are to ride back to the southeast and find him and bring him to this spot. Or, if you see the Nez Perce herd being driven off, the same applies. The top of that butte will make a good lookout point to keep an eye on things. Here," and Morgan reached across and handed Pocket his field glass, "don't lose it. It was given to me by my grandfather, and it has great sentiment with me."

"Rest easy, lieutenant," Simon said, "I'll look after it like it was my own."

"Good. Dodd, you and Mr. Pocket are to work as a team. Do your best, keep an eye on the herd, and stay out of sight."

"Yes, sir!" Dodd said gravely. He and Pocket turned their horse and mule, and, leading Pocket's pinto, they worked their way back down the slope to intersect the depression in the brown rolling hills that would shield their approach to their assigned vantage point.

Beck and Morgan headed in the opposite direction, descending the bluff to the northeast, and they turned up a long, winding creek bottom in the general direction of the plateau where the Nez Perce horse herd grazed. From time to time, Beck eased Bill up the side of the creek bed to peer over the rim at the surrounding country, looking for any sign of movement. Then he would ride to the bottom again, and they would proceed another few hundred paces, and Morgan would repeat the process on the other bank. They constantly watched the rim above them, and their back trail. The gully had no cover in it, just the brown, dry grass of the plains, and an occasional low shrub or bush. They knew that if they were discovered here, they would have to run for it or die.

Late afternoon found them at the head of the draw where the banks were low and sloped shallowly. To go on they would have to expose themselves in the open to cross a low saddleback ridge ahead. They dismounted and crouched together, holding their horses.

"We must wait for dark," Morgan said. "I think we are about a mile from the herd, maybe a little less."

"I've seen a rider or two on the hills," Beck said, "probably hunters. They don't seem to be excited about much. Wonder where our Cheyenne brothers are about now?"

"Brothers?"

"Scouts, ain't they? Brothers in that sense."

"Never ceases to amaze me," Morgan said, in low tones barely audible even at three feet away, "how one tribe can spy on another tribe for the army, even fight Indian on Indian for the army. Don't they have any loyalty at all?"

"Loyalty?"

"As one Indian to another."

Beck chuckled a bit. "You figure all Indians are the same, is that it? I thought we talked about this way back yonder."

"Oh I know they have tribes, and the tribes can have enemies. But you would think that when the white man comes into their lands, they would forget their differences and unite against him."

"Sort of like some of them did at the Little Big Horn?"

"Well, yes."

281

"It just don't work that way," Beck said, his eyes scanning the surrounding hills. "These folk live on the land. They take what they need from the land. If the land don't provide, they starve and die. Having someone else, another tribe, say, come onto your land and take your game, well, it's like they were taking the food out of your mouth, out of the mouths of your children. Doesn't matter that the invader is Indian or white, it's a matter of life and death. Another tribe, or a white man and white men, come to your house and demand all you have. If you don't give it up, they will take it by force. What man will stand for that?"

"But you said before that the Indians don't own the land."

"That's right, they don't own it. What I mean is, they defend their territory, sort of. They defend their right to be on the land, to hunt there, to exist. When you take an Indian's land, you don't take the dirt from under his feet. What you take is his life, his whole ability to exist, to make a living, so to speak. Indians have lived as independent souls for thousands of years. To tell an Indian you're going to take his life from him and give him your food and your goods in return, would be like putting you in a small room, and promising that you'll be fed and clothed, taken care of. No matter that you don't particularly want to spend the rest of your life in a small room. You'll have security, you see, and no need for anything other'n what you're given. How would you like that?"

"I would rather die first."

"So would they, lieutenant. So would they."

Morgan remained silent for a time, and they listened to the wind in the grass.

"But what I meant was," he said finally, barely above a whisper, "why is it that some tribes fight the white man for a time, but then turn around and scout for the army against their own...well, their own race, I guess you'd say. Is there no mutual sympathy among them, for their own kind?"

"Sure there is, after a fashion," Beck answered softly. "But you have to look at it like we do, you and me, you know, other white folk. After the war, quite a few southern boys come west, and some of those ended up in the U.S. Army. I dare say you most likely have a few in your own command. These fellers fought the blue coats, and now they wear one. Each man has to eat, has to live every day, and some have families to feed. They do what they must. Same

282

with the Injuns. Just because the army whipped his particular tribe, doesn't necessarily mean any particular Indian brave wants his traditional enemy to succeed. He may hate another tribe far more than he hates blue coats. It comes down to family first, and then tribe. Any other tribe is competition, and most likely an enemy."

"So they don't think of themselves as Indian, then, in the broader sense of the word?"

"Actually, not really. You know, Hardy made a point about that once, and he's been out here among these noble savages a lot longer than your or I. He said that most of the languages for each of the various tribes have a term or phrase or word in them that designates that particular tribe as "The People," or "The True People." Meaning, that tribe is made up of the real human beings, and all the rest of the world, including other tribes, is something…less."

"Sort of like a one true religion," muttered Morgan. Beck grunted.

They crouched there in the gully, waiting out the falling light, and as dusk was hastened along by the low clouds, they moved on in the darkness. It was slow going, and they stopped and listened often, peering into the night, alert for any movement. Several times they came upon some beast in the dark, horse or mule or bear they could not say, which, when startled, thumped away quickly. Several times they heard voices, but the words they could not make out. Using the wind as a guide, they cut to the north and west, and after several hours of stealthy going, lay down on the top of a rolling hill and gazed to the east upon a shallow valley blinking with cook fires.

"Got 'em!" Morgan whispered, "By God we've got 'em cold!"

Beck looked over at Morgan, smiled a bit in the dark.

"And what do we do with 'em, now that we've "got 'em"?" he asked.

"We—" Morgan began, but Beck jammed out his arm to grip Morgan's shoulder. Morgan froze.

"Look to your right!" Beck said so softly that Morgan could barely hear him over the rustle of the wind. Morgan slowly turned his head. Darker shapes than the night materialized on the slope of the hill, coming at them. Morgan counted, one, two, then two more. As the shapes closed, the scouts could see the faint glint of rifle barrels, and then they could hear the soft thud of hooves in the grass as the riders came up and passed across the hill, barely a dozen feet in front of them. Neither man dared to breathe, each tensed against the moment when they might be discovered. But the riders, apparently looking at the fires in the valley as the scouts had been, passed on along the slope, and were soon enveloped again in the darkness. Beck tapped Morgan's shoulder again, and they slid backwards off the brow of the hill, and silently eased on back to the horses.

"They nearly rode right over us!" Morgan whispered. "Were they Nez Perce?"

"Don't know," Beck said, taking Bill's reins and mounting up, "but whoever they were, if they'd of seen us, there'd a been shootin' for sure. Let's get on back to the others, and get word to Miles."

They moved off in the darkness, the wind at their backs, and carefully guided the horses south and east, skirting the pony herd plateau to the south. The first light of dawn found them near the long, grassy gully that had fed them north the evening before, but they had to cross the same low saddleback ridge to enter it. Beck and Morgan looked all about in the faint first light, and could see no other riders. They urged their horses forward, up the slope toward the ridge, then over it. They had nearly reached the head of the gully when a shot cracked, faint with distance, and a bullet whizzed past their noses. Up the long slopes to the right, on the foothills of the Bear's Paws, three riders were seen coming down on them at a gallop. As they looked, the white puff of smoke of a rifle shot blossomed from one of the horsemen, and another bullet sang by the rumps of their horses. The boom of the gun followed, faint against the steady north wind. The scouts set the spurs to their tired mounts and raced for the gully.

They descended into its bottom as several more bullets whizzed and whirred overhead. Then they were in the creek bed and following its curved course, Beck in the lead and Morgan's horse thumping along after. The Indian riders could not see them below the rim of the gully, and Beck felt they had a chance, even with tired horses. No bullets buzzed after them for a time, and the horses were churning along steadily.

Then the firing began again, for the pursuers had come up on the gully rim, several hundred yards behind. They raced straight along the hillside above the gully, and as the fleeing scouts became visible in the twists and turns of the gully bottom, the pursuing Nez Perce fired at them. The Indian's course was straighter, and they began to close the distance.

Beck glanced back again and again. He could see that the enemy was gaining. Bill had been ridden all night, and though he was a stout animal and gave his master more than he had at times, he was tired now and slowing. Morgan's horse was even worse off, and the lieutenant fell further and further behind. As they pounded along, Beck began to look for a side gully on the south, a place he could dodge into and make a stand. Morgan had to get back to the other scouts, and the message had to be sent to Miles. Then he saw it ahead, a steep sided arroyo angling away toward the mountain, and slowed Bill a bit. Morgan gained, and then was along side, as two more bullets whined around them and kicked up dirt from the gully side ahead.

"I'm going to make a stand of it!" Beck hollered, "It'll give you time to break away and get back. Don't stop for anything, if they get around me they'll be on you right quick!"

"I can't leave you!" Morgan protested. The gully Beck intended to occupy was close now, and Beck cried desperately, "Don't be a damned fool! You've come all this way as a scout, act like one now! You have to get the word to Miles!" And then the gully was abreast of them and Beck hauled Bill to a stop and then wheeled him aside up the gully. Morgan pounded on down the arroyo, slowly at first, then spurring his exhausted mount desperately.

Beck dragged the long Springfield out of the scabbard and leapt off of the big horse, then scrambled up the gully side. At the rim, he cocked the rifle and threw it up, sighted on the nearest horseman galloping toward him less than fifty yards out, and fired. The rifle bucked, smoke billowed out to block his vision, and he halfcocked the piece, slammed open the breach block, sending the empty cartridge case tumbling over the side of the receiver, and grabbed a new cartridge from his bandolier. The smoke was gone as he inserted the round, slapped the breach block home, cocked the piece and fired from the hip at a second warrior sliding his horse to a stop ten yards in front of him. The man screeched, his horse stumbled, and the man tumbled forward from the saddle, hit the ground an arms length from Beck and slammed into him, sending them both over backward into the gully.

The rifle was torn from Beck's hands by the impact, and he rolled halfway down the slope. As he sat up, a sharp rap on the side of his head tore off his hat and sent him tumbling across the slope, as the Indian's horse came thrashing and sliding past him. Beck's vision exploded in stars, and he shook his head and blinked. He jumped up, dove his hand under his coat and came up with his Colt just as another warrior appeared to his left up the hill on the gully rim. The warrior fired and Beck felt a tearing sting across his ribs and belly. He whipped up the Colt, cocked and steadied it with his off hand, and fired at the Indian.

He moved quickly back up the bank as the gun smoke wafted away on the wind, and looked over the edge. The first Nez Perce pony lay out on the prairie. The second horse, without a rider, stood thirty yards up the gully, at its rim. He could see a body lying beside it. Just as he turned back to his front, a screeching Indian appeared in midair, like a stooping hawk, falling down on him. He tried to swing the Colt as he cocked it, but the warrior hit him before he could point the pistol, and it boomed out harmlessly to one side as the Nez Perce brave clung to him like a panther, and they went over and back and rolled down the slope again.

Beck dropped the revolver and grabbed the Indian's wrist where a gleaming blade was poised to strike. They came to rest at the gully bottom, the brave on top, each man gripping the other with their free hand, the other hand locked with the knife. Beck shifted to one side, the warrior shifted with him. Beck's heavy coat was holding him like a leaden second skin, binding his movement, and the Nez Perce on his chest and middle felt like a catamount, flexible, fiercely strong, and intent on his death. The man was using his superior position to press the knife point home. His face, wearing a vicious snarl, was nose to nose with the scout. Beck looked at the face, and studied it almost detachedly, holding the wrist with the knife from him. The warrior shifted his weight, trying to get the knife directly under him so that his full body would help to press it down. Beck came back to the moment, and felt the urgency of the fight flood through him, the fight for his life.

He wrapped his right arm around the outside of the Indian's left arm, hooking it solidly, and squirmed and shifted to get the warrior onto his right hip. The Indian squirmed, and screeched, and lunged on top of the knife. Beck's left arm, his pillar of strength, held the man and all of his weight up.

Suddenly Beck turned left, drew his right arm holding the warrior's left across his chest, and threw his hips to the right. He scrabbled and jerked and then the Indian rolled out of his grasp to his left. Both men were on their feet in an instant. In that instant, blackness clouded Beck's vision, and he blinked desperately, trying to clear his head.

His vision returned just as the Nez Perce came in fast with the knife out front, slashing at Beck's head. Jon ducked back, then reached out a left jab into the Indian's face, crossing over the man's right arm holding the knife. The Indian took the blow and hesitated for a second, then tried for a backhand swipe with the knife. As the blade swung past and wide, Beck stepped in with a straight right to the man's face. The Indian's head snapped back, and he took a step backward, off balance. Blood started from his nose. And in an instant he leaned in and dove for Beck's middle, leading with the knife, and Jon took the point of it on his left arm before he could react. He swiped his left arm up, taking the knife with it, and slammed a hard right uppercut into the Indian's middle. The brave "whoofed" as the breath went out of him, but he withdrew the knife arm, and crouched again, ready to spring.

Beck knew his enemy was probably unable to breathe for a few seconds, for his eyes, though fierce and black and narrowed, also showed a trace of uncertainty. Beck had seen that look in many an opponent, after they had gone a round or two with a thick, red haired man who had looked at the outset to be an easy mark. He stepped in, but the warrior took a step back. He was playing for time, just to get a breath in him. Beck went at him then, avoiding the slashing knife, whacking the Indian's face with a left, another left, then a right. The brave went down, splayed out against the gully bank.

Jon looked quickly about, and saw his pistol lying twenty feet away. He walked over and picked it up, turned, and the warrior was in mid stride coming at him, the knife held high. Beck cocked and fired the big Colt as the brave slammed into him sending both men sprawling. Only Beck got up.

He looked quickly around. The Indian ponies were visible, one at the rim of the gully, one standing at its bottom. He walked over to the brave and turned him over. His eyes were glassy, half closed.

The .45 slug had taken him through the heart. His nose and mouth were bloody. Beck could see that he was a youth, maybe twenty years old. He sighed.

Carrying the Colt at the ready, he scrambled back up the bank, and carefully peered over. The third Indian horse lay dead thirty yards out on the grass. He walked out and had a look. The first shot he had fired had hit the horse instead of its rider, and the horse had gone down with the back of its head blown off. Chance had spared its rider, who afoot had come up to be the last of the three to die.

Beck scanned the hills around him, looking for anyone who might have become interested in the gunfire. He could see no other riders. He holstered his pistol and slid back down into the gully, fetched his rifle, reloaded it, slipped it into the scabbard on Bill. He found his hat, and feeling at his scalp with his fingers, found a lump that caused him to winch as he touched it. There was blood on his fingers. He put his hat on so that it was cocked to one side to avoid the wound. He gathered up all of the Indian rifles and lashed them to the Indian ponies. He mounted up, collected the two Indian horses, and leading them, reentered the main wash and trudged Bill along its bottom to the south.

His chest burned, and blood soaked this left arm. When he held the arm down, blood dripped from his sleeve. He could feel the wet of the blood on his belly, coming from his chest wound. His head was numb on one side. He did not have time to stop and tend to the wounds, and though they ached and burned, he did not think they were serious. And even if they were, to stop now was to invite yet another attack, one he was not sure he could beat off. He knew his arm would stiffen quickly, and that would make the use of the rifle a clumsy thing. He knew he had to ride, and not stop.

He steered Bill with his wounded left arm, and pulled the Nez Perce ponies along with his right. The rising sun was full in his face as he headed east and south, and though it was warm on his skin, the cold wind at his back cut at his neck. Then he was out of the gully and crossing the rolling grassland toward the little chimney-topped butte where he thought to find the rest of his scouts.

In the sun over the next ridge he caught a glimpse of dark shapes. He lowered his hat brim to get beneath the glare, and there, arrayed against him, were dozens of horsemen lining the brow of the ridge. He pulled Bill to a stop. The sun was behind them, and all he could see were the dark shapes. Then they started off the brow of the hill in his direction, the horses moving fast, running. He glanced left and right, looking for cover, but the rolling grass stretched out for miles. They had him for sure, what with Bill being worn out. He thought of the Indian ponies he led, but by the time he had mounted one of them, they would be within rifle shot. He dropped their reins, pulled out his Colt, and spurred Bill forward. The big horse reluctantly started an exhausted canter toward the oncoming riders.

Then they were on him and he pulled Bill up and laughed. As the cavalry troopers streamed past, the guidon of the Seventh Calvary snapped in the breeze, its bearer leading the men in a column of fours. Off to his right another column of soldiers, a quarter of a mile away, streamed out from behind a low hill, paralleling the Seventh. Then Morgan materialized from the mass of blue coats and pulled up before Beck.

"Look what I found!" he said grinning and waving at the passing soldiers, "I'm leading them in...my God, man, are you shot?" he said, looking at the blood on Beck's front and saddle.

"Winged a little," Beck said, smiling. "Get up there and guide 'em to it, you've certainly earned the chance!"

"But what about you, can you ride?"

"I'm riding now, ain't I?" Beck said gruffly. "Get the hell out of here, you're needed at the head of that column!"

Morgan hesitated briefly, then spurred his mount to overtake the leaders. Beck turned his head and watched him go. He felt the urge to turn Bill around and go after them, but he knew the horse was played out. The Indian ponies, freed from his hand on the reins, were cantering off after the column of soldiers. Beck holstered his revolver and switched his reins to his right hand. His left was stiff now, and felt numb and ached at the same time. His chest burned with every breath. He had to get to ground soon, or he would stiffen up and fall out of the saddle. As the last of the troop galloped by, he started Bill again for the little mesa.

He knew the cavalry would make a charge into the Nez Perce camp, and within hours it would all be over. He wanted to be in on it, but at the same time he was satisfied not to be. And over all he wanted to be off his horse and lying down. The side of his head burned, and his vision seemed to sharpen and fade in turns.

He reached the butte and circled it, and found the place where the scouts had waited. There was a small pool at the base of the rock, with water seeping out of the rocks and gurgling into the pool. The path of the seep was laced with ice, and half of the pool was iced over. He swung down off of Bill, and let the horse drink. He sat heavily at the edge of the little pool and shrugged off his buffalo coat. The front of his shirt and the left sleeve were soaked in blood. He unbuttoned the shirt and pulled it off. Then he peeled off the top of his long johns.

His chest was crossed by a red welt where a bullet had furrowed the flesh. The wound was not deep, but it was bleeding steadily. His left forearm was gashed to the bone along the outside, and that wound, too, was bleeding. He rinsed out his shirt in the pool, and swabbed the wounds. The icy water soon numbed the fire of the gashes, and gradually the bleeding lessened.

He heard the faint rattle of gunfire coming down the wind. The cavalry had struck. He knew that he had but to bind his wounds and mount up, and by the time he got to the camp it would be over. He could get help from whatever army surgeon was with the command. But he was tired, so very tired, that to even rise and get back into his clothes seemed an impossible task. He sat and thought over again what he must do. But he still sat. He began to shiver in the cold, as the sun climbed in the sky, offering a weak promise of warmth against the constant bite of the wind.

Beck knew he had to move. To remain as he was meant death. He would simply go to sleep and die of exposure. He willed himself to become angry with his complaisance, and so began to move with great effort.

He cut up his shirt and made a bandage for his left arm, tying it tight with his right hand and teeth. He used the rest of the cold, wet shirt to form a pad across his chest, buttoned up his bloody long johns to hold it in place. He rose and found a spare shirt in his saddlebag, and put that on. He wrestled the great, heavy buffalo robe coat on again, and taking down his canteen, drained it down his throat in great, thirsty gulps. He refilled the canteen from the trickle feeding the spring, and laid it beside the pool.

He sat down again next to the pool. His left arm was nearly useless. His chest ached. He was incredibly hungry. He had jerky and biscuit in the saddlebag, but he could not get the energy to rise.

He wanted to go to sleep. Just a little nap. The idea seemed so delicious to him, so overwhelming.

Beck growled like a bear, and rolled to his feet. No sleep yet. He got the food out of his saddlebag, and set the packet on the rocks next to the icy rivulet. Then he gathered buffalo chips and small twigs and little branches from the several shrubs growing in the little swale where the pool lay. He got a fire going, and sat before it while he ate. He opened his coat to the warmth, and could feel it seeping into him like a live thing. He washed the food down with icy cold spring water. He ached all over. He felt magnificent. He slumped over on his side and slept.

Chapter 33

The sun had sunk below the little butte where Beck lay, leaving him in shadow. The fire he lay beside had burned itself out. Bill grazed a short distance away, chomping the dry brown grass slowly. The rustle of the wind was punctuated by the distant popping of gunfire. Beck became aware of something gripping his shoulder. He opened his eyes.

Morgan knelt at his side. "Jon!" he was saying, "Jon, wake up!"

Beck rolled into a sitting position.

"God, man, I thought you were gone!" Morgan said, sitting back on his haunches.

"Not quite yet," Beck said, rubbing his eyes with his working hand. He listened for a moment, then said, "What's the shooting about?"

"They turned our charge!" Morgan said bitterly, "They shot us up something fierce, and we have lost a dozen good men! Now we pop at them from long range, our boys having given up the horses and taken to ground. We ran off their herd, though, and some of them are pursued off to the northwest. Without their horses, they will not get far. We finally have them, Jon, we've caught them for sure!"

Beck stared at him dumbly, and it took a few moments for him to realize what Morgan had said.

"Not over yet, then?" he said.

"Not yet, but tomorrow, certainly. The infantry is coming up, and then we'll have it done!"

Beck nodded, rolled back onto his side, and closed his eyes.

"Jon!" Morgan said urgently, "You must not stay here! There is a surgeon with the troops, you must let me get you to him!" He shook Beck's shoulder roughly. "Jon, you must come with me!"

Beck opened his eyes again. He could not be certain of what the urgency was, but a feeling ran through him of dread, of need. He must rise. He did not know why. Someone was shaking him.

"Jon! You've got to get up! You must come with me. Jon!" Morgan was saying, at him like a terrier on a rat.

Beck sat again, and blinked to clear the clouds from his vision. Morgan found the canteen, and forced Beck to drink. Then with great effort the lieutenant dragged the scout to his feet, and worked to shove him up onto Bill. Beck just sat there, blinking a bit. Morgan mounted his own horse, took Bill's reins and led them off toward the sound of the firing.

The sun was in the mountains in the west, its long rays like fiery lances spiking across the purple folds of the land. Clouds were coming down the wind from the north, and the sun lit the undersides to a golden glow. They headed north toward the battle, Morgan leading Bill, while Jon Beck clung to the saddle horn, hunched against the pain on his chest. His vision seemed to come and go, awareness fading to a red tinged haze that brought with it the nearly irresistible urge to relax, sleep, let go. But the swaying of the horse jerked and jolted him awake again and again, as the animals plodded along to the north.

It was nearly dark when Morgan brought them to the south side of a brown grass knoll, where men were in blankets on the ground, lanterns were lit, and a rude canvas shelter had been rigged. There a doctor was examining a man shot in the arm, his assistant holding a lantern. Some of the men in the blankets were groaning, others snoring.

Morgan helped Beck roll out of the saddle, and brought him staggering to the shelter, where he seated Beck on the grass. The doctor glanced over at him.

"Are you shot?" the doctor said.

"Some," Beck said. "And stabbed, and I do believe a horse made a fine attempt to kick my brains out. But, all in all, I am in capital condition." Beck flopped back on the grass, out cold.

The doctor finished sewing up and dressing the wound of the man he was working on. He gave him a draught of laudanum, and an orderly led him away while helping him put on his shirt.

The doctor came to Beck, and he and Morgan got the unconscious man into a sitting position, and stripped off his upper clothing. The man with the lantern held it where the doctor directed.

"Who is he?" the doctor said as he worked.

"Jon Beck, my chief scout," Morgan said. "He saved my life today."

"And you? Who are you?" the doctor said. He examined Beck's head, feeling of the skin under the hair, bringing the lantern in closer.

"Lieutenant Morgan, Fifth Cavalry. We have been trailing the Nez Perce for weeks, scouting in advance of General Howard and Colonel Sturgis."

"I'm Major Tilton. The hospital tents have not come up yet, so we make do here on this hillside. The fighting seems to be dying down now, with the darkness, so I expect we must now tend to what wounded were left on the field, if we can locate any of them in the dark.

"Your scout has a serious head wound and no doubt a concussion. That arm wound is deep, and already inflamed. The bullet wound across his chest is not so serious, though it has bled a considerable amount. I will do what I can, but your man must remain here with my wounded for several days."

Morgan watched as Beck's arm wound was opened, washed out with alcohol, and stitched up. A dressing was applied. The chest wound likewise was cleansed, and the right side of it was stitched closed. A dressing was wound around Beck's middle and tied in place. The doctor cut away some of Beck's hair, washed out the scalp wound, and stitched it up.

"Will he recover, Doctor?" Morgan said.

"I cannot say," Tilton said. "The head wound is the question, the swelling is remarkable, and is no doubt putting pressure on the brain. If it does not subside within twenty four hours, I may have to trepan the skull to relieve the pressure. At this point, he must be bedded down with the rest, then we shall see."

The orderly brought a dose of laudanum, which they eased between Beck's lips, and he swallowed it. Morgan went to Bill and got down Beck's bedroll, and Morgan and the orderlies carried Beck over to it. They rolled him up in his blankets, in a row with other wounded, and spread his canvas bedroll cover over him.

Morgan took the horses and found the holding area where other stock had been picketed, and, stripping the gear from them, added them to the herd. When he got back to the hospital, the pack train had come up and the men were busy unloading the hospital tent and supplies. Extra blankets were handed out, and the wounded made as comfortable as possible. Morgan went to check on Beck again, and the big scout was snoring peacefully. He went back to Dr. Tilton, who was supervising the placement of the hospital tent.

"You mentioned wounded to be found in the dark," Morgan said. "If you have a man who knows where they might be, I would be happy to assist you in going after them."

"Johnston!" the doctor called to one of his orderlies, and the man came over.

"Take the lieutenant here up to the lines, find out where you can do the most good at finding and bringing in the wounded."

"Yes, Sir," said Johnston. "This way, lieutenant."

They walked up the low grade over the grass in the darkness. The wind had taken on a new bite, and Morgan could feel the snowflakes nipping at his cheeks. Johnston led them to the Army lines, where the cavalry had dug rifle pits and some troopers were still there, watching for the enemy or digging at the soft earth to deepen the pits.

"Any of you men want to come with me?" Morgan said quietly to the few soldiers still on the line at that point. "We're going out after the wounded." No one said anything.

"I'll go!" came a voice from behind them. Corporal Dodd materialized out of the darkness, grinning.

"Dodd!" Morgan said, "Where…?"

"Came up with the mule train," Dodd said, "Didn't have time to report to you, I was busy with the mules. But I'm here now, and I'll go with you."

"That's the spirit!" Morgan said. And then more loudly, "It would appear that once again the Fifth Cavalry must come to the aid of the Seventh!" But no reply came back from the exhausted men of the Seventh.

Morgan advised the men in the pits what they were about, and asked wryly that they not be shot upon returning to the lines. Then he and Dodd and Johnston went forward, across the grass now wet with the new snow and sleet that came down with it. They spread out in the darkness, just far enough so that each could be seen by the other in the soft light from the underside of the clouds. But the snow thickened, and the darkness became complete, and soon Morgan had no idea where the others were. He tripped over something, and on his knees felt about for what it was. The limb of a dead horse.

"Anyone here?" Morgan called softly. No answer. Then again, "Anyone here?" a little louder.

"Here, for God's sake!" came a weak reply.

Morgan moved in the direction of the voice.

"Where?" he said.

"Here!" came the reply. "If you're a white man, tell me who is in command!"

"Miles, and I'm as white as they come!" Morgan said, moving toward the voice.

"Come on, then, for God's sake," the man said, and then Morgan found him. The trooper was laying on his side, and uncocked his revolver as Morgan reached him.

"Where are you hit?" Morgan said.

"My leg!" the man said. "I bound it up some, but I cannot walk."

"Then I shall drag you back, trooper," Morgan said.

"God bless you, man!" the trooper said desperately.

Morgan gripped the man by his coat shoulders and began to drag him down wind. He ran into the dead horse again, stumbled and fell, got up and dragged the man around the carcass. The sleet and snow pelted him in the face as he staggered backwards with the wounded soldier. He slipped from time to time and stumbled onto the wet grass. His arms ached with the effort, and be began to despair of ever finding the lines. Then he heard voices, and a bit later, the cocking of a rifle hammer.

"Lieutenant Morgan here!" he said loudly over his shoulder, "I have a wounded man."

The soldiers came out from the line and helped drag the man in. Morgan collapsed on the edge of a rifle pit, done in. The sleet had wet him thoroughly, and the cold was stiffening his uniform coat. The snow was finding its way down his collar, and he began to shake.

A faint voice came down the wind, and several of the soldiers went out to investigate. Soon they came back with Dodd and another wounded man, and some of the men of the line carried the wounded back toward the hospital area.

"Well done, Dodd!" Morgan said, as Dodd dropped into the sodden grass by his lieutenant. "Any sign of Johnston?"

"No, sir, saw no other soul out there. Dead horses aplenty, and found one dead trooper."

They huddled in the blowing sleet and snow, and after a time Johnston came in down the line a hundred yards, then worked up the line to them.

"Nez Perce are out there, sir, among the wounded," he reported.

"My God, are they scalping our men?" cried one of the soldiers in the rifle pit next to them.

"No, I do not believe that they are," Johnston said. "I heard several of our wounded speaking, but they were very near to the Nez Perce position, and I dared not go after them. They did not act like men who were being scalped, although they certainly cried out as the wounded often do."

"We shall have to leave them there for the time being," said a voice from the darkness. A dark figure loomed over the rifle pit.

"But we may be able to—" Morgan began.

"No. I'll not risk the lives of men in the dark on a chance. Who among you brought in those wounded just now?" the voice said.

"Myself and Corporal Dodd, here," Morgan said, rising. "And I do not believe it to be pure chance at all, if we—"

"You have acted most commendably, lieutenant, and I shall certainly include your actions in my report." In the darkness, Morgan could make out the dim gleam of shoulder markings on the form before him. "What is your name, lieutenant?"

"Morgan...sir. Fifth Cavalry."

"Colonel Nelson Miles," said the officer, and felt for and took Morgan's gloved hand in his. "I had heard that scouts had come in from Sturgis and Howard. That would be you?"

"It would, colonel!" Morgan said, wanting to have his hand back to salute, but he shook hands with the colonel anyway.

"Good! I have work for you to do. Get back to the camp and get some sleep, then report to me at first light."

"Yes sir, of course, colonel."

"And again, lieutenant, well done. Now, who can lead me along the line of our positions?" Miles said. A trooper stepped up out of the darkness, and they moved off.

"Well don't that beat all?" Dodd said, looking after the departing Miles.

"Come on, corporal," Morgan said, "Mr. Johnston, can you get us back to the hospital area?"

Johnston led them back, and when they had come down the hill they could see several small fires going as well as the glow of the lanterns. They found the snowy mound that was Beck under his canvas cover, and next to him sat Simon Pocket. Simon sat with a blanket wrapped around him, his wide plains hat pulled low against the blowing sleet and snow.

"You heard what condition he's in?" Morgan said to Pocket.

"Yep. Doctor told me about it. Think he'll make it?" Simon said.

"It'll take more'n that to put down that ol' bull!" Dodd said, grinning in the lantern light.

"We're to report to Miles at dawn," Morgan said. "More scouting, I would think. Get what sleep you can."

"I'll be here. Just come and get me at first light," Pocket said.

Morgan looked about at the camp. Three small tents were up, and the orderlies were working to get the most badly wounded into them. A layer of snow was already on most of the blankets, including the canvas over Beck. The wounded being moved were often roused from their stupors and some cried out, some moaned, some complained loudly. When the orderlies came for Beck, Pocket held out his hand.

"Don't move him!" he said. "He's been in that bedroll for weeks, and he'll do just fine as he is. I'll make sure he's taken care of." They hesitated, glanced at Morgan, then moved on to the next man.

Morgan nodded, then moved off to the picket area with Dodd, where they retrieved their own gear, and found a spot on the grass to unroll their bedding. They slipped in among the blankets, but sleep did not come. The groans and cries of the wounded filled the night wind as did the blowing snow and sleet. Before first light the snow stopped, but the bitter wind continued, and anything wet by the snow or sleet froze solid.

At first light a trooper came for Morgan, and as he peeled back his canvas bedding cover, it crackled and popped, stiff with ice. He was shivering even as he rose. The headquarters tent had been set up fifty yards across the hillside, and Morgan left his gear and walked over to it. At the door the man who had waked him bid him enter. Miles was sitting at a small table, maps covering its surface. He rose when Morgan entered.

"Good morning, lieutenant," Miles said. Morgan then noted what the Cheyenne scout had said, for Miles wore a blood red shirt under his buckskin campaign jacket. "May I interest you in a cup of coffee?"

"That would be most welcome, sir!" Morgan said, and instantly the orderly pressed a steaming cup into his gloved hand. He sipped at it, burned his lips, but sipped again, eagerly, letting the scalding liquid encroach upon his tongue. It was exquisite torture.

"How many men in your scouting group?" Miles said.

"We are down to myself, Corporal Dodd, and the civilian scout, Simon Pocket. Our chief of scouts, Jon Beck, is out there among your wounded."

"Is he hit bad?" Miles asked with casual interest.

"Gunshot wound, knife wound, and kicked in the head by a horse," Morgan said. "We can only hope for his recovery."

"God willing it shall be so, as with all of those brave men he lies with."

"He saved my life yesterday," Morgan said. "I owe him more than prayer."

"And what more can you give to him than prayer?" Miles said, noncommittally. "There is much to be done, for we are just begun, here. Our assaults have had little effect, that we can tell, and it has come down to a siege. What we face is not just the Nez Perce dug in among the gullies to the north, but the possibility of the Sioux coming south to aid them. Sitting Bull must know by now of the battle here, and if he is coming he will do so within this day or the next.

"First of all, tell me of Howard and Sturgis. Where are they, what resources do they command, and when do you opine they can come up?"

Morgan reported all he knew, which amounted to the fact that the main command was two days behind. He noted he had received no dispatches from Howard or Sturgis, and his own couriers had not returned, save those sent out who met Miles' own command.

"So we may assume that the general will come up within two or three days," the colonel mused almost to himself. "I must have warning if Sitting Bull comes south. If we are prepared for him, we may make a fight of it."

"Against five thousand Sioux?" Morgan said.

"Oh he would not have that many warriors, lieutenant," Miles said, "only two or three thousand of those." He smiled slightly. "And we have only to hold out for two days. How many men does General Howard command?"

"I do not know, sir!" Morgan stated. "I have never met the general, nor seen his command."

"Hmm," Miles murmured, and studied the maps on the table.

"I must know if the Sioux are moving against us. Take what men you have and head north of the Milk River, here, and along here," the colonel said, pointing to areas of the map. "I will organize two other patrols, one in this area, and one about here. Stay out there until you are recalled, and send word at first contact with any sizeable party of Sioux."

"Sizeable?" Morgan said.

"Half a dozen warriors, or more. I expect you will see the occasional party of scouts, so be wary of being fooled. If Sitting Bull comes, I firmly believe he will come in force. But there is always the possibility some of his hot heads may form a war party and come south, even if Sitting Bull does not. Use your judgment, and send warning if you sight the main body."

Two officers entered the tent then, and Morgan took his leave. He walked back toward the hospital area. The camp was alive with men going about the tasks of tending small fires, heating coffee, water, and soup. More wounded were brought in, men who had been out on the field all night and managed to drag themselves to friendly lines. And he could hear the popping of gunfire coming down the wind as the two sides began the deadly game of siege for the day.

Morgan found Beck sitting in his blankets, Pocket at his side.

"Well, Jon," Morgan said, kneeling, "how's that head?"

"Feels like a wagon rolled over it," Beck said. "I been sewed up?" he asked, looking at his left arm, bulky with its dressing under his shirt.

"Like a trussed turkey!" Morgan said, grinning. "Your job now is to rest here for a few days, with the other wounded."

"And you?" Beck said, "What will you be doing?"

"We have been detailed to scout north of the Milk River, keep an eye out for the Sioux," Morgan said. "I would rather be here, take the fight to its end."

"Well, we have to do what we are ordered to do," Beck said, peeling the blankets off of his lap. He rolled over to rise.

"Now Jon!" Pocket said, putting a hand on his shoulder, "You ought to stay put, you're in no condition to go anywhere!"

"He's right, Jon!" Morgan said on the other side of him, "Get back into your bedroll and stay quiet. Or better yet, let's get you into one of the tents out of the weather."

Beck rolled his head first to one, then the other. He grinned, then lurched to his feet, and stood swaying as the last of his blankets dropped from him.

"Jon, for the love of God!" Morgan said, rising beside him.

"God ain't got nothin' to do with it!" Beck growled, blinking back the haze that still haunted his vision. "There's scoutin' to be done, and I'm your chief scout! That God of yours only knows you ain't got that many men left to push around, Lieutenant, so I'm going with you!"

"No!" Morgan said. "You're staying, and that's an order!"

"Make you a deal, lieutenant," Beck said, grinning. "If you can knock me down, I'll stay. But if you try, and you don't get 'er done, I'll wipe up this camp with your carcass, stitches and busted head and all!"

Morgan looked at Beck, then at Pocket, behind him. Pocket shrugged, then shook his head. Morgan looked back at Beck.

"Jon, I wouldn't take to fighting with you for any reason at all," Morgan said. "You saved my life out there, and I owe you that life.

I ask you to stay behind for your own good. We can do the job without you, and—"

"The hell you say!" Beck growled, grinning no longer. "I've had to wet nurse you from the first moment we rode out on this trip, and you still ain't got half the sense a 'coon pup's born with! If'n I let you two greenhorns—"

"There'll be Dodd along with us, too," Morgan said.

"Three greenhorns, then! If'n I let the three of you tender footed, half baked nincompoops ride out into Injun country alone, I may as well dig yer holes and write yer kin right now, for all the chance you got of comin' back with yer hair! And I don't like writin' all that much!"

Morgan looked at Pocket again, who was grinning now.

"Very well," he said with a sigh, "But we'll not wait on you, nor coddle you along—"

"Coddle!" Beck roared. Several men about the camp looked at the three of them. "I'll show you some God damned coddle—" and he stepped toward Morgan, his face beginning to show red. Simon reached out and grabbed his good arm, stopped him.

"Jon!" Pocket said, "Jon, simmer down. Take it easy now, pard. I figure we all need some coffee, and they have soup, all hot off the fire. Let's just take it easy and get some breakfast into our bellies, and then we can talk about this some more, Come on, pard, you too, lieutenant, let's us just mosey over to the cook fire there, and see about some chuck."

Pocket herded the other two along, prodding gently with his words and his hands, and they moved along like wary wolves, eyeing each other as if ready at an instant to leap snarling at the other's throat. Beck was also nearly smiling, for he saw Morgan's readiness to stand up to him, to lead. And Morgan felt a sense of relief in his heart, for he knew that Jon Beck was up and growling, and would live. Simon Pocket was just moving the herd as he had done since he was boy. And hot food loomed at the end of a very short trail.

Chapter 34

The army cook tending the hospital cook fires was a good one, and rations brought up by the mule train provided bacon, biscuit, and coffee. He made up soup for the wounded as well, and the scouts soon had their fill of hot food. They gathered up their bedrolls and met at the picket area. Jon went out to get Bill, and the others their own mounts.

He pulled Bill's picket pin and stood at the big horse's head, patting his neck. Bill nuzzled him and Beck rubbed his ears. Jon was having second thoughts of his going. His gut was warm with food, but the rest of him hurt like the devil. What worried him most was the cloudiness of his vision. The knife wound and bullet wound burned, and he could feel a throbbing in his head that pounded out all thoughts but what was immediately before him. He had to make a great effort to think of what to do next. The pain made him angry, but he could control that. Or thought he could. But he could not see clearly. He gritted his teeth, and knew he must go on, and knew he must not appear to the others as weak or wounded, though wounded he certainly was. It was the instinct of the wolf, of the pack leader. To show weakness was to die. Or in his case, he thought wryly, to be left behind.

He led Bill over to the gear pile, and got him saddled, working methodically, wiping his back first, then throwing on the saddle blanket, then the saddle, which he swung up using only his good arm. He favored the left, and though it took a little longer to do the work with only his right, he managed it. Then it came to tying on the bedroll, and he realized he could not do that with only one hand. He finally succeeded by using his right hand and his teeth to set the knots. It was a sloppy job, but it would hold.

Dodd and Pocket brought in their mule, and they loaded it with their gear. Pocket's little paint was saddled up, and then they were off. The paint seemed to walk normally, and Simon was smiling at the prospect of his pony being sound again.

They made their way to the west, skirting the fighting, hearing the muffled report of the rifles in the distance as the two sides took pot shots at each other. A mile to the north of the creek they came on a dispersed troop of the Second Cavalry, and Morgan stopped to talk with its commanding captain for a time.

Beck sat atop Bill, his head pounding. His wounds ached, and he could feel wetness against this forearm and belly. He knew the wounds were seeping, but there was nothing he could do about it. He felt the urge to turn back, to find a place to rest, a place to put down his head and let go. But he would not let go. He would not let Morgan win, he would not let Morgan or any man tell him what he could and could not do. He would take orders according to his job, but he would not be told what he personally was capable of. If he died in the attempt, so be it. Infection had taken stronger men than he, as he had seen in the war. There was nothing for it but to keep going, to grit his teeth and just keep going.

And soon they were indeed going, moving north into the bitter wind and flurries of snow. They walked the horses over the prairies and rolling hills all of that day, and crossed the Milk River late in the afternoon. Evening found them just below where they thought the Canadian line to be, and they camped at a small creek in a hollow out of the wind. The best grass was just over the brow of a steep little hill, so that the horses had to be picketed out of sight of the camp. One of the men had to be with the horses at all times. The first duty fell to Dodd.

They collected buffalo dung and some small brush from along the creek, and soon had a cook fire going. Simon got a pan of bacon on the flames, and the coffee pot. He also had beans cooking in short order. Morgan and Beck got the gear sorted out, Beck using only his right hand to lift and carry. Each movement brought fire to his chest, and his head throbbed ever more deeply. He could feel his face flushed with the heat of fever. But he set his face in a mask of indifference, and did his share.

They ate, and Pocket went out to relieve Dodd. Beck laid out his bedroll, asked Morgan to wake him for his guard shift, and crawled into the blankets. He was asleep in an instant.

Morgan and Dodd sat at the fire, coffee cups in hand. They looked at one another, then at the flames, low and flickering out of the wind.

"He is one stubborn sonuvabitch," Dodd said.

"They don't come much tougher," Morgan said.

"You taking the next guard duty, or is he?" Dodd said.

303

"I will. And don't wake him at all, he needs a night's sleep more than the rest of us. I'll take his shift."

"You know, Simon stayed up most of last night looking out for 'im," Dodd said.

"Then I'll relieve him early, and take the rest of his shift, too."

"You can't do it all, lieutenant," Dodd said, smiling.

"If he can ride all day all battered up and cut up and shot up like he is, I can lose a little sleep," Morgan said.

"I know that, sir," Dodd said. "Just let me help out."

"I'll do that, corporal. You turn in now, and relieve me at four in the morning."

"Yes, sir. Gladly, sir."

Light was full and grey, and the wind still brought snow with it, dusting the canvas over Jon Beck's bedroll, when Beck's eyes opened in the morning. He sat up suddenly, his head spinning, then his vision cleared. He looked up at Morgan, Pocket and Dodd, as they were putting the finishing touches on packing the animals. Bill stood to one side, saddled, loaded save for Beck's bedroll, ready to go.

The three looked at Beck, and Pocket grinned.

Beck grew red in the face. He threw off the bedding, a light flurry of snow scattering in the breeze from his covers, and rumbled to his feet. Pocket walked over to the fire, picked up the coffee pot, and, grinning, said, "Coffee, Jon?"

"Damn you to hell!" Beck started, "Why didn't you—"

"Call you for your watch?" Morgan said, stepping up to Beck. "I made the decision not to. It was my call, and I was right in making it. You came along on this trip to scout, and I need my scouts in top condition. Which you clearly are not. I have watched you grit it out all of yesterday, and I decided you needed the rest."

"I pull my weight—"

"Yes, Mr. Beck, you do. And I pull mine. I will make the decisions as to who does what, and who goes where, and when, and how, and anything else that needs deciding. If I need your thoughts on any matter, I will ask for them. Do we understand each other, sir?" Morgan's gaze was clear and direct, and he stood within easy reach of the bigger man.

Beck looked at the lieutenant for a long moment, his jaw working. Then he relaxed. He looked at the others, eyed the coffee pot, then back at Morgan.

"It's my command, Jon, small though it is," Morgan went on, quietly. "I need you, and I need Simon, and I need Dodd over there. I can't afford to lose a single one of you. I will do what I think best for the command. That's it, pure and simple. Do we understand each other, then?" he said again, more gently.

"I believe we do, lieutenant," Beck said. "I just don't want any favors—"

"And you'll get none. But we work as a team, like four fine matched bays pulling a coach. We all look out for the team, and the team looks out for each of us. And I, with your fine judgment as a scout and guide to aid me, am the lead horse."

"Well, all right. As the lead horse, where we goin' today?" Beck said, turning to roll his bedding.

"Have some coffee and breakfast, and we'll work that out," Morgan said.

Jon Beck accepted coffee in his cup, and Simon slid the last of the bacon onto a plate for him. He added hard tack to the plate and handed it over. Beck began to eat hungrily, the cold wind on his face, and he felt better than he had in days. The fever was nearly gone, and he could see clearly. He smiled inwardly, though his chest and arm were stiff and burned when he moved. The throbbing in his head still intruded, but it was much muted and seemed like an afterthought.

They worked out a route to patrol, two of them going to the east in parallel of the Milk River, and two going west. They expected to meet up with patrols sent up to either side of them by Miles. They would then reverse course and meet in the middle, thus be constantly moving across the area to be patrolled. Beck thought it best if a camp was maintained in the middle of the patrol area, with two of them there at all times, and the other two making the circuit, then switching off. Two would be resting their horses at all times, two would be moving across the plains watching for the Sioux. Morgan thought it best for the moving segment to have two men, with no set camp until the end of the day.

"We might be up here for a week, or more!" Beck said. "The horses are none too spry even now, and if the Sioux show up, will our horses be able to outrun the Sioux to get back to Miles in time?"

"But if we send out only one rider, what does he do if he sights the enemy?" Morgan countered. "If he rides directly south to Miles, the rest of us won't know what's going on, and may be surprised by the Sioux, or cut off. If he rides back to camp to give us warning, we lose the time it takes to do that, and may even lose any advance warning we can send to Miles."

"We just got too much country and too few men," Beck said. "I see no easy way."

"Then we'll do it my way," Morgan said. "Dodd, you'll come with me, and Simon, you and Jon will go together. You two go out to the east, we'll go west. When we meet up with whatever patrols are out there, find out what men they have, and see if we can pry a few loose to help us. Failing that, come on back to this spot for tonight's bivouac."

"Who gets the mule?" Pocket said.

"Who wants the mule?" Morgan said. No one spoke.

"All right. Simon, if you'll drag the mule along with you on the first leg, we'll take it on the next one. I don't know how far we'll have to go before we hit the other patrols, so we'll just work it out as we go. All right with you, Jon?"

"Ah, well…" Beck sighed. "Sounds like a plan, lieutenant," he said, nodding.

They split up and headed east and west as agreed. The country was flat into the distance, but not flat close at hand. The rolling brown grass hid depressions and little valleys and gullies, and clumps of scrub oak and willow, bare and grey or with a smattering of withered brown leaves, showed the random water courses of dried up streams or seeps. Occasional ponds lay hidden in the hollows, with stunted trees like picket fences around them.

Beck and Pocket soon lost sight of the army men behind them, and plodded their horses along in a grey, wind whipped light snow. The wind had shifted into the northwest, so they, heading east, had the worst of it at their backs. As the morning wore on, they saw riders in the distance on several occasions, in ones or twos, some going north, some going south. Once they saw people afoot, about a dozen of them, going north. By the time they had come up to their trail, they were long gone in the nooks and crannies of the folded brown land, the snow already blown over their tracks. Beck pulled big Bill to a stop, looking over his left shoulder at the dim trace winding off toward Canada.

"You figure they's Nez Perce?" Pocket said, coming up beside him.

"Most likely," Beck said.

"We gonna chase 'em down?"

"Tain't our job," Beck said. "We're here to watch out for the Sioux. This bunch," he said, nodding to the trail, "probably already in Canada anyway. I figure they slipped out of the Bear's Paws camp last night, or maybe the first day. Wouldn't take much to get by them soldiers."

"We might be able to round 'em up and head 'em back. Who's gonna know where the line is, out here in all this grass?"

"What for?"

"What for? Why, ain't that what all this is about, catchin' them renegades and herdin' 'em back to their reservation?"

"Maybe for the army. Not for us. Our job was to locate the main bunch, and we did that. Now our job is to keep a look-out for the Sioux. I figure if the army wants 'em bad enough, they'll come get 'em. I'd just as soon get shut of the whole damned business, to tell you the truth." Beck eyed the country round about, sighed. "I had friends in that bunch. Women and kids. They made a game try at it, and now it's got dirty. I don't want to see the outcome, 'at's why I came north on this last scout. Just don't want to see what happens to them. They'll fight it out, they're that kind of people. And there's no good ending when both sides think they're right. I seen that in the war, seen men of good character, brave men, run at each other and die. They all thought they were right. I would imagine some of your Texas kin was there, and did that. Were they slave owners?"

"No. Not a one. Had several uncles went off to the war. One came back."

"And did he think he was right? Fightin' for a good cause?"

"Yep. Did then, and does now."

"Same with these Nez Perce. No, it ain't gonna end well. And I'd just as soon be up here prancin' around in front of a Sioux war party than down there at the Bear's Paws watching women and kids and men I lived among get shot down like vermin."

307

"Well, speakin' of prancin', who d'ya figure that is?" Pocket said, nodding off to the east. There, on a hill some miles distant, several dark figures could be made out through the thin, blowing snow. As the scouts watched, several others came over the crest.

"Let's go find out," Beck said. "And if they be Sioux, we ain't gonna want that mule to hold us back. When we get up to 'em, you hang back with the mule, just in case we got to run fer it."

They walked the horses east again, and eyeing the half dozen horsemen on the slope ahead, and very soon made them out to be U.S. Army troopers. The soldiers waited for them to come up. A lieutenant walked his mount out to meet them.

"You must be Beck," he said, smiling. "I'm Anderson, Seventh. See anything?"

"Few riders here and there. Seen some folk on foot, most likely Nez Perce, headin' north. Couldn't get up to 'em though, figure they're in Canada by now."

"Same for us, no Sioux. Lucky for us, eh?" Anderson said, grinning.

"Any word on what's going on at the Bear's Paws?" Beck said.

"We came up this morning. They've been talking, some. Still shooting, mostly. They put the Hotchkiss gun in place, tried shelling the camp, but the Nez Perce made it too hot for the gunners, so they were going to re-site the gun. Runners say Howard and Sturgis coming up, no sign of them by this morning. I had heard they have a Napoleon with them, that should get the job done!"

"What's your patrol area?" Beck said.

"We'll leave a couple of men on this hill, spread the rest out back to Saugus Creek. Use a line rider to link them all. Where's the rest of your command?"

"The other two are patrolling out to the west," Beck said.

"Two?"

"That's it. Can you spare us a few men?"

Lieutenant Anderson thought for a moment. "No, I can't" he said reluctantly. "We've a lot of ground to cover, and it'll be pretty thin as it is. But, I will send my two end pickets a mile or so further west, so you won't have to come so far to sight them."

"Good of you, lieutenant," Beck said. "We'll be in touch."

The scouts wheeled about and headed back the way they had come. By mid afternoon, they were in sight of their original hillock and the little stream-fed basin where they had camped. The top of the hillock was a high spot for the surrounding country, and would make a good lookout for the rest of the day. The blowing snow, though light, made any object beyond a mile or two away blurry, so their range of observation was limited to what the snowstorm allowed.

They unloaded the animals, watered them, and moved them over the crest into the little grassy paddock and picketed them. Simon got the fire going again, and both men scoured the area for fuel. Further down the shallow valley, where the stream had broadened the wash a bit, Beck could see some brush that he thought might yield added fuel. The light was beginning to go, and before he could go off to look, Lieutenant Morgan and Corporal Dodd rode in.

"See anything?" Morgan said as he swung down off of his tired mount.

"We found the next patrol, about ten, twelve miles out. They couldn't spare any men. No Sioux, did see a few riders in the distance, and a bunch of folks on foot. Couldn't get close enough to figure 'em, though."

"We linked up with the next patrol, too," Morgan said, stripping the gear and saddle from his horse. He turned the reins over to Dodd, who led the mounts off to the meadow.

"They couldn't spare a man either," Morgan said, a little bitterly. "We did see a group of horsemen several miles to the north, but they did not approach us. There were about half a dozen of them. Not the Sioux war party we are to watch for, but I would not doubt it for a moment that they were indeed Sioux."

"You think they'll come south after dark?" Pocket said.

"Might. Whoever stands guard tonight must be very alert," Morgan said.

"If'n they's looking to lift our hair, they won't have any trouble finding us. I suggest we post two guards, one up on that hillock, the other watching the horses. We can take turns, two on, two sleeping."

"Yes, by all means," Morgan said.

"Lieutenant, I think there's a lot of firewood down the gully a few hundred yards. Care to go get some with me?" Beck said.

"Indeed, I would," Morgan said. "My butt has seen too much of my saddle for one day, and a good stretch of the legs would be just the thing."

They stepped over the hill and asked Dodd to stay with the horses, as Simon got the pans out and started supper. Morgan and Beck worked their way down the draw to the brushy area, and began foraging for wood, bringing a small log here or an armful of sticks there to a central staging spot at the bottom of the gully. The evening turned darker, and the light faded to a grey gloaming, softened by the lightly blowing snow. In the bottom of the gully the snow eddied and turned on the shifting wind, and made the black shapes of the sage brush and bushes less distinct. Beck was working beside a large sagebrush, loosening a dry, twisted root from the ground, when he heard a thump. He looked in the direction of the sound, but Morgan was off to his left, and he could see that Morgan had heard the sound, too, and was looking down the gully. The pile of wood they had been accumulating was before them, then more brush beyond. Beck froze, thinking perhaps a deer was close at hand, and that meant fresh meat if they were lucky enough to get a shot. He slowly unbuttoned his coat, reached around to grasp his army Colt, his chest aching with the movement. He slowly drew out the gun and waited.

Morgan had crouched into the brush, and had also drawn his revolver. In the dim light they could make out the dark shapes of the brush, but little else. Soon that would be all darkness as well. Then, as they watched, a dark form detached itself from the rest of the black bushes and moved up the draw, approaching the brush pile. It materialized into the figure of a man, and Beck could see that he carried a rifle. The man dropped to one knee, set the rifle butt on the ground and leaned on the rifle barrel, gripping it with both hands.

After a moment, several more forms came out of the brush and moved up to sink down beside the man with the rifle. Two of them were very small. Beck heard the sound of low voices, and the whimper of a child.

"Halt!" Morgan shouted. "If you move, we will open fire!"

The man holding the rifle instantly sprang to his feet, bringing up the rifle as he did so to hold it across his chest. Beck heard Morgan cock his pistol.

"Lieutenant, there's kids down there," Beck said over his shoulder to Morgan, while keeping his eyes on the figures in the gully.

"Lay down your arms!" cried out the lieutenant.

"Hey, that you Jon Beck?" said the man in the gully. "Throw me down some bullets, so that I can fight you like a man!"

"Men, hold your fire!" hollered Morgan. "You there in the gully, bring out the rest of your people, and throw down your guns!"

"The rest of my people are dead!" the man said, "I lead my woman and my children. Throw me down some bullets, and we will end this thing."

"Two Shirts?" Beck said loudly, lowering his pistol.

"So Jon Beck, you remember your old friend. If you are my friend, throw me down some cartridges, so that I may do what a warrior should do."

Beck stood up and slipped his revolver under his coat, slid it into its holster.

"Throw down that rifle!" demanded Morgan, aiming his pistol at the forms who were fast fading into darkness. The man laughed, and threw down his rifle. Beck and Morgan went down the side of the gully to stand before them. In the semidarkness, Beck could see Two Shirts, and his woman, and two small children. He knelt and took up the Winchester repeater, levered open the action, and found the gun empty. Morgan still held his cocked revolver, muzzle pointed at the Indians.

"Where are your soldiers?" Two Shirts said.

"We are the soldiers," Beck said.

"Just two of you? We should have run away," the Indian said.

"It is done," Beck said, "finished. No more running. Come to our fire, we have food, and blankets for the little ones. If that's all right with you, lieutenant?"

Morgan looked down at his gun. He un-cocked it, replaced it in his holster.

"Yes. Of course. Let's get the children to the fire," he said, and led the way up the gully. Beck came along behind, carrying the rifle. Within a few yards they could see the blaze up ahead, and soon the little party had trudged through the snow-smeared landscape up to the fire.

"My God!" Morgan muttered, "They have no shoes!" He was looking at the children's feet in the firelight. Simon had looked up from his pots as the group came in. He smiled. "Four more for supper, then?" he said.

Blankets were unrolled and the children, two little girls, wrapped up and placed near the fire. The squaw wrapped a blanket about herself and tended to the children, rubbing their feet before their toes disappeared into the folds of blanket. Simon dished up hot food, looked to Lieutenant Morgan, who nodded, and gave the plates to the children first.

They in turn looked to their mother, who nodded, and then they dug in with all the ferocity of starving puppies. Simon smiled.

"At least somebody in this world appreciates my cookin'," he said.

Beck went out to find Dodd, and together they went back down the gully and retrieved armloads of wood. Beck had Dodd heap his chest and right arm with wood, his left not yet able to grip. The burden of limbs and sticks on his chest was painful, but he carried a fair load back, and Dodd came in with a heap of his own. They dumped it onto the pile of sticks and buffalo dung already near the fire. Two Shirts and his woman were eating from the plates, both trying to maintain dignity and restraint, but both clearly desperate for hot food.

Dodd ate and then went back to the horses. Morgan and Beck had their suppers, and lingered over a cup of coffee, Two Shirts accepting a cup as well. His squaw and children all sat in the warm glow of the fire, out of the wind in the little hollow, more asleep than awake in the mellow draining of their exhaustion.

"Where is your son, Two Shirts?" Beck said.

"I do not know. He was with the horses when the pony soldiers came. Many were driven off with the horses."

"He is probably with the Sioux even now," Beck said.

"I do not know. He may be with the Great Spirit as well."

"Why did you come north, when your children have no moccasins and there is snow?"

"All who stay will die. I did not want my children to die."

"They will not die if they give up," Morgan said.

"Some want to give up. Some do not. They know that it is ended. They fear that if they give up, the soldiers will kill them. They have been killing them for three moons, and they will kill them until none are left."

"You are left" Morgan said. "You will not be killed."

"If I go back, I will be killed. My woman, my children will be killed."

"No!" Morgan stated, "None of you will die. You have my word on it. I promise you this, none will die. You have my word."

Two Shirts looked up at Morgan from where he squatted by the fire. The flames flickered in his black eyes. He looked at the Lieutenant's face for a time, then back at his steaming cup of coffee.

"Perhaps it is as you say. I see that you are a man with a good heart. You believe what you tell me, and you would make it so. But you are not the chief among the whites. The whites have too many chiefs. Each one of them speaks with a new tongue, and tells me that what he says is the best word. Then another chief comes, and he says a new thing, and tells me that it is the best word. But I know there is another chief. And another. When Toohoolhoolsote was among us, he warned that the double tongued chiefs were too many to count. As the birds of the air, as the buffalo in the long grass country. I know that this is true. I cannot hope against so many chiefs."

Morgan did not reply at once, but looked over the little family before him. Two Shirts' clothing was in tatters, his old hat drooping and holed. An eagle feather stuck in the hatband was broken, its tip drooping. His coat was coming apart at the seams. He wore boots, with the toe worn out of one, the other missing its laces.

His wife wore a blanket about her shoulders, and a hat also, pulled low against the cold and snow. Her moccasins, showing beneath the blanket, had holes in the soles. The children wore buckskin overshirts too large for them, and buckskin skirts torn away and ragged at the lower edge. Their bare feet peeked out of the blankets now, seeking the warmth of the fire. The family carried nothing with them, save the rifle that Two Shirts had thrown down in the gully.

"You are right," Morgan said at last. "There are too many chiefs. Too many white men who speak only for their own gain. Not from the heart. But what I tell you is from my heart. Come back with us, and you will live. Your wife will live, your children will live. We are not all liars. I cannot guarantee you, I cannot promise you, that you will always have enough to eat, or warm clothes to wear. But you will live, that I can promise you. The army, my chiefs, the men who command me, are men of honor. They will fight your people to the end, as they are bound by duty to do. But when your people stop shooting, when your people surrender, they will stop shooting, too. They will not kill those who do not try to kill them. Just as you would not, Two Shirts.

"I have heard that your people went out among the wounded the first night of the battle. Your people did not kill the wounded, and some of your people even helped some of the wounded soldiers. This is known in the camps of the white men. Many of the soldiers respect your people for this. Many of the soldiers do not want to fight your people any longer. But they will do what they must, what they are ordered to do. Your people will surrender, sooner or later. When they do, they will be treated decently. They will not be killed, they will be allowed to go home again. You will be allowed to go home again, too. Is this not what you want? For your family?"

"What will you do if I say no? You have my gun. You have my family. You have me. Why do you even ask me to agree with you? You can do what you want to do."

Morgan thought for a time, watching the fire. He looked into the eyes of Two Shirts.

"I say these things to you because once I hated you. I did not know you, and yet I would have shot you dead with happiness in my heart. And your wife, and your children! I would have killed you all and thought myself a great warrior for doing it.

"But that was a long time ago. A lifetime ago. I have seen your people fight and die, kill and be killed, flee and turn to fight again. It is war. One of those countless chiefs you spoke of once said that war is hell. We have walked through hell together. My men have been slain, and wounded, and your people have been slain, and wounded. We have walked through this hell we have made together, and I for one am sick of it. I had hoped that you might feel the same. So I tell you these things from my heart, so that you will believe them, and we might go back in peace and leave hell behind us."

Two Shirts stared into the fire, sipped from his cup. His wife murmured something to him. He chuckled.

"What does she say to you?" Morgan asked.

"She says you make a pretty good speech," Two Shirts said.

"Well, there's a hard part to it," Morgan said. "You asked why I bother saying all this, when I can do what I want to do. I will take you back, one way or the other. It is my duty, and I must do it." He looked over at Beck, who was about to speak, but thought better of it. "But I am saying to you that I will lay my life on the line to see that you are not harmed, nor your family. I think it is important that you know this."

"Well, I didn't think you would let me go," Two Shirts said. "It's just that I don't like having a white man tell me what to do."

"Nor do I," Morgan said. "But sometimes, we do what we must."

Two Shirts rose to his feet. "Then it is decided," he said, "I give you my word. You do not need to bind us, we will stay with you and go back with you." He held out his hand, and Morgan took it. The wife of Two Shirts spoke again, glancing at Jon Beck.

"She wants to know if you have taken a woman yet," Two Shirts said.

"Her sisters are all married," Beck said, "what am I to do? All the beautiful women among the Nee Me Poo have thus been spoken for!"

The wife of Two Shirts hid her face in her blanket and laughed.

Chapter 35

The men among the scouts took turns on watch through the cold, windy night, and when it was Beck's turn, he went to the top of the knoll and huddled in his great buffalo coat against the wind. Simon had drawn the watch on the horses. Beck could look down into the little gully and see the glow of the fire, with the forms of Two Shirts and his wife huddling in blankets next to it, each cradling one of the children. Dodd was stretched out beside them in his blanket, and Morgan stayed with the Indian family, talking with Two Shirts.

The night retained a ghostly light in the snowstorm, as the clouds seemed to offer a pale light that came from everywhere and yet nowhere. Beck could make out the gentle rolling forms of the grassland around him, muted in the near distance by darkness and the pastel of falling snow. He hugged his coat about him, cradling the long Springfield rifle to his chest.

His left forearm was stiff, but the pain was subsiding. His chest wound throbbed. His head still ached in its deepest recesses, but his hat fit better now that the swelling had gone down. His vision was clearing, though at times he had to blink and stare at an object to sharpen his image of it. But he knew he was healing, and the progress made him glad.

But his spirit was not glad, only his feeling of his own physical self was sparked by hope. His spirit was tired. He thought of the men who had died, of the men he had killed. He knew that in his capacity for the job at hand, it was what he had to do. And he did not shirk from the responsibility of it. But now, with the Nez Perce cornered, and the end in sight, he thought it a terrible waste. The Indians had ravaged the country, and had been ravaged in return. What had been gained? Not a damned thing. The Nez Perce would be sent back to Idaho, and made to till the ground, and that would be that. Hundreds dead and wounded, and all for what? Not a damned thing.

Beck shook his head, scattering snow from his beard. And what would he do now? Perhaps it was time to find a new profession. As a young man growing up, he had worked with his uncle as a stone mason, and with another uncle in his smithy. He had become a scout when asked to do so by men he knew in the war. At the time, it had seemed a fine way to make a living. And when he had found Bill, and tamed him and trained him, the combination was a natural. A big horse to carry a big man and all his gear. Beck sighed at the thought of Bill and all that the animal had gone through, stepping up time and again to do the bidding of his master as if he was a voting partner in the company. He found the thought of Bill immensely satisfying as he tried to burrow deeper into the shaggy great coat that shielded him from the soft, bitter wind.

He blinked his eyes and found that dawn had appeared as if by magic. The snow had stopped, and in the east the first golden rays of the sun were lancing over the rim of the world and dancing in his blinking eyes. The low, grey clouds reflected the sun in warm gold and pink splashes, and the sight was like a dawning of heaven.

On a knoll a quarter of a mile away stood a pinto pony, and standing on its back a man. Beck blinked into the blinding light of dawn and could make out that the man had removed his hat and was using it to shade his eyes against the flat light of the newly rising

316

sun. Then the man waved the hat over his head as he looked out to the south, and slapping the hat back on his head, dropped into the saddle and spurred the horse down the knoll toward the camp. Beck got stiffly to his feet, shook the snow from his coat, and started down his own slope toward the fire below.

As Beck approached the fire and the figures tending it and huddled about it, Simon Pocket came over the rim of the gully and slid his horse to a stop.

"Rider coming in from the south," he said as he hopped down from the saddle, "looks to be army."

"How far?" Morgan said, rising from the fireside.

"Mile or so. Only one, so I doubt its reinforcements," Pocket said. He stepped to the flames and held out his hands. Dodd and the Indian woman were tending the pot and skillet. Beck laid aside his rifle and squatted at the fire, opened his coat to the blaze. The two children came to him and eased into the folds of his coat. He wrapped them up and sat, they on his lap, and they leaned back against him and soaked up heat from the fire. The woman looked at them and smiled ever so slightly.

"The Red Bear has no honey stones," Beck said to the children, "and he is hungry. Perhaps a squirrel for breakfast would be good to eat." One of the girls giggled.

"Squirrel Tail remembers how to speak the white man's tongue," said Two Shirts from across the fire. "She will make a good prisoner."

"And what of Soft Fire? Does she remember?" Beck said, glancing at the top of the head of the other girl.

"She is like her mother," Two Shirts said. "She speaks to nobody."

Dodd had finished frying the bacon, and the Indian woman put hardtack into the pan to soak up the grease and soften. Soon the food was put on plates and passed around, first the children and the army men eating, then the plates reloaded for the others. Dodd went to the top of the gully wall, and watched for the incoming rider. He waved him in just as the plates were passed to Beck, Simon, and the adult Indians.

The rider was a soldier, who dismounted at the gully rim and walked down. He approached Morgan and saluted.

317

"You're to bring in your patrol at once, lieutenant!" he said as Morgan returned the salute. "General Howard has come up, and the fighting is ended. They are negotiating the surrender. Colonel Miles feels he has a force large enough to meet any threat from the north."

"What's your name, trooper?" Morgan said.

"Oh, ah, sorry, sir. Trooper Smith reporting," Smith said, straightened to a stiff attention.

"At ease, Smith. Join us in some breakfast?" Morgan said.

"I should be on my way, sir. I am to bring in the patrols to the west of you, as well."

"They can wait a few moments. Have something to eat, and some coffee. That's an order."

"Well, sir, since it is an order..." Smith said with a grin, and as soon as a plate was free, he gladly accepted the last of the bacon and fried hardtack. As he waited for the first plate to be emptied, he sipped coffee from a cup fetched from his own saddlebag.

Smith ate, mounted, and rode off to the west.

"Well, with Howard and his men joining Miles, it's only a matter of time," Morgan said. "Let's break camp and head south."

The fire was left burning until the last possible moment as the animals were saddled and packed. The Indians were left to bask in its heat, but the woman insisted on washing up the dishes and helping to pack the food. When all was ready, Beck mounted Bill and hoisted up the little girls one at a time, which he cradled in his lap, wrapped in the folds of his buffalo coat. The woman was helped up to the saddle cantle behind Morgan, wrapped in a blanket against the cold.

"That horse of yours can carry much," Two Shirts said as they crested the wall of the creek and headed south across the grassland. "My best pony was like that, too. He could go all day long and never by weary."

"Your best pony?" Beck said from atop the plodding Bill.

"He was my war pony," Two Shirts said, "and he could run buffalo pretty good, too."

"Which one was that?" Beck said.

"The grey with white stockings," Two Shirts said, "the one you killed at the buffalo spring."

"Oh. That one," Beck said. He sighed and shook his head.

"That was a good shot, when you killed that one," Two Shirts went on, "broke his neck."

"Not a good shot," Beck said. "I was aiming at you, not the horse."

Two Shirts chuckled. "But I was hidden behind him. You could not have seen me. I was riding like a warrior should. The white man cannot ride like that. You are all sitting up straight in the saddle. Only an Indian can ride a horse and not be seen."

"Maybe," Beck said. "But I could see you peeking over the top of his neck. I tried to put a bullet in your left eye. It was a new rifle, and I misjudged it by an inch or two."

"Lucky for me," Two Shirts said. "Not so lucky for my horse. And your bullet stung my ear after it passed through his neck. Would you have shot me if I had not run away?"

"If you did not surrender."

"I didn't surrender. I ran away."

"Yes. And so I did not have to shoot you."

"You are still my friend, Jon Beck."

They trekked in silence most of the day, and the wind, though bitter, was gentle and at their backs. They crossed the Milk River after mid day, and stopped at a small stream to build a fire and eat. Then they all mounted up again, this time one of the children riding with Dodd, the other with Pocket, and the woman rode on Beck's cantle. Two Shirts refused Beck's offer of a ride and plodded on at Bill's side, keeping pace with the walking animals without complaint.

The Bear's Paw Mountains were tall in the late afternoon sun as the little procession came in sight of the first of the troops surrounding the battle site. Morgan rode to meet them and came back with the location of General Howard and his headquarters. They swung wide around the little valley where the fight had been, and came up on the several command and hospital tents as dusk was deepening. Wood had been brought up by wagon from the mountains, and cook fires threw up bright, glowing beacons all through the camp.

A sergeant and several soldiers came to meet them as they pulled up at the edge of the encampment.

"Caught some more of 'em, eh lieutanant?" grinned the sergeant as Morgan swung down tiredly from his horse. "We'll just herd 'em over with the rest of the bunch for you."

"Is this the way you greet the officers of your command?" Morgan said gruffly.

The sergeant looked at him, blinked, chewed, and straightened to attention. He saluted. Morgan returned it.

"Sergeant Gilcannon, sir. At your service. May we relieve you of your prisoners?" the sergeant said in formal tones.

"You may, sergeant, and thank you." The sergeant saluted again, Morgan did likewise, and the sergeant directed his men to take Two Shirts and his family to the place where the surrendered people were being held. Beck handed down Two Shirt's woman, and as she lit upon the ground still clinging to the strong right arm that lowered her, her eyes held Beck's for a moment. In that moment he glimpsed the terror of a trapped animal, the silent plea of the condemned.

"It will be all right, Moon On The Snow, they will not harm you," he said to her. She opened her mouth, but did not speak. Then she smiled ever so slightly and looked away, and let go of Beck's arm. As she gathered up her children, the soldiers closed in around the family and they moved off. Beck watched them go. He sighed, and slowly dismounted as did the rest of the scouts.

"I'll go report in, find out what the situation is," Morgan said. He handed the reins of his horse to Dodd. "See to the animals, Dodd."

"Certainly, lieutenant!" Dodd said. Morgan headed off toward the small cluster of tents where officers could be seen coming and going. Dodd watched him go.

"Seems a little testy, don't he?" he said to no one in particular.

"Too much fraternizing with the enemy," Beck said. "I do believe he's comin' 'round."

The scouts found a likely spot over the brow of a low bank, out of the wind. The horses and mule were unloaded, and Dodd took the mounts off to be watered in the creek which wound through the low valley and picketed on good grass. The others went to the nearest wood wagon and came back with armloads of wood, and soon a fire was going and Simon was readying the pot and pan for cooking.

"What'll happen to that little family?" Pocket said, as Beck brought him the bacon and the biscuit tin from the pile of supplies.

"They'll go back to Idaho with the rest," Beck said.

"I mean tonight. You know, it's cold, they gonna get blankets and food and such?"

"I'm sure the army will see to that," Beck said. "But there wouldn't be any harm in us going down to the Indian camp a little later to make sure of it."

"Nope, be no harm in that at all."

"'Specially if you make enough food so's there's a bit extra, if you know what I mean."

"Was plannin' on it," Pocket said with a grin.

Dodd came back in, and Simon cooked up a supper. It was nearly ready when Morgan found them. Simon began to dish up the chow onto the tin plates, and each of the men held out a coffee cup to him to be filled. They settled around the fire to eat. For a few moments the sound of spoon or fork on the tin plates, the crackle of the fire, the murmur of soldiers in nearby circles of firelight were the only noises in the deepening dusk.

"Joseph surrendered this morning," Morgan finally said. "They've been coming out of their entrenchments all day, a few here, a few there. Pretty sad lot, according to my brother officers. But there may be some hold outs in their rifle pits, or so they say. No one seems to know who is giving up and who isn't."

"That's the Indian way," Beck said around a mouthful of grease-soaked hard tack. "No warrior speaks for another, unless they agree before hand to make it so. If Joseph surrendered, then he was probably speaking for himself alone, or just the Wallowas. And whoever decided to go with him. Each of them has to make up his own mind if he'll give up or not. But they're not stupid, if they see that the cause is hopeless, they'll come in. Eventually."

"Doesn't Joseph speak for the whole tribe?" Dodd said, "I mean, isn't he their chief?"

"Maybe," Beck said. "Sometimes they have a war chief, and maybe a traveling chief, and maybe a negotiatin' chief, so to speak. They might have a council at any time and pick a man who is good at the next thing they got to get through, sort of a chief for that day. Usually the fighters will follow a man they trust, a man who has been blooded in a fight, who shows good judgment, or whose medicine is strong. When I spent time with the Nez Perce some years ago, they had a leader for each of the bands. But that man spoke only for his own band, he had no power to bind any other

321

band to anything. Sure, they were all Nez Perce, but no man spoke for them all."

"Well, Joseph seems to have spoken for most of them today," Morgan said. "More than two hundred have come in, given up, laid down their arms."

"How many of these were warriors?" Beck said.

"Not sure. They recovered about sixty or seventy rifles, I was told."

"Well, there should be another sixty or seventy on top of that," Beck said.

"They may give up tonight. Or in the morning," Morgan said.

"Maybe. Or they may not give up at all. They may go the way of Two Shirts and his family."

"How could they?" Morgan said. "We have the whole valley surrounded."

"How did Two Shirts do it?" Beck said. "With two small children, at that."

"But wouldn't they all feel obligated to go with Joseph?" Morgan said. "I mean to say, what hope would there be for those left, if most of the warriors have given up, if their leader has given up?"

"Only the hope of the damned," Beck said, forking the last bit of bacon into his mouth.

Morgan and the others finished up their food as well. Then Morgan said, "By the way, General Howard asked after you."

"He did, did he?" Beck said, handing his plate over to Pocket. "You think he'd mind if this old scout paid him a visit tonight?"

"Why, I don't know," Morgan said. "I suppose it wouldn't hurt to go find out."

"Think I'll do that," Beck said.

Darkness was complete when Beck had finished his second cup of coffee, and, reluctant to leave the warmth of the fire, stood and wrapped his coat about him once more. He crunched over the cold-stiffened grass, through the firelight and camps of groups of soldiers, and approached the tents where wagons were drawn up and kettles were set over larger fires, men busy tending the fires and pots. From one of the tents came loud talk and laughter, from another low groaning and muted cursing. The officers were having dinner in the first tent, the wounded were dealing with their reality in the second. Beck approached a sentry slouching at one of the wagons.

322

"Howdy, sergeant," Beck said to the man, "Is it all right to go on in?"

"Wall sar, let me inqware," drawled the man. He called to a lieutenant who was talking to two soldiers near the officer's tent. The lieutenant came over.

"What is it, sergeant?"

"Man here to see the gen'l, I'm guessin'," the sergeant said.

"The general is at supper, Mr...?" said the lieutenant.

"Beck. Chief of Scouts, Fifth Cavalry."

"Fifth? Man, you are a long way from home!" the lieutenant smiled.

"Ain't we all," Beck said.

"I'm Jerome, Second Cavalry," the officer said, extending his hand with a grin. Beck took it and they shook. "I was in the Indian camp during the fight," Jerome said. "Those Nez Perce are a tough bunch."

"That they are," Beck said. "When you figure the general will be available?"

"I will go and find out for you," Jerome said, grinning again. He turned and went off toward the officer's tent.

"Proud little peacock," muttered the sentry. "You hear what he did?"

"No."

"Rode right into the Indian camp to have a look around. Ol' Joseph came out for a parley, and that little popinjay just took the opportunity to go have a look see. That's balls fer ya. But the laugh was on him, 'cause Miles arrested that ol' Joseph and took him prisoner. Was gonna use him to get the rest of 'em to give up. Only Jerome got took at the same time, they had to swap 'em out in the end! Man, I tell you, Miles was fit to bite a cannon ball in half, he was gonna have that little cock shot at sunrise! You could hear him screechin' all the way to the Missouri!" the sergeant chuckled.

"Well, I see he still wears his ears," Beck said.

"That he do," the sergeant said, "but I will bet you a sawbuck to a side a bacon he'll be pullin' Officer of the Guard every night for a month!"

"Don't seem to gall him none."

"That's the thing about that little peacock, he just grins about it and goes on about his merry way!"

"Bother you?"

"Hay'll no!" the sergeant said, "Next time he goes off an' does somethin' like that, I'd shore as hell go with 'im!"

Beck leaned against the wagon, and soon the lieutenant came back, with another lieutenant in tow. The second man stepped up to Beck, put out his hand.

"Mr. Beck, I am Lieutenant Howard, aide to the general," said the new lieutenant as they shook hands. "He is at mess with his officers at present, but has expressed the wish that you bear with them for a short time, as he would very much like to see you at the conclusion of the meal. Have you eaten?"

"I have, lieutenant, and thank you. Howard, eh. Any relation?"

"I am the general's son," said Lieutenant Howard.

"Of course."

"He has spoken of you to me," said Lieutenant Howard. "During the war there were few men he regarded as his good friends. You seem to have been one of them."

"I am flattered, lieutenant," Beck said evenly. "I was a bugle boy and afterward one of his messengers, when he commanded the Eleventh Corps. But I am not certain he would call me his friend."

"I am surprised," Howard said. "Why is that?"

"As you well know, your father is a very religious man. I am not."

"Yes," said Howard with a smile, "that he is. But how would that fact prevent him from calling you his friend?"

"We had a chance to talk of God on many occasions," Beck said, looking out over the camp, the fires, the men moving through the smoke, "and we never came to much agreement. I am afraid I offended him, deeply, more than once. When we last saw each other, during the war, I had requested reassignment back to my regiment. He had reluctantly granted my request, but I know in my heart he took it personally. As though I was in some way rejecting him as well as he beliefs. Or so was my impression."

"Well, I would say you were most likely mistaken!" Howard said. "All my life I have known him to be a man of indomitable good will, even to those who despised him. If he remembers you as a friend, then it is so!"

"You are as kind as he is," Beck said, looking the young lieutenant in the face.

The two lieutenants took their leave and went off about other tasks. Beck chatted with the sergeant about the details of Joseph's surrender. Within the half hour, officers began departing the commander's tent. Soon, Jerome returned and escorted Beck to the tent flap. He ducked through it, and stood just inside the entrance. Two orderlies were clearing away plates and platters from a long table in the center of the tent, beneath the light of several kerosene lanterns. In one corner a writing desk was set up, and a man sat before it, pen in hand, another lantern hanging from a cord near his shoulder. He wore a full beard, neatly trimmed, and still had on his blue military blouse, with small silver stars glinting from his shoulders in the lantern light. He turned his head as Beck straightened up from coming through the tent flaps.

"Jon!" the general called out, laying down his pen. He stood and hurried around the table, dodging one of the orderlies, and held out his left hand to Beck, smiling broadly. Beck took it and smiled in return. The general was a slight man, shorter than Beck by several inches. His right sleeve was empty and the cuff of it was pinned to the side of his jacket.

"It's been a long time, general," Beck said, awkwardly shaking with his left hand.

"That it has, that it has!" Howard said. "Come on over and set with me." He led the way to the desk, and pulled up a camp chair for Beck. Jon sat in it, unbuttoning his buffalo coat as he did so. The general sank back into his own chair.

"I had heard that you had accepted my request and were scouting for the Fifth," Howard said, "but I did not expect you to end up all the way up here. And that lieutenant of yours, ah, Morgan, quite a remarkable young man. A mark of the quality of the young men coming from the academy these days, don't you think?"

"As is your son, general," Beck said.

"Yes, yes, he does me proud every day. Still a lot to learn, but then, we all have to start somewhere."

"How is the family?"

"Very well, thank you. Although I must say their patriarch is somewhat the worse for wear," the general chuckled. "But now all is done, we have caught them, they have surrendered, and it is but for gathering the last of them out of their works and off to the Missouri we shall go!"

"Back to Idaho, I take it."

The general looked at Beck for a time, saying nothing.

"Perhaps. It is what we promised them, of a certainty. But as you know, General Sherman is commander of the department now, and his will be the final say in the matter. For the time being, I must assume they will eventually be transported to Idaho. For my part, we will get them to the Missouri, then to Fort Benton, and perhaps they will be able to winter there. After that, we await the spring and the general's pleasure."

"Well, after all that has happened, it will be good to see it finally come to an end."

"And you, Jon, what of you? Have you married yet?"

"Why no, general, I have not."

"You must think of it, Jon. Life is too short to go scouting forever. The Indian wars are winding down, and apart from the Sioux in Canada, most of the tribes have accepted the inevitable and are giving in to the reservation."

"So it would seem."

"I recall that you once worked as a blacksmith. Or was it a stone mason?"

"Both, actually."

"Well, there are two fine professions for a young man in fine health. I encourage you to settle down in one or the other of them, and find a fine Christian woman as your helpmeet."

"Or a fine Crow woman whose father has many horses," Beck said.

"Come, Jon, surely you can't be serious."

"But of course I am. In my last visit to the Crow camps, I was approached by one of the chiefs on behalf of his daughter, and a comely lass she is indeed. This chief has many horses, and so I thought that I, as a poor scout, might be able to negotiate the bride price down a bit. We talked it over. I thought he, being already rich in horses, would not demand such a stiff price for his lovely daughter. I was wrong. The price was beyond me."

"Barbarous custom, the buying of women! I can understand it among the savages, but you, Jon? Surely you would not?" the general said, shaking his head. "But if you don't mind my asking, what was the price?"

"One horse."

"One?"

"Only one. The mount I have been riding for the last eight years or so."

"You mean that huge stallion, ah, Bill, I think you call him?"

"The very same."

"Well, I surely could not condone anyone buying a woman for horses, but it would seem to me that the price was actually quite reasonable."

"It is everything I own. Or at least everything I care about."

The general looked at Beck again, his eyes glittering in the lantern light. He shook his head.

"Jon, I said it just now and I will say it again. You need to settle down and find yourself a good, Christian woman. This fixation you have on a horse—"

The orderlies were carrying the table out of the tent when Lieutenant Howard burst in past them. "General!" he said quckly, "I am sorry to interrupt, but news has come to me this instant that a large party of the Nez Perce has broken the treaty and they have departed for the border tonight!"

The general rose quickly.

"Damn them!" he growled, "How did you discover this?"

"One of the Indians who surrendered told one of the soldiers, who went to his sergeant, who came to me."

"Do you think the information reliable?" the general asked his lieutenant.

"Yes, sir, I do," Lieutenant Howard said, "I thought at first that it might be one of their jokes, to get us out running about the countryside in the middle of the night. But I found and questioned the man myself, and I am certain he is telling the truth. It was White Bird and his clan, perhaps fifty or sixty souls, according to the Nez Perce. They left at dusk."

"And no word of their passing from our surrounding troops?"

"None, sir."

General Howard looked down, sighed, shaking his head.

"All right, lieutenant. Here is what I want you to do. Send couriers to the several commands on the perimeter, alert them to the situation. Mount a patrol, no more than one company, and head due north. It will be futile to search in the dark, but have the patrol in

327

position as far as they can travel by first light. If they find nothing by mid day, they are to return to camp."

"Yes sir!' the lieutenant said, straightened, snapped off a salute, and darted out of the tent.

"Damnable treachery!" growled the general, and sat heavily once again in his camp chair. "White Bird! I should have suspected it! It was at his camp it all began, so I suppose it is only fitting that he be the last holdout. This changes everything! All that Joseph said was a lie, nothing can be trusted. We will double the guard on the prisoners, and at first light go into their works and pry the rest of them loose with the bayonet!"

"But general, you know how these things work," Beck said. "Joseph was speaking for himself, maybe for his own clan. He could not speak for all the others, every warrior and sub chief—"

"But he did!" stated Howard, "He sent word that the fighting was over! That meant all of them, every last one! I relied on that statement, and I trusted him! Well, no more! From this moment we will treat every man jack of them as hostile, every step of the way! I will not be tricked again!"

Howard rose to his feet, then seemed to see Beck for the first time in several minutes.

"I am sorry, Jon, but I have work to do, as you may well suppose. It was a pleasure seeing you again, all too briefly, I must confess. On your way out, would you ask Lieutenant Jerome to report to me."

"Certainly, general," Beck said, holding out his left hand, which the general took and shook. "I wish you luck."

"God is on our side, what need do we have of luck?" smiled General Howard.

"Luck all the same, sir," Beck said, and left the tent.

Chapter 36

Jon Beck made his way back to the scout's camp, past men moving urgently to and fro, horses being moved up, orders being

328

shouted. When he found their fire again, Dodd was the only one present.

"They've gone off to see the prisoners," he said when Beck asked about the others.

Beck thought about going there too, to see if Two Shirts and his family were being treated well, but his heart was not in it. He sagged onto a piece of firewood next to the fire and stared into the coals.

"What's all the hullabaloo about?" Dodd asked across the fire.

"Seems it's not over yet," Beck said. "Some of the Nez Perce have slipped out of the camp tonight, I figure they're bound for the Sioux camps in Canada. White Bird and his band, or so it was said. I figure they are not the first this night, nor will they be the last."

"Well if they are bound to surrender, why don't they do it?" Dodd said.

"They don't trust the white man," Beck said. "Most of them figure they will be killed sooner or later by the white man if they give up. So, when it comes down to it, to walk out and lay down their guns before the soldiers isn't just admitting defeat, it's accepting death at the same time."

"But we wouldn't kill them after they've given up…would we?"

"Maybe not right off," Beck said, stirring the coals with a stick. "But there are many ways to kill, and many deaths to die. Going onto a reservation is death to some of them."

Beck and Dodd sat at the fire, its sparks twisting up against the night, listening to the sound of a company of soldiers being mounted, formed up, and trotted out of the camp to the echoing commands of its officers.

"Think they'll catch them?" Dodd said.

"Maybe. But I doubt it. They're Indians. It's what they're good at."

Shortly Lieutenant Morgan and Simon Pocket came back to the camp, Pocket carrying a blanket folded over his shoulder. The two squatted at the fire.

"They doin' okay?" Beck asked the lieutenant.

"Yes. Army has provided blankets, wood for the fires, and food. They were putting up tents for the prisoners when we were ushered out of the camp. New orders, no visitors, no gifts, no one in or out. While we were there, several more Nez Perce were brought in."

329

Morgan sighed. "I am hoping they will be cared for as human beings, as prisoners of war. So far, that seems to be the case."

"Hear about White Bird?" Beck said.

"Yes. Can't say as I blame him much."

Beck looked over at the lieutenant, smiling a bit.

"Why lieutenant," he chided, "I do believe you have come full circle at last! Only a few short weeks ago, your favorite word was extermination—"

"It would please me immensely, Mr. Beck, if you would be so kind as to cease your self-righteous, condescending tone with me concerning my attitude toward the Indians!" Morgan protested, but tiredly. "Yes, in the past I would just as soon have killed them all out of hand. Every one of them, every man, every squaw, every child. I freely admit it. But that is not the case now. I have changed my opinion. One can do that, you know, I am living proof that one can do that. If you feel that is wrong of me, then damn you hell, I do not care for your opinion on the matter one whit!"

"Spoken like a true officer!" Beck said, "But I do not condemn you, lieutenant. Matter of fact, I kind of admire this...new you. A man can grow here in the west, can change and expand what he is and what he thinks. And what he feels about things. Nothing like a good campaign to put a true temper on a soldier. And you, Lieutenant Morgan, have come to understand your demons."

No one about the fire spoke for a time.

"It's disgusting," Morgan said finally. "It's pathetic and disgusting. This whole fight is for nothing, all this suffering, all the killed, for nothing at all. Two Shirts, much less his wife and his daughters and his son...did you know he has a son--?

"Yes. Walks In The Light. He's about thirteen, now."

"They had no part in the killings that started this war, they had no part in the first battles, they did not even fire a shot, Two Shirts did not, until the Big Hole battle, and only then because the camp was attacked and he had no choice. All of this time he and his family were simply following the chiefs, running with the rest because they had no choice in the matter. Or thought they had none. And why? Because a few hot heads took it upon themselves to take vengeance on those who had wronged them. The whole war is simply a testimonial to fear and distrust and injustice."

"Did Two Shirts say where his son is now?"

"He does not know. He was with the pony herd when the soldiers attacked."

"Perhaps he lives. I had heard that some of the herd, and the herders, got away."

"How about you, Jon?" Morgan suddenly said, looking at Beck sharply. "How can you, who lived with Two Shirts and his family, you who know the names of his little girls, how can you go about hunting these people down and killing them?"

Beck looked in turn over at Morgan. He pursed his lips, and looked back at the fire.

"First of all, it's what I was hired to do. Secondly, I do believe that if you think back on it, I never killed a man wasn't trying mighty hard to kill me. Thirdly, every man makes up his own mind. The Nez Perce, and Two Shirts, are here because they chose this trail. Others of the Nez Perce did not. A man makes his bed, and must lie in it, as they say. A man chooses his trail, and must ride it. Whether they were right or wrong is something I cannot say for them. What I can say is that powers bigger'n them determined that they were indeed wrong, and I am part of the...machine...that was constructed to put it all right.

"You're asking yourself, most likely, if I would kill Two Shirts, or harm his family, in the way of doing my duty, of doing what I was hired to do. Well, I would kill him, if he was tryin' to kill me. Would I harm Moon On The Snow, or Squirrel Tail, or Soft Fire or Walks In The Light? Not if I could avoid it. But I would do what I was hired to do, first and foremost.

"But I will say to you, lieutenant, that had I killed Two Shirts, and you will recall a time back at that hilltop spring where we found that buffalo, when I shot his favorite pony out from under him, had I killed him then, I would have felt bad about it. But not regretted it. At least not the killing of Two Shirts. Sort of pains me to think of killing that pretty little grey, though."

"You are a hard man, Jon Beck," Morgan said, his face in his hands, the warm yellow light of the fire reddening his features.

"Mebbe so," Beck said. "I've had me a few wars here and there to sorta help tone down the flames of my forbearance, you might say. I have come to admire efficiency over luck, expediency over bravery, and yes, compassion over glory. Give me good tactics,

331

every time, over a hasty charge and a prayer. Do you think it evil of me to put my trust in what I have seen to be successful?"

"No. I do not."

"I would expect you to say that, otherwise all those years at West Point were for naught!"

"But sometimes a hasty charge and faith in God are all that will do! What then?"

"Then by all means, do! I am only telling you that I do what must be done, and whether I regret the things that have to be done or don't regret them is unimportant."

"And I, Mr. Beck, think that it is very important!"

"So we disagree. Mr. Dodd, any more coffee in that pot?"

"Why, yes, Mr. Beck, here is your cup." Dodd handed it over, then filled it from the pot at the edge of the fire as Jon held it. The others decided on coffee too, and soon all of them were sipping the hot brew around the glow of the fire.

"So where you figure we go from here, Mr. Beck?" Simon said.

"Well, it will take a few days to round 'em all up, get 'em all out of the pits down there," Beck said. "Howard was mighty burned up when he heard White Bird and his band had flown the coop. May take a day or two to find them and bring 'em back, if they can. Then the whole kit and caboodle will be drug off to the Missouri, then onto the steamers and down the river to the forts. Probably winter there, then back to Idaho in the spring."

"And us?" Dodd said.

"We have the option," said Morgan, "of traveling with Howard's command and the prisoners, or we can strike out on our own. We can take the river down to the forts, then strike out cross country for Camp Brown and home. Being scouts, our job is done, and we are not under orders to assist with the prisoners in any way."

"What about our pay?" Simon said.

"Well, you can come to the quartermaster at Camp Brown for it, or, if you return to Quandry, we can arrange to have it sent there," Morgan said.

"I guess that'll have to do," Simon said, "not much out here to spend a dollar on, anyway."

With plenty of firewood provided by the army woodcutters, they kept a good blaze going through the cold night. Beck slept soundly, but was awake in the first light of dawn. The rustle of cookware awakened him, for Dodd was up getting breakfast started.

He soon had coffee on, and Beck accepted a cup before the first rays of the sun sliced over the eastern horizon.

The others rose to the sounds of cavalry bugles rousting out the troopers. Again there was hustle and bustle with the soldiers and they were formed into squads and marched to gather in long lines near the headquarters tents. Several hundred men were soon formed up in three companies, and Jon Beck went over to the command tents. Morgan caught up to him as they came up to the tent flaps. The sentry at the corner of the tent ignored them. They ducked inside.

Howard, Miles and Sturgis were all talking together in the corner near the desk. Half a dozen other officers stood waiting, along with another half dozen civilians and scouts. Soon Howard turned to the group.

"Gentlemen, as you know, White Bird and his band escaped the camp last night. We have sent out a company to look for them, but as yet no word has returned. This morning we are going to form a skirmish line and advance into the Nez Perce positions, and ferret out each and every one of the remaining enemy. Captain Snyder, I would like your men—"

"Excuse me, general," Beck said, elbowing his way through the officers to stand before Howard, "but do you intend to take the position by force?"

"Good morning, Jon!" beamed General Howard, "That is precisely what we intend to do!"

"May I remind the general that a surrender is underway, and that these people believe you will not harm them now that word has been given—"

"Word which White Bird has broken!" Howard cried out. "This treachery has negated all that has gone before, we are back to a state of war! We will go into their camp and end this farce once and for all, not one more of them will slip out of here in the dark."

"General, if you march your men into their camp, they will fight! They fear you more than they trust you, and if you show them the rifle at this point, they will be convinced that their holdouts are right, that you intend to kill them all!" Beck said.

"All they have to do is lay down their guns and come over. We will not harm the ones who do that."

"But how do they know that?" Beck said, "If you come at them with hundreds of armed men, they will know they are dead men, and they will fight to the last bullet. Even a trapped wolf will fight until you kill it! You will force them to die fighting, and they will take many of your soldiers with them! Don't do this, for the sake of your men, as well as that of the Indians!"

Howard looked up into the eyes of Jon Beck. Not an officer offered even a loud breath. Finally Howard said, "What do you propose?"

"Let's go over there and talk to them. Let them know you will not tolerate any more slipping off into the night. Let them know that by, say, mid afternoon, they must all come over, or you will attack. Let's you and me, and whoever else you say, maybe a few others, just walk over there under a flag of truce and spell it out. They know they have to surrender. But they are afraid to do it. They think they will be killed after all, that's why many have not come over, they are afraid to die. If you go over and talk to them, I think they will believe you, and I think they will all give it up and come over. And it won't cost you one casualty. On either side."

"That would be taking an unnecessary risk!" Miles said.

"I don't believe it is, colonel!" Beck said, looking Miles in the eyes. "These people know General Howard, they know he is a man of his word. They have not always liked what that word has been, but they believe the general means what he says. They have not heard the words of the general in person, only the messengers we send over. Joseph came to meet Howard and tried to surrender to him personally, for he knew that Howard would speak with a true heart and not deceive him. If the general goes to them now, in his person, and shows that he is willing to risk standing before them all, they will have no choice but to believe him and come over. I know these people, I know how they think. They will see that the white man's chief is so sure of his victory that he does not fear to stand before his enemies. That will mean everything to them."

"But what of White Bird?" Miles said. "I am sure there are other hold outs like him. What if one of them decides to use his last bullet on General Howard?"

"That's not the way they think," Beck sighed. "They know they're beaten, what they don't know is what will happen to them when they lay down their rifles. I say let the general tell them in person. They will accept that, I know it."

"And if you are wrong?" Miles said, a look of stern rebuke upon his face.

"I will be standing at his side," Beck said.

"General, this is not—" Miles began.

Howard raised his hand, stopping Miles. The colonel clamped his jaws shut and shook his head a bit.

Howard looked about at his officers, then back to Beck.

"You have a good point, Jon," he said at last. "I would ask that you step outside the tent while I and my officers discuss it."

"Thank you, general. You will not regret this, I know it!" Beck said, and turning, moved through the officers and out of the tent. He stepped a few paces away out of hearing of the argument he heard rising in the tent at his back.

Before him the three troops of soldiers were drawn up, the men at ease, rifles grounded, the steam of their breath flowing away like a thin fog on the cold morning breeze. He doubted they had had time for breakfast. The mounted infantry troopers carried the long Springfield rifles, while the two troops of cavalry bore the shorter carbines. Though they wore the uniform of the United States Army, each man seemed to be rumpled in a slightly different way, so that the crushed hats and too big or too small coats and trousers set each man off as a unique specimen. At casual glance they did not seem to be of the same body of troops at all, but each and every one of them put up singly to be somehow lately come to the gathering.

At last Beck turned at the sound of boots on the grass, and General Howard himself came to him, smiling.

"Good advice, Jon!" the general said, "Although some of my officers, especially those who have lost men in the fight, were eager to wreak a bit of vengeance. But we have come far, and we have suffered much, and if we can conclude this affair with no more blood, then so be it. I hope in God that you are right!"

"Thank you, general. And may I suggest two things?"

"Certainly."

"That the truce party be small. And that we take along a Nez Perce that I know can be trusted, to accurately convey your words to the people."

"But I have two such men in my command, who have come all the way from Lapwai with me. They are Captain John and Old George, who they style a captain also, but Nez Perce and quite reliable."

"But they have come with you, as part of your command."

"Yes, they each have kin with the rebellious bands, and have been trying to find out their fate. They have helped negotiate the surrender, and have behaved splendidly, I might add."

"I suggest we use one of the men who has been with the non-treaties from the start, a man known to me, and to you, as a reliable speaker. You remember him as Two Shirts, who worked as scout for us during the Cayuse war."

The general thought for a second, then said, "Of course! I believe you lived in his village for a time after that."

"I lived in his lodge. I know him to be an honest man. He understands what we are about. He can speak to the holdouts as a reliable witness to what it is like in the surrendered camp, for he is there now with his family. I think the last of the holdouts will believe him, where they might mistrust your own scouts."

The general again thought for a few seconds, then said, "I agree. If you will go fetch him along, assuming of course he will agree to act as a Judas goat to his people, I will arrange the party to go over from our side. What I will do is send over Captain John and Old George to let the Nez Perce know we are coming. We shall follow momentarily upon their heels, as soon as you can bring up Two Shirts."

"I'll go get him now, then," Beck said, and tramped off down the line of waiting soldiers toward the prisoner camp. He made his way among the soldiers' fires and bedding camps to the small depression in the creek bed where the new tents rested, and the smoke from the cook fires curled up and bent off down the wind.

He explained to the lieutenant in charge what he had come to do, and was directed into the camp. Using what few words of Nez Perce he could, he soon found that many of the natives were willing to speak English and soon directed him to the fire of Two Shirts. Moon On The Snow was working over a pot on the fire with another woman, and Two Shirts was squatting at the blaze. He rose as Beck came up.

"I have a job for you, Two Shirts, if you will take it," Beck said.

"What work cannot the white man do that he needs an Indian to do it?"

"The general is going into the fighting camp this morning, to tell the people who remain that they must come out now, or face an attack at noon. We do not want any more killing, either Indian dead or white dead. We need someone who has been with the traveling Nez Perce to tell them what kind of treatment they will get when they come out. I ask that you tell them this."

"Why is the white man going to attack at noon? Were not promises given? Did not Joseph put down the rifle, and all of these," and he waved his hands about at the Indian fires around them, "did they not also put down the rifle? Yet now you say the white soldiers are getting ready to attack again."

"White Bird left the camp last night with many of his people. General Howard thinks that this is a breaking of the treaty that Joseph gave, and he is ready to fight again because of it."

"Joseph speaks only for Joseph, and his Wallowas. You know this. One Arm must know this! There is Joseph, over there by that tent," Two Shirts said, pointing across the little valley at one of the tents. "Go and ask him. He will tell you. He did not speak for me and my family, we left the camp before he could speak at all. Yet we are here. I knew the whites would kill all who stayed, and I could not stay and see my family butchered by the white man. But I am here. If One Arm is ready to fight again, what is to stop him from killing all of us?"

"Two Shirts, do you trust me?"

Two Shirts looked at Beck, then looked away. He faced Beck yet again.

"You are not the soldier chief," he said to Beck. "You do not tell the soldiers what to do. If the soldier chief comes here to kill us, what medicine lies with you to stop them?"

"That is true," Beck said. He looked out at the huddled figures close to the fires, the new blankets on the shoulders of the Indians moving about the camp, the new tents to one side of the little valley. He turned back to Two Shirts.

"General Howard has given his promise that there will be no more killing if we can get the rest of your people to lay down their rifles. To do that, we, that is myself and General Howard, are going into the camp of your people and tell them the truth. I know that the Nee Me Poo believe that when Howard speaks, he speaks with a true heart. He goes now to say the words. I want you there because your people trust you to tell them the truth. You are the key to keeping the last of your people alive. Will you come?"

"Why not get Joseph to come? He laid down his rifle first. His medicine is greater than mine."

"I do not believe General Howard trusts him now. When White Bird left last night, Howard wanted to attack your camp at dawn, kill all the rest of the people who did not lay down their guns at once. He thought Joseph spoke for all of the Nez Perce, and White Bird had broken the promise. You and I know that is not so. I have persuaded Howard that it is not so. But he still does not completely trust Joseph.

"But I trust you, Two Shirts. I don't want any more of your people to die, nor any of the white soldiers. I beg you, come and help us."

"I don't know what to do," Two Shirts said, looking down. "I don't want any of my people to die, either. But if I go, my people will see me as a white man. The young warriors, Yellow Wolf, White Bull, He Who Sits, they will never listen to my medicine again."

From the fire, Moon On The Snow spoke up, a rapid string of Nez Perce words, among which Beck could only make out "warrior" and "sheep." Two Shirts looked at her for a long moment, sighed. He answered back slowly, but she whipped another sentence at him like a lash across the flames, and her black eyes flashed in the firelight. Then she looked down at the pot, her teeth clenched.

Two Shirts' eyes widened as he looked at his wife, then he grunted.

"I will go with you," he said, looking again at Beck.

"Good!" Beck said, "We go now. The general waits for us."

They moved off through the camp together, and came to the lieutenant of the guard and his sergeant. Beck explained the errand again, and the soldiers passed them out of the camp. As they moved over the slope toward the distant formation of soldiers and command tents, Beck said, "What did she say to you?"

"Oh, nothing much" Two Shirts said slowly. "She reminded me that other warriors would like to see their daughters at the camp fires tonight."

"I heard the word for sheep…?"

"Yes. She was referring to being a sheep alive, rather than a dead wolf. She is a woman, she does not know what it takes to make a wolf into a sheep. It is not an easy thing."

Beck walked beside Two Shirts in silence for a moment, as they moved over the grass among the little camps and fire pits of the soldiers. "And the last part? What did she say then?" he asked finally.

"Be a man. Do what must be done. Your chief has shown the way, honor him."

"And that decided you?"

"No. I thought that you and I had better go finish this thing, or I wouldn't get any supper tonight."

Beck chuckled as they came up to the soldiers. General Howard stepped out to greet Two Shirts, and offered his left hand with a smile. Two Shirts took it.

"Thank you for coming to help," the general said, "We want to end this matter with no further bloodshed. Can you talk to them for us, let them know that what I say is the word of my true heart?"

"Yes," Two shirts said, "I will do what I can."

The negotiating party was quickly formed of General Howard, Colonel Miles, Beck, Two Shirts, and Arthur Chapman, who had been with Howard since the start. The two treaty Nez Perce, Jokias and Meopkowit, had already gone into the Indian camp. Several lieutenants made as if to go, and General Howard, surveying the little party, asked them to stay in camp. He also asked Beck to stay behind.

"I do not want to present a picture of strength," the general said to them all. "The fewer the better, as you insisted, Jon. Now, is everyone ready?"

They walked off over the crest of a shallow slope and down into the little valley where the entrenchments of the Nez Perce were constructed. Beck watched them go from the crest of the hill, as did others of the command. He felt stunned by the general's refusal to take him along, but he had not the will to protest the general's order. A job is a job, he thought, you do what you are told.

"We had quite a fight after you left the meeting this morning," said Guy Howard at Beck's elbow. "There is still an appetite for blood among the unit commanders. They would as soon make an all-out attack and end it in one final bloodbath."

"I am surprised your father listened to me," Beck said.

"As I said to you before, he does not dislike you, Mr. Beck. And, as you know, he has always been quick to find a less violent solution, when possible. Sometimes he has little patience, which is the only fault I can lay to him. But your ideas had a ring of truth to them, and so he had only to persuade Colonel Miles of the efficacy of your argument."

"Colonel Miles?"

"Yes. You see, the general left command of this situation with Colonel Miles, and refused responsibility for the field operation. He felt that Miles had shown initiative and leadership in catching the Indians, and should be given the credit for bringing them to bay and eventually inducing their surrender."

"Then why is he even going over there today?"

"Why, because of you, certainly!" Lieutenant Howard said, smiling. "You convinced him that his presence would go a long way toward persuading the last holdouts that they will not be killed. He knows full well that many of them hate him, many of them fear him, and many of them see him with contempt."

"Contempt?"

"Of course. He did not, after all, catch them. But from very early in the chase he knew that such would be the case. He also knew that he had to be relentless in his pursuit, so that they would know that he kept his word, no matter the circumstances. He has done that, and so was willing to relinquish command to Colonel Miles as was the colonel's just due. But as you so stated, he knows his presence will have some effect on these heathen renegades, and he is not a cruel man. If his form will influence them in any way to end this affair, he will provide it."

"Even if, as Miles so eagerly suggested, they take a shot at him?"

"Even so. And I would not fault the colonel for suggesting such a thing. You know full well that it would be a possibility, do you not?"

340

"At this point I am certain of nothing."

"Two-Days-Behind. It's what they call him, you know. The Nez Perce, I mean," said Howard absently.

They waited on the crest, in the wind, listening for the sound of shots, hoping they did not hear them. The unit officers went back to their troops, and Colonel Sturgis had the men formed into a long skirmish line of battle just under the crest of the hill. There they were allowed to be seated, most of them huddling into their coats against the cold. Then, after an hour of tension in the grey morning light, the watchers could see the small group of army men and scouts come out of the creek bottom and stride up the hill. They had come less than half way when several of the Indians came out behind them, following them up the slope to surrender.

The officers rejoined their comrades at the hilltop, orders were given, soldiers went forward to receive the surrendering Nez Perce. They came out of the trenches in ones and twos and small family groups, straggling up the hill. They lay down their rifles at the line of soldiers, and were herded into clusters and taken under guard off toward the new camp. Some rode horses, thin, gangly beasts that seemed bedraggled and tired. Wounded came with them, some limping, some on travois made from the lodge poles of the tepees that were left, some carried by their fellow tribesmen. Dr. Tilton had come up to the hilltop, and directed the soldiers to take the wounded down to his hospital compound. Women and children and warriors trickled in, muddy, their buckskin clothing torn, some without shoes or moccasins, every one with the look of a cornered beast in their black eyes.

Two Shirts had come with the officers, and stood beside Beck watching the trickle of surrendering Indians as they came.

"Looks like you did good," Beck said him after a time.

"If this is good, I don't want to see the bad," Two Shirts said.

"But it's over," Beck said. "They'll get food and blankets, and they will be well treated. You will see. All of you will go back to Lapwai, and there will be peace in the land of the Nez Perce."

"Good for you to say," Two Shirts said. "I have the taste of bitter gall in my mouth."

Lieutenant Howard stepped up to Beck.

"The general would like you to join us in his tent, if you don't mind," said Howard.

"Certainly," Beck said. The lieutenant led off toward the command tents a quarter of a mile away down the rolling slope of the grassland. Trailing off toward the Indian's new camp was a long line of Indians being escorted by soldiers. It reminded Beck of ants returning to the colony with bits and pieces of forest debris held high. Only this debris was the brown and red blanket clad members of a shattered tribe.

At the commander's tent, several officers were in attendance. Howard, Sturgis and Miles were inside with three captains and five lieutenants, all seeming talking at once. Howard and Miles were receiving the congratulations of their subordinates, and most of the officers were smiling in great good humor.

"Ah, Mr. Beck! Jon!" the general said, moving through the uniforms to reach out his hand to Beck, "You were right, sir, absolutely! Once the situation was carefully explained to them, they cheerfully gave it up! Peace is ours at last!"

Miles stepped over to them also. "I commend you, sir!" he said to Beck, also extending his hand, this time the right, which Jon shook. "Once they saw that we meant business, they surrendered. Your idea was the clincher, certainly!"

"Meant business, or meant them no further harm?" Beck asked, releasing Miles' hand.

"No further harm, of course, of course," Howard said, patting Beck's elbow.

A louder murmur arose from the gathered officers, as someone brought in a bottle of champagne, and tin cups were produced, the bottle popped open, and the wine poured out. The general cheerfully refused his portion, but took water in his cup instead. As the toasts to their bravery, skill, and efficiency began to flow, Jon Beck slipped out of the tent and walked off toward the soldier fires. The scanty line of Indians and soldiers moving down toward the refugee's camp flowed lumpily along. Jon found his own campfire, and around it Dodd and Pocket perched. He pulled up a chunk of firewood and sat on it next to the warm glow.

"So that's it?" Pocket said. "They all comin' in?"

"It would seem so. I expect it's finally over," Beck said tiredly.

"You don't seem all that happy about it," Pocket said.

342

Beck looked at the coals, reached over the tossed another stick on the flames. It sizzled a bit, and finally began to flame up. He sighed.

"Guess it's just that I'm tired," Beck said. "Aren't you?"

"Man, I'll say!" Pocket said. "I could sleep for a week, if only 'twere warm enough."

"And a bath!" Beck said. "And something to eat but bacon and biscuit."

"There's gonna be buffler tonight!" Dodd said. "Woodcutters shot some critters up on the mountain, they're gonna share it out so's we all get a bit."

"And something to eat but bacon and biscuit and goldurned buffler!" Beck growled.

"I heard the army's bringing up some beef. That would help," Dodd said.

"Yes it surely would!" Pocket said.

"Where's the good lieutenant?" Beck asked absently.

"Don't know," Dodd said. "We was up on the ridge awhile back, and he was talking to Two Shirts. Ain't seen him since."

The since turned into the rest of the daylight hours. Midday passed and afternoon, and then the long grey of the winter evening encroached upon the camps. More wood was brought in, the buffalo meat secured by Dodd, water brought up from the creek in the valley floor, and Beck took the time to clean his guns and look to his wounds. The welt on his left arm was an angry red, but had become somewhat numb to the touch. The slash across his chest still wept a yellowish pink fluid, and he went down to the hospital tents for a fresh dressing.

As he was being bandaged up again by one of the orderlies, he could see Indians in the tent, several squatting along one wall awaiting treatment. One of them was on the doctor's operating bench, with the doctor busily probing an upper chest wound for a bullet. The warrior on the bench looked at the ceiling of the tent with no expression on his face. The doctor finally exclaimed, and, looking more closely, yanked a bullet out of the man's shoulder with his forceps. He dropped it into a bucket at the base of the table. The bleeding was staunched with a fresh bandage and the man helped from the table to have the wound dressed by an orderly. The next man squatting along the tent side arose, came to the table and lay down. His arm was shattered below the elbow, and the doctor began to work with the wound to find the extent of the damage. The Indian examined the ceiling as had his predecessor, without uttering a sound.

His own wound dressed, Beck buttoned his shirt, pulled on his buffalo coat, and left the tent. He found his way back to the fire, where Dodd and Pocket still orbited in its warmth. Lieutenant Morgan was still absent.

"Morgan?" Beck said to Dodd. Dodd shrugged, looking up from the buffalo meat he had spitted over the fire for a slow roast. The aroma of it caused Beck's stomach to churn hungrily. But it would be awhile before the meat was done.

Beck decided to go see how the Indian camp was sorting itself out, now that refugee's were added to it by the dozen. When he arrived he saw that new fires were blazing in addition to the several dozen that had been there before. He paid his respects to the officer on duty and got permission to enter the camp. Wagons had been brought up, and blankets and food were being distributed. Another new tent was up, and it was already crowded with the sick and the elderly.

Jon threaded his way to the cook fire of Two Shirts and Moon On The Snow. Their two daughters huddled at the fire, wrapped in a new Army blanket each. They smiled as his face materialized in the firelight.

"Where is your father?" he asked them. "Where is your mother?"

They just smiled at him. He crouched and warmed his hands at the fire. A pot had been slung over the coals, and a coffee pot sat on a rock beside the flames. One of the girls, Squirrel Tail, sat beside the small pile of fire wood, and added a stick to the flames.

Beck was about to ask the girls again where their parents had gone, when Moon On The Snow stepped into the ring of golden light.

"Two Shirts?" Beck asked, rising.

"Gone," she said.

"Visiting?" Beck said, thinking he had gone among the new arrivals, searching out family members, looking for word of his son.

"Gone!" Moon On The Snow said sharply, making the sign for far away.

Beck looked at her blankly, then remembered that the last he had seen of Two Shirts was on the ridge, just after the officers came back from the Nez Perce camp.

"Did he return from helping One Arm?" he said.

Moon On The Snow looked at him for a second, then shook her head.

"How do you know that he is gone far away?" Beck said.

She paused. "Others say!" she said then, sweeping her hand across the camp in general.

Beck felt a cold lump form in his belly. Surly Two Shirts would not have left the camps entirely, not with his family here. Why would he do so?

"I will find him!" Beck said to Moon On The Snow. She looked at him for a moment, and her eyes softened, and she nodded quickly.

Beck left the camp, stopping at the officer in charge's post, and briefly inquiring about Two Shirts. But the officer had no idea who Beck referred to, as he had seen hundreds of new faces that day, and was not on post when Beck had left with Two Shirts that morning. Beck hurried back to his camp. Morgan was now at the fire with the other two.

"Chow's ready!" Dodd said with a smile. Beck squatted at the fire, and Dodd dished up a slab of buffalo meat on a plate, added beans and fresh biscuits, and handed the plate to Beck. He followed that with a cup of steaming coffee.

"Buscuits?" Beck said, "Where the hell...?"

"Feller next door has a Dutch oven!" Dodd grinned, "I fetched him a couple of loads of wood in trade for some of the second batch. They're a bit warmed over, but they sure do beat hard tack all to blazes!"

Beck agreed by attacking the food with a vengeance, savoring the hot, juicy meat with closed eyes and a shake of his head, then the biscuits, sopping up beans with them, washing it all down with hot coffee. He barely had time to breathe as he ate and ate and ate, and in a few moments was looking at an empty, biscuit wiped plate.

"More?" Dodd said, and Beck looked up to see all three of the others grinning at him.

"Seen a wolf eat like that, once," Pocket said, casually, "gnawin' on an elk he was. Had a belly on him the size of a prize pumpkin afore he crawled away in the brush fer a nap."

"Wolverines," Morgan said, "they're like that, too. Once they get onto a carcass they'll just go at it 'till nothing is left. Hide, bones, horns and tail, every bit of it gone."

"I seen a wild boar, once, 'at—"

"Shut up, Dodd!" growled Beck, as Dodd handed him back his plate with another biscuit on it, and more beans.

"All out of buffler," Dodd grinned. "And that's the very last biscuit."

"This'll do just fine," Beck said, and dug in again, but with less ferocity.

Beck eyed the fire as he chewed, thinking of Two Shirts. Where would he have gone? If he had indeed left the camp, would he try for Canada and the Sioux camps again? But why, if his family was here, and his people had given up, why would he leave? To get to Canada without his family would be unthinkable. At least unthinkable to Beck. He had lived with Two Shirts for one winter, he had seen a man who had a great fondness for his wife, and an open love for his children. It must be his son, Walks In The Light. He must have gone off to find out what happened to his son. Beck could think of no other reason why Two Shirts would abandon his family.

He cleaned his plate again, and rose from the fire.

"Simon, where did you picket the horses this afternoon?" he asked Pocket.

"I moved 'em to a little meadow just over the knoll there," Pocket said, point off into the darkness. "What you got in mind?"

"I've got to go out and do a little scouting," Beck said. "Show me."

Simon rose and led Beck out into the darkness, through the rim of soldier camps, and finally to a grassy swale where many horses grazed. They found two sentries watching the herd. Pocket went out into the meadow and came back shortly leading Bill and his own pony.

"You won't need that little pinto," Beck said, taking Bill's reins.

"I'm going with you!" Pocket said.

"You don't even know what the hell I'm going to do!" Beck said.

"Don't matter," Pocket said, falling into step beside Beck as they began leading their horses back to the fire. "You hired me to scout. Well, let's go scout."

"Something I have to do of a personal nature," Beck said.

"Fair enough. You just tell me at the proper time, and I'll look the other way."

"I'd just as soon you didn't come along," Beck said. But he was tired, and he didn't want to argue the matter. And, he could use the help.

"I know. But I'm comin' just the same."

At the fire, they saddled up the horses, and Dodd wrapped up some bacon and hardtack for them, which Beck slipped into his saddlebag.

Morgan sat at the fire and did not say a word. The two men mounted, and Beck looked at Dodd, then at Morgan. A question seemed to gnaw at his consciousness, but he could not name it. He turned Bill into the darkness and moved off, Pocket following on his pinto. Morgan looked after the spotted horse, watching until the last splotch of white was swallowed up by the night.

Chapter 37

Beck skirted the camp and came around to the headquarters tents, where the sergeant of the guard watched he and Pocket ride up and halt. Lieutenant Jerome materialized out of the darkness, and, grinning, said, "Ah, Mr. Beck! Going, or coming?"

"Came for a rifle," Beck said. "Any of those guns turned in by the Nez Perce available for use?"

"Why yes, as a matter of fact they are," Jerome said. Beck swung down and followed him to the quartermaster's tent. They ducked through the flap, and inside were barrels of flour, sacks of bacon, chests of ammunition. The lieutenant led the way to a heap of rifles stacked next to biscuit tins and crates of canned fruit. He stepped aside and fetched one of the lanterns over, lowering it toward the guns so that Beck could have a better look.

"Pretty much picked over by the officers," Jerome said, "they all want a souvenir, you know."

Beck knelt and began to move aside guns, pulling others from the stack, looking at each one carefully. There were many Winchester repeaters, several long barreled buffalo guns, muzzle loaders, shotguns, revolving rifles.

"No Springfields?" Beck asked.

"Oh, we took those out of the stack right away," Jerome said. "Army property, you know."

Finally Beck slid a long Winchester repeater from the stack, looked it over carefully, worked the action, opened it again and put his thumb in the breach, held the thumb to the light so that a faint gleam was reflected down the bore, which he eyed from the muzzle. He closed the action and lowered the hammer.

"This one will do. Any ammunition for it here?"

"I believe so," Jerome said. He thought a second, then moved to another crate and placed the lantern on a box next to it. He lifted the lid, revealing a conglomerate of cartridges inside, some in boxes, many loose in heaps, some in belts. He found two boxes of the .44 WCF cartridges fit for the gun Beck had chosen, and handed them over.

"That should do it!" he said with a grin, and closed up the crate again.

"Thank you, lieutenant. Do I need to sign for any of this?"

"No one else did!" Jerome said. "If that changes, I will come find you."

"Again, thanks," Beck said, turning to leave the tent. He paused and turned back to Jerome. "Oh, one more thing. Did Lieutenant Morgan come for his souvenir, like all the others?"

"Why, I do recall that he did. Sort of strange, though."

"How so?"

"He seemed to be looking for a particular rifle, knew exactly what he wanted. Not one of the best, either, an older model 1866 Winchester, the rimfire one. I would have thought he would want one of the newer '73's, like yours."

"Did it have tacks on the stock, shaped in a double row?"

"Yes," Jerome said, "why, yes it did! Do you know that rifle?"

"I do. It belonged to...well, a friend of mine," Beck said.

"Did the Indians kill him to get it?"

"No, not exactly," Beck said. "Anyway, thank you, Lieutenant Jerome, and I do hope that you see an end to your Captaincy of the Guard in the near future."

Jerome laughed. "Oh, I don't think I will ever see daylight again, Mr. Beck! At least not while I am in the command of our illustrious Colonel Miles, bless his soul."

Beck chuckled in turn and left the tent. When he got to Bill, he slid the Long Tom Springfield out of his saddle scabbard and handed it over to Lieutenant Jerome, who handed it to the sergeant of the guard, who handed it to a private at his elbow. Beck opened one of the boxes or cartridges, and, while Jerome held the box, he loaded the magazine of the Winchester, then slid it into the saddle scabbard. He took the box and dug out a handful of cartridges and shoved them into the pocket of his coat, then closed up the box and put it in his saddle bag, along with the unopened box. He pulled a sack of .45-70 cartridges out of the saddlebag and handed them over to Jerome.

"You may miss that Springfield if you come upon buffalo, Mr. Beck," Jerome said as Beck swung up into the saddle again.

"Ain't after buffalo," Beck said, turning the big horse toward the darkness again. "May find a wolf or two, though."

Jon Beck and Simon Pocket rode slowly through the night, not pushing their mounts in the darkness, letting the horses feel their way. They headed west in the direction that was taken by the pony herd on the first day of battle, scattered by the attacking soldiers. As the first grey hint of dawn seeped into the eastern sky, they swung to the north for the Milk River.

The weather had turned a bit warmer, but with the change in temperature came more snow. It fell in flurries as the grey clouds scudded overhead on the north wind, stinging their faces and causing the horses to walk with their heads low. At mid morning they found a brushy draw where they could get to the bottom out of the wind, and there built a fire. Beck got out the small fry pan he carried, and some of the bacon and hard tack. He soon had the bacon sizzling in the pan, as the snow, deprived of its wind in the creek bottom, drifted down to lightly powder the shaggy shoulders of his buffalo coat. The horses grazed on the brown grass of the gully bank. Simon crouched at the fire, warming his hands.

"I suppose you'll tell me where it is we're bound in good time," he said to Beck.

"Wolf huntin'," Beck said. He sighed. "It's that durned Two Shirts again," he went on. "Never went back to his camp after he talked his people out of their trenches. I figure he snuck off again, trying to find out what happened to his son. Or, after thinkin' about it, he may have just lit off for Canada, I don't know. I do know he wasn't too proud of his part in the surrender."

"But the way I figure it, he saved his people!" Pocket said. "I mean, isn't that exactly what Joseph did, too?"

"You and me see it that way. Maybe he doesn't."

"Well why are you out here, I mean, why you? Ain't it the army's job to round up the strays? At least, that's the way you put it, awhile back, up north of the Milk--"

"That was up north of the Milk!" Beck growled. He sat silent for a time. "I sort of promised his wife."

Simon shook his head. "It's a mighty big country out here," he said, looking around the arroyo, "God only knows where he is. What chance you figure we got of seein' hide nor hair of him?"

"Next to none, most likely. But, I've got to give it a go. I talked him into helping the white man get the last of his people to give up. I knew he would trust me, as I also trusted him. Now it don't set too well with him, I'm thinkin'. If he's out here, and if he isn't planning on coming back, I owe it to him and his wife to do what I can." Beck shook his head, and sighed. "I guess I'm going out after wolves, and hope to be coming back with sheep."

"What?"

"Something Two Shirts said to me. It's hard to turn a wolf into a sheep. It's what we're expecting of his people, now. And of him. He's a proud man, he's always made his way on his own terms. This whole rotten war has been about wolves and sheep. It's just that there isn't room for the wolves any more."

The bacon fried, they sopped up the grease with hard tack, and ate breakfast there in the gully in the snow. Beck wiped out the pan with brown grass and put it away. They mounted up, spurred the horses over the brow of the gulley, and once more faced the never ending prairie wind.

They moved steadily north throughout the day, found the Milk River and crossed it on solid ice. By mid-afternoon they had swung to the west for several miles. It was there they found an old man and a young girl, Nez Perce people who were crouching in a ravine out of the wind. The old man stood as they approached the rim of the ravine on its south side.

Beck drew up Bill, leaned on the saddle horn with crossed arms. The pressure on his left arm caused a jolt of pain in the forearm, and he sat up again.

"How'd you get here," Beck said to the old man.

"Walked." The girl got up and stood beside him.

"Where headed?"

"Grandmother's land," the man said, jerking his head over his shoulder.

"Need help?"

"Maybe a little food," the Nez Perce said.

Beck got down and retrieved the bacon from his saddlebag, pulled out his knife and sliced off a third of it. He handed it down into the gully to the old man, who gave it to the girl. She slipped it into a pouch at her belt. Beck put away the bacon, got out the biscuit, broke off a chunk and handed it over. The old man broke off a smaller chunk and began eating it, handing the larger portion to the girl.

"When did you leave the camp?" Beck said, wiping his knife on the grass and sheathing it.

"Soldiers attacked the horses. We were among them. We rode with the herd, but the horses ran off in the first dark. We thought to slip back into the camp, but after a few days, we saw that most of the people were coming out, so we went with them. They all go to Grandmother's land, we go too. Then Indians shoot at us, and we run away."

"When did they shoot at you?"

"One day gone."

"Was Walks In The Light with you?"

The old man stopped chewing on the hard tack and looked hard at Beck.

"Yes!" the Nez Perce said, "He was the only one who had a rifle. When the Assinaboin started shooting at us, he shot back! He was the one who told us to run and hide!"

"Where was this? Where did this happen?" Beck said urgently.

"That way!" said the old man, pointing to the northwest.

"Can you lead us? Will you help us to find them?"

The old man shook his head. "We have run and run. We are tired. It is cold...."

"Come, up on the horses!" Beck said, "You can ride with us and show us the way. If we get there in time, we might be able to help."

The old man looked at the girl, who stared back at him, then nodded slightly. The Nez Perce stuffed the piece of hard-tack into his hunting shirt and the two of them scrambled feebly out of the gully. Beck swung up on Bill, then bent down his right hand, the old man grasped it, and Beck swung him up neatly to the cantle. Pocket did the same with the girl, and they started off by skirting the gully and then lining out for the northwest.

The old man hung onto Beck as Bill worked up into a canter beneath them. The Indian muttered directions into Beck's ear as they rode, and nearly an hour later they topped a rise and halted.

"I think it was down there," the Nez Perce said, and then the girl, perched behind Simon on his little paint beside them, spoke to the old man in Nez Perce.

"No, she says. One more ridge."

Then they all heard the very faint sound of a rifle shot coming down the wind. Beck spurred Bill, who jolted into a gallop, and the old man nearly tumbled off behind, catching Beck's coat to cling barely to the burly rider. Simon's pony was instantly alongside the pounding Bill and they rode into the little valley, then up the far slope as another rifle shot drifted down the wind. Then they crested the ridge and Beck reined in the great, panting Bill.

Below them in another of the hidden scars of the land, several heads bobbed up over the edge of prairie grass, and one of them brought up a rifle, laid it along the slope toward the far ridge, and fired. The white puff of smoke wafted away in the wind, as the report rolled up the valley and barked faintly in Beck's ear. On the far slope, other puffs appeared, one, two, three, then a fourth, and the clatter of rifle fire followed. As they watched, a dark figure clambered out of the hidden arroyo and started running up the long slope toward the riflemen on the ridge. The figure, a man, was carrying a rifle, and would raise it to fire as he went. Answering fire popped out from the ridge.

"It's Two Shirts, by God!" Beck cried. "Here, old man, get down!" and Beck reached around with his right hand and the Nez Perce behind grabbed his forearm and Beck swung him off of Bill to the ground. "Simon, get these two down to that gully, see what you can do for them." Beck spurred Bill and the big charger was off again down the slope, angling after the running man on the far bank.

"Jon, let me help you!" Simon called after him, but Beck was already far enough into the wind that he may not have heard.

Beck reached back to the rifle in the saddle scabbard as Bill carried him into the bottom of the shallow valley. He drew out the Winchester and levered a round into the chamber. Bill was on the up slope then, and climbing hard, his great form fairly leaping over the prairie grass and patches of snow, clods and clumps of snow showering out behind from the gouging of his hooves. The running man was approaching the top of the ridge, and firing as fast as he could lever his gun. Bill narrowed the gap, his hooves thumping hard on patches of the semi frozen ground, the sound of muted thunder, the creak and squeak of saddle leather punctuated by the rasping breath of the huge horse. As they came up to and then were on the running man, whose pace had slowed to a controlled stumble, Beck raised his rifle and fired.

Two Shirts turned his head at the sound and saw Bill rush past on his right, Beck levering and firing again, and again, at the spots where moments before the opposing fire had puffed out its white smoke. "Come on!" Beck called back as Bill pulled away, "Now ain't the time to peter out!"

Two Shirts let out a war whoop that sounded like seven cats dying, and redoubled his efforts. Beck reached the crest, slid Bill to a stop and tumbled off of him in one motion, losing his balance and flopping on his face in the process. But he rolled over and sprang up, and looked wildly around as Two Shirts came huffing and puffing up beside him.

On the grassy slope sliding away before them, they could see three figures, running. Two Shirts threw up his rifle and fired. He wracked the lever, pulled the trigger again, but only a hollow clink sounded. Beck said, "Here!" and tossed him the Winchester as the Nez Perce dropped his own rifle. Two Shirts began levering and firing at the three running men, and one of them fell. The other two disappeared over a small rise, and then another running man appeared from the left and also went over the rise. Two Shirts levered and fired again, but again the hollow clink sound brought him to a stop.

He lowered the rifle, looking after the retreated enemy, then tossed the gun back to Jon Beck. He sat down, breathing hard.

Beck sat as well, and began to reload his Winchester with the cartridges in his pocket.

"Who were they?" Beck said.

"Stone People," Two Shirts said. He sat, looking out over the rolling country, his black eyes glistening. Far out over the land, four horsemen broke from a depression in the plain and galloped away to the north.

"Why do the Assiniboine attack you?"

Two Shirts did not answer for a time. His breathing gradually slowed. Then he said, "My son went to their village, asking them for meat. They took his gun, and gave him food. When he had eaten, they told him he must leave. He asked for food to take back to the others. They did not give him food. When he left the village, some of their young men went out to kill him. He saw them coming and hid. He was lucky, it was nearly dark. He was unlucky, for they found him and shot him anyway. But he took a rifle from one of his enemys and they ran from him. He ran into the brush near a stream, and they could not find him in the dark. He found the people and warned them. In the morning the Stone People's young men tracked him to this place. Some of the old men and children ran away. But there were old women and young children, very young, and they could not run. One of the women has broken her leg, and could not run. Walks In The Light had the rifle he had taken in the fight. He kept those cowardly dogs away until I could find him. Then he died."

Beck gritted his teeth and sighed.

"I am sorry to hear of this, my friend," he said.

Two Shirts watched the horizon to the west and northwest. The snow had nearly stopped, and the wind was getting colder. In the west, the sun was edging down below the grey overcast of snow clouds, and a stray ray or two gleamed silver, as if probing the cloud underworld for depth.

Two Shirts picked up his rifle and rose. He turned and began walking over the crest of the ridge and back down the long slope he had run up moments before. Beck got up, ran his rifle into its saddle scabbard, and swung up on Bill. He turned the horse and followed Two Shirts, staying a few yards behind him. By the time they had reached the gully where the others waited, the underside of the lowering clouds was painted crimson by the setting sun.

Simon Pocket's pinto stood munching grass at the top of the gully rim. Pocket was in the gully, binding a woman's leg. Two Shirts slid down the gully wall, walked over to the body of his son. He tossed his rifle onto the bank, and kneeling, took his son into his arms. He began to sing the death song, the red light of the last rays of sun turning his face redder than the sky to which he lifted it.

Beck sat atop Bill, atop the gully rim, noting the tears that ran down the cheeks of his friend, the half dozen bedraggled Indians in the gully, the bloody body of the Nez Perce boy that he had played with and ridden with and hunted with that cold winter so long ago, it seemed, when finding out about what an Indian had for dinner was important to him. He had learned about the dinners, and about everything Nez Perce that he could take in, and he had come to the conclusion that Two Shirts was a friend worth having. As was his son.

His vision was blurred when he looked at the rifle Two Shirts had tossed to the ground, but not so blurred as to see the two lines of tacks on the stock, and the sunburst of tacks at one end of it. Several of the tacks were missing from the sun figure. The sign for hope, the road to happiness.

Chapter 38

A camp was made in the little arroyo of death, and a grave was dug while those who could manage it went about gathering buffalo dung and twigs and small branches for a fire. Living things bigger than the grasses were not in abundance, and Beck and Pocket took the horses several miles away to a small creek bed and roped together several bundles of firewood and dragged them back. It was full dark by the time they found the camp again. Two Shirts had buried his son on a little flat above the bottom of the arroyo. He sat beside the grave, head down, motionless in the night. The others had started a small dung fire, and with the newly arrived firewood, a good blaze was soon crackling.

Beck got out his small pan and began to cook what little food they had. The girl who was with the old man and had put the bacon Beck had given her into her pouch, produced it for cooking also. Beck shared the water from his canteen, as did Pocket, and it was soon gone down the throats of half a dozen exhausted people. The food suffered a similar fate, and Pocket refused a portion as did Beck. Jon got his bedding poncho down and used it to bundle up the children before the fire, and the old people crowded around the blaze as best they could. The rest of the bedding went to the old women, who huddled together under the blanket. Simon picketed the horses on the south rim of the gully.

When he had come back to the fire, he and Beck squatted beside the blaze.

"Think we can keep it going all night?" Simon said.

"We'll do what we can," Beck said. "No way to find more wood in the dark."

"What do we do with 'em?" Simon said.

"Do with them?"

"Whal, do we take 'em back, or let 'em go on to Canada? Or just leave 'em here. I can't say we should leave 'em, I don't figure half of 'em would make it north. Prob'ly all freeze to death, out here in this gol durned wind!"

"We'll let them decide," Beck said.

The fire wood ran out before dawn, and as the fire cooled the bodies huddled around it seemed to get smaller and smaller as they shrank into whatever clothing or blankets offered them the last vestige of warmth. Finally, as the glimmers of a new dawn glinted grey in the east, Beck rose to stand by the fire.

"Hear me, people of the Nee Me Poo!" he said firmly. Some who had been dozing started awake, others turned fearful eyes to him. Two Shirts, a few yards away at the grave, still sat unmoving. "It is time to decide," Beck went on. "I have no more food to give you, no water...," he said, as if giving a speech. The old man intoned the words in Nez Perce. "The Grandmother's land is far. The camp of the soldiers is not so far. If you go to the Grandmother's land, I have nothing to give you to help you. If you come to the soldier camp, where I and my friend are going, we can share the horses. The little

356

ones can ride. The old ones can ride. She who has the hurt leg can ride. If you go back to the soldier camp, I can help you. If you go to the redcoat's land, I cannot. You must decide."

There was murmuring among the Indians. For several minutes they talked, until finally Two Shirts raised his head and said one word. He rose and came to stand near the fire. He did not look at Jon Beck, nor at the members of his tribe.

"They are afraid of the soldiers, Red Bear," he said to Beck. "They do not want to die. But it is cold. They are hungry. They see death whichever way they turn. They talk now about which is the better death."

"Do you believe there is death in the soldier camp?" Beck asked.

"It doesn't matter to me," Two Shirts replied. "I must convince them to stay alive one more day. That is all that matters." And he spoke in Nez Perce to the people, who listened without a sound. After a few moments, several of the Indians looked at each other, and finally the old man nodded.

"We will go to the soldier camp," Two Shirts said.

"What did you say to them?" Beck asked.

"I reminded them that you are the Red Bear, and that you give the honey stones to the children. That you should be trusted. That you would not lead them to a death. They trust me in this. I trust you." And for the first time, Two Shirts looked at Jon Beck. His black eyes seemed to hold a universe of sorrow. Beck clenched his teeth. He nodded.

"We'd best get started as soon as we can," he said. "This cold isn't going let up."

They brought in the horses, saddled and packed them quickly, and got the children up on the pinto pony in front of and behind Simon. Beck climbed aboard Bill, and hoisted up the squaw with the wounded leg to sit is his lap. The other old woman refused to ride, so the young girl was pulled up to ride Bill's cantle. The rest of the party trudged off south as the horses led out.

Within the hour an army patrol sighted them and came up in a column of fours, a young lieutenant in the lead. He halted the column fifty yards out and came on with his sergeant.

"Mr. Beck, isn't it?" he said to Jon as the two of them halted before the scouts and their charges.

"It is," Beck said. "And you would be?"

"Lieutenant Maus," the officer said. "I was in the tent when you explained to the general that offering himself as a target would be of benefit to the situation." The lieutenant was smiling as he said this.

"That was not exactly my point," Beck said, a small smile of his own forming.

"Yes, Mr. Beck, I know. A small joke. But, I see that you have been doing my job for me," he went on, looking over the several Nez Perce with the scouts. "May I offer my assistance in herding these renegades back to the camps?"

"First of all, they are not renegades, Lieutenant Maus," Beck said evenly, "they are prisoners of war, if you consider that the United States Army makes war on women and children. And old men. And one mangy wolf who would slip on a different suit of clothing if you will allow it."

Two Shirts looked up at Beck, and nodded slightly.

"And secondly, they require no "herding," as you phrase it," Beck went on. "They are coming into the soldier camp of their own accord. We are simply assisting them in that endeavor."

"Well, so be it," Maus said lightly. "But what is that man doing with a rifle in his hands?" he said, nodding at Two Shirts. "If you describe these people as prisoners of war, certainly a man with a rifle is no prisoner yet."

Beck shook his head a little and rolled his eyes. He looked at Two Shirts, who handed up the rifle to him. "Satisfied?" Beck said.

"Completely, Mr. Beck," grinned the lieutenant. "Well, we have other reneg--, that is, prisoners of war to round up, so, if you will excuse me, I must be on about business." He gave Beck a mocking salute, wheeled his horse, and he and the sergeant returned to the head of the column. They thundered off in the direction from which the scouts had come.

Beck handed the rifle back to Two Shirts.

"Just like a white man," Two Shirts mumbled as the little procession started once more toward the looming Bear's Paw Mountains, "make the red man do all the work." Jon Beck chuckled, glad to see his friend could still joke at something.

They reached the camps after dark, guided in the last few miles by the lights from the soldier's cook fires. As they came up on the Indian encampment, the Indians slid from the horses, and Two Shirts handed Beck his rifle once more.

"I will keep it for you," Beck said. "You will need it for hunting at Lapwai."

"It doesn't matter to me," Two Shirts said. "Give it back to the lieutenant. Tell him I made good use of it, killing those stone eating Sioux."

"I'll come by a little later, see how you're doing," Beck said.

"It would be better if you did not," Two Shirts said, looking out over the fires and smoke and moving people in the camp. "I must tell Moon On The Snow about her son. I will tell the story of his defending the old ones and the children, and of his brave ride to seek food at the camp of the Stone People. I will let her know that he died helping his people. She will not hear any of it. She will only hear that he is dead. She will need time to sing the death song. It would be better if you did not come."

Two Shirts turned and went to the officer in charge of the camp guards, and then was walking into the midst of the fires and the smoke and the people. Soon Beck could not be sure which of the people he was, walking there among them on his way to his own cook fire. On his way to the mother of his only son.

Beck and Pocket rode back to the soldier camp and found their own fire. Morgan and Dodd were there, sitting at the flames, and when Dodd saw them enter the firelight and dismount, he got out the pans and nudged the coffeepot closer to the coals.

"Bet you boys could use a little grub, eh?" he said with a smile.

"If we don't get something soon, ol' Bill here's in mortal danger," Beck said, loosening the saddle girth, "I feel like I could eat a horse at least as big as him!" Bill turned his head and looked at Beck, then snorted.

Beck tossed Two Shirts' rifle across the firelight, and Morgan caught it in a startled reflex. He looked down at the stock.

"Yep, it's the same gun you dug out of the pile and gave back to 'im," Beck said.

"How'd you get it?" Morgan said, standing up, letting the rifle dangle from one hand.

"He gave it to me, just before he went back into the prisoner camp," Beck said.

"He's...still alive, then?"

"Yep."

"And the boy? Did he find Walks In The Light?"

359

"Yes," Beck said, sliding the saddle off of Bill. "But he was too late."

"Damn!" Morgan muttered, settling down to sit again at the fire. He pulled the rifle across his lap.

"He says you can have the rifle," Beck said. "And he told me to tell you he made good use of it, killing a few of those who murdered his son."

"He said that?" Morgan said.

"His way of thanking you, I suppose," Beck said.

Pocket took the horses away to picket them for the night. Beck stepped to the fire, squatted and held his hands to the flames.

"The army is moving out in the morning," Morgan said. "I have decided that Dodd and I will travel south with the column, and though you are technically still working for the Fifth Cavalry, that is, me, you may do as you please. I will release you from service at any time you choose. If you come with us, I will see to it that the army still considers you under my orders, and thus eligible for continued pay. You can travel with us all the way to Camp Brown, if you wish."

"Generous of you, lieutenant," Beck said, "I think I'll take you up on it, at least as far as the river. I've got to find Mr. Hardy, see how he is doing with that bullet-holed foot and all. If he needs further medical attention, we may indeed stay with the column for the trip down the river. We shall see."

"In the mean time, I don't believe there will be much for you to do, of a scouting nature, that is," Morgan went on.

"Not unless you turn any more of the Nez Perce loose," Beck said. "Was it your idea or his?"

Morgan watched the fire, and Dodd added beefsteak to the skillet, and began to shave off slices of a potato into the pan. Beck saw the potato, raised his eyebrows.

"Came in on the supply wagons just today," Dodd said.

"His idea, mostly, at first," Morgan said. "He didn't want to go back into the Indian camp right off. Started talking about finding his son. I knew it was a long shot, I knew he probably just wanted to get out of here, at least for a time. He felt bad about helping the white man bring in his people. So I asked what I could do. He said he needed his rifle. Told me what it looked like. I knew other officers

360

were cadging souvenirs, so I went to the quartermaster and found his rifle. And half a box of shells."

"How'd you get him past the lines in the daylight?"

"Oh, easy enough. I took my horse, he came along on foot, we explained to the officer of the guard we were going to the pony herd that the army has pastured to the east, to look for a new mount for me. Two Shirts was to pick out a good one, being familiar with the stock. I carried the rifle. Once we were out of sight of the sentries, I gave him the rifle and he disappeared down a gully. I had thought he would come with me to the horses and get one, but he must have figured he could travel more easily without being seen if he did it on foot. Where did you find him?"

Dodd flipped the steak, and stirred the frying potatoes. The aroma caused Beck's stomach to growl.

"We ran into an old man and a girl. They had been with a larger party, heading for the Canada line. Assiniboines attacked them, scattered the lot, had some of them pinned down. Turns out one of the Nez Perce had a wounded leg, and Walks In The Light had been with them. He had gone to an Assiniboine village to get food for them. They gave him nothing, shot him, but he got away. He made it back to the others, but the Stone Sioux tracked him, attacked the group. That's when some of them ran off, the ones we found. They led us back to the others, and apparently Two Shirts had found them in the mean time. He was there in time to see his son die. Made him crazy. There was five or six Assiniboines shooting at the camp, and Two Shirts charged them! We got there just then, and I took Bill off to help him out. We drove them off, sure as hell, and he got at least one of them. Then we had to come back and bury his boy."

They watched the fire for a time, and Dodd dished up the beef and potatoes and handed the plate over to Beck. He found a fork and handed that over too, and Beck pulled out his belt knife and attacked the food. Pocket joined them at the fire, and Dodd started a fresh skillet of food for him.

"What were the chances of him finding his boy out there in all that endless country," Morgan said absently.

"And just in time to watch him die," Beck said. "Wasn't he lucky."

The first bugles sounded before dawn, and the soldiers rose all about the camp to the barked orders of corporals and sergeants.

361

Breakfast was hastily prepared, and the business of packing up the camp began in earnest. Dodd and Pocket went off to find a pack mule for their gear, and Beck cleaned the rifle he had recently acquired. Morgan cleaned the yellow-bodied Winchester that had belonged to Two Shirts. The two men returned with a mule and pack saddle, and then brought in the horses. The animals were saddled and packed, and then they waited at the fire.

Wagons were brought up to the hospital tents, and lined with willow branches and dry prairie grass. The seriously wounded were loaded aboard. Two wagons were allotted to the Indian wounded, and any one whose wound allowed them to ride was provided a horse. It was not until late morning that the command was loaded up and formed up and ready to move. General Howard took his place at the head of the column, and off they moved toward the southeast and the Missouri. Beck and the party of scouts lagged behind the column, watching it snake its way though the creek bottom and over the backs of grassy ridges which ran up to the Bear's Paws miles away.

Travois had been rigged up for some of the wounded, and many of the Indian prisoners were mounted on horses from the captured pony herd. The procession strung out for miles, with knots of blue coated soldiers here and there like blue stones on a dropped necklace draped across the folded land.

The column made ten miles that day, and came to rest at a camp already chosen for them by an advance party coming from the Missouri in the south. Food and wood were brought up with the soldiers, and the creek chosen provided fresh water. The weather continued cold and the wind never stopped. Soldiers and Indians alike huddled around fires that were kept burning all night. The next day the long serpentine procession stretched out its supple form once more and crawled east and south beneath silver clouds and the unrelenting wind at their backs.

In camp that night a storm swept in, lightning and thunder causing the horses to cast wild eyes all about and jitter nervously. The men found what shelter they could in tents hastily thrown up, and in the grey cold light of dawn a steady rain pelted the camp. Orders were passed to stay put, and Beck and Pocket rigged up a shelter from Beck's canvas sleeping cover and a tent half that Dodd had commandeered. They managed to keep a small fire going under one edge of the shelter, all of them crowded under its meager protection like squirrels under a pie plate.

The rain gushed steadily all day, and rivulets of water ran off the frozen ground and into the nearby gullies. The sound of the rain was like a great sigh blanketing the land and the huddled soldiers and their prisoners.

Beck dozed off and on, his body glad of the halt. The other three were sort of heaped up against his great shaggy coated form, like a hairy boulder. No one said much, and at times this or that man would snore for a time, then awaken with a snort. The little valley where the halt had been made was dimmed by the lowering grey sky and the falling water, and here and there wisps of smoke trailed away low across the grass from a campfire.

In the evening rain Dodd reluctantly stirred and extracted himself from the warm pile of bodies to make supper. He got out the pans and coffee pot, and Beck put most of the last of their firewood, upon which they were sitting, into the fire. The flames took hold on the new wood, and licked higher giving new light to the little shelter. Dodd had to cook from the outside of the tent, as the fire was built at its edge, and the three other men crowded around the blaze under the shelter. Beck finally rose, and slipped out of the awning.

"Dodd, you go ahead and do your cooking under there," he said, "I've got to go check on the horses." Dodd smiled a little and gratefully transferred his gear and food under cover.

Jon Beck walked up a shallow slope and over the brow of the hill to the paddock area, and soon spotted Bill and Pocket's pinto in the growing gloom. The horses were on their feet, heads down, munching grass. Beck untied the picket lines and led the two of them down to the creek, skirting the camp and the clumps of sodden men at their smoky fires. At the running water the horses eagerly slurped up a belly full, and Beck led them back to the pasture and, after searching a bit for their pins in the semi darkness, picketed them again. He found Morgan's horse and Dodd's, but could not locate which of the animals in close proximity was their mule. He finally gave up and led the two army mounts down to water, then back to the grassy slope. It took him some time to locate the last picket pin and get the horses tethered, for he could not see the pins in the darkness, and had to swing his foot around in the grass to locate them by feel.

When he returned to the fire he found the others finishing up, and Dodd had a plateful of food ready for him. The rain had nearly stopped, so he squatted outside the tent at the fire and ate. Morgan turned his empty plate over to Dodd, crawled out of the tent, and went off toward the headquarters camp to see about marching orders.

"Horses doin' okay?" Pocket said.

"Yep," Beck said. "They're still pretty much beat out, though. Like to see 'em get a solid week of good hay and oats."

"I'll second that," Simon said, "and I wouldn't mind a solid week of something else 'sides bacon and hardtack."

"Aw whatcha' itchin' 'bout?" Dodd said, reaching over with the pan and sliding the last of the bacon and grease soaked hard tack onto Beck's plate. "Didn't I rustle up some beef and spuds awhile back? And I hear they got eggs at the river, come up on the boats. Can you even remember what an egg tastes like?"

"Oh I ain't poppin' at you, Dodd!" Simon said, smiling a little, "You done a peach of a job with them pots and pans. And while you happen to have your handy little mits in the general vicinity, could you pour me a drop more of your fine coffee?" He held out his cup and Dodd obliged, then poured more for Beck as well. "Thankee, sir, very much appreciated, and I mean that. No, sir, I do not slight your cookin' a'tall, it's just that a man can only take so much bacon and hard tack a'fore he starts lookin' fondly at anything else to eat, anything a'tall. Remember that buffler we et up on that little knoll by the spring? Now, that was fine eatin'! T'weren't fancy no how, but it surely wasn't bacon, and that made all the difference."

"Well," said Dodd, "I hear tell that at the river they have eggs—"

"So you said, so you said," Simon interrupted a little impatiently.

"And butter, and salt, and real flour, you remember them biscuits we had at the last camp? I know how to use a Dutch oven, and I'm gonna keep us in biscuits for a week! Can't you just taste it, fresh, lightly browned, soft in the middle, slather on a big dollop 'o butter, then jam, I hear there's jam, too, at the river."

"Damn you, Dodd!" Pocket said with an exaggerated grimace, "For the love 'a gawd shut up! Even on a full belly, you're torturing me worse'n a redskin with a hot iron!"

"Well I hate to drag you down none," Dodd went on, "But they got beans in that supply boat as well. And if I don't miss my guess, after a few weeks of them beans, you might just wish the bacon and hard tack was back!"

Beck and Pocket chuckled. Dodd gathered up the plates and utensils and went off to the creek to wash them up.

"Sounds like a little bit of heaven at the river," Pocket said, "at least for an eatin' man."

"Mebbe so," Beck said. "I do hope they have brought up something for the horses."

"You're always thinkin' on that big stallion of yours, ain't ya?"

"He and I go back aways," Beck said.

"How'd you come by him, anyhow?"

Beck stirred at the glowing embers of the fire with a stick.

"Well. He and I met up at Fort Riley some years back. I was working there for the post command as a blacksmith and farrier. Sort of stayed in that end of the business after the war, before scouting came along for me. Anyway, they had brought in a herd of horses for a new artillery regiment they were forming up. They were all big horses, they like the bigger animals for hauling the guns, when they can't get Morgans. I was supposed to check out all their hooves, get them rough shod to be broken to harness. Well, right off, they was having trouble with big Bill, seems as if he had a stubborn streak in him that they just couldn't break. And those army breakers was a tough lot, I'll guarantee that. One of 'em, a sergeant, took over working on Bill. Figured he knew it all, and Bill was just another mean horse to be broken. Turned out he was wrong. Bill got a hoof into him first thing, broke some ribs, they carted him off to the infirmary. They teamed up on him, had two or three mounted men hem him in while others tried to get a halter on him, and he knocked one of the horses down, would have done fer the rider if'n that man didn't know how to scramble.

"Now, I'm watchin' all this from the corral fence. I could see that the horse was just being bullied, and he wasn't takin' to no bullyin'. Sometimes, a horse like that can be reasoned with."

"Reasoned with?" Simon chuckled.

"Well, yes, after a fashion. Those breakers kept at it, finally had half a dozen ropes on Bill, three horses pinning him in, got ropes on his legs, drug him over. While he was down they got a halter on him, tied a long lead to it, then let him up. Three men on the lead, guess they figured they needed all that weight cause he was gonna buck some. Well, he didn't buck, he came right at 'em! He wasn't afraid of men, if fact, he'd just as soon hunt one up and get into a fight! He charged those breakers and scattered 'em, not a one held onto the lead. I was laughing so hard I nearly fell off the fence!"

"What'd they do then?"

"Oh they were circling him, half a dozen of 'em, trying to get to the end of that rope. Any one of 'em step out, Bill would just go at 'im. Finally I climbed me down off of that corral rail and walked right out there to him. He saw me comin' and made his little charge, and I just stood there. He came right up, half reared a bit, then he just stood there. We looked at each other, eye to eye so to speak, and came to an understanding. I stepped over, careful like, never leaving his gaze with my own, and took up the halter rope. I patted his nose. All them breakers was standing around, jaws dropped to the dirt, looking at us and each other like it was the second coming."

"How'd you do it?"

"Don't know. Just figured if he got whiff of a man who was a stubborn as he was, he'd figure we was pals. And I meant him no harm, he could smell that, too."

"And he's been tame ever since?"

"Oh hell no!" Beck said, laughing. "I stepped out of that corral and he was back to hurricane strength in a flash. Took them better part of a week just to break him to harness. When they brought him in for shoein', though, I was ready. Had me an apple, couple of carrots. He was still a little wild eyed by then, for they were none to gentle on him. But he remembered me. Gave him the apple, went to work on him, then the carrots when I was through. He behaved like he'd been doing it all his life. And, as it turned out, he was one of the best pulling animals they ever had on them guns."

"But how'd you come to own him?"

"Well, the following year, after the artillery had been up and down the country some, they cut the unit back. Turned out cannon wasn't such a great advantage against the plains tribes, and the Gatlings they converted to wasn't much better. So, it was decided to halve the strength of the regiment, and so they had surplus horses. They got rid of the worst of the lot, and the ones that weren't a color match and same size as the others on the teams. Colonel liked his animals to be all alike, that way. Bill was about the biggest of 'em, and being a roan like he is, he didn't match no other horse in the outfit! So they turned him out. And I bought Bill as a surplus animal."

"But I thought you said he was a good puller?"

"Oh, he was that. But he also was a reluctant soldier, so to speak. If the wrong man laid a whip to him or abused him, he would start all over again from day one. Give him a man with a soft touch, he'd pull his heart out for 'im. Just picky, I guess."

"He ever been ridden afore you got him?"

"Just a bit. They tried him as the lead on the gun team, but he didn't like it. Tossed a few soldiers into the dirt from time to time, just to remind them he still had heart. So, when I wound up with him, we had to start all over."

"So the army sold him 'cause he was mean," Pocket said, "and unpredictable. Don't sound like the horse I been ridin' next to for the last month or so."

"Well, he isn't mean at all," Beck said. "He requires respect. Demands it. Won't work for a boss he doesn't respect in return. So, when scouting came along as a profession, I needed a mount that could go the distance. Bill showed up, and we joined forces. I spent a week getting him used to a saddle, then another week getting used to me. I'm no bag of bones cavalry trooper, I got me some meat and bone on me! He sort of watched the process like he was looking at some other horse being broke to saddle, it was sort of puzzling. Like he was thinking it out as we went along, figuring if the next step was a good thing or a bad thing. By the end of it, he'd hang around the smithy during the day, hoping for another apple or carrot or whatever I could rustle up for 'em, like a big dog."

"I know that kind of horse!" Pocket laughed, "You know, I taught my little paint to fetch, just like a dog?"

"Naw!" Beck said, feigning incredulity, "'Tain't possible!"

"Heck, that's just the start! That little pony's one of the best cuttin' horses you ever seen, and she can go at it from sunup to dark, never a hitch!"

"You been cowboyin' long?"

"Ever since I was old enough to saddle a horse," Pocket said with a grin. "We come out of the war with cattle run wild, ranch all ramshackle, hardly more'n a garden and two cow ponies on the whole spread. When they started drivin' cattle up to the railheads in Kansas, I was too young to go, but I stayed behind and worked the

367

cattle and the ranch and learned. But couple of years later, I made the drive, bein' sixteen and nearly growed. Following year my brother came too. My uncle was one of the best, was foreman on couple of drives, then took up a herd of his own. We heard about the need for cattle up in Montana, so we took a herd up there in '75. On the way back, we wintered over on the T Bar W, ol' Mr. Tarn bein' a straight up cattleman, and from Texas, too! He needed experienced cow men, so we set a spell, 'til this job come along."

"Why'd you come scoutin'?" Beck said.

"Well, it bein' winter comin' on, and not much to do at the ranch, my brother and I sort of had the time. And besides, everybody had the Injun fever, and we wanted in on the fight! And you might say we wore out our welcome at Quandry, what with Zack carrin' on so about that fool girl."

"Zack? Zack Tibbits? You mean, Zack Tibbits is your brother?"

"Why, shore! I thought you knew!"

"But he's a Tibbits, and you're a Pocket! And, apart for a shared tendency to run wild, you two don't bear much of a family resemblance."

"Oh, that. Well, ya see, my pappy died while I was still a baby, and my ma remarried. First off she bore Mr. Tibbits a son of his own, Zack. He's been my little brother all his life. I taught him to ride and to shoot, and even told him all about girls."

"And what do you know about girls?"

"Wall, they had some of them up there at the railhead. I even talked to some of 'em, and it only cost me the price of a drink!"

"You manage to find out anything more about 'em, other than what they cost?"

Simon looked at the fire for a time. His face seemed to take on a redder glow than that provided by the flames.

"Well, one of 'em let me have a little kiss," Pocket said.

"And then what?"

"Ain't sure. Wasn't used to that whiskey, and it sort of snuck up on me 'bout then."

"It'll do that."

"Wall, I don't drink it no more, not like that."

"Should have been one more lesson you taught your brother."

Simon sighed. "I s'pose so."

Dodd returned from the creek and stowed the gear away. Simon went off to find more firewood, and then Morgan came back.

"We pull out at first light," he said to Beck, "assuming the rain is done for now. You have any plans once we reach the Missouri?"

"Still don't know," Beck said. "Thought I might try to find out where they've taken Hardy, see what can be done to get him back to the Crow camps. May stay on there, or I may try for Quandry. See if I can't rustle up some pay for this job."

"Suit yourself. But the offer is still open. If you want to come on to Camp Brown, I can see that you are paid for your time. I would imagine the heights will have snow by now, and more coming all the time. I have discussed the route with your general's people, and it looks as if Dodd and I will have to circle south of the Bighorns and come up on the railway. A better trip than chancing the passes in winter, even with that huge beast you ride."

"What is General Howard going to do?"

"The Indians will be taken to the cantonment on the Tongue River for the winter, then removed back to Lapwai, or so I understand it. The riverboats will see us safely down the Missouri at least as far as the nearest rail head. If it means anything at all, I would welcome the pleasure of your company."

Beck looked at Morgan in the last glow of the fire.

"That's real white of you, lieutenant," he said. "I'll think on it."

Chapter 39

The wind with its icy talons returned on the following day. The column sluggishly unreeled itself toward the south once more by mid morning. The early going was through mud churned up by the passing horses and mules, and the wagons had a hard go of it in the beginning. By mid afternoon the ground had drained and solidified to some degree, and the cold had begun again to freeze it up. The wind nipped and tugged and dug in its icy points where it could find flesh to bite. Low clouds scudded down the sky, robbing the day of all but a dim silver hue devoid of any warmth.

The weather held until the column reached the Missouri River on the thirteenth. The men were allowed to hunt, and antelope had been harvested and brought in. Dodd worked his magic on their share of the meat, coming up with salt and spices to render the flesh tasty and less like broiled sagebrush.

At the river, the steamers were landed and the prisoners were taken across. Howard and his troops embarked and departed down the river. Sturgis stayed behind on the north shore, tasked with gathering up any stragglers and forming the bulwark of defense should the Sioux decide to come south after all. Miles shipped his troops and the prisoners across the river, and after the last of the wounded had been dispatched down the river on the steamer *Silver City,* the troopers and their charges started the overland journey toward the Yellowstone.

Jon Beck inquired of several of the steamer crew as the troops were being ferried over as to the fate of Elijah Hardy. He found that several boatloads of wounded had been taken down the river over the last several weeks. No one could speak directly of Hardy.

Lieutenant Morgan was making arrangements to have the scouts taken aboard the last steamer, when an Indian approached Jon Beck as he stood on the high ground on the south bank of the river.

"Red Bear," said the Indian, a Crow. "The man of Magpie Woman sends me."

"Well I'll be," Beck said. "I was just asking around after that old reprobate. Does he live?"

"He lives. He has been taken to the Crow lodges."

"Well then," Beck sighed, "he's in good hands."

"He is in the hands of Magpie Woman," the Crow said, looking out at the river, "and he came without horses. Others have returned to the lodges too, but they bring horses. The man of Magpie Woman comes only with a bloody foot. All is not peace in the lodge of Magpie Woman."

Beck chuckled. "What is your name?"

"I am Swift Water. I have been sent to ask if you will come."

"To the lodge of Magpie Woman?"

"Yes."

"Who sends you?"

Swift Water looked back at Beck for a moment. "The man of Magpie Woman," he said finally.

"Not Magpie Woman?"

"No. She is content to make war on the man. He is content to wiggle before her tongue. He is caught by the foot in a trap, like a wolf, and daily the trapper comes to taunt him. I think he needs the final shot."

"The final shot?"

"As you would the wolf in the trap," said Swift Water, pointing a finger at his temple and jerking the hand.

"Well, I can ease his pain. I cannot release the trap."

"Then you will come?"

"Will you guide me?"

"I will guide you."

Beck sought out Morgan, and found him talking to the captain of the steamer. He came up just as Morgan turned away.

"All arranged!" Morgan said, "He'll have the steamer up here in two days, and we can go down with the next load of wounded and stragglers."

"Sorry, lieutenant, but I have to go the other way. Hardy has got himself taken home to the Crow village, and he has sent for me."

"Well, Jon, I regret to hear it. Oh I don't mean that he's safe and all, I mean that we'll be parting ways here. I was looking forward to our trip." He stuck out his hand, Beck took it.

"Once I'm done at the Crow camps, I'll be along," Beck said.

"Unless you get snowed in. But, nonetheless, come when you can. I will arrange to have your pay, and that of Mr. Hardy and your other men, sent to you whenever you get back to civilization. What of Simon, by the way? Will he come with us, or go with you?"

"Don't know. I'll go find out."

Beck, trailed by Swift Water, found Pocket near the horses. He was brushing out his paint pony. Simon took no time to think it over, volunteering to go with Beck instantly. Beck spoke on about the possibility of getting snowed in, being in the Indian lodges all winter. Pocket just grinned.

"Ain't never done that afore!" he said, "Could be right interestin'."

Beck visited the quartermaster in charge of the supplies that had been landed, and directed Pocket to follow the man and collect traveling victuals. Permission was granted them for the loan of an

Army mule, and by mid afternoon they were saddled and packed and ready to depart.

Morgan and Dodd stood beside the horses as the scouts mounted up. Swift Water led out of the camp. Beck said, "You wouldn't by any chance be willing to part with Corporal Dodd, there, for a week or two, would you?"

Morgan laughed. "Not on your life! He's the only command I have left!"

"Well, we have certainly got used to his cooking," Beck said, "Dodd, you ever need a job, you come and see me. Long as I got use for a cook, you're my man!"

"Thanks, Mr. Beck. Glad I could be of some use."

Beck gave them a little salute and moved Bill off after the departing guide and Pocket. Morgan watched them go, heading for the rising land to the south.

"There goes one hell'uva scout," Morgan said.

"Good eater, too!" Dodd put in with a grin.

The three travelers made ten miles that afternoon, winding up the valley of a little creek. The land was rolling grassland, and dirty mounds of snow lurked like hiding beasts in the pockets and crevasses of the land, behind boulders, bushes, out of the wind. The weather held cold, cloudy, but no snow for the first two days. Then, in the middle of the third morning, a blinding fury of flakes came roiling down the wind. They had camped and cooked as they had traveled, Simon taking over the tending of the skillet at first, tempting Swift Water to leave his jerky and hard tack in his saddle pouch and taste the hot beef he broiled up from the fresh supplies they had secured at the river. The Indian did not comment on its taste, but ate all that was given him. Beck tried to take over the cooking on the second night out, but Pocket would not allow it. Beck shrugged, let him have it.

When the snowstorm hit, they traveled through it for the rest of the day, and by that evening the snow was nearly a foot deep on the flats, and drifted by the wind into three and four foot depths in places. They took turns forging the trail through the deeper stuff, letting each horse work at it until it became tired or winded. When they finally began to lose the light, the snow stopped, and they took shelter in a wooded ravine out of the wind. They had plenty of firewood, and melted snow for water. They even found a sheltered slope that had escaped the worst of the blizzard, and staked the horses out so they could get at the dry, brown, wind-flattened grass.

That night the clouds cleared, the temperature dropped still further, and the stars burst forth like a mist of droplets on a raven's wing. They huddled close to the fire for warmth.

The fire died away in the night, and pre-dawn cold drove them from their blankets to get warm by saddling and loaded the horses and mule. Simon poked up the fire long enough to get a pot of coffee made, and they drank it up to warm their insides and their fingers on the tin cups.

That day was clear and the sun brilliant off the new snow as Swift Water led them into the hills. They tried to travel on clear ground and hillsides where the snow was not as deep, and made good time. Beck had to lower his hat on his brow, and raise the wool muffler that he wore about his neck up over his nose, so as to narrow to a slit the view his eyes had of the world. He knew about snow blindness from his youth in Pennsylvania, and he did not want the glare of the sun off of the white world around him to blind him now.

They made good progress that day, and on into the next, the clear, cold weather holding. The day after, it clouded up again, and then they were at the Yellowstone. Swift Water led them up river for several miles until they found a broad, shallow ford that would allow them to cross without swimming the animals. The horses crunched through sheet ice for yards on either shore, and they dodged small floes of ice coming down the low-water current. The horses got wet to their bellies, but the men stayed dry.

Up into the snowy hills led Swift Water, and they climbed and crunched through the flats and the drifts. The horses slowed and panted more often, even Bill pausing more frequently to rest. Lack of forage, hidden by the snow layer, was beginning to tell on the animals. Whenever they found any pocket of snow-free grass, they let the horses eat what they could. But the higher they went into the mountains, the fewer such patches could be found. On the second day after crossing the Yellowstone they crested the final ridge and began the descent into the valley of the Stinking Water River. Two days thereafter the Crow camp was in sight.

They came off of the final ridge, the horses easing down the slope through the drifts, the valley of the river spread out blow. The sun was bright, and the wind in the valley gentle. The smoke of the cook fires trailed away on a gentle arc down wind, grey against the white of the slopes. The trees were weighted with snow, and their branches sloping down to match the slopes of the hill covered in white, all of it sliding the eye down, down into the valley and the dark stream of winding water still unfrozen curling through its bottom. By mid day they were on the river, and then the camp was before them, dogs barking, heads poking out of the tepees to see what the clamor was all about. Swift Water gave a small sign with his hand, and turned his horse toward his lodge. Beck and Pocket pulled up before the lodge of Magpie Woman. They swung down. No one came out of the lodge. Beck handed the reins over to Pocket, and knelt at the entrance to the lodge.

"A hungry man waits at your door!" he said loudly.

"Well get yer butt in here, then!" came the muffled reply. Beck ducked into the lodge. The light was dim, and the fire pit in the center of the tepee gave off a lazy curl of smoke that rose toward the smoke hole in one side of the top.

"'Bout time you showed!" growled Hardy from a bed of skins across the fire. Beck straightened up inside the entryway, letting the flap swing closed behind him.

"Well glad to see you too!" he said, grinning. "How's that hind paw doin'?"

"Could be better," muttered Hardy. "Thought I was gonna lose it there for awhile. Got all infected, burned me up with fever. I was looking every day for gangrene. That durned woman of mine wouldn't let me rest, kept chasin' me out into the snow every day so's she could clean, she said. Clean! Why that woman ain't swept out a tea pot in ten years, now she's all het up about cleanin'? Hunh! Anyways, the infectin' went away, the oozin' stopped, the dressin's she puts on it helps the pain, and all this stompin' 'round has kept me blood up! So, apart from being prodded like a holed-up badger, I is feeling prime!"

"Good to hear," Beck said. He turned and ducked back out of the lodge. He and Simon unloaded the animals, and Beck took them to a corralled area where the Indian ponies were pastured. Back at the lodge, they carried the gear into the tepee and stowed it along one wall. Then Beck squatted at the fire.

"You haven't by any chance seen my Winchester?" he asked Hardy. Pocket dropped his saddle next to the fire and sat on it.

"There in the corner next to that box," Hardy said, pointing behind Beck. Jon rose, moved aside some skins, and found the rifle. He turned with it to the fire. The stock was broken off as he recalled, but some of the wood still clung to the wrist area.

"Like I told you before, you leave that with me, and I'll whittle you a new piece of lumber for it," Hardy said. "Ain't got much else to do."

"Well, it won't do me much good as it is. You got a deal." He turned and put the rifle back where he found it, and noticed the broken off stock was there as well. He returned to squat by the fire.

"Where is She Who Has The Voice Of A Magpie?" he said.

"She's gone down river to visit relatives. And listen to all the war talk. Lotta new horses around the camps these days. Damn if I understand that woman, she's already married, and yet she's pissed I didn't come home with no horses. I tried to tell her, it ain't the job of an army scout to count coup and steal horses! But she's off on a wild hare nonetheless. Go figure."

"Mebbe she's hankerin' after a young buck, someone who'll bring her gifts, like, well, horses," Beck said, grinning.

"There ain't a buck within thirty miles of here that'd have anything to do with that woman, horses or not! If she hadn't fished me outa that durned river, I'd be one of 'em!"

"What, a horse?"

"No! Thirty miles away!"

Beck had a good laugh, and Pocket. Hardy wanted to know all about the campaign after he had been wounded, so the rest of the day was spent in story telling. Finally, Beck mentioned that they could not stay with the Crow for long.

"What'cha figurin'?" Hardy said.

"Don't want to get snowed in here. Not that I don't enjoy your company, ol' Pard, but a winter cooped up with you would be a chore."

"You mean with Maggie, don't cha!"

"Now, I'm not going to go and cast disparagin' remarks on your woman, Lige," Beck said, "I love Maggie, I truly do. Best cook I ever did see. But this here tepee of yours is nice and cozy—for two. Me and Simon living here for months on end, well, the mere thought of it curdles my blood! No, we're striking out for Quandry, if the weather holds and the snow doesn't get any deeper. We'll be here

375

just long enough to rest the horses and get used to a little hot food, then we got to be movin' on."

"Well that's a fine howdy do!" Hardy said. "You just gonna leave me alone with her—"

"With who?" came the voice of Magpie Woman, as Beck turned to see her coming through the tepee flap.

"Why, with lady fortune, my sweet," said Hardy with a hasty smile, "we was just talking about my foot and the sweet embrace of lady fortune that has allowed it to heal!"

"You speak with the tongue of the snake," Maggie said, standing at the fire. "And it is my special wrapping that has healed your foot, not some white man's very godmother!"

"Very godmother?" laughed Beck

"The mission woman tells us of this godmother. Very strong medicine. But I have not seen this godmother, and no one can tell me where to find her. I think she is white man's spirit ghost, something to tell the little ones around the fire."

"Call it lady luck, then," Hardy said, "that and your special bandages. I am forever grateful to you."

"Aayii! Be grateful enough to fetch in more firewood, my worthless husband! I have been a bad wife and have not offered these travelers any food!" She found a spoon and stirred the pot hung over the fire beneath an iron tripod. "You will eat with us?" she said, looking at Beck and Pocket.

"Of course!" Beck said, "After all, when your worthless husband has told us you are the best cook among all of the Crow, how could we refuse."

Magpie Woman beamed out a smile. Hardy rolled to his knees, then grabbed a home made crutch and hoisted himself up to his feet. With a wink he crutched himself to the tepee flap, and slipped out into the snow.

"Sit!" said Maggie, and got out gourd bowls. Soon she had steaming stew in the hands of Beck and Pocket, as firewood sticks and split log chunks came flying in through the entrance flap. She moved around and tossed the wood into the pile along one wall as it came in. Then Hardy came in after it, and hobbled around to his bed again, sank down on the skins, and laid the crutch back along the wall.

Maggie handed him a bowl of stew. She sank down to sit by the fire.

"Now, tell me the truth," she said to Beck, "what really happened to this one," and she tossed her head at Hardy, "did he shoot himself in the foot, or did someone else do it for him?"

"Has he not spoken of the battle?" Beck said, shoveling in the hot stew as if he had not eaten all day.

"He speaks with the tongue of a snake!" she said. "Who can believe him?"

"Perhaps that very godmother?" Beck said.

"Perhaps. But not this woman! Tell me!"

Snow set in the following day, but it was light, dry, and soon stopped. The day after dawned grey and windy, with the temperatures soaring above freezing. By noon the snow was dropping from the trees as it melted, and the river had begun to rise. Every creek and gully ran roiling with snowmelt, and before the day was out, the horse paddock was free of snow, and much of the Indian camp was down to bare gravel. The lodges had been sited on high ground on the inside of a river bend, and gravel from the old bar was under them. The high water of the river, running milky grey with silt, swung around the bar and piled up on the opposite bank, flooding up the side of the bank several yards with its momentum. Ice flowed down with the torrent, rolling up by the slab and chunk to form a pile high on the north bank.

"Chinook coming," Maggie had said the night before, and the warm winds had proven her right. Beck looked at the river and the valley, and decided.

"We'll be riding out in the morning," he told Hardy that night. "Chinook has cleared the high ground of snow, the horses will be able to get grass. I figure by the time we get over the hill into the Wind River breaks, we'll just beat the next storm."

"May be," Hardy said. "Or you'll get snowed in on the heights, and we'll find what's left of you in the spring. I think you ought to consider stayin' on."

"Have. Don't want to eat you out of house and home."

"Wall, there is that. You got the grub to make the trip?"

"Yep. I could leave you some of the bacon, if you'd like it."

"May as well." Hardy sat silent for a time, watched the flames. Maggie was out at another tepee, visiting.

"Come spring, I'll come up again," Beck said. "Bring your wages for this scout. Who knows, may have work for ya, dependin'."

"And you'll need to pick up your rifle," Hardy said. "Maybe I could send along a list of things, you know, things you might buy with the wages, some things Maggie might like."

"Why, sure enough. Be happy to do that."

The next morning the weather was still warm. Beck and Pocket rose well before dawn, fetched and packed the animals, and as the first hint of light winked over the valley summit, they waved farewell to Hardy, propped on his crutch beside the tepee door, and Maggie, standing at his side.

"It is good you are not going too," she said, slipping an arm around him.

"Even though I bring no horses?"

"Even no horses."

Pocket and Beck traveled up the river, crossing gushing creeks and melt water gullies splashing with brown water. They had to circle up the valley wall from time to time to find places to get across some of the heavier rushing streams, but the weather held and they made good progress. The horses found good grazing on the brown mountain grasses, and though they worked hard, at least held their own. The pace was deliberate, careful, chosen by Beck to offer the least effort to their mounts.

Five days saw them to the summit, and then the weather had a change of heart. A blizzard caught them on the first down slope, with the snow coming over the ridge behind them like a thin avalanche on the wind, and within an instant they were in the midst of a white world where it was impossible to see anything beyond a few feet. They rode close together as the horses worked their way down the slope, for to move more than a few feet apart would be to lose touch completely. The temperature dropped thirty degrees in a matter of minutes. Beck had been looking over the long slope before them when the storm hit, and he thought they could get into trees in the creek bottom without danger. He had not seen any drop-offs or rough going, but he had no time to really examine the valley into which they were now descending. The longer they traveled, the more uneasy he became, worried lest the horses step over a hidden ledge or into some ravine which he had missed seeing before the

378

storm. He knew that Bill was sure footed over rough ground, but in this white on white world, even a good horse could be fooled.

Then they passed a tree, so close to the trunk before they saw it that the snow clad branches were in their faces. They ducked, and moved on, and then more trees, and they were among the tall pines in the creek bottom. The snow was light there, as the treetops caught some of it, and muffled the wind, so that what remained came swirling down more vertically. Beck drew up as did Pocket.

"We either hole up or keep moving," Beck said, "and it's risky either way. If we keep moving, we don't know what the ground is like, the horses may fall, hell, anything could happen. If we hole up, we don't know how long the snow will fall. If the storm drops more than two or three feet, we're trapped."

"I say we keep on," Simon said, "I sure as hell don't want to spend my winter up here!"

"Nor do I," Beck said. So on they went.

The land sloped down, and they needed to go down, so they kept to the creek valley and descended. The snow kept up its fury, swirling through the trees, whistling by them on the open stretches, never allowing more than twenty or thirty feet of view, often less than ten. The snow began to deepen underfoot, and within a few hours the horses were knee deep in it. Beck's neck muffler was stiff with the ice from his breath, his hands ached with cold, he was beginning to lose the feeling in his toes. And the light was going. He began to look for a likely place to camp for the night. The twilight had deepened to a dense gloom when they found a little flat in a copse of pine, where the snow had seemed to bypass and the ground could actually be seen. Beck steered Bill in among the trees, Pocket followed, and they swung down in a lighter snowfall.

They quickly stripped the saddles from the horses, and got the gear off of the mule. They left the saddle blankets on the animal's backs for what little protection they would provide. Stripping dead branches off of the lower parts of the trees, they soon had a crackling blaze going. Even the horses crowded close to the fire for warmth. Simon looked up at his pony in surprise.

"I thought horses was afraid of fire," he said, grinning at Beck.

"Shows she trusts you," Beck said. "Where you are, it's safe to be."

"Little does she know," Pocket said, looking out at the snow. "If it don't let up soon, we're dead men."

"It's downhill from here, Simon," Beck said cheerily, "that'll make all the difference, you'll see."

"I hope you're right."

They passed a fitful night in their blankets around the fire, the horses just beyond them, standing three-legged, tails into the wind. They did not see the snow cease in the early hours of the dawn, but when they woke at first light, they smiled. The remaining snowfall had partly filled in their back trail, but they could still see it leading into their little enclave of shelter. Which meant the trail ahead would still be passable, even if it was going to be a lot of work.

They rose and rolled the bedding, and Simon cooked while Beck packed. They ate a hasty breakfast of bacon and biscuit, then rode out through two feet of gleaming white.

Their shallow valley soon closed into a deeper cleft, and through its bottom ran a gurgling stream. It was iced over in places, but for the most part was open and not deep. They followed its course, riding in the water when the drifted snow blocked easy passage or deadfalls or outcroppings of the rocky hillside proved impassable. The little stream opened into a larger valley, an open blanket of white that stretched for miles, the dark course of the stream snaking through it.

"I do believe we've hit Station Creek," Beck said as they rested the horses on the rim of the broad expanse. "Those hills off to the south, just beyond should be Quandry. Maybe twenty miles, give or take." The southerly sun gleamed off of the snow, and Beck pulled his hat low once more, edged up his muffler against the glare, and they descended onto the valley flats. The snow proved deeper there than they had thought, and the horses were belly deep in it. Soon one horse followed the other, the first breaking trail for the second. When the first tired, the other took the lead. The mule had it best of all, always being led at the end of the line.

Five miles of trail breaking had the horses blowing. They were only halfway down the valley, but the animals were nearly played out. Beck got down off of Bill, and leading the animal, he broke trail himself, nearly waste deep in the drifts. He only made it a few hundred yards before he, too, was gasping for breath. Pocket then took a turn, and he in his turn was stopped by the seemingly endless white barrier. Beck mounted Bill and took the big stallion another half mile before he simply would not go further. Pocket forged ahead on the pinto, crashing through the flat white mass. Then Beck again on foot, then Pocket. Then the horses again, the men again, each time just a little less distance than before. Finally they had come within a mile of an easy slope, and they could see tips of grass poking through the snow on that hill, where the wind had scoured away some of the white and they might find easier going. But it was still a mile away. Men and horses were exhausted. It may as well have been the moon.

Finally Beck went to the mule and unpacked the saddle. He stripped off the pack saddle and led the mule to the end of the furrow. He clambered up atop the animal, which skittered a bit in the snow. And then Beck set his spurs to the mules flanks. With a squeal of protest the mule lunged forward, leaping like a deer, then again and again. Beck kept at it, driving the animal as far as he was willing to go, then as far as he would unwillingly go. When they finally halted, the mule trembling and heaving with exhaustion, the beginning of the slope was only a hundred yards away. Beck got down and left the mule and began to bull his way though the snow again. At one point the ground rose to within a foot of the level top of the white, and Beck began to grin. Then he descended into the cold mass again, sinking further down with each step until he was chest deep in the fluffy white. He began to think that he would go under completely, but he could not stop even if he had to burrow his way along. His breath came in heaving sobs as he fought his way forward, and the ground began to rise. He growled savagely and surged through the nearly solid barrier, gaining higher ground with each stride and then he was on the slope, and snow was only six inches deep and he could see and feel the grass under it and through it and he was laying in it and laughing. And gasping.

He sat up, and turned to look out over the white desert of cold. The mule had not moved. Simon was piling gear on the horses. It wasn't done yet. And to the north, stacked up like piles of dirty cotton, banks of clouds poked their roiling heads over the mountain ridges they had just crossed. Another storm coming down the wind.

Chapter 40

The storm had blown for two days, hard, from the north, and the streets of Quandry were swept clear of most of the snow where the wind whistled between the buildings and got a clear shot down the open expanses of the town. What snow remained in the roadways was packed hard by the wheels of wagons and carts, and the hooves of hauling horses and mules. None of these animals had been seen on the streets for half a day, as the town and its people were holed up like hibernating beasts, peering out of windows and cracked doors at the storm and wondering when it would slacken.

Where the buildings blocked the blast, the drifts piled up in the lee of the wooden barriers, the snow sculpted like long bones lying across the roadways, down the alleys, heaped up on porches and boardwalks. At the start of the blow two days before, some intrepid souls had shoveled and broomed it from their thresholds, but now no one bothered, for it just piled up again, almost faster than it could be shoved aside. Better to wait it out, then tackle the chore when the icy wind wasn't whining past their ears and biting hard at any exposed flesh.

The light was dim with the storm, a pewter glow that blended the drifts and the buildings in a twilight of blowing gloom. Several brief snowstorms had struck in the last several weeks, which most folks who had lived long in the country knew and expected, but then a Chinook had rolled through and given the latter part of November a brief remembrance of the balmy days of fall. But there was no balm in the blizzard that had come after, only the howl of an almost vindictive wind and the scraping rush of the snow as it tore over the land and lashed the town with its violence.

Mrs. Eugenia Robinson Ransom moved the curtain aside slightly and peered out of the jailhouse window at the storm-shrouded street, and sighed. It was past the noon hour, and her relief was due at noon. She sighed again, and turned back to the room. Across from the marshal's desk was a bed along the wall, and in the bed a man. The black potbellied stove stood near the head of the bed, and next to it a pile of wood. Two buckets stood at the foot of the bed, and trailing from one were the tails of several bloody bandages.

Mrs. Ransom crossed the room to the stove, picked up a piece of wood and used it to lift the stove door handle, swinging it open to reveal a hot glowing blaze within. She tossed in the chunk of wood, then another, and used a third to swing the little door shut again.

She tossed the stick back on the pile and stepped to the bed. The man lying there had a folded cloth across his forehead, and his midsection was bandaged. The red of blood and the yellow of puss stained the bandages over his belly. He lay with his eyes closed, and his lips parted. Beads of sweat glistened on his cheeks, though the room was slightly cool. She bent closer to his mouth to listen for the least breath. Then she removed the cloth from his forehead, stepped to a second bucket next to the one with old bandages in it, and dipped the cloth in water. She wrung it out partly, leaving enough water in the cloth to keep it wet and cool, refolded it and draped it over the man's brow once more. A small groan issued from the man's throat, almost a sigh.

She crossed again to the window, and peered out. Still no one stirred in the blowing bluster of the street. She turned back to the room, and shook her head, pursed her lips.

It was a small jail, more of an office in fact, with the actual jail cells through a closed door out back. The town had built the original cells, two of them, out of hewn railroad ties, so that the walls were eight inches thick of solid wood. The floor was of the same material, as was the ceiling. Over the top had been laid a shingled roof, when the office was added a year later. She wondered if the railroad workers, for whom the jail was built and intended, appreciated the irony of its being constructed out of railroad ties. But now it did not matter, with construction of the rail line being terminated for the indefinite future. The workers had begun to leave the country, and with them went the Saturday night brawls and the stabbings, and the occasional shootings, and the need for the jail at all. And at the same time, the jail was now, suddenly, needed more than ever, and should have been in use at that moment, except for the fact that the marshal himself was the victim of the crime that cried out for incarceration.

Mrs. Ransom's husband had been talking with the other town business owners, workers, residents, about what to do. They knew what to do. They knew how to do it. But the object of their concern was not going to be easy to apprehend. They knew where to find him. But for five days, they had not dared. The also knew that some of them would most certainly be shot in any attempt at justice. They were not cowards. They just didn't like the odds.

The local horse doctor had been called in to tend to the wounded marshal. He did not think it was worth going after the two slugs in the victim's gut. A real doctor had been sent for, down the rail line. He was expected. In the mean time, the women tended the shot-up marshal as best they could, but he was fading. She had seen it before. With the appearance of puss seeping from the wounds and the fever, she knew the doctor would not come in time. Even if he arrived momentarily. They could only try to make the man's last hours comfortable.

She turned again to the window, and movement caught her eye. Horses came into view, one being led by a large man, walking, the other ridden, and a third animal, bearing packs, being led. She could not make out through the blowing snow who the men were. They were heading for the depot at the end of the street, or perhaps the livery to one side of it.

Could it be the doctor? But no, he was to arrive by rail. If the train was still running. Snow drifts might have blocked the tracks. She watched the little procession out of sight. Then, from across the street, another figure materialized from the darkness of the bulk of a building, and Mrs. Ransom could see that the hurrying figure was her relief.

She quickly went to the door, unlatched it, waited until she heard footfalls on the porch boards outside, then swiftly jerked the door open and stepped aside. A muffled figure bearing an armload of parcels and a basket rushed into the warmth of the room, and Mrs. Ransom slammed the door and latched it.

The other woman quickly placed her load on the desk, and unwound the woolen wrap from her neck and face.

"Oh Gina, I am sorry I am late!" said the woman. "I had three students who actually came to school this morning, and I had to prepare some home work for them and shoo them off home again! It took longer than I had anticipated. How is the marshal?" she said, turning to the man on the bed. She began pulling off her gloves.

"About the same I am afraid, Miss Bertram. He lapses in and out of his sleep, but now he seems to sleep longer than before. His fever is increasing, too. At least he is not constantly moaning with the pain of it, as he was."

"Is there anything different that we must do?" Miss Bertram said, her brow wrinkled with the question.

"No. Nothing else is possible. Did you bring the fresh dressings?"

"I did, here in the bundle. May I help you with them?"

"Of course. Perhaps a bit of supper first, for I am famished!"

"Yes, here in the basket. Mr. Ransom put it up just for you. He certainly does love that new stove of his, I do say."

"Yes, that he does. Although now that the Indians have been driven off and captured, we haven't nearly the trade we once did. I suppose I should thank the Lord for this storm, as it has brought us travelers seeking shelter from it. But that is as it may be. It seems now there are new perils, and much closer to home."

"What is to be done about him? The killer, I mean. Oh, I don't mean killer, for Marshal Gerline is not dead, but...."

"Not yet." Mrs. Ransom looked at Miss Bertram and shook her head sadly. "But something must be done, and soon!"

Outside in the raging blizzard Jon Beck led his exhausted mount down the street to the stable. He had taken to his feet two miles out, just to get the circulation going again in his toes. They had struck the road east of town, and nearly missed it for the wind-whipped and drifting snow had hidden its presence. But Bill had paused, and tried to turn, and Beck, knowing the big horse did not deviate from his directed path without good reason, took a second look about and could barely discern the road. They had turned west, and within an hour the lights of the town had squinted faintly from the wall of whisking white.

At the stable, Beck paused at the large sliding door of the main entrance and shoved it aside. He led Bill inside, and Pocket followed, still aboard his pony. The mule crowded close behind, smelling the hay and oats within and needing no urging in that direction. Beck went back and rolled the door closed behind them.

A lantern was hung on the other side of the large room, and coming down the ladder from the loft, a second lantern in his hand, was the stable owner, Mr. Pickworth. The stalls along two walls of the building were all full, and a pile of hay, just pitched down from the loft, lay near them. Bill smelled the hay, and took a step toward

385

the pile, snorting a little. Pickworth hit the floor and came hurrying over.

"Gentlemen!" he said coming up to Beck, who was slapping the snow off of his shoulders, and lifting the lantern, "Welco—" He froze, his mouth dropping open. "It's you!" he finally said.

"Yes, indeed," Beck growled, "weary travelers, cold and hungry. Is there room at the inn?"

"Well, I, uh, er, you see, I don't, ah…"

"I take that as a yes," Beck said, reaching under Bell to loosen his cinch.

Pickworth paused, pursed his lips. "Yes!" he spouted, "You mean here! Oh yes, of course! Yes indeed! You are welcome, sir! There is room enough for your horses, but I must turn your mule out into the corral, I am afraid, as I have three other mules here, and there has been trouble…."

"Is there shelter for the animals in the corral?" said Pocket, swinging down off of his paint horse.

"Oh yes!" the owner said, "We have put up a shed out there, and mounded it with hay, and they can stay out of the wind."

"Good enough," Pocket said. He, too, began to wearily unsaddle his horse. Beck got the gear off of Bill and the saddle, and stowed the tack along the wall with other gear. They unpacked the mule, and Pickworth led it out the small door to the corral, then returned with the halter in his hand.

The horses walked over to the hay pile and began to eat. Several horses in stalls nickered and snorted, hungry too. Pickworth took up a pitchfork and began forking some of the hay into the various mangers in the stalls.

"You have oats, and corn?" Beck said to him across the room. He found a pile of sacking and took some over to Bill, and began to rub him down.

"Yes sir!" Pickworth said over his shoulder as he worked at the hay.

"See to it they have what they want," Beck said.

"Of course Mr. Beck. Consider it done!"

Beck looked at Simon over his shoulder as he worked. "Well, we made it, Simon. We're back. What you figure, a bath first? A drink? Food? Or about a week's worth of sleep?"

"Yep," Pocket said.

Beck chuckled. "Yep what?"

"All of it!" Pocket said.

"All right then," Beck chuckled, "once more into the jaws of death. Or at least the teeth of the wind." He tossed aside the sacking, shouldered his saddlebags, took up his rifle. "I figure we'll make the hotel our first stop, see about food and a bath. Then, if we're still awake, maybe a drink over at the saloon. Sound about right?"

"Does to me," Pocket said. "Only one little hitch in that rope, I ain't got the price—"

"You leave that to me!" Beck said quickly, "Besides, we'll both be paid soon enough, you can catch up to what's owed then. Come on, lets get this over with," he said, and slid the big door open just far enough to slip through. Swirling snow billowed through the opening as Beck and Pocket quickly stepped out into the storm, and Beck slid the door shut again.

Heads down against the wind, holding their hats, they trudged up the street toward the Ransom House. Lighted windows cast a warm yellow glow into the gloom along the street, but half the town was invisible in the swirling white. They climbed the porch steps at the hotel, and then they were through the door and into the little lobby, shaking snow from their coats as they set down their gear.

Mr. Ransom came up the hallway to the lobby, and quickly slipped behind the little desk, a smile on his face.

"Gentlemen, welcome, welcome!" he beamed. "Will you be staying with us this evening?"

"Yep," Jon Beck said, taking off his hat and slapping it against his thigh to shake off the snow and wet. "Got the fires hot out back? We're looking for a hot meal and a tub full of water, as well!"

"Of course, of course, we can provide all you ask," Ransom said, turning the ledger around and setting out an ink bottle with a pen sticking out of it. He eyed the two men in his lobby, cocked his head slightly.

"Airn't you the Indian scouts what lit out after those renegades a few weeks ago?" he said, as Beck stepped over and took up the pen. A drop of water from his thawing hat fell on the ledger as he bent to write his name.

"The same," Beck said. He handed the pen to Pocket, stepped aside.

"Tell me, were you in on the kill? Did you take vengeance on them for Custer?" Ransom said, his eyes bright, eager.

"They had nothing to do with Custer," Beck said, tiredly. "And most of them were taken alive."

"Oh," Ransom said, turning the book back to him when Pocket had replaced the pen in the well. Ransom blotted the drip of water that had fallen from Beck's hat with his sleeve. He looked up again, and said, "Not many scalps taken, then?"

Beck looked at him levelly. "No, I am sure you are sorry to hear. The Nez Perce do not take scalps."

"No, no, I meant Indian scalps, didn't the soldiers...?" Ransom said expectantly.

"None there either," Beck said. "Now, how about some supper? And that bath?"

"Of course, I have food on, if you don't mind beef stew, fresh buttermilk biscuits, butter, Mrs. Ransom's berry preserves, potatoes, green beans, carrots, apple dumplings, and coffee. And I will have my girl get the bath ready. We have a bath room now, you know, heated! And I can have your clothes laundered for you, for a small additional charge...?"

"That would be just fine," Beck said.

"This way, then," Ransom said, leading off down the hallway toward the back of the building, "I will show you to your room, number seven, just at the top of the stairs. You don't mind sharing a room, do you? The storm has brought us travelers, stranded by the snow, and—"

"Don't mind at all," Beck said, taking up his gear and starting after Ransom. Pocket did the same.

"I didn't mean any offense to you, Mr. Beck, about the scalps, I mean," Ransom said over his shoulder at the stairway, "it's just that some folks place great store on the taking of scalps, and consider it the badge of a warrior. Why, just the other day—"

"More like the badge of a vulture!" Beck said. "No more talk of it, Mr. Ransom, or on my honor I shall become agitated. And, sir, you do not want to be in the vicinity of my agitation, I guarantee you that!"

Ransom paused on the third step, turned partly to look down upon the face behind him. What he saw in the grey eyes uplifted to him sent a shudder down his spine. He turned and quickly scurried up

388

the stairs, the two weary scouts at his heels. He showed his guests to their room, and just as quickly scurried off to see about the supper.

The room was as before, one bed, a small table, one chair, an ewer and basin for water. But the bed now had a comforter, and a pillow. The scouts dropped their gear in the corners, and Beck heaved his shoulders out of the bushy buffalo coat that had kept him alive over the last several days. He draped it over the chair to dry.

Simon sat on the bed, patted the comforter. He flopped backward across it, closed his eyes. "Mebbe I'll just stay right here," he said, dreamily.

"Suit yourself," Beck said. He went to the door, looked back. "It's a plate of biscuits for me, and all the stew I can hold! Then I'm going to scrape some of this stink off me with a good ol' soaking!'"

"Hummmm," Simon murmured, his eyes closed. Beck smiled and went out.

He passed a family of four on the stairs as he went down, tipping his hat to the woman, and then found the new dining room out of what used to be the back door. Ransom had built the new room onto the back of the hotel, with a kitchen at the back of that. Half a dozen patrons sat here and there at two long tables running down the room. As Beck looked about for a seat, Mr. Ransom came out of the kitchen.

"Please, sir, sit here near the door," Ransom said, indicating the last chair next to the kitchen door. "Warmer here, and you are the last for lunch, easier for us to serve you." Beck moved down the room as others rose to leave. He eased into the chair. Ransom ducked back into the kitchen.

Jon Beck tilted his hat back on his head. He felt dirty. His clothing itched. His toes tingled. His belly growled. He had not sat in a proper chair for what seemed like a lifetime. Within moments, Ransom came back with a large bowl of stew, plates of corn bread, butter, jam. He provided a big tin cup of beer, cold from its storage in the winter weather. He clanked down fork and spoon, and finished it off with a folded napkin. Beck looked it all over from a half daze of rest and warmth.

Ransom stood by his chair for a moment. "Is there anything...?" he said. "Is it all right?" He wiped his hands on his apron.

"Mr. Ransom," Beck said with a sigh, "it is more than all right. It appears, from where I sit, to be a grand slice of heaven." And he picked up a spoon and dug into the stew. Ransom smiled and went back to the kitchen.

Beck buttered up the hot cornbread, and dipped it in the thick, hot stew, bit and savored the flavor of it, spooned the stew into his mouth, chewed it all slowly, washed it down with the cold, clear bite of beer, and then Ransom brought in plates of beans, carrots, and small potatoes. "Had these left over, so if you don't mind helpin' me finish them off...!" he said, smiling at the obvious pleasure with which Jon Beck decimated the victuals before him. "Don' min' if I do," Beck mumbled through his chuck.

The last of the other guests had long departed the dining hall by the time Beck had progressed to fresh fluffy buttermilk biscuits, buttered and jammed and washed down slowly, Beck savoring the exquisite sweet-salty flavor of each and every morsel, with hot black coffee. At last he could hold no more, and thunked his cup back to the table to put a period on the long, wonderfully wrought sentence of his first civilized meal in many long weeks.

Ransom appeared again from the kitchen. "Anything more I can get you, sir?" he smiled, wiping his hands again on his apron.

"There was talk of a bath. Bath room, you said."

"Of course! I can have the bath ready for you in fifteen minutes!"

"If you please. Oh, and I congratulate you, sir, on a most excellent stew."

And pleased Ransom was, as he scurried back into the hotel to arrange the bath. Within the promised fifteen minutes, Beck was shown to the new bath room, which was located through a side door just off the kitchen, in which a tub of galvanized iron sat gleaming securely on four stubby legs shaped like lion's paws. Water had been added, soap and a cloth placed on a chair beside the tub, and towels hung from a handy wall rack.

Beck made arrangements to have his clothing cleaned, and as Ransom left the room, he quickly stripped and stepped into the hot water. He eyed his long johns and other clothing in a heap on the floor, and wondered if it were not a better idea to simply burn everything and buy new. But as he sank into the hot water of the bath, he quickly lost all interest in what happened to his clothes, and Ransom was back a moment later to collect them and hurriedly depart.

Jon grabbed the soap and went to work. The wounds on his arm and chest were still red and somewhat swollen, and he washed tenderly around them, dabbing at the stitches carefully. After he had washed and scrubbed and scraped months of grime and sweat and dirt from every other part of him, he tossed out the soap and folded the cloth into a pad, laid it against the end rim of the tub, and settled his head back against it, relaxing in the still warm water. Another door opened, this one to the exterior, and a young boy came in up some steps, lugging a bucket. He brought it to the tub, heaved it up with all his might, and poured hot water into the tub. Then he turned and left with the bucket without a word, closing the door with a bang.

The new influx of hot water washed over his body as it mingled with the tepid, soapy dirty water in which Beck lay. Although Ransom had boasted of the bath room being heated, it still remained cool to Jon's face. One window brought in the grey afternoon light, but the window was iced over on the inside, and Jon could not determine if it was still snowing. It did not matter to him. He let his mind sweep over his full belly, his clean belly, his warm belly.

Outside the entrance door in the dining room he heard the sound of boots on the new flooring, the screek of chairs being moved about, the murmer of voices. He drifted in and out of a dazed luxuriance, the glow in his middle like a stove heating his well being. The voices mumbled on beyond the door, and at times he could hear a word or two. Then, loud enough to hear clearly, came "Shoot the son-of-a-bitch!" and then another voice, "Well who's gonna do it, you?" Then "Gentlemen, gentlemen, we've been over this a dozen times!" came Ransom's voice, "Gentlemen, please!' and the sound of the voices subsided again to a dull murmur. Jon Beck dozed off.

When he woke, the water was cool, the light fading, and the room had a definite nip in its atmosphere. He sighed, rose out of the water, reached over a towel, and dried himself. Then he realized he was standing in a room with no clothes in sight. He went to the door to the outside, opened it a crack. The storm howled in streaking white down the alley in his view. He closed that door, went to the door into the dining room. He opened it, stuck his head out. The lamps had been dimmed, the kitchen appeared quiet, and no one was in sight. He grunted.

He wrapped the other towel about his waste, then stepped through the door into the dining room, then crossed it to the hotel hallway, then up the stairs. At the top of the stairs two guests were coming down, a man and a woman. Beck edged past them, smiling, "Excuse me, please, do," he muttered, turning a bright crimson from the neck up. The woman averted her startled eyes, eased past on the stairs. The man grinned, tipped his bowler hat as he also stepped past. Then Beck was in the upper hallway and into his room.

Simon still stretched across the bed where Beck had last seen him, snoring. Jon got his spare clothing out of his saddlebags and dressed. Then he grabbed Simon's shirt and swiveled the young cowboy lengthwise on the bed. Pocket sawed on without missing a snort. Beck went around to the other side of the bed and got in, slipping under the sheets in his long johns. He jostled Simon a bit to find comfort, then relaxed and let his mind roam. He recalled the conversation in the dining room, and had just began to wonder who it was that needed shooting when sleep washed over him like a warm, black wave.

Chapter 41

He heard, or felt, a tapping on his skull, behind his eyes, against his brow. He shook it off and burrowed deeper into the feather comforter his mother had thrown over him as she kissed him good night. The room was full of light, and he tried to burrow deeper yet, to block off the light, to go back into the depths of oblivion, the warm dark of no caring, no need to go or do or be.

The tapping came again, this time with a sharp claw on it that pecked into his brain, jabbed at his eyes, irritated his forehead. His eyes cracked open, reluctantly, his inner self crying out no, no, there was still sleep to be wrapped in like a feather comforter, tucked into it by a loving—

Tap tap tap! His eyes opened fully. He was in a strange room, harsh grey light streaming in through an iced-over window, and someone was banging on the door. Then it all flooded back, and Jon Beck sat up. He was alone in the bed.

"What is it!" he demanded loudly.

"Begging your pardon, Mr. Beck," came the voice of Ransom the inn keeper from the other side of the door, "but I have an urgent matter to discuss with you. And your clothing, I have your clothing all cleaned and ready to go. May I come in?"

Beck yawned. "Yes, you may as well, since I am now awake," he growled loudly.

Ransom came in bearing an armload of folded clothing, Beck's hat atop the load. He placed the pile on the end of the bed.

"Mr. Beck, I am truly sorry to wake you, ah, at this hour," he began.

"And just what hour is it?" Beck said.

"It is just past ten o'clock. In the morning. Of the next day. I mean, I saw you last in the bath room yesterday afternoon, and this is the next day. Tomorrow. From yesterday," Ranson stammered on and on. Beck held up his hand.

"Whoa, there, pardner, just hold on. It's all right. 'Bout time I was a'risin' anyway."

"Yes sir. Except that man you rode in with, Mr. Pocket, told me when I passed him in the hall last night that to wake you would mean my sudden death! He said you were meaner'n a poked grizzly if anyone were to wake you at all, and he said he had the scars to prove it! He even offered to show them to me, right there in the hallway, and I—"

"Oh hush yourself!" Beck said, chuckling. "That durned kid was just funnin' with you, that's all. But what's this urgent matter you need me to hear about? Clothes not come clean or somethin'?" Beck said tightly.

"Oh no, sir, the clothing came back nicely done! They even plugged the holes in your hat! No, not that. But it seems that the town council wishes to have a word with you on a most urgent matter. Could you meet with them this morning, perhaps after breakfast, in our dining room?" Ranson was wringing his hands, in deference to having no apron to wipe them on.

"What sort of urgent matter?" Beck said.

"I am afraid I cannot say," Ransom said, trying to smile a little.

"Can't, or won't?" Beck said.

"It is not my place to broach the subject, Mr. Beck, no, not at all. But I beg of you, please, at least meet with us, er, them, and hear us out. It is of the greatest urgency—"

"Yes, yes, so you say!" Jon Beck said, rolling out to sit on the side of the bed. "All right, I will be down shortly."

"Thank you, sir!" Ransom fairly shouted, "I will have your breakfast hot and ready the moment you step down. Thank you, Mr. Beck, thank you!" He bowed several times and backed out of the room, closing the door as he went.

Beck shook his head, wrinkled his forehead, and sighed.

"Whatever it is, I don't think you're gonna want in," he muttered to himself.

He washed up in the bowl on the side stand, using icy cold water from the ewer, then dressed in his newly washed clothing. His boots had been cleaned and greased. His hat had been brushed and blocked, and as he looked it over, he could barely tell where a Nez Perce bullet had passed through it, parting his hair in the process. The clothing made him feel like a new man. He buckled on his gun belt, and with his buffalo coat over one arm, left the room.

As he stepped into the dining room, the late morning light streaming through the windows, and six men sat along one of the tables. They all looked at him as one when he came through the door. His first instinct was to reach for his pistol. They looked like a posse, or a jury. And he felt like the verdict had already been pronounced, and that he was not going to like the sentence.

They rose as one as he crossed the room and laid his coat across the back of a chair. The six men were all dressed in suits, save Pickworth, who among them alone wore the breeches and shirt and short coat of a working man. All six had removed their hats. Beck did the same. Ransom stepped in from the kitchen.

"Mr. Beck, this here's Mr. Connolly from the bank," Ransom said, indicating the first of the six, who stepped up and offered his hand. "Pleasure, Mr. Beck!" he said as Jon shook it. Connolly took over the introductions.

"Mr. Pickworth, you already know," he said, "And here is Mr. Dowdy and Mr. Bolt, from the General Store and Merchantile, Mr. Bridge who owns the Downspout Saloon, and Mr. Marchand who runs the Feed and Tack." Beck shook hands with each of them in turn.

"Pleasure, gentlemen," he said, "and just what is it I can do for you?"

"Oh please, Mr. Beck," Ransom blurted, "have some breakfast first, then we can talk business. That's all right with you gentlemen, is it not?" he said, his eyes darting along the line of businessmen.

"Why, certainly!" Connolly said with a smile.

Jon Beck seated himself at a table, his back to the wall. The six men seated themselves along the other table, facing Jon Beck. Ransom scurried into the kitchen and came back with plates and platters, setting hot cakes and butter and syrup and ham slices and coffee before Beck. He took his tray back into the kitchen, came out with coffee in tin cups for the six men.

Beck attacked the food before him, and the six men sipped their coffee. All six watched Jon eat. Beck watched the six sip coffee. Not a word was spoken. Beck slowed in his work as the pancakes went down and the ham, and Ransom brought biscuits and jam, and Beck slathered butter on the creamy white, still warm biscuits, then the jam, and ate. And ate. Ransom kept Beck's coffee hot and offered more to the others, who either nodded or shook their heads, but said nothing. Finally, Jon pushed his plate back and, with a hand on his cup, leaned back in his chair and waited.

His grey eyes sought out the eyes of each of the six men facing him in turn, and what he saw there was doubt. Uncertainty. Fear. Even their leader, Connolly, for he took the man's forward manner as that of their leader, even his eyes showed a hint of fear. But something else that the others did not show. Beck thought of it as cunning. The view that wheels were turning behind the façade, that something was going on. Yes, Connolly would be the one to reckon with.

"More coffee, anyone?" Ransom said after ten minutes of complete silence while Beck looked at the six, and they at him.

"No, I think not," said Connolly. He glanced at the others, then faced Beck. "Mr. Beck, let us come to the point. We represent the commercial interests of Quandry, more or less, although there are a dozen other men of property in the town who believe as we do. We are the men who made this town what it is, and we all have a vested stake in the community. And the public safety. Certainly the public safety. Each of us has roots that go back—"

"Thought we were coming to the point?" Beck interrupted.

"Yes. Well. What we have is a problem. A...person, a man, who is causing a problem. We don't know what to do about this man, and unless he is stopped, he may in fact cause additional mortal harm to our citizens here in Quandry, even to us," and Connolly glanced about at the other six.

"Who is the man and what has he done?"

"He has been on a rampage for more than a week now!" Dowdy cried, "He's been shooting up the town, and in fact has shot down several citizens!"

"He's the one who shot Marshal Gerline!" put in Bolt.

"And right at this moment he is camped in my saloon!' said Bridge. "Not another customer will even enter the place while he's there!"

"He's a mad dog, and he's got the whole town treed!" cried Marchand.

"Gentlemen, please," Connolly said, holding up his hand. The others quieted, though Beck could see the tension in them wanting to spill out their hatred of the interloper, the fear, wanting to scream out their case for begging assistance.

"All this is true," Connolly went on, "he has been in town for weeks, most of that time spent drinking. About ten days ago he ran out of money. That's when it all began. He went about to persons on the street, begging first, then robbing them. The bartender over at the Downspout tried to put him out. He was the victim of the first shooting. Then another customer didn't like his drunken tirade. He was the second. Marshal Gerline was out of town for a brief time, and when he came back and found out about the shootings, he went to the Downspout to do his duty. The man shot him down. And shot him again, for God's sake, as he lay there on the floor! He is a mad dog, cold blooded killer, and we have no way to stop him!"

The others all murmured assent, nodding their heads rapidly.

"And I would imagine having him around is a little tough on business," Beck said wryly. The six looked at each other, and down, and at each other. "So why don't you just form up a vigilance committee and go get him?"

"We thought of that," Connolly said. "But you see, he's ready. He's always waiting for the next one to come through the door. We could rush him, of course, but some among us would be shot. There is no getting around it, someone would most likely die in the attempt."

"Does he never sleep?"

"We don't know. We have sent scouts to the saloon to find out, but it seems no one has yet found a time when he is not ready. And shooting, I might add. The last man sent over barely got a peek in the window before a bullet nearly took his ear off!"

"You think about peppering the saloon with gunfire?"

"That would destroy my business!" burst out Bridge. "And that's no guarantee of anything. Why, it just might make him angry enough to go on another rampage and shoot us all!"

Beck shook his head. "Well, I declare. I don't think I have ever witnessed a bunch of western men with so much to lose and so little gumption to save it." He sipped his coffee.

"You may try all you please to shame us, Mr. Beck," Connolly said evenly, "but we are realists. To flush out this man may involve great loss of life. It will surely cost the first man through the door his. We are not gunfighters. None of us, it turns out, saw service in the war. We are merchants and men of business, and we have families to think of. We found a fine man in the person of Marshal Gerline to keep the peace with the railroad workers, and he did a grand job of work there. For which we are grateful. But this matter is a shooting matter, and we believe this miscreant, this mad dog, must die in the end. If not by a bullet, surely by a rope. We don't know where to turn, or didn't, until it was brought to our attention that you are a man who…well, who is used to violence, so to speak. And as much as I hate to say it, we need a violent man at the moment."

Beck eyed the six of them levelly. He said nothing for a time. The thought that he should be sought out under these circumstances set him to thinking. Was he a violent man? Certainly he had done what had to be done in his life. And yes, he had relished the rough and tumble fighting at the fairs and jubilees of his youth, but that had all been at least semi-organized, each man knowing what he was volunteering for. He had never fought unless provoked, his tussle with the stable owner notwithstanding. Pickworth.

Jon let his eyes rest on Pickworth.

"And who, might I ask," he said slowly, "suggested me to you? Who is it that names me a violent man?"

397

Pickworth would not meet his eyes. Ransom looked toward his kitchen, and nearly made a move toward its door, but stopped, and looked at the floor.

"The fact is, Mr. Beck, you are an Indian scout, or an army scout, as it were," Connolly said hastily. "As such you have seen fighting, and I am sure have participated in fighting, am I wrong?"

"You are not wrong."

"And I am told you came through the war, as an infantryman."

"With the 81st Pennsylvania, it was, and I started as a boy, a bugler."

"Well, you have seen your share of blood, then—"

"That's exactly it, Mr. Connolly!" Beck said. "I've seen my share of blood. And I'm not hankerin' to see any more, especially my own! I'm not a lawman, and I don't live in your town. At least not regular. I don't much give a damn who shoots up the place, as long as they're not shootin' at me! Marshal Gerline seemed like a good enough man, but he's no kin of mine and I never rode with him, official like. Sure it's a pity he got killed, but it still isn't my fight."

"We'll pay you five hundred dollars to kill that cowpoke!" blurted out Bridge.

Silence again seized the room. All eyes were on Beck. He sipped at his cup. Finally he shook his head.

"'Tisn't the money," he said at last. "I'm no lawman, and I am certainly no killer. I have just got into town after weeks on the trail, weeks of watching' good men on both sides of the fight get shot down into the mud, and I am just sick and tired of it. Do you men hear what I am saying? I am just goddamned sick and tired of it!"

"We'll make it seven…" Connolly began, looking at the others, then, "no, we'll give you one thousand dollars to do it!" The look of desperation in their faces would inspire pity in an inquisitor. Beck had no pity left.

"Take your money and shove it up your ass!" he growled, thinking once more that a revolver would deal with this bunch in a most efficient way.

Connolly flushed pink in his fat cheeks. He looked at the others, gritting his teeth.

"Then if it's not to be money, what about your responsibility?" he said.

Beck just stared at them.

"If you hadn't run him off, he wouldn't be here now shooting up our town!" Connolly said accusingly.

"What the hell are you talking about?" Beck said, setting down his cup.

"When you fired him he came back here so full of rage we thought—"

"Who, goddamn you! WHO?" Jon Beck nearly shouted. But he knew the answer before they could spit it out.

"Why, it's that Tibbits fellow, Zak Tibbits! You didn't know?" Connolly said.

Beck sat back, blinked, sighed. His jaw clenched, then relaxed. His eyes focused once more on the men before him.

"One thousand dollars," he said. "Dead or in jail."

"Agreed!"

Chapter 42

The business elite of Quandry, Wyoming Territory, spent some time relating the details of Zak Tibbits' return to the town. He had scalps in his possession, and while the Nez Perce to the north remained on the run, and the town stayed full or nearly so of frightened farmers and ranchers, Tibbits was full of tales of how he had obtained the scalps, and congratulatory whiskey flowed freely. Then news came of the Bear's Paw fight, and the war fever subsided. The frightened bucked up and left town, back to their ranches and farms and hill side mining or timber cutting, and Zachary Tibbits was left to drink alone.

Or nearly so. The railroad workers had completed their spur, and now they were packing up the gear and machinery for the trip south to the main line. A crew had finished this work, and half a dozen of them had hung around Quandry before striking out for the next job down the line. Some of these found company in the young Indian fighter and scout extraordinaire, and for a few days the whiskey still dribbled if not flowed. Then the workers had grown tired of Zak's boasting, and the same stories over and over, each time told a little differently, so that soon the railroad men knew a fable when they heard it. So they found standing room at the other saloon, even though it did not have a fine nude above the back bar nor offered Irish whiskey.

Tibbits owned the Downspout, or so he was willing to assert when anyone asked why he never left. He had sold his scalps to pay for whiskey, to the very bartender he later shot. Then that money ran out, and he spent his time wandering about the streets and businesses looking for anyone who might have a dollar on him. He begged, he pleaded, then he just robbed the weak by physical violence and the stronger at the point of a gun. The bartender tried to throw him out, and was shot for his trouble. The railroad men came back to the saloon, and one of them ended up with a bullet in his gut as well.

Gerline had come back to Quandry then, and upon being informed of the situation, confronted Tibbits in the saloon. He had expected to find a drunken sot, one who might be trigger happy but sloppy, and he had hoped to get the drop on Tibbits before shots were fired. What he found was a red-eyed, hair trigger demon who was ready for him even as he walked through the door. Gerline saw that Zak's gun was in his holster as he stood at the bar, and took his chances. Tibbits got a slug into the mashal's belly before Gerline cleared leather. As the marshal lay on the floor, Tibbits walked up and shot him again in the belly, then smirked at the two men watching through the window. Tibbits sat drinking at a table as they timidly sidled in and dragged the marshal out.

A vigilance committee had indeed been formed, and several attempts had been made. No one had the courage to actually show themselves to Tibbits, save the gentleman who managed to save at least part of his ear through the use of silk thread and a good needle.

And there it lay. Tibbits still holed up, and Gerline in his office, dying.

"Dying?" Beck said. "You mean he's still alive? What about a doctor?"

"Bender looked at him," Connolly said, "said there's nothing anyone can do. One of the bullets hit his spine."

"How about a real doctor?"

"We sent for one, down to Rock Springs."

400

"My God, that'll take a week, even on the railroad!"

"And it's been that, and more. But it was the first place we could find a doctor that would come. Two others heard of the wounds and said it was no use."

"Well, first off, I must talk to Gerline."

"If he's still among the living. He's over at the marshal's office. We have some ladies who have volunteered to nurse him through it."

"Through it?" Beck said, rising and picking up his coat.

"Well, to the end," Connolly said. "Shall we go with you?"

Beck looked at the reluctance on their faces.

"I believe I can find my way to the marshal's office," he said wryly, and started across the room.

"There is one thing," Connolly said behind his back. Beck paused at the door, half turned to look at them.

"The money," Connolly said, "what should we do with it, if you don't...I mean, if he...."

"Kills me? Hell, what do I care. Give it to Simon Pocket, tell him to buy some cows and settle down." Beck turned and left the room.

He walked up the hallway through the middle of the hotel, and into the lobby. Mrs. Ransom was behind the counter, working on the business ledger. She looked up and smiled at him, then realized who he was, and the smile faded just a touch.

"I'm going over to see the marshal," he said to her, "If you see Simon Pocket, would you ask him to come on over. I need his help."

"Why, yes, Mr. Beck. I will do that," she said. "Are you going to do it, then?"

"Do what?"

"Why, I thought the committee talked to you, I guess I may have been mistaken...."

"Oh they did that, Mrs. Ransom. And yes, I am going to see what I can do to help out. Your man, Mr. Ransom, certainly does have a knack with that stove of his, I grant you that. I have enjoyed my stay with you, as always."

"Oh. You'll be leaving us, then?"

"Not just yet, Mrs. Ransom. Not just yet."

Beck heaved himself into his buffalo coat, wrapped his muffler taken from one pocket around his neck, turned up his collar, nodded

401

to Mrs. Ransom as he pulled his hat tighter, and stepped through the door. The wind had stopped. Everything was a shade of milk or dirty milk or grey milk or buttermilk. Drifts streaked down the street and blocked alleys and piled up against wooden walls. No one was on the street. One horse stood at a hitch rail two doors down.

The jail was to the east, across the street. Beck carefully stepped down from the hotel porch, feeling the slippery, uncertain footing beneath his boots. There was loose snow over packed snow and ice, and his leather soles would slip a little here and there as he made his way toward the marshal's office.

The sky was filled with low, dark grey clouds, and they came down to horizons all around, so that in whatever direction Beck looked down the alleys between the buildings or down the streets, the snowy landscape and the sky blended together so that he seemed to be walking inside a ball of white. The buildings along the street were roofed in snow, their porches neatly piled with it, windblown snow filling every crack and slit and piled on windowsills. As Beck approached the marshal's door, he heard footsteps at his back. He turned.

A woman, bundled in a shawl against the cold, came crunching up the street to him. Her face was muffled, and he could not identify her, but it was sure she was headed for the same destination, so that Beck stepped up on the porch and reached for the door to open it for her. The door seemed to have a mind of its own, and sprang back from his grasp. He stepped aside, surprised, and the woman whisked by him into the office. He followed.

Another woman quickly closed and latched the door behind them. She straightened and turned to Beck.

The bright, grey eyes grabbed his attention like a slap in the face, and for a moment he stared into them, nearly on a level with his own. Her eyes were the color of a drop of meltwater at the tip of an icicle, a hint of blue sharpening the sparkle he saw there. She was tall, nearly as tall as he, and gradually his attention widened to the chestnut locks framing her pale face. And freckles, splattered athwart a strong, straight nose. The eyes scrunched a little in a look of curiosity, and he realized he was staring.

"—isn't it, your name, Mr. Beck?" the woman who was unwrapping her muffler was saying at his side.

402

Beck shook his head a bit as if waking from a vision, and looked at her.

"Yes, yes, of course," he said formally, looking at the woman who spoke, "and if I recall correctly, you are Mrs. Pickworth?"

"I am," Mrs. Pickworth said primly. Beck glanced back at the tall slim woman who had let them in. "And this is Miss Bertram, our school teacher." Mrs. Pickworth scurried around in front of Beck and made a motion with her hand to indicate the grey-eyed woman.

"I am pleased to meet you," said Miss Bertram, extending her hand with a little smile at the corners of her full, wide lips. Beck looked at her lips, and the smile they held, and after a second took her hand. She gave his fingers a slight squeeze, and tried to withdraw the hand, but he held it, gently, gazing into her face.

"Please forgive me," he said, releasing her hand after another long moment. "I do not mean to stare. But you remind me to my very soul of my own lovely mother, back in Pennsylvania."

"Be that as it may," cut in Mrs. Pickworth, and she turned to Miss Bertram. "How is the Marshal doing?"

Miss Bertram tore her bemused gaze away from Jon Beck's face, and the two women quickly stepped to the dying man's side while Beck stripped off his heavy coat, and laid it over the marshal's chair behind the desk. The ladies discussed the marshal's symptoms, his heightening fever, his greater delirium, what Miss Bertram had done on her watch, and then Miss Bertram retrieved her own coat, put it on, and went to the door. Beck was quick to step in behind her and grasp the door handle.

"If I may, Miss Bertram?" he said, close enough to her to breathe in the slightly scented heat of her. She looked over her shoulder and smiled a bit, and said "Thank you, sir."

Beck opened the door, and Miss Bertram launched out into the cold. Beck watched her step carefully across the porch and down into the street.

"Ahem!" came a grunt from Mrs. Pickworth, and Beck once more came back to the instant and closed the door.

"We must keep the heat in!" Mrs. Pickworth stated. Beck nodded as he followed her to the marshal's side.

"How long has he been…here, like this?" Beck said.

Mrs. Pickworth opened her mouth to speak, but was interrupted by a gruff, gritty tone from the cot.

"Long enough to die twice over!" said Marshal Gerline.

"He is lucid!" said Mrs. Pickworth. "Good, marshal, you can help me to help you. I need to change your bedding and attend to your cleanliness. Mr. Beck can help, and you can help, too."

As Mrs. Pickworth worked, Gerline looked up at Beck.

"Yer Beck, ain't you? The scout?"

"Yes. Tell me what happened."

"Somebody's got to go deal with that little rattler," Gerline said, then he groaned as Mrs. Pickworth and Beck turned him on his side to uncover and wash him.

"I know. They've asked me to do it," Beck said.

"They? Those peddlers and piss-ants who run this town?"

"Those would be the ones."

"Well to hell with them!" Gerline groaned and gritted his teeth as they turned him the other way. "Are you gonna do it?"

"I'm going to try. But I need your help. Tell me what happened when you went after him."

"You'll need more than that," Gerline sighed as they got his long johns back on his shoulders, and Mrs. Pickworth began removing the bandage about his middle. "Over in the left top drawer of my desk. A badge. Get it."

Beck stepped to the desk, got a badge out of the drawer. It said "Deputy Marshal" in an arc across its starred shape, and stamped unevenly at the bottom, "Quandry, WT."

He took the badge back to the cot.

The bandage was off of the marshal's middle, and Mrs. Pickworth was bathing the wounds. The bandage was lying at the foot of the cot, and was saturated with yellow fluid and blood. The belly was slight distended, and the wounds, two black holes with puckered flesh surrounding them, were seeping yellow and red as the woman wiped it away. Beck looked at the wounds and pursed his lips.

"Yes, I'm a dead man," Gerline said, and Beck looked at his face to find him staring at Beck's own. "But before I go, I'd shore like to see that little viper put down. Now, raise your right hand."

Beck did so.

"By the power vested in me as Marshal of the City of Quandry, Wyoming Territory, I hereby authorize you to be deputy marshal, with all of the—ouch!" he grimaced, as Mrs. Pickworth scrubbed a little too hard. "With all of the authority, under the law, as befits the office and oaths emanatin' therefrom and thereto. And Mrs. P, here, is our witness."

"All right," said Beck. "Now, tell me what happened."

"You heard the tale from our gutless wonders, I 'spect?"

"Some of it."

"Well, I'd been out of town on business, got back to find the town shot up and all them foundin' feathers clamoring for action. They told me where he was, and they said he'd been drunk for days. I figured I'd move straight in, get the drop on him before he could get a clear thought into his pin head. But he wasn't drunk, nor close to it, and he was layin' for me. I was three steps in the door before I even saw him, and he was waiting. Coiled like a snake. I could see it in him, just see it, clear like, he was gonna shoot no matter what. I knew I'd been stupid, and I knew I was gonna take lead. So I went for my gun, but he was way ahead of me. Shot me down, then shot me again while I was on the floor. And not to kill me, right then, but just to make sure I'd die, the little yellow bastard! He was laughing while he did it, I could see it in his eyes. He wanted me to know just how stupid I had been, and wanted to make sure I gave it careful thought."

"Well, the vigilance committee hasn't had any luck with him, either, and there's a site more of them than the one of you."

"Oh those spineless toads—youch!" the marshal yelped again as Mrs. Pickworth finished tying up the new bandage. "Mrs. P, I don't mean yer man, it's the rest of 'em ain't worth the spit to shine a boot!"

"I am taking no offense, Marshal Gerline!" Mrs. Pickworth said as she cleaned up the old bandages and placed them in a bucket at the foot of the cot. "But those men have families, and they are not trained in the use of weapons. That is why they hired you."

Gerline lay quietly for a moment.

"Yes, it certainly is. And here I am. Beck, I just wanted you to know, he's quick. He's snake quick, and he's a killer, right down to his rattlin' little tail! Don't go after him face to face, back shoot the sonuvabitch, if you will excuse the language, Mrs. P. I mean it, Beck, if you go after him face to face you're a dead man!"

The sweat glistened on Gerline's brow, and Mrs. Pickworth took a cloth and daubed it away. His eyes stared fiercely at Back, eyes red with his fever, and his lips were drawn back in a near snarl. Beck thought of a fox he had seen once, caught in a trap, snapping at him as he approached, no give and no surrender whatsoever.

"Marshall, is that fine Greener gun of yours about the premises somewhere?" Beck said, glancing around the room. A gun rack on one wall was empty.

"Them damned fools borried it. I believe Nate Chalkin had it with him when he got his ear shot off. I believe he left it behind when he ran screaming down the street, or so I am told. I figure that goddamn snake has it now. If you will excuse the language, Mrs. P."

"No offense taken, marshal."

"All right then," Beck said. "I best be getting' to it." He placed the badge on the desk, reached his coat over the desk and shrugged himself into it. He started for the door.

"Ain't you forgettin' something?" Gerline growled. Beck stopped and looked at him.

"That badge ain't just fer show," Gerline went on. "You got to do it proper like, otherwise it ain't right. If you wear that badge, that means I'm there, too, a piece of me is in on it. Will you give me that much?" Gerline's eyes wore a pleading look behind the fierce effort his face displayed.

Beck stepped back to the desk, picked up the badge, and pinned it to the left breast of his shaggy buffalo coat.

"Thanks," Gerline said, lying back. "And one more thing."

"What would that be, marshal?" Beck said, moving to the door.

"You said once you don't take scalps," Gerline said weakly. "Make an exception in this case. Bring me his."

"I'll see what I can do," Beck said, opened the door and walked out. Mrs. Pickworth came to the door behind him as he looked back, her stern face softened a little about the eyes. She shook her head slightly and closed the door.

The two saloons of the town were on South Street, one on the east side at the intersection of South and Main, and the Downspout fifty yards further south on the west side of the street. Beck made his way on the slippery snow blown street to the corner, turned south, and stepped up on the boardwalk in front of the Treadwater Saloon. He moved to the window, peered in. The room was empty. He went to the tall double doors, tried the knob, found it unlocked, opened the door and went in. He quickly glanced around the room, and it was indeed empty. The half dozen tables were clean, the chairs neatly placed. He walked to the bar. As he glanced back at the door, he heard a sound and turned to find the barkeep coming out of the back room carrying a box.

"Well howdy, sir," said the barkeep, setting the box on a bench behind the bar. He turned to face Beck. His eyes rested on the badge. His smile faded.

"He ain't here," said the barman.

"I know. Or at least I figured as much. Just making sure he hasn't shifted his hole."

"How's Gerline doing?"

"He's dying. Even if a doctor could get to him, I don't see he's got a chance. And he knows it."

"Damned shame. I'm just lucky that little coyote ain't camped out in front of my bar!"

"Seems that way. He still across the street?"

"Far as I know." The barkeep eyed the badge. "You going after him?"

"That's the plan."

"Well good luck," the 'tender said and stuck out his hand. "I'm Elroy Blanchard. You make it back alive, I'll stand you to whatever you want, as long as you want!"

"That's mighty generous of you, Elroy," Beck said. "I'm Jon Beck."

The barkeep's eyebrows shot up. "Oh!" he said, "You're somewhat famous around here. After a fashion. In the short time that little coyote's been drinking up the town, he's been talking about you! Seems he saved your hide on several occasions, from those bloodthirsty Nez Perce and all."

"You don't say."

"I do! Or, he did."

"Well, I guess I'll have to go thank the man." Beck turned from the bar, and across the room the door opened, and through it stepped five men. The last two were Downs and Pearly, the railroad men. The first three went immediately to the bar, and ordered whiskey. The barkeep got busy. Beck started for the door, and Pearly stepped up to block the way.

"Why if it isn't Mr. Beck, the famous scout and Indian fighter," he said in a thin Irish brogue, a smile upon his lips.

"Pearly, isn't it?" Beck said.

"That would be correct, Mr. Beck, and let me buy you a drink in remembrance of our past friendship."

"Sorry to say I am little busy at the moment—"

Pearly lashed out a short, chopping right hand blow that smashed Beck on the mouth, setting him back a step with the suddenness of it. Pearly also stepped back, removed his hat and tossed it onto a table, quickly stripped out of his coat and tossed that to Downs, all the while keeping his eyes locked on Jon Beck.

"We have a little matter to discuss," he said, rolling up his sleeves.

Beck felt of his lip, his fingers coming away with blood.

"Wouldn't sway you none if I said I needed to slip away and go kill a man first, would it? Be happy to come back and continue our chat, after," Beck said.

"Ah, but what if the little bugger kills you?" Pearly said, sneering a little. "There goes all me fun!"

Beck peeled off his buffalo coat, walked over and draped it over the bar, then placed his hat atop it. He reached for his big army Colt with his right hand, and the gun belt buckle with his left. He heard a commotion off to this right and glanced over to see the three railroad hands facing him with drawn pistols.

"Now boys," said the barkeep, standing at the other end of the bar, behind the railroad men, "I'm asking you nicely to put those pistols on the bar, like good little fellers." The sound of hammers locking into full cock froze the pistol pointers, and Beck glanced over at the barkeep and the sawed off double barrel he held leveled at them.

"All right with you, Mr. Beck?" said the barkeep.

"First rate, Mr. Blanchard," Beck said, and finished unbuckling and taking off his pistol belt, which he placed on the bar next to his coat. The three railroad men carefully reached over and placed their smaller revolvers on the bar. The barkeep lowered the muzzle of his shotgun and collected the guns and placed them on the back bar.

"Now, gents," he said, "anyone for a refill?"

"Thought you railroad boys was all done here and gone south," Beck said, walking into the center of the room.

"Oh we are, after today," Pearly said, stepping up. He was half a foot taller than Beck, with wide shoulders and a slim, fashionable waist. He wore a linen shirt, and a vest that was still neatly buttoned. His watch still resided in his vest pocket, and the chain traversed the cloth in a golden arc. He had a thin mustache, a sturdy, square jaw, and bright blue eyes. They seemed to twinkle as he fainted with the right again, and jabbed out a quick left to stab Beck in the nose.

Beck circled to his left, looking over the battery of fists and forearms Pearly held before his face. Pearly seemed an experienced fighter, and quick. He tried the feint and jab again, and Beck slipped the punch.

"Was that one of your men that Tibbits shot?" Beck said, stepping in for a roundabout left. Pearly neatly ducked it.

"'Twas indeed," he said. Three lefts came in then, one landing on Beck's forehead. None of them were thrown with any force. Pearly was testing the range.

"You felt no need to set things right?" Beck said.

Pearly opened his mouth to reply and Beck moved in two steps, ducking below the right Pearly jabbed in reaction and uppercutting a left right left into Pearly's vest. The bigger man grunted, stepped back, snuck his own roundhouse left into Beck's right ear.

A little lightning flashed across Beck's vision.

"We'd already paid him off, you see," said Pearly, "so at that point he was not one of ours. Like those gentlemen there at the bar."

Pearly let fly a combination, left and right, but Beck got under the right and landed another right to Pearly's middle. And he noticed that Pearly dropped his left a bit when he went out with the right. The thought had barely registered when Pearly came in with all fists swinging, driving Jon Beck back and back, then they were at the bar and Beck could feel the wood in the small of his back, crouched, hands up, taking blow after blow, but most of them glancing. Using the wood to push off from with his hips, he lurched forward and hooked into Pearly's middle again and again and again, feeling the taller man's hands smacking his head and the stinging pain of his ears being battered by right and left cross punches. He kept his head down and his legs driving him in and under, staying in tight, slamming punches into Pearly's gut, blows that were causing Pearly to grunt each time he took one. Then Pearly sprang back, panting. The mischievousness was gone from his eyes.

Jon Beck looked at him through red fire behind his eyes. Little stars were blinking in his vision, and things seemed a bit blurred.

Pearly circled, lashed out a left, another left, Beck slapping aside the punches. His arms were shorter than Pearly's, and he knew he could not spar with him at long range. Pearly kept on with the lefts, Beck dodging and slapping them aside, and one or two got through, jarring Beck's head, bringing out the stars. Pearly tried to set up a right or two with a left lead, and one of those got to Beck as well. Beck let his hands fall a little as this went on, and then Pearly threw another left and right, his left dropping just a little as he followed with the right as Beck had noticed, and Beck counter punched the right with a right of his own, feeling his fist connect with solid jaw, and Pearly rocked back. He shook his head. Beck did not pursue.

"Good one, that," Pearly said.

"Glad you liked it," Beck said, raising up his hands again.

He started for Pearly then, circling and stepping in, left and in, left and in, Pearly going round the other way, slinging left after left, always just an inch out of Beck's reach. Beck feinted the next step left, then two quick steps in and right and he was in under Pearly's hands again, upper cutting and hooking with all of his strength into Pearly's middle. Two of his blows were solid, and Pearly grunted hard. Then the taller man danced away into the center of the room.

Both men stood looking at the other, both panting. The left side of Pearly's face glowed bright red. Beck was red all over. Blood trickled down the side of his face from a cut brow. He could taste blood in his mouth. Pearly was not standing perfectly erect, but seemed to be crouching ever so slightly.

"Have you had enough fun, then?" Beck said.

"Not entirely," Pearly said, raising his hands again.

"It gets rougher from here," Beck said, lifting his own fists.

"I would imagine so," Pearly said.

The two men closed, both crouching and wary. Pearly stabbed out the lefts, looking for an opening for his right, throwing it where he thought he'd found one. Jon Beck countered every time, taking the punches and giving back his own, stepping in again and again to try and come within range. Pearly wasn't having any of that, and kept the fight at distance, hoping for a kill shot that would not cost him. He could not find it.

Not a word was spoken by the spectators, the three railroad men standing slack jawed, drinks in hand, fascinated with watching their boss in action. Most of them had seen him bully or beat other workers, and never had a man stood with him toe to toe for more than a minute. And here was a squat little man not only holding him at bay, but very nearly rolling over him.

Downs watched the fight with mechanical disinterest. He had his own theories about what Pearly was doing, and he would have done it another way. In the back of his mind he was thankful that he did not have the opportunity.

The barkeep kept his eyes on the railroad men, and the fight. He had seen Pearly's work before, seen him methodically beat down several men. He knew Pearly to be a trained fighter, and he had always marveled that a railroad engineer, a man adept at planning and building and overcoming natural obstacles, could be so good at violence. But he could see that Beck was no novice at battle, and he marveled at the patience of the man. He waited patiently as well, wondering what Beck would do to pull it off. For, from his place behind the bar, he had no doubt that Beck would do just that.

In the center of the room the two men circled, the shorter, thicker man dodging and slapping punches, the taller, lankier man lashing them out, and then the two of them tore at each other like tigers, the sound of bone and flesh smacking together loud in the room, the grunting of punches given and taken, the scuffing of boots on the floor, and then Pearly broke from the clinch and stepped back, his arms just a bit wide and Beck got a left up into Pearly's jaw, lifting it, and then the right followed after and Pearly's head snapped back hard and he went down on one knee, and the momentum of Beck's attack carried him over Pearly and the two of them tumbled to the floor.

Pearly sat up, shaking his head. Beck rested on his back momentarily, then rolled to his hands and knees, and got to his feet, panting. He stepped over to his sitting adversary, and after a moment reached down his hand. Pearly eyed it, then wearily grasped the forearm. Beck hauled him to his feet. Pearly grabbed on to Beck, his knees gone to mush.

"Had enough fun now?" Beck said, gasping for breath.

"I believe I have experienced enough joy to last me the week," Pearly said.

"We done, then?"

"We are done, sir," Pearly said. "May I buy you a drink?"

"I have business to attend to," Beck said. "But I'll be back shortly, and then I would be happy to accept your invitation." Beck helped Pearly to the bar, and draped him over it.

"Then in the mean time," Pearly said, leaning on the bar, "drinks for all the rest of you!"

The railroad men cheered. The barkeep carefully let down the hammers of his shotgun and laid it behind the bar, and handed over the small revolvers to the rail workers. Downs stepped up to the bar beside Pearly, a look of mild disgust on his face, and laid his coat on the bar.

"We'll be here for an hour," Pearly said, pulling his watch out of its pocket by the chain. Several bits and pieces of it fell tinkling to the bar. "Ah, well, we'll be here until you hear the noon train whistle."

Beck stepped to the end of the bar and asked the barman for a bucket of water. This was brought to him, and he washed his face and hands, turning the water pink with his blood. Blanchard brought him a clean towel, and he daubed at the cuts on his brows and lips until the bleeding stopped.

Beck slipped on his gun belt, but pulled the pistol from its holster and laid it on the bar. He slowly heaved the heavy coat about his shoulders, buttoned it up, pulled on his hat. He took the pistol in hand and started for the door.

"And gentlemen," said Pearly loudly, "I give you Jon Beck, the only man who has ever beaten me in a fair fight!" They all turned from the bar and held up their glasses and mugs in salute.

"And a grand time was had by all," Beck said wryly. Pearly chuckled.

Jon Beck slid the big army Colt butt-first up the right sleeve of his coat, resting the muzzle in his cupped palm. He turned and went out the door, closing it behind him.

The cold was like a splash of icy water on his battered face. He stood on the saloon porch, looking south across the street to the Downspout Saloon three doors down. No other person was in sight. He had no plan. The hidden gun was his only hope, and the trick had worked before with his knife. He only had to get close enough to be sure of one shot, for that would be all he would get. He was counting on the fact that Zack knew him, and if he hated him, or liked him, it did not matter. Beck was fairly certain it would be the former. And that fact might cause Zack Tibbits to hesitate long enough for Beck to get in close. That and the second fact that Beck was wearing a heavy coat, buttoned, impossible to get at his belt gun in a hurry. He hoped that Tibbits would see that, and feel comfortable enough to let his enemy come, knowing he had the advantage, knowing that he could draw and shoot Beck at any time, and Beck could do nothing about it. Jon would start off with a plea to get Tibbits to surrender, he would bring up the scouting trip and the chance Beck had given him to make good. Yes, he would appeal to the young man's sense of the right, at least long enough to get close. Maybe three paces. He knew Tibbits would not allow him to come within arm's length. But three paces. That would do it. He would have to drop the gun into his palm and bring it up and fire all in one motion. He could not simply present the gun and depend on the young man to back down, to surrender. Not now. Too many men had been shot. No, as much as it pained him, Beck knew he would have to try and kill the man without waiting for a response. Without a trial. Without a moment's hesitation. All the reason and justice and right of it pinned to his left breast. And poised over his right hand. He just had to get close enough.

He stepped down into the snowy, slippery street, and wobbled a bit on the slick surface. His vision had not cleared completely from the beating he had just taken, and this worried him. Should he go on now, when in fact he could not see clearly? He cursed that damned Indian pony for the hundredth time. And started down and across the street toward the Downspout Saloon.

He had not gone twenty paces when the entry door to the Downspout flew open and slammed into the outside of the building with a crack. Zack Tibbits bolted across the boardwalk and down the steps into the street, slipping crazily as his boots slid on the hard packed snow and ice under the thin layer of new snow.

"Goddamn you Jon Beck!" he screamed, trying to run in Beck's direction, his boots gaining no traction on the slick roadway. Beck stopped, then started on again. He didn't know what was happening,

413

only that suddenly his target was in sight and coming at him. No choice now but to go on.

"Zack, for God's sake don't do it!" came another shout. Simon Pocket appeared at the Downspout's door. "Zack, don't!"

"You holier-than-thou sonuvabitch!" Tibbits screamed, slipping a little less, but coming. "I should'a shot you back there on the trail when I had the chance!"

"Well Zack, pleasure to see you too!" Beck called out. Walking.

"Pleasure my ass!" screamed Tibbits, scurrying over the snowy street, his arms out, waving for balance. Coming.

They were ten yards apart, then eight. Beck let the pistol drop into his hand, shifted the grip slightly to firm it up. Zack Tibbits saw the gun drop, and a snarl instantly contorted his face as he remembered the same trick Beck had pulled with his knife months ago. He slapped for his holstered gun, slipping as he did so, and got it out as Beck's hand rose to level the big Colt at Tibbits' chest. Zack fanned the hammer back with his free hand and a shot barked out, the bullet exploding the ice just to the left of Beck's left leg. Jon thumbed back the hammer of his gun and began to squeeze the trigger, fighting to line up the sights with his indistinct vision, when Tibbits' second shot broke and a hammer blow smacked Beck's left leg. Beck's balance was thrown off as the leg jerked but his own shot broke and white erupted in front of him as the flash of his muzzle came and went and with it another hammer blow to his right shoulder, turning him, twisting him, his mind frozen in time as he toppled over and down. His mind thinking of how quiet it was, that he had not heard the shot, that he was falling, that he must have slipped on the ice, that it was so quiet, that he could hear the wind about him as he fell through the air, and then the impact of his head on the icy roadway that blotted out all other thoughts save the blinding flash of lightening in his vision and the galaxy of stars that flashed and fizzled before his eyes.

Jon Beck lay on the road, staring up at the dirty milk sky, a searing fire in his left thigh and right chest. He mind could not think of why he was lying here, why he hurt. Bright flashes of fire danced in his eyes. He could hear voices, but he could not determine words. Then a blurred face appeared in the sky.

"Jon!" a voice said from far away. Slowly he could make out t[he] fuzzy image of Simon Pocket's face. The sky was turning pi[nk] around him.

"Jon!" Pocket said, and Beck could see that it was Simon wh[o] said the word.

"Simon," he whispered. "I'm sorry."

"Jon, for God's sake, lie quiet! We'll get you inside, just take it easy!"

The sky was red now, and Simon's face less distinct. Beck blinked but it did not help.

"Simon," Beck whispered. Pocket bent low.

"Take care of Bill for me, won't you?" Beck said.

"Sure Jon, anything you want. I'll even kiss the big bastard for you, just lie still! We'll get you inside, we'll get you some help!"

But Jon Beck did not hear him, for the sky was red and redder still, and then he could not tell the red from the blackness that welled up and put out the stars dancing in his eyes.

e
k

Made in the USA
Lexington, KY
10 April 2012